SAVING MAX

This Large Print Book carries the
Seal of Approval of N.A.V.H.

SAVING MAX

ANTOINETTE VAN HEUGTEN

WHEELER PUBLISHING
A part of Gale, Cengage Learning

GALE
CENGAGE Learning

Detroit • New York • San Francisco • New Haven, Conn • Waterville, Maine • London

Copyright © 2010 by Antoinette van Heugten.
Wheeler Publishing, a part of Gale, Cengage Learning.

Wheeler Publishing Large Print Hardcover.
The text of this Large Print edition is unabridged.
Other aspects of the book may vary from the original edition.
Set in 16 pt. Plantin.

LIBRARY OF CONGRESS CATALOGING-IN-PUBLICATION DATA

Van Heugten, Antoinette.
  Saving Max / by Antoinette van Heugten.
    p. cm.
  ISBN-13: 978-1-4104-3453-1 (hardcover)
  ISBN-10: 1-4104-3453-2 (hardcover)
  1. Single mothers—Fiction. 2. Asperger's syndrome—Patients—Fiction. 3. Mothers and sons—Fiction. 4. Psychiatric clinics—Fiction. 5. Large type books. I. Title.
  PS3622.A585493S38 2011
  813'.6—dc22   2010044292

Published in 2011 by arrangement with Harlequin Books S.A.

Printed in the United States of America
1 2 3 4 5 6 7 15 14 13 12 11

For Bill, who has made all of my dreams come true.

PART ONE

Part One

PROLOGUE

She walks down a deserted hallway of the psychiatric hospital, her heels tapping a short staccato on the disinfected floor. She pauses; pushes open a door; and steps inside. The room is red, all red, with dark, sick spatters of blood. They stab and soar at the ceiling and walls, pool on the floor. She claps both hands to her mouth, trying to stifle the scream that tears at her throat. Her eyes are pulled to the body on the bed. The boy lies gaping at the ceiling, his eyes blue ice. Her fingers, slick with his blood, find no pulse. She scrambles for the nurse's button — and freezes.

There, on the floor next to the bed, lies a huddled form — a boy not so different from the corpse above him. His face and hands are smeared with blackened blood, but this time her frantic search for a pulse is rewarded with a faint throb. It is then that she sees it.

Clutched in his hand is a long, spiked object, covered in the slime and blood that lacerates the room. Grasped in that hand, as tightly as a noose, is the murder weapon.

CHAPTER ONE

Danielle falls gratefully into the leather chair in Dr. Leonard's waiting room. She has just raced from her law firm's conference room, where she spent the entire morning with a priggish Brit who couldn't imagine that his business dealings across the pond could possibly have subjected him to the indignities of a New York lawsuit. Max, her son, sits in his customary place in the corner of the psychiatrist's waiting room — as far away from her as possible. He is hunched over his new iPhone, thumbs punching furiously. It's as if he's grown a new appendage, so rarely does she see him without it. At his insistence, Danielle also has an identical one in her purse. The faintest shadow of a moustache stains his upper lip, his handsome face marred by a cruel, silver piercing on his eyebrow. His scowl is that of an adult, not a child. He seems to feel her stare. He looks up and then averts his lovely, tenebrous eyes.

She thinks of all the doctors, the myriad of medications, the countless dead ends, and the dark, seemingly irreversible changes in Max. Yet somehow the ghost of her boy wraps his thin, tanned arms around her neck — his mouth cinnamon-sweet with Red Hots — and plants a sticky kiss on her cheek. He rests there a moment, his small body breathing rapidly, his heart her metronome. She shakes her head. To her, there is still only one Max. And in the center of this boy lies the tenderest, sweetest middle — her baby, the part she can never give up.

Her eyes return to the present Max. He's a teenager, she tells herself. Even as the hopeful thought flits across her mind, she knows she is lying to herself. Max has Asperger's Syndrome, high-functioning autism. Although very bright, he is clueless about getting along with people. This has caused him anguish and heartache all his life.

When he was very young, Max discovered computers. His teachers were stunned at his aptitude. Now sixteen, Danielle still has no idea of the extent of Max's abilities, but she knows that he is a virtual genius — a true savant. While this initially made him fascinating to his peers, none of them could possibly maintain interest in the minutiae Max droned on about. People with Asperger's often wax rhapsodic about their specific obsessions — whether or not the listener is even vaguely interested in the topic. Max's quirky behavior and learning disabilities have made him the object of further ridicule. His response has been to act out or retaliate, although lately it seems that he has just withdrawn further into himself, cinching thicker and tighter coils around his heart.

Sonya, his first real girlfriend, broke up with him a few months ago. Max was devastated. He finally had a relationship — like everybody else — and she dumped him in front of all his classmates. Max became so depressed that he refused to go to school; cut off contact with the few friends he had; and started using drugs. The latter she discovered when she walked into his room unannounced to find Max staring at her coolly — a joint in his hand; a blue, redolent cloud over his head; and a rainbow assortment of pills scattered carelessly on his desk. She didn't say a word, but waited until he took a shower a few hours later and then confiscated the bag of dope and every pill she could find. That afternoon she dragged him — cursing and screaming — to Dr.

13

Leonard's office. The visits seemed to help. At least he had gone back to school and, in an odd way, seemed happier. He was tender and loving toward Danielle — a young Max, eager to please. As far as the drugs went, her secret forays into his room turned up nothing. That wasn't to say, of course, that he hadn't simply moved them to school or a friend's house.

But, she thinks ruefully, recent events pale in comparison to what brings them here today. Yesterday after Max left for school and she performed her daily search-and-seizure reconnaissance, she discovered a soft, leather-bound journal stuffed under his bed. Guiltily, she pried open the metal clasp with a paring knife. The first page so frightened her that she fell into a chair, hands shaking. Twenty pages of his boyish scrawl detailed a plan so intricate, so terrifying, that she only noticed her ragged breathing and stifled sobs when she looked around the room and wondered where the sounds were coming from. Did the blame lie with her? Could she have done something differently? Better? The old shame and humiliation filled her.

The door opens and Georgia walks in. A tiny blonde, she sits next to Danielle and gives her a brief, strong hug. Danielle smiles. Georgia is not only her best friend — she is family. As an only child with both parents gone, Danielle has come to rely upon Georgia's unflagging loyalty and support, not to mention her deep love for Max. Despite her sweet expression, Georgia has the quick mind of a tough lawyer. Their law firm is Blackwood & Price, a multinational firm with four hundred lawyers and offices in New York, Oslo and London. She is typically in her office by now — seated behind a perfectly ordered desk, a pile of finished work at her elbow. Danielle can't remember when she has been so glad to see someone. Georgia gives Max a wave and a smile. "Hi, you."

"Hey." The monosyllabic task accomplished, he closes his eyes and slouches lower into his chair.

"How is he?" asks Georgia.

"Either glued to his laptop or on that damned phone of his," she whispers. "He doesn't know I found his . . . journal. I'd never have gotten him here otherwise."

Georgia squeezes her shoulder. "It'll be all right. We'll get through this somehow."

"You're so wonderful to come. I can't tell you how much it means to me." She forces normality into her voice. "So, how did it go this morning?"

15

"I barely got to court in time, but I think I did okay."

"What happened?"

She shrugs. "Jonathan."

Danielle squeezes her hand. Her husband, Jonathan, although a brilliant plastic surgeon, has an unquenchable thirst that threatens to ruin not only his marriage, but his career. Georgia suspects that he is also addicted to cocaine, but has voiced that fear only to Danielle. No one at their law firm seems to know, despite his boorish behavior at the last Christmas party. The firm, an old-line Manhattan institution, does not look kindly upon spousal comportment that smacks of anything other than the rarified, blue-blooded professionals they believe themselves to be. With a two-year-old daughter, Georgia is reluctant to even consider divorce.

"What was it this time?" asks Danielle.

Her azure eyes are nebulous. "Came in at four; passed out in the bathtub; pissed all over himself."

"Oh, God."

"Melissa found him and came crying into the bedroom." Georgia shakes her head. "She thought he was dead."

This time it is Danielle who does the hugging.

16

Georgia forces a smile and turns her gaze upon Max, who has sunk even lower into his leather chair and appears to be asleep. "Has the doctor read his journal?"

"I'm sure he has," she says wearily. "I messengered it to him yesterday."

"Have you heard from the school?"

"He's out." Max's principal had politely suggested to Danielle that another "environment" might be more "successful" in meeting Max's "challenges." In other words, they want him the hell out of there.

Max's Asperger's has magnified tenfold since he became a teenager. As his peers have graduated to sophisticated social interaction, Max has struggled at a middle-school level. Saddled with severe learning disabilities, he stands out even more. Danielle understands it. If you are incessantly derided, you cannot risk further social laceration. Isolation at least staunches the pain. And it isn't as if Danielle hasn't tried like hell. Max had cut a swath through countless schools in Manhattan. Even the special schools that cater to students with disabilities had kicked him out. For years she had beaten paths to every doctor who might have something new to offer. A different medication. A different dream.

"Georgia," she whispers. "Why is this happening? What am I supposed to do?" She looks at her friend. Sadness is one emotion they mirror perfectly in one another's eyes. Danielle feels the inevitable pressure at the back of her eyes and fiddles with the hem of her skirt. There's a thread that won't stay put.

"You're here, aren't you?" Georgia's voice is a gentle spring rain. "There has to be a solution."

Danielle clenches her hands as the tears come hard and fast. She glances at Max, but he is still asleep. Georgia pulls a handkerchief from her purse. Danielle wipes her eyes and returns it. Without warning, Georgia reaches over and pushes up the sleeve of Danielle's blouse — all the way to the elbow. Danielle jerks her arm back, but Georgia grabs her wrist and pulls her arm toward her. Long, red slashes stretch from pulse to elbow.

"Don't!" Danielle yanks her sleeve down, her voice a fierce whisper. "He didn't mean it. It was just that one time — when I found his drugs."

Georgia's face is full of alarm. "This can't go on — not for him and not for you."

Danielle jerks back her arm and fumbles furiously with her cuff. The scarlet wounds are covered, but her secret is no longer safe.

It is hers to know; hers to bear.

"Ms. Parkman?" The bland, smooth voice is straight from central casting. The short haircut and black glasses that frame Dr. Leonard's boyish face are cookie-cutter perfect — a walking advertisement for the American Psychiatric Association.

Still panicked by Georgia's discovery, she wills herself to appear normal. "Good morning, Doctor."

He regards her carefully. "Would you like to come in?"

Danielle nods, hastily gathering her things. She feels hot crimson flush her face.

"Max?" asks Dr. Leonard.

Barely awake, Max shrugs. "Whatever." He struggles to his feet and reluctantly follows Dr. Leonard down the hall.

Danielle flings a terrified glance at Georgia. She feels like a deer trapped in a barbed-wire fence, its slender leg about to snap.

"Don't worry." Georgia's gaze is blue and true. "I'll be here when you get back."

She takes a deep breath and straightens. It is time to walk into the lion's den.

Danielle files into the room after Max and Dr. Leonard. She takes in the sleek leather couch with a kilim pillow clipped to it and

19

the obligatory box of tissues prominent on the stainless steel table. She walks to a chair and sits. She is dressed in one of her lawyer outfits. This is not where she wants to wear it.

Max sits in front of Dr. Leonard's desk, his chair angled away from them. Danielle turns to Dr. Leonard and gives him a practiced smile. He smiles back and inclines his head. "Shall we begin?"

Danielle nods. Max is silent.

Dr. Leonard adjusts his glasses and glances at Max's journal. Dense notes cover his yellow pad. He looks up and speaks in a soft voice. "Max?"

"Yeah?" His scowl speaks volumes.

"We need to discuss something very serious."

Dr. Leonard takes a deep breath and fixes Max with his gaze. "Have you been having thoughts of suicide?"

Max starts and looks accusingly at Danielle. "I don't know what in the hell you're talking about."

"Are you sure?" Leonard's voice is gentle. "It's safe here, Max. You can talk about it."

"No way. I'm gone." Just as he starts for the door, he catches a glimpse of the leather journal on the corner of Leonard's desk. He freezes. His face a boiling claret, he whips around and shoots Danielle a look of pure hatred. "Goddammit! That's none of your fucking business!"

Her heart feels as if it will burst. "Sweetheart, please let us help you! Killing yourself is not the answer, I promise you." Danielle rises and tries to embrace him.

Max shoves her so hard that she slams her head against the wall and slides to the floor. "Max — no!" she cries. His eyes widen in alarm, and for a moment, he reaches out to her, but then lurches back; grabs the journal; and bolts out of the room. The slamming of the door splits the air.

Dr. Leonard rushes over to Danielle; helps her to her feet; and guides her gently to a chair. She shakes all over. Leonard then takes a seat and looks gravely at her over his glasses. "Danielle, has Max been violent at home?"

Danielle shakes her head too quickly. The scars on her arm seem to burn. "No."

He sits quietly and then puts his notes into a blue folder. "Given Max's clinical depression, suicidal ideations and volatility, we have to be realistic about his needs. He requires intensive treatment by the best the profession has to offer. My recommendation is that we act immediately."

She tries not to let him see that her

breathing has become irregular. Like an animal trapped in another's lair, she has to be extremely careful about her reaction. "I'm not certain what that means."

"I mentioned this option earlier, and now I'm afraid we have no choice." His usually kind eyes are obsidian. "Max needs a complete psychiatric assessment — including his medication protocol."

Danielle stares at the floor, a prism of tears clouding her eyes. "You mean . . ."

His voice floats up to her very softly, very slowly. "Maitland."

Danielle feels her stomach free-fall. There is that word.

It is as final as the closing of a coffin.

CHAPTER TWO

During the trip from Des Moines to Plano,
Iowa, she drives as Max sleeps. Despite the
chaos of suitcases, cabs, traffic and night-
marish arguments, they somehow caught
the flight from New York. She had tried
every form of plea and coercion to get
Max's agreement to go to Maitland. It was
only after she broke down completely that
Max relented — just barely. She didn't wait
for him to change his mind. She stayed up
all night, constantly peeking into his bedroom to make sure he was . . . alive. The
next day they were on that plane.

Her anxiety lessens as she settles into the
thrum of the road. She lights a cigarette and
lowers her window, hoping that Max won't
wake up. He hates it when she smokes. The
landscape is a flat, weary brown. It is only
after they reach Plano and turn off the
highway that all around them explodes.
Every broad leaf is a stroke of green, burst-

ing with liquid sun. She smells the aftermath of swollen showers and imagines a flood of expiation that wipes the world clean, leaving one incorruptible — the black, secret earth. It is a sign of hope, she decides, a presentiment that all will be well.

As she drives on, she turns her face to the sun, relaxes in its warmth, and thinks of Max as a small boy. One afternoon in particular flashes in her mind. At her father's farm in Wisconsin, shortly before he died, Danielle rocked gently in the porch swing and watched as the afternoon sun burnished gold into the summer air and turned her bones to butter.

As she sank deeper into the worn cushion, Max clambered up and sprawled across her lap. They had been swimming all morning and, exhausted, Max wrapped his arms tightly around her neck and fell into that syncopated stupor unique to young boys. She breathed deeply of the heady scent of magnolias that hung over them — voluptuous, cream-colored blossoms so heavy and full that their tenuous grip upon stem and branch threatened to drop them softly onto the lush green below. Their scent was interlaced with her son's essence — a mixture of boy sweat, sunburned skin and dark spice. As she held him closer, she felt his heart echo the strong beat of her own. Eyes closed, she gave herself up to the languid moment of mother and child, perfect in its communion and impermanence — so intense as to be indistinguishable from piercing sadness or exquisite joy. They would always be like this, she had thought. Nothing, she vowed, would ever tear them apart.

It is then that she looks up at the white, arched gate. It is then that she reads the weathered sign. Faded words hang in black, metal letters, pierced against the sky.

Maitland, it says, swinging in the breeze.

Maitland Psychiatric Asylum.

CHAPTER THREE

Danielle and Max sit in a bright orange room and watch the group leader arrange a circle of blue plastic chairs. The linoleum is a dizzying pattern of white-and-black squares and smells of disinfectant. Parents and awkward adolescents file reluctantly into the room. Danielle's heart twists in her chest. How can she possibly be in this place with Max? The faces of the parents all reveal the same ugly mixture of hope and fear, resignation and denial — each with an unholy, tragic story to tell. They look like burn victims steeling themselves before another layer of skin is stripped away.

Max is by her side, angry and embarrassed because he's old enough to know exactly where he is. He has not spoken since they arrived. He looks so — boy. An oversize polo shirt finishes off rumpled chinos and Top-Siders with no socks. The sports watch he wears is too big, as if he's playing dress-up with his father's watch. Unbidden, he shaved off the wispy moustache the night before they left New York. His mouth is a small line, the width of a piece of mechanical pencil lead. His one act of defiance remains — the cold, ugly piercing on his eyebrow.

Suddenly, the door swings open and a woman rushes in, pulling a teenaged boy by the hand. She stops and surveys the circle. Her blue eyes make direct contact with Danielle. She smiles. Danielle glances left and right, but no one looks up. The woman makes a beeline in her direction. She sits next to Danielle and pulls the boy down onto the chair next to her. "Marianne," she whispers.

"Danielle."

"Good morning!" A young woman with wild red hair and a name tag that says Just Joan! stands in the middle of the circle. Her voice batters the ear like hail on a tin roof. "This is our group session to welcome new patients and parents to Maitland and, well, to just share our feelings and concerns."

Danielle hates group therapy. Anything she's ever "shared" has come around to bite her on the ass. She casts about desperately for an exit sign. She needs a cigarette — badly. Just Joan! claps her hands. Too late.

"Let's pick someone and go around the circle," she says. "Introduce yourself and tell us why you're here. Remember, all conversations are strictly confidential."

The tales of heartache are overwhelming. There is Carla, the rickets-thin waitress from Colorado who gives her son, Chris, loving glances as she tells of how he snapped her wrist and purpled her eye. After her is Estelle, an elegant black grandmother who tenderly clasps the hand of her doll-like granddaughter, whose pink taffeta Sunday dress only partially veils the crazed, ropy scars that run up and down her coffee-colored legs.

"Self-inflictive," whispers Marianne. "The mother ran off. Couldn't take it."

Just Joan's sharp eyes troll the room for a victim and then rivet upon Danielle. She stiffens.

Marianne pats Danielle's hand and quickly raises her own. "I'll go." Her voice is a honey-coated drawl. "My name is Marianne Morrison."

Danielle's sigh echoes around the circle. She leans back and tries to put her arm around Max, who shrugs it off. She studies the woman who has saved her.

Marianne looks like the bright center of a flower. The pleats of her claret skirt are

28

Gillette sharp, forming a perfectly pointed circle around her knees. A shimmering blouse reflects the gleam of a single strand of pearls and draws the eye to the single gold band on her left hand. Her simple, blond pageboy frames her oval face. Her flawless makeup reflects a level of detail and attention seemingly innate in Southern women. In her case, it enhances her features, particularly a wide, generous mouth and intelligent blue eyes. Next to her, Danielle is aware of her own *de rigueur* black-on-black pantsuit, her severe dark hair and pale skin. She wears no jewelry, no watch, no makeup. In Manhattan, she is an obvious professional. Next to Marianne, she looks like a pallbearer. Danielle glances down. A bag next to Marianne's chair overflows with all manner of crafty-looking things. Danielle's depression deepens — like when she sees the pre-prison Martha Stewart on TV stenciling an entire room with a toothbrush or casually butchering a young suckling pig with an old nail file. Or when one of the mothers at Max's grade school brought a homemade quilt that had the handprints of all the kids on it for the school auction and Danielle gave money instead.

"This is my son, Jonas." Hearing his name, the boy shakes his head and blinks rapidly. His hands never stop moving. Fingernails scrape at scarred welts on his arms. Danielle instinctively pulls her own sleeves down. Jonas rocks back and forth, testing the chair's rubber stoppers as they squeak against the floor. All the while, he makes soft, grunting noises, a perpetual-motion-and-sound machine.

"If I have to say something about myself, I suppose it would be that I'm from Texas and was a pediatric nurse for many years." This does not surprise Danielle. What Marianne says next, however, surprises her deeply.

"I actually finished medical school, but never practiced." She inclines her head toward her son. "I decided to stay home and take care of my boy. In fact, that is the most important thing about me." She clasps her hands and then flashes what Danielle believes must be one of the most beautiful smiles she's ever seen. Her attitude is infectious. The parents all smile and nod, like a bobblehead dog in the back of a '55 Chevy.

"Jonas's diagnosis is retardation and autism, and he doesn't speak, not really." Marianne pats the boy's knee. He does not acknowledge her. His eyes roam the room as he taps and scratches. The reddening on his arms deepens to a frozen cranberry.

30

"He's been this way since he was a little boy," she says. "It's hard, you know, to deal with the challenges our children have, but I do the best I can with what the good Lord gave me." As sympathetic glances pass from the parents to her, Marianne brightens like a rainbow after rain. "His father . . . well, he's gone, bless his heart." She averts her eyes. "Recently, Jonas started getting violent and self-destructive. I want him to have the very best, and that's why we're here."

After she finishes, everyone applauds, but not too much. It's like being at the symphony. Once or twice — that's polite. Anything more would be disrespectful. Marianne then whispers to Jonas in some kind of gibberish. In response, he whirls around and slaps her face so hard with a flat, open hand that it almost hurls her from her chair.

"Jonas!" Marianne cries. She covers her scarlet cheek as if to ward off further blows. A male attendant appears; yanks Jonas to his feet; and pins both arms behind his back.

"Nomomah! Aaahhnomomah!" The attendant pushes him roughly into his chair, gripping his hands until he quiets. Everyone sits, stunned. As soon as he is released, Jonas bites the knuckles of his right hand so hard that Danielle winces.

Marianne seems inconsolable; her veneer of optimism shattered. Danielle leans over and embraces her awkwardly as the woman sobs in her arms. Normal mothers are oblivious to their enormous, impossible blessings, she thinks. To have a child who has friends, goes to school, has a future — these are the dreams of a race of people to whom she and this woman no longer belong. They are mere truncations, sliced to so basic a level of need that their earlier expectations for their children seem greedy to them now — small, mercenary — almost evil. Their one hope is sanity. Some dare dream of peace. As Danielle tightens her arm around this destroyed woman, she knows that the communion between her and this stranger is deeper than sacrament. She feels the holiness of the exchange, however alienated and bereft it leaves them. It is all they have.

Danielle stares up at the forbidding sign posted on the thick glass doors. *Secure unit. No unauthorized persons. No exit without pass.* The black, merciless eyes of one of the 24-hour security cameras glare down at her from a corner of the room. They learned at orientation that they are installed in each patient's room and in the common areas.

This is supposed to make them feel safe.

It is late afternoon. Danielle stands at the reception desk, but Max hangs back. He is terrified. Danielle can tell. The more afraid a teenager is, the more he acts like he doesn't care. Max looks bored shitless.

Danielle doesn't blame him. By the time the group session was over, she was ready to slit her throat.

"Ms. Parkman?" The nurse waves her over with a big smile. "Ready?"

Oh, sure. Like mothers in the Holocaust about to separate from their newborns. She squares her shoulders. "I'm at the hotel across the street — Room 630. Can you tell me when visiting hours are?"

The nurse's smile fades. "You're not leaving tomorrow?"

"No, I'm staying until I can take my son home."

The smile dies. "Parents are not encouraged to visit during assessment. Most go home and leave us to our work."

"Well," says Danielle, "I suppose I'll be the exception."

The nurse shrugs. "We have all the pertinent data, so you can go back with Dwayne to the Fountainview unit." The enormous attendant who came to Marianne's aid with Jonas appears. Dressed in blinding white,

33

his chest is so big that it strains against the unforgiving fabric of his shirt. As he comes toward them, Danielle thinks of football players, heavyweight wrestlers — men with abnormal levels of testosterone. She looks at her pale boy, who weighs no more than two damp beach towels, and imagines this man pinning him to the ground. If Max bolts, this guy will snap him up in his jowls like a newborn puppy and carry him down the hall by the scruff of his neck.

"Hi, I'm Dwayne." The wingspan of his outstretched hand is larger than Danielle's thigh.

"Hello." She manages the smallest of smiles. Dwayne grasps her hand, and she watches it disappear. In a moment, he returns it.

He turns to Max. "Let's do it, buddy."

Danielle moves forward to embrace him, but Max charges her — fist raised, face enraged. "I'm not going in there!"

Dwayne steps in. With one elegant motion, he yanks Max's arms in front of him; slips behind him; and envelops Max's entire upper body in his massive arms. The ropy muscles don't even strain. Winded and trapped, Max flails and twists. "Get your fucking hands off me!"

"Give it up, son," growls Dwayne.

34

Max shoots Danielle a look of pure hatred. "*This* is what you want? To have some ass-hole put me in a straightjacket and lock me away?"

"No, of c-course not," she stammers. "Please, Max —"

"Fuck you!"

Danielle is rooted to the floor as Dwayne drags Max down the hall. They come to a menacing red door that buzzes them through. Her last glimpse of Max's contorted face is seared into her mind. He stares at her with the betrayed eyes of an old horse at the glue-factory gate. He is gone before she can utter the words that strangle in her throat.

At the far end of what appears to be a TV room are four women dressed in jeans and T-shirts — undercover nurses in casual disguise. A large whiteboard hangs on the wall. It unnerves her that Max's name is already there with ominous acronyms scribbled next to it — "AA, SIA, SA, EA, DA." The black letters hang final, immutable. She sneaks a look at the typewritten sheet pasted on the board. "AA — Assault Awareness; SIA — Self-Infliction Awareness; SA — Suicide Awareness; EA — Escape Awareness; DA — Depression Awareness." The words slice her heart.

Danielle glances around the room and notices Marianne chatting with an older doctor. She smiles warmly at Danielle. Jonas plucks at his clothes and twitches his feet in an odd, disturbed way, as if he's doing the flamenco sitting down. Then she sees Carla and her son go into one of the bedrooms. Her heart sinks. She would do anything to prevent Max from being on the same unit with a boy who would break his own mother's arm and purple her eye.

An older woman with a shock of short, white hair enters the room and walks up to Danielle. She exudes a calm authority. A conservative, navy suit matches feet shod in dark, sensible flats. Behind small, gold-rimmed glasses are very, very green eyes. Her doctor's coat is Amway white. Red embroidery on her lapel says *Associate Director — Pediatric Psychiatry, Maitland Hospital.* She holds out her hand with a smile. "Ms. Parkman?"

"Yes?"

"Dr. Amelia Reyes-Moreno," she says. "I'll be Max's primary doctor while he's here."

"Nice to meet you." Danielle stares as she shakes the woman's hand. Her long, fine fingers are cool to the touch. Intensity and intelligence are evident in her gaze. Danielle's research of Maitland revealed

36

that Reyes-Moreno is one of Maitland's most valued psychiatrists, nationally renowned in her field. She glances at the old doctor with Marianne, his veined hands folded as he listens. Both are smiling. Danielle wants him. Someone who looks as old as Freud and who'll take one look at Max and say, "Of course! I see what they've all missed. Max is fine, just fine." Then he'll nod his head wisely and go on to his next miraculous cure.

Dr. Reyes-Moreno catches the arm of a young, dark-eyed man who looks like a pen-and-ink rendering of Ichabod Crane. "Dr. Fastow," she says, "would you mind my introducing you to Ms. Parkman? She is the mother of one of our new patients, Max."

He nods curtly and fixes Danielle with a milky stare. "Ms. Parkman."

"Dr. Fastow is our new psychopharma-cologist," says Reyes-Moreno. "He has just returned from Vienna, where he spent the last two years conducting exciting clinical trials of various psychotropic medications. We are honored to have him."

Danielle takes the hand he offers. It is cold and dry. "Dr. Fastow, are you planning to significantly change Max's medication protocol?"

His gray eyes are limpid. "I have reviewed

Max's chart and ordered extensive blood work. I plan to take him off of his current medications and put him on those I believe will better serve him."

"What meds are those?"

"We will provide you with that information once we are more familiar with Max and his symptoms." He gives her another cold stare and takes his leave.

Put off by his antiseptic manner, Danielle turns to Reyes-Moreno, who nods reassuringly. "Don't worry, we'll take good care of him." Danielle panics as she watches Reyes-Moreno disappear through the malefic doors of Alcatraz. Only the dominating truth — that Max wants to kill himself — prevents her from breaking down those doors and fleeing with him back to New York. She takes a deep breath. There is nothing to do but go back to the hotel and work. She turns to go.

"Who are you?" A muscular girl with thick, oily hair stands before her with clenched fists.

Danielle tries to walk around her, but she blocks her path like a defensive back. "I'm a . . . mother."

"I'm Naomi." Her eyes snap like a bird whose nest has been threatened. "You that new kid's mom?"

38

"Yes."

"He's a real brat, that one. I can tell." She swaggers her hips back and forth and smirks. "He just better stay out of my way, that's all. I'm dangerous."

Danielle blinks, rooted where she stands. "What do you —"

"I cut people."

"What?"

Naomi lifts up a greasy lock of hair and reveals a ruby keloid the size of a fat caterpillar on the side of her neck. "I practice on myself first." Her fingers let the fatty strands fall back into place. Coal-pot smudges under her eyes look like permanent bruises and are an odd contrast to her light eyes and gray skin. Danielle has one thought: *this ghoul is going to be with Max every day.*

"Boundaries, Naomi." It is big Dwayne. He inserts himself between Danielle and Naomi and points a large finger down the hall. "Move it."

"Yeah, right, Duh-wayne." Her eyes glitter like a raccoon holding a silver spoon in the dark. "Why don't you get your sorry fucking face out of my *boundaries,* okay?"

"Get to your room. You know the drill." Dwayne has the hardest soft voice Danielle has ever heard.

"Fuck you."

"An hour. Solitary."

Naomi skulks down the hall.

Dwayne turns to Danielle with a big grin.
"Welcome to Fountainview, Mom."

CHAPTER FOUR

Danielle spends an exhausting morning at the hospital giving Reyes-Moreno Max's life history. It so debilitates her that she goes back to the hotel, takes off all her clothes and sneaks between the cheap sheets like a downtown hooker on a lunch break. Marianne, who is staying at the same hotel, rousts her after only twenty minutes and hustles her off to the Olive Garden on Main Street.

Danielle settles into the fake leather booth, which exhales as she sits. The Olive Garden may be the only restaurant in Plano that actually serves wine with names on it, not just colors. Danielle is relieved to find that they have real knives and forks — not the antisuicide plastic of Maitland. The waitress takes their drink order and disappears.

Danielle sneaks a sidelong glance at Marianne's ensemble. She wears a crisp, navy pantsuit with a cream-colored blouse. A diaphanous scarf with paisley butterflies is wound loosely around her neck and is held in place by a simple gold pin. Her blond hair is freshly coiffed. Her short nails are painted a demure beige that matches her bag, which brims with needlepoint and vivid yarns. Marianne appears supremely calm and composed in her femininity. Danielle glances down at her own pantsuit. Is everything she owns black?

They have been discussing their sons' disabilities and disorders, their medications and Maitland. Danielle learns that Jonas has pervasive developmental delay (PDD), oppositional defiance disorder (ODD), and is profoundly autistic. The prospect of a premature exchange of private information about her son — anathema to any New Yorker — keeps Danielle closemouthed. She does disclose that Max has Asperger's, but does not reveal that Dr. Reyes-Moreno did her level best to persuade Danielle to go back to New York until the assessment is concluded. She cited the needs of the "process" — observation, transference, medication, testing — all of which apparently cannot take place effectively with her in the wings. Danielle had smiled politely, but has no intention of leaving.

As Marianne goes on with the litany of medical minutiae only mothers of these children find remotely interesting, Danielle hears something that catches her attention. "What did you say?"

Marianne snaps open a starched red napkin and fans it on her lap. "I was talking about a new drug Dr. Fastow, the über-psychopharmacologist, has prescribed for Jonas. I'm very excited about it, even though the potential side effects are disturbing."

"What are they?"

Marianne shrugs. "Liver damage, heart problems, tardive dyskinesia."

Danielle is alarmed. Long-term use of some antipsychotics — even the newer atypicals — can result in permanent physical problems, like irreversible rigidity of the extremities. Danielle imagines Max with his tongue stuck out in a frozen sneer or his arm jutted at a permanent right angle to his body. "Aren't you scared?"

Marianne runs her finger down to a menu selection and holds it there. "Not really. It's more important to be willing to take risks when you're at this level."

Danielle isn't sure what she means. Maybe Max isn't at the same level — whatever that is.

"So, tell me," says Marianne. "Has Max

ever been violent? I know that's an issue for so many special-needs boys."

Danielle feels her face flush. "No, not really. A few incidents at school." And tearing at her arms.

Marianne squeezes her hand. "It's okay. Jonas has been violent, too, but more in the nature of self-infliction. You know. Clawing at his arms, biting his knuckles — all perseverative behaviors." She shrugs. "Besides, Jonas has had such severe problems since the time he was born that it's a miracle we've made it this far. He was cyanotic as an infant — turned blue, you know. I had to sleep next to him night and day. One minute he'd be fine, and the next he'd be purple and cold as ice. I can't tell you how many nights we spent in the emergency room." She looks up. "Not exactly lunch conversation — sorry."

"Not at all. How often do you see him? I get short visits in the morning and afternoon."

Marianne's eyes widen. "You're joking, right?"

Danielle frowns. "No, Max's psychiatrist says that anything more will interfere with his assessment."

"Well, Dr. Hauptmann gives me unlimited access."

"Dr. Hauptmann?"

"You saw him with me the other day." Marianne gives her a surprised look. "He's the foremost child psychiatrist in the country. I'm sure you researched all the doctors here, as I have." Marianne accepts a white wine from the waitress with a big smile. "Dr. Hauptmann and I have been in contact for some time, and he agrees on the nature of my involvement in the assessment." She shrugs. "I think it's because I'm a doctor. We talk about things he can't discuss with just any parent. If it were up to the staff — especially that Nurse Kreng — I'd never see Jonas."

Danielle feels the effects of the wine. She sits back, finally unwinding. "Where are you from, Marianne?"

"I was born in a little Texas town called Harper — way up in the hill country. My daddy was a rancher." Marianne laughs at Danielle's raised eyebrows. "He said I was just like his cattle. I matured early, with a high carcass yield and nicely marbled meat. So I wouldn't end up in a hayloft with one of those Harper boys, he shipped me off to the University of Texas." She shrugs. "When I graduated, I applied to medical school and got in."

"Where?" Danielle can't help it. Pedigree

means a lot to her.

"Johns Hopkins."

"That's very impressive."

Marianne gives her an amused look. "Southern girls do have brains, you know."

Danielle blushes. "What happened to your plans to practice medicine?"

"A month before I had Jonas, my husband, Raymond, had a massive coronary and passed away."

Danielle grasps her hand. "How awful for you."

Marianne gives Danielle's hand a squeeze. "Thank you. It was difficult, but I have Jonas. He's such a blessing." Danielle nods, but can't help thinking how blessed she would feel if her husband had died right before she gave birth to such a damaged, fractured child.

"So," she says, "once I began to appreciate the extent of Jonas's challenges, it became clear that I had to give up my dream of becoming a doctor. I couldn't justify that path if it meant turning over my son's care to a stranger, no matter how qualified." She smiles at the waitress as she serves the entrées. After she leaves, she looks at Danielle with her beautiful blue eyes. "So I took on part-time jobs as a pediatric nurse. It hasn't been easy, but it gives me the flexibility I need."

Danielle tries to think of something meaningful to say. Her respect for Marianne has grown commensurate with her quiet, dignified tale of self-sacrifice and love. She feels a stab of guilt. Would Max have had all these problems if she had stayed home? She looks at Marianne. No matter what her difficulties with Max, they are child's play compared to this poor woman's lot.

Her face must reflect her dismay. Now it is Marianne who reaches over to pat Danielle's hand. "It's not so bad. We all have our trials and joys."

"I just want you to know how much I admire you," says Danielle. "You seem so strong and . . . balanced."

"You're stronger than you think." She flashes her brilliant smile. "And we're going to be great friends — I can tell."

Danielle smiles back. Maybe she's right. Maybe she does need a friend.

CHAPTER FIVE

Danielle looks up. Marianne catches her eye and smiles. They sit in companionable silence in a secluded area of the Fountain-view unit called the "family room" — a misnomer if Danielle's ever heard one. It is, however, the only place where they have any privacy and can avoid the daily traffic of nurses and patients going to and from their rooms. It is the only hideaway where they can pretend that everything is normal. Danielle closes her laptop for a moment. She is seriously behind in e-mailing a draft brief to E. Bartlett Monahan, her senior partner and the bane of her existence. He is the head litigation partner and a member of the management committee — one of the firm's five powerhouses who rule them all. "King Prick," as he is referred to by the associates, is forty-eight, a bachelor and a not-so-secret misogynist. E. Bartlett, as he insists on being called, doesn't believe that women have the balls to be litigators, much less partners. Women are secretaries, mothers, other men's wives and — when the urge strikes — to be slept with and discarded.

He has not taken kindly to her absence — not that she expected a whit of understanding from him. He has no experience with kids — and he certainly has no clue about special-needs children.

She rubs her eyes and takes in the scene. Marianne sits across from her, knitting what appears to be something complicated, while Jonas holds a ball of yarn, which he bounces in his hands. He mutters and shakes his head in that odd, rhythmic way that Danielle has come to recognize as his attempt to communicate. Marianne, dressed in a perfectly creased white pantsuit and silk scarf, appears not to notice Jonas's machinations as she calmly knits and purls. Danielle has always avoided engaging in the domestic arts. Her experience has been that professional women cannot risk being perceived as weak or too feminine in any way — at least not litigators. Danielle has always secretly looked down upon women who stayed home as inferior in both position and choice. As she watches Marianne and Jonas and sees the love and devotion that binds them, she feels herself color and repents.

She certainly can't claim that she has been the best parent in the world if Marianne is the benchmark. Unlike her, Danielle never contemplated quitting her career to take care of Max — not that she had the choice. The money had to come from somewhere. Still. She turns and takes in the sight of Max, pale and sprawled across the sofa next to her, sound asleep. Anyone looking at the two of them would probably only see the distance between them. Seeing him this way tears at her heart and gives way to the crushing panic she has felt since they came here. *What is wrong with her child?*

Her cell phone vibrates. Maitland does not permit the use of cell phones — probably to keep the schizophrenics from believing they're on the line with God, she thinks. Sighing, she takes her phone, laptop and purse and walks out of the unit. She plops down on a white cement bench far enough out of sight so that Max can't see her through the window as she shakes a cigarette from the pack. She lights it; inhales deliciously; and touches the iPhone's various Apple icons to access her recent calls. *Shit. E. Bartlett's secretary.* Another touch of the screen. A nasal voice announces that her brief is expected no later than tomorrow morning. She groans. Another late night downing hotel-coffee dregs.

She takes in the brilliant sunshine and vibrant blue sky. She relaxes body and mind, letting the warmth spill over her in golden waves. The last puff of her cigarette is a reluctant one. She has to go back into that sterile, unnatural place. It is agony to sit and not be able to do anything. She sighs and goes back to the unit, where one of the young nurses buzzes her in. As she walks down the hallway toward the family room, she hears shouting and wailing. Her heart slams in her chest as she breaks into a run. The sight that greets her is complete bedlam.

Dwayne, the gigantic orderly, has Max in a Mandt hold. He sits on the floor behind him with his burly arms cinched tightly around Max's chest, his tree-stump legs preventing Max from moving. "Get off me, you son of a bitch!" He writhes, kicks and screams. "Motherfucker!" Dwayne holds him easily, his face impassive, as if he cradles a wild animal every day.

Naomi, her greasy, black hair flying, faces a young orderly who is trying to capture her. She lands a flying kick at his groin. He crumples to the ground, moaning. Another orderly, this one older and bigger, comes up behind her and twists her arms behind her back. Naomi breaks free and circles around him, her hands making swift slicing motions. Her voice is a crow screech. "You want what he got? Bring it on, dickhead!" Her Goth-black nails bite into her palms. She turns around and lands a powerful high kick on the orderly's shoulder. He, too, is implacable as he hauls her kicking and screaming down the hall.

Jonas lies unconscious on the floor. Blood gushes from his forehead. Marianne is on the floor as she cradles his head and wails. Nurse Kreng towers over her. "Stand back, Mrs. Morrison! I cannot ascertain the extent of his injuries unless you *desist.*" Sobbing, Marianne pulls back and covers her mouth.

Danielle rushes over to Max as Dwayne rises to his feet, Max still chained in his arms. "Mrs. Parkman," he says calmly, "I'm taking Max back to his room."

"Let me go, you bastard!" Max bends over and kicks him with his heel. Dwayne merely shifts position, disabling Max once again.

Danielle grabs Max's arm and crab walks with the pair as they make their way down the hallway. She hears her own voice — high-pitched, desperate. "Max! What in the world happened?"

Max twists his face toward her. "That

freak Jonas came at me — that's what happened!"

"What do you mean?"

"I was sleeping on the couch, and the next thing I know the creep's got his arms around me! He got what he deserved!"

Terror strikes black into Danielle's heart. "You hit him? Max —"

"Let go now, Ms. Parkman," says Dwayne, puffing slightly with the effort of dragging Max down the hall. "I've got to get him out of here."

Danielle watches helplessly as he hauls Max into his room. She rushes back to Marianne and, for the first time, notices spatters of bright red blood on Marianne's white pantsuit. Jonas lies prostrate on the floor, partially hidden by the couch and coffee table. Nurse Kreng helps a groggy Jonas up and lays him on the couch. His eyes open briefly, register fear, and then close again.

"Jonas." Nurse Kreng's voice is loud and firm. "Open your eyes." Jonas's eyes open immediately. "Now, look at my fingers. How many do you see?" Jonas's terrified eyes scan her hand. He shakes his head, moans and buries his face into Nurse Kreng's ample bosom. Kreng looks up accusingly at Danielle. "Do you see what your son has done? He has *mauled* this poor boy!"

Danielle kneels before Jonas. Tears well in her eyes. "Oh, Jonas, I'm so sorry! I —" Her hand is slapped away.

"Sit *down, Ms.* Parkman!" Nurse Kreng's eyes fire the command with such urgency that Danielle recoils and almost falls onto the couch. Three clucking nurses help Kreng take Jonas to his room.

Marianne wails and clutches her throat. She is so white that Danielle is afraid she may faint. Danielle rushes to her. "Marianne, oh, God — what can I say?" Marianne falls into Danielle's arms, sobbing uncontrollably.

Nurse Kreng returns, casts a scathing glance at Danielle, and places a firm hand on Marianne's arm. Marianne looks up, dazed and confused. Kreng pulls her free from Danielle's embrace and gives her shoulders a slight shake. "He'll have to be taken to the emergency room, Mrs. Morrison." Marianne looks at her blankly. Kreng raises her voice, as if Marianne is deaf or dying. "He needs stitches. Don't worry. The ambulance is on its way."

Marianne seems clearer. "Are you sure? Can I go with him?"

Kreng shakes her head. "It's best that you wait here. You need to collect yourself so

54

you can comfort him when he returns." She whips her head around and glares at Danielle. "Perhaps you can speak to Mrs. Morrison about who is going to cover the emergency room costs."

Danielle takes a frightened breath. "But, Nurse, what about Max? Is he all right?"

Kreng turns so quickly on her eraser heel that it emits a loud squeal. She shoots Danielle a malevolent look. "Of course. He's the *attacker* — not the *victim*." She walks over to a white cabinet and unlocks it with one of perhaps twenty keys that dangle from a metal ring fastened to her belt.

Danielle takes a frightened breath. "But can't I —"

"No, you can't." Kreng swiftly removes a small brown bottle filled with some kind of liquid. She then yanks out a plastic bag and rips it open. Danielle watches with horrified eyes as Kreng removes a menacing-looking syringe and holds it up, as if she wants to make sure that the needle is long enough.

Danielle's eyes widen. "What are you doing?"

Kreng ignores her as she plunges the needle into the rubber top of the bottle. When she is finished, she holds the syringe; flicks it with a fingernail; and inspects it. Only then does she turn to Danielle. Her words are clipped. "I am sedating your son, Mrs. Parkman. He is completely out of control, and I must ensure that he will not endanger another patient on this unit. He will be restricted to his room until he can prove to *my* satisfaction that he is capable of civilized behavior. In any event, he will no longer be permitted to venture into the common areas without staff supervision." Her eyes are as mean as a vulture's before it plunges down for the kill. Her white heel squeaks violently as she turns to march down the hallway.

Danielle's heart falls. What has happened to Max? Has he really become so violent that he would do such a thing? She can't believe it, but there is apparently no denying that he viciously attacked poor Jonas. Marianne is now crying quietly, gelid tears streaming down her face. She raises her head and gives Danielle an imploring look. "Oh, God, Danielle, you've got to help me. Promise me that you'll keep your boy away from Jonas." She stares down at the blood on her shaking hands. "This is a nightmare."

Danielle pulls Marianne gently down on the couch next to her, far away from the place where Jonas fell and where his precious blood has formed a dark pool on the white, cold floor. She tries to keep the fear and horror out of her voice. "Marianne, tell me what happened."

Marianne nods and takes a deep breath. "We were just sitting here. I was distracted by my knitting, I suppose, and didn't notice when Jonas went over to Max. All he did was try to hug him, Danielle — I saw it with my own eyes!"

"What did Max do?"

Marianne twists her hands in her lap. She raises miserable eyes to Danielle. "He beat him. First he threw him against the coffee table, and then he beat him." She points to the low coffee table that is now at a crazy angle to the sofa. Marianne points. "See that? See Jonas's blood? He hit his head on the corner and split it wide open."

Danielle recoils. She still can't believe it. She knows Max. He has never harmed another human being. Her heart sinks. Well, there were a few altercations at school, but those were just hormonal clashes. As Danielle moves forward once again to comfort the shaking Marianne, a thought sears through her brain. Her boy has truly spiraled out of control. She doesn't know him — this violent stranger. A wild, primitive terror grips her. *Where is Max?* Her heart whispers the truth. He is in a place she can't reach him. *Will she ever get him back?*

CHAPTER SIX

Danielle and Max sit on a bench in the hospital courtyard the next morning. He seems groggy from whatever monster sedative Kreng injected into him. Danielle puts an arm around his shoulders and gives him a squeeze. As she looks at him, so subdued and sweet, she believes that he must be terribly remorseful about his behavior yesterday. After considerable thought, she has dismissed the horrible incident as a fluke. She knows that Max is terrified that he may be like the other patients in the unit, and Jonas is, sad to say, the very worst example for him to see every day. Danielle is certain that when Jonas surprised him, Max's retaliation was merely a knee-jerk response. That must be what happened.

"How are you doing, sweetheart?"

Max moves out of her embrace and turns to her, his face pale and anxious. "I feel — weird. Like things in my head are sort of scrambled."

"What do you mean?" She keeps her voice nonchalant.

His face closes. "Never mind. It's nothing."

"Max, we need to talk about what happened yesterday."

He glares at her. "What about it?"

"Why did you attack Jonas?"

Max's face flares red. "It wasn't my fault! The guy came at me while I was asleep. I just pushed him off of me and he fell. He's a freak — always mooning around and driving everyone nuts."

"But Marianne says you hit him."

Max jumps up from the bench and points an angry finger at her. "Then she's a goddamned liar!"

Danielle decides to switch the subject. They won't get anywhere this way. "Okay, Max. Come sit down."

He sits, but this time at the end of the bench, as far away from her as possible.

Danielle sighs. "Are you feeling okay physically?"

He shrugs. "I guess so. Kind of sick to my stomach."

"It's just the new meds." She avoids mentioning the sedative. There is no need to set off another outburst. She pats his arm. "The doctor says you'll feel better in a few days." Max grunts, leans back, and closes his eyes. Danielle takes a deep breath and then asks the real question. "Are you feeling less . . . depressed?"

Max opens his eyes wide enough to glower at her. "Don't go there, Mom."

Danielle nods and tries to look as if everything is all right. She turns her face up to the warm sunlight, and they sit like that in companionable silence. Then Max moves closer and lays his hand on her arm. "Mom?"

"What is it, honey?"

His eyes are wide with a fear he can't hide from her, although he's trying to do exactly that. The piercing on his eyebrow looks particularly cruel above the dark smudges under his eyes. "Dr. Reyes-Moreno said she has some tests for me today — if I'm not too sleepy." He is quiet a moment, hands folded on his lap. He raises sad eyes slowly to hers. "After I finish those, will they tell her if I'm nuts?"

Her spine stiffens as she fights to speak in a normal voice. "You're not nuts."

Max slumps down farther on the bench, refusing to meet her gaze. Danielle tries to take his hands in hers, but he pulls away. "Yeah, right," he mutters. "That's why I'm

60

here. Have you noticed how sane the rest of these geeks are? Not to mention that creep yesterday."

Danielle cannot disagree, so she does what she usually does in such situations. She bullshits. "You're different from those kids, sweetie," she says softly. "All they're going to do here is fine-tune your medication and get to the bottom of your . . . depression."

Max lowers his head like a veal calf that's been lied to about its imminent slaughter. "Sure."

All Danielle can think about is how awful it must be for him to watch these terribly disturbed children and to worry if — or when — someone is going to tell him how screwed up he is. She holds out her hand, palm up, their secret sign of solidarity. He places his on top, and they link fingers. His hand is almost bigger than hers now.

"Mom?"

She takes a deep breath. "Yes, baby?"

His green eyes stare directly into hers. "What do we do if they say I'm really crazy?" He turns away quickly, as if he can't bear hearing the question out loud, much less the answer. Danielle takes him in her arms and holds him to her. His thin body quivers like a mouse caught in a trap. She

squeezes him tighter.
She doesn't have any answers.

CHAPTER SEVEN

Danielle manages to slip a twenty-dollar bill to the bartender and grasp the icy double vodka he offers. Anything more than this is beyond her physical or emotional capabilities. Witnessing Max's fear and pain this afternoon proved more than she could bear. After they went back to the unit, Danielle deposited Max into the care of a chipper Reyes-Moreno, who bustled him off for testing. The backward glance Max gave her tore a fresh slash in her heart.

She takes a healthy sip of her drink. The cold and wet of it jump-starts her, the alcohol producing a welcome effulgence that shimmers down her body. She relaxes enough to take in her surroundings. Plano is a one-horse town, and the hotel is modest, but the bar is a thing of beauty. Soft chandeliers bathe the room in forgiving pools of light as soft music slips through hidden speakers. The carpet, thick and luscious, mutes the murmur of guests who sit around low, glass tables, conversing in small tribes. Danielle drinks steadily until the glass is empty and then holds it up, ice cubes tinkling. The bartender catches her eye and nods. Just as he slides the next glass of elixir across the slick wood of the bar, someone touches her elbow.

"Excuse me."

Danielle turns. A man stands before her. She puts him at about six foot three and fiftysomething. He has white hair at the properly distinguished places around his temples. All-starched white shirt, designer tie and custom suit, he is the epitome of a successful businessman. It is only the kind, brown eyes that prevent Danielle from giving him her customary terse dismissal. "Yes?"

"This is a bad cliché, but may I buy you a drink?" His voice is deep, mellifluous. "I promise — if you don't want company, just say so, and I'll go sit in a corner and drown my proverbial sorrows."

Danielle regards him for a long moment. Her choice is the same as his. Either she can sit here and run the miserable reel of her life over and over, or she can talk to someone else and try to forget about Max for a few minutes. She is suddenly aware that the black dress she slipped on after her shower clings closely to her body. She forces a small smile. "One drink — and then back to your corner."

The smile he flashes back seems genuine. He takes the seat next to her and raises his index finger at the bartender. "One of what she's having. When hers is empty, bring another."

"This is already my second."

He turns and fastens mesmerizing brown eyes upon her. "Then I'll have to catch up."

She holds out her hand and makes a split decision. "Lauren."

"Tony. It's a pleasure to meet you." There is an awkward silence as they wait for his drink to arrive. When it does, he raises his glass to hers. "To a better evening than the day before it."

"I'll certainly drink to that." They clink.

"So," he says, "what possible reason could you have to be in Plano, Iowa? You've got big-city girl written all over you."

She smiles. "Good guess. Manhattan."

"Aha." He reaches over the bar and relieves a plastic container of its olives. He lays a few on her cocktail napkin. "The question still stands."

Danielle dodges his glance. "You first."

"It's too clichéd," he says. "I'm going

65

through a divorce. My wife prefers that I live elsewhere until it's final."

Danielle raises an eyebrow. He laughs. "No, really — it's the truth. I have family and friends here."

"So, what are you doing at a hotel?"

He gives her a wry glance. "Would you stay with family when you're the one who wants the divorce?"

"Point taken." Danielle takes a sip of water, flaming the small hope that it will cut the vodka already swimming around in her head. "Do you have children?"

"No." His voice has something bitter and raw about it.

"Sorry. I shouldn't pry."

"Not at all. And you?" He takes off his jacket and folds it crisply over the back of his chair. Danielle catches a waft of something — Old Spice mixed with man, perhaps. It creates an urgent longing in her, one she immediately dismisses. She can't afford these selfish thoughts, not while Max is in that terrible place. As if he reads her thoughts, he touches her hand. "Listen, if the subject makes you uncomfortable, let's talk about something else."

She looks at him gratefully. "Thank you."

"Are you married?"

She laughs. "I thought you were going to

change the subject."

"I did," he says. "Now we're talking about you."

She swivels a bit toward him and crosses her legs. "Let me try to cut right through this. I'm not married; I have a son; and I don't want to be in Plano, either."

"Hmm." He slowly unknots his tie and leans back in his bar stool. Everything about him exudes a quiet confidence. "Which begs the question — why are you here?"

Danielle blushes. She set him up for that one. "Is it important?"

"No, not really," he says. "Except for one aspect."

"And what might that be?"

"Do I have to dazzle you tonight, or will I have another chance tomorrow?"

"I'm afraid not." She is surprised by the playful tone of her own voice. "This is your only shot."

He shakes his head. "Damn!"

Amazingly, she feels lighter than she has in months. She dismisses the possibility that she is also drunker than she has been in months. She doesn't care. "Where do you live when you're not hiding out in Plano?"

"Des Moines," he says. "So tell me, what is it you do in Manhattan?"

Danielle is uneasy. She doesn't want to

talk about Max, her work, her problems — anything about her real life. Her grip on her emotions is a frayed thread. If she even mentions Max's name, she will burst into tears. The alcohol is already fomenting feelings she hasn't permitted herself to have in years — a yearning for intimacy with a man who could love and support her during these grueling times with Max.

She hasn't had a real relationship since Max was born. Her short affair with Max's father — an unhappily married lawyer at an ABA convention — ended in a pregnancy he never knew or cared about. Since then, no potential suitor was permitted entry into the inner circle reserved to her and Max. Tonight there is no possibility of complication — not with this kind stranger at the bar.

"Let me make a proposal," she says. "No questions about the real world — kids, marriage or work. And no last names."

He raises his eyebrows. "Isn't that usually the man's line?"

"Maybe, but those are my ground rules."

"Then you've got a deal." The brown eyes twinkle. "Are books and music okay?"

The tension in her neck subsides. "Absolutely."

They spend the next hours in rapt conversation. He loves opera; Danielle has a subscription at the Met. She is an avid hiker; he goes white-water rafting every summer. They are both amateur chefs. Danielle's specialty is Indian; his is Thai. His humor and warmth enchant and delight her. When Danielle finally checks her watch, she is shocked to see that it is almost midnight.

"It's getting late," she says.

"I know."

"I think I should go." Her voice is flat.

He leans closer and takes her hand. His touch is electric, synaptic. The air between them is dry powder hungry for the flame. Danielle can hardly breathe. His deep brown eyes are intent upon hers. When he speaks, his voice is hoarse. "Please don't leave."

Danielle hesitates. She should walk away — before she can't. Those eyes, his caress — they mesmerize and enthrall. Her whisper is a feather in the wind. "I . . . don't know what to do."

He rises from his bar stool, still holding her hand. "Come with me."

There is no question where he wants her to go. Spellbound, she stands before him. He grasps her elbows and pulls her lightly toward him. As if her body already knows his, she leans forward into his embrace. As his arms envelop her, she does not question or falter. She is lost, yet found.

The darkness is voluptuous velvet. Danielle hears the click of the lock and watches the smoky outline of his body make its way to the bed, where she lies under the sheets. As he removes his clothes, the spicy ambrosia of his naked body reaches her before he does. As Victorian women swooned, Danielle reels from the essence of this man — unfamiliar, but known. There is no thought other than to have him touch her, know her, consume her. The moment that he lies next to her and their bodies cleave for the first time, she is aware only that she has never been so completely vulnerable, so friable. She simultaneously craves and fears.

Danielle can barely see his eyes, but what she sees is intense and yearning. She moves her hands to his face and holds them there, the roughness of chin against her palms, the softness of cheeks against her fingertips. He whispers something and moves his lips to her neck, throat, breasts. She wants to remember him — every detail of his body, his smell, the feel of his hands on her.

She runs her fingers down his body, shaken with a desire so strong it seems like molten silver streaming from her. His chest is covered with thick, fragrant hair. It is pure male, a luxurious field — all hers. She slides down farther, wanting to feel his pleasure and to have him feel her desire to please him. He stops her and lays her gently on her back. He lowers his mouth to the soft of her stomach. It continues its journey until he reaches the soft folds, the secret middle of her. She opens herself to him and closes her eyes, relinquishing all but the pulsing of her body and the sweetness of his tongue. It is a slow, maddening, upward spiral of sensation — an unbearable yearning and then a height, a reaching, an explosive burst at the pinnacle. She cries out, writhing and peaking, again and again.

As if he can wait no longer, she feels the thrust of him inside her as she clings to him, moving in time to the ancient dance, a single pulse. At the moment of release, she rises — hips, mouth, arms, thighs — to meet his arching abandon with a fierce climax of her own. Afterward, they lie in each other's arms. He holds her tightly to him, his breathing irregular, his heart beating strong against her own. As she meets his mouth, she tastes herself, him, them, on her lips. Something breaks inside her, and tears stream from her eyes. Her sobs are ragged, rough blows that rack her body. They are Max, her loneliness, her pain — her joy.

"Shh, shh," he whispers. "It'll be all right." His words are a balm, his arms strong and solid around her.

"No, no, it won't," she whispers back, her voice thick, throttled.

"Then hold on to me." He squeezes her tighter.

She clings to him as the dying cling to life.

CHAPTER EIGHT

Danielle awakens slowly. The room is dark, the curtains drawn. She groans as she thinks of the day ahead — the stultifying boredom whenever she isn't with Max; her unsuccessful attempts to work; and the constant anxiety about what the assessment will ultimately reveal. Then her eyes fly wide open. She remembers — everything. After their incredible lovemaking, they talked for hours. Tony talked about the disappointment of his divorce and his regret that he had no children. She told Tony about Max (using another false name) — his problems, her fears, her loneliness as a single parent. She did not reveal that she was a lawyer or that Max was at Maitland. Danielle could not bear to speak of the fresh agony of a hospitalized Max. She finally drifted off, awakening before dawn to an empty bed. Embarrassed and not a little piqued at having been loved and left, she got up hastily and dressed. Before she left, she caught a glimpse of something white next to her pillow — a sheet of hotel stationery.

Hate to go, but have to be in Des Moines this morning. Could not disturb your sleep. You look beautiful in my bed. Dinner tonight? Yours, Tony

Danielle sits down at the small writing desk. She reads and rereads the note. Reluctantly, she turns it over and writes. "I can't tell you what last night meant to me. You are a wonderful, lovely man, but my life is far too complicated for a relationship that has nowhere to go." She pauses. The memory of his hands upon her and the absolute safety she felt in his arms flood her with warmth and desire. She balls up the page and picks up another piece of hotel stationery. "I'd love to. See you downstairs at seven." She signs her false name. "Lauren." After that, she takes one last look at the deliciously mussed bed and walks out.

Back in her room, Danielle pulls on her jeans and makes a cup of vile hotel coffee. No sooner does she take a scalding sip than there is a knock on her door. "Damn."

"Hey, you. Let me in."

That voice couldn't belong to anyone else. Danielle grabs the knob and flings open the door. "Georgia!"

Dressed in a dark, navy suit, Georgia walks in and gives Danielle a big hug. "Surprise!"

"My God! What are you doing here?"

She grins. "Just passing through."

Danielle pulls her farther into the room. "I can't believe you're here."

Georgia sits on Danielle's lumpy couch. "I can't believe it, either. Just when you think it's over, there's that drive from Des Moines to scenic Plano."

"Coffee?" She gives Georgia a broad smile.

Georgia peers into the paper cup Danielle offers. "I'll pass."

They sit, and Georgia squeezes her hand. Danielle is thrilled to see her dear friend. "Why are you here, by the way?"

"Because I'm worried about you and Max." She takes a deep breath. "And I have some things to tell you that I felt needed to be said face-to-face."

Danielle feels a fresh uneasiness. "What things?"

"Later." Georgia settles back into the couch.

Danielle waits. Their specialty is shorthand

speech. Georgia begins the beguine.

"How are you?"

"Okay."

"Max?"

"Not great."

"He hasn't tried to —"

"No!" She pulls back. "Of course not!"

Georgia places a cool palm on her arm. "I'm sorry. It's just that you don't always tell me the worst."

Danielle gives her a miserable smile. "It's because I can't even bear to think about it."

"Do you have a diagnosis?"

"No." Before she lets Georgia continue her cross-examination, Danielle changes the subject. "Tell me something about the outside world."

Georgia doesn't let her down. There is the latest office gossip — who's sleeping with whom; who made a fool of himself at the summer recruiting party; which associate is brown-nosing which partner; which partners are trying to screw around other partners.

"So," says Danielle, "how did you manage to get away from the office? From Jonathan and Melissa?"

Georgia's lovely face bleeds from blushed pearl to arsenic white. "Oh. That."

"Oh, what?"

Her deep indigo eyes fall to the floor. "Well, like I said, there are a few things I have to tell you."

"A lot, I'd guess." Danielle's voice is dry. "And don't try to put a good spin on it, Georgia. You look like shit, and I want to know why."

Georgia meets Danielle's eyes. Brilliant tears, unshed, skate on her lower eyelids. "It's Jonathan," she whispers. "He's been . . . fired."

Danielle thinks of the cutting-edge plastic surgery group in which Jonathan has been the boy genius. "What are you talking about? He became a full partner last year, didn't he?"

"Yes." Her voice trembles.

"So what happened?"

Wet diamonds course down her cheeks. "They found out."

"About the drinking? Well, that's not exactly —"

"He's been doing cocaine — a lot of cocaine." Her voice is flat, dead.

Danielle is stunned. "But how did anyone find out?"

Georgia gives her a look of shame and fear. "He operated on a woman while he was high. Everyone in the operating room could tell." She closes her eyes. The rest comes out in a whispered staccato. "Her face is horribly disfigured. There's going to be one hell of a lawsuit. It could ruin their practice."

"When did this happen?"

"A month ago," she says miserably, her face deathly pale. "He never said a word."

"Did his partners turn him in to the police?"

"At first they were in damage-control mode, but then they searched his desk and found a huge stash." Her words are hollow reeds in a blistered wind. "They say he was dealing, Danielle. Can you believe that? Jonathan — a coke dealer!"

"God, Georgia, what now?"

"They reported him to the medical board and fired him immediately. The board suspended him pending a complete investigation." She shakes her head. "There's no question that they'll jerk his license. He's finished."

"Where is he now?"

"The last time I saw him, he was in the apartment, locked in the bedroom — drunk. He told me to get out." The thin thread that held her snaps. Georgia's head falls into her hands as brutal sobs pound her small frame. Danielle holds her dear friend until they subside. Georgia looks up with frantic eyes.

"What am I going to do? What about Melissa?"

"Where is she now?"

"I grabbed her; took her to my mother's house in the Bronx; and came here." Georgia's face is titanium white. "I didn't know what else to do."

Danielle pats her hand. "You did the right thing. Can you stay for a few days?"

Georgia shakes her head. "I have to leave at noon. I start trial in the *Simmons* case on Friday."

"What timing."

"No kidding."

Danielle retrieves her keys from the desk and takes one off of the ring. "Stay at my place for as long as you want. When I get back, you two can have the guest bedroom. We'll figure something out. Right now you need to concentrate on Melissa and that trial."

Georgia takes the key with a grateful look and wipes away her tears. "I may just use your place as a getaway from the office. I'm desperate for some peace and quiet." She sighs. "Melissa and I will stay with my mother until I can figure out what to do. Thank God Mom is retired, and Melissa isn't in school yet." She takes a deep breath. "Okay, enough about me. What's going on with Max? How are you holding up?"

"Oh, Christ, Georgia, let's not." She hears the tension in her voice.

"Okay." Her voice is as patient as Danielle's is not. "I won't demand ugly details. Just tell me one thing. When are you coming home?"

Danielle shoves an ashtray full of cigarette butts across the coffee table. "In a week, maybe two."

"You're coming back for the partners' meeting, aren't you?"

"Absolutely. I don't want to leave Max, but I'm sure as hell not going to risk my partnership."

"That's my girl. You'll be our first female partner. How can they not anoint someone who won a fifteen-million-dollar case in front of the Supreme Court? Still, you'd better put in some face time very soon."

Danielle shakes her head. "Not now. They're having trouble titrating Max's medication, and he needs me here. He looks terrified every time I even suggest that I have to go back to New York."

"How often do you see him?"

"Mornings and afternoons."

Georgia glances around the room. "What do you do the rest of the time?"

A migraine blooms somewhere behind

Danielle's left eye, enveloping her forehead in a deep, twisting pain. She thinks briefly about Tony but doesn't mention him to Georgia. It already seems as if it were a dream. "I work. That's not entirely true. I try to work."

Georgia leans back. "Well, that's good, because things are heating up at the office."

"What do you mean?"

Her blue eyes cloud. "It's another reason I came out here. You need to know what's going on. That worm, Gerald Matthews, is sucking up to every partner in his usual unctuous manner, letting them all know he's the natural choice for your spot."

"I'm not worried about him," says Danielle.

"Well, worry about this." Georgia gives her a pointed look. "E. Bartlett is up to something, and it isn't good."

Danielle is silent. E. Bartlett again. His unpleasant countenance appears in her mind's eye. The last few years have been tough on Danielle, now officially designated as his personal lackey. She knows that some of the powers-that-be at the firm hope she'll give up and go elsewhere — once they've made enough money off of her. But they don't know her. She never gives up. Slowly, grudgingly, E. Bartlett has been forced to acknowledge her talents. Although he will never admit it, she is the associate he turns to when a crisis erupts; when a complex case presents an esoteric legal issue; when an important client from overseas must be wined and dined. He even leaves matchbooks on her chair from the all-male club where he takes the prep boys for lunch. It's as close as E. Bartlett comes to having a sense of humor. Despite his currently favorable assessment of her, she knows he will use any excuse to keep her from joining the fraternity of the testicularly anointed. E. Bartlett also has a W. C. Fields view of children. If she hadn't already billed thirty-two hundred hours this year and wasn't due two years' worth of vacation, he would have already dropped her in the dirt. She lights a cigarette, ignoring Georgia's disapproving glance. "Okay, let's hear it."

"It's the *Sterns* case."

"What about it?" *Sterns* involves Danielle's biggest client. It is a juicy class-action suit that has all the earmarks to make the firm millions. That, coupled with her big win in the *Baines* case, is her ace in the hole for partnership. Michael Sterns, the young CEO of the company, loves Danielle's aggressive litigation style and has, thus far, refused to be represented by any of her partners.

Georgia glances away. "The bastard turned over the next slew of depositions to Matthews."

"But that's *my* client —" Danielle cries. "I spent two years wooing that company."

Georgia shrugs. "Too true, my dear, but you are a mere associate."

Danielle slaps her hand to her forehead. "Goddammit."

Only partners are allowed to put their names on the case-generation form. Her initials appear in small type as the assigned minion. E. Bartlett has been getting credit for *Sterns* for over a year now. That, coupled with the fact that her billable hours have dropped precipitously since Maitland, puts her into the average category. And average won't make her a partner. Panic rises in her throat. She can't let this partnership slip through her hands. She's earned it — not to mention the fact that she needs the extra income to help pay Maitland's phenomenal bill. As usual, insurance only covers the bare minimum, and there is no way she can cover the uninsured portion on her salary and savings. She also has Max's future expenses to consider — whatever they might be.

"That's not all," says Georgia. "Last night I stayed late to work and ran down to Harry's for a drink and a sandwich. You know the scene — the whole firm crawls over there before the partnership meeting — boozing it up while they bullshit each other about how great their candidates are." Harry's is a terrific place for lawyers to gather. Danielle almost feels the cool dark of the room; the huge oak bar with brass bar stools; the rows of dusky liquor bottles; the deep, red leather booths; the blurred light from the candles on the tables.

Danielle puts her bare feet on top of the cheap coffee table. She wishes she were half as relaxed as she appears. "So this year is exactly like any other."

Georgia frowns. "You're wrong there, I'm afraid. Guess who I saw — all closed off and cozy?"

"Who?"

"E. Bartlett and Lyman — two snakes in a pit."

Danielle sits up straight, her eyes wide. "But that's impossible."

Lyman and E. Bartlett started with the firm in the same class and have been bitter rivals ever since. E. Bartlett made partner a year before Lyman, and he's never forgotten it. The lengths to which the two go to stab each other in the back are legend.

Georgia takes the cigarette out of

Danielle's hand and stubs it out. "Well, the impossible has occurred. They were knocking back a bottle of single malt and grinning from ear to ear."

It doesn't take a clairvoyant to know what's happening. Her absence has so pissed off E. Bartlett that he's agreed to let Lyman's boy leapfrog her. She wraps her sweater tighter around her. "I don't like the sound of that."

"No kidding," says Georgia. "I also overheard one of Lyman's lackeys saying that Lyman didn't trust E. Bartlett farther than he could kick him. It would be just like E. Bartlett to put on a great friendship act with Lyman and then totally screw him over at the partners' meeting."

Danielle feels a flicker of hope and grabs Georgia's hand. "It would be just like him, wouldn't it?"

"True." Georgia gives Danielle's hand a firm squeeze, but something is very wrong with her voice. "Look, E. Bartlett isn't all you have to worry about. The scuttlebutt is that the partners met last week and decided that, due to financial concerns and low billable hours, they're considering firing some associates."

"What?"

"The goal is to get rid of four of us by

January," she says softly.

Danielle's heart lurches until she runs the numbers through her head. "Well, at least you and I are in the clear. We're the top producers of the whole damned section."

"Exactly — and the most expensive." Georgia sighs and hands her a piece of paper. "There's more. I got a copy of the latest musings of the partnership committee yesterday — from the trash can of E. Bartlett's secretary."

Danielle doesn't comment on Georgia's methods. "And?"

"And . . ." Georgia draws a deep breath. "You're up — or you're out."

CHAPTER NINE

Danielle sits in a battered vinyl chair, jacked up with a hydraulic thing so the flashy hairdresser with the flaming red lipstick can get a good look at her. Country music blares as the woman pops her gum and delivers her verdict.

"Cut." She wheels Danielle around. "Perm."

Danielle sees her eyes in the mirror, as large and wild as a religious zealot who shows up on your doorstep to pray for your soul. *Oh, well,* she thinks. *Drastic times require drastic measures.* She nods her assent.

After Georgia left, Danielle worked like a madwoman, making client calls; following up on court and deposition dates; catching up on her billing records. Georgia's visit struck terror into her heart. She *has* to make partner. If she doesn't, there will be no way to fund Maitland's expenses, much

less the special schools and future treatment
Max may need.

She is bleary-eyed by the time Marianne
shows up at her door and asks if she would
like to escape for a while. Danielle grabs
her bag and hops into Marianne's car. They
laugh and chat their way across town to a
small beauty shop with the name Pearl's
above the door in faded red letters. Danielle
so thoroughly enjoys herself that when the
pedicures are over, she lets Marianne whirl
her in front of a mirror and convince her
that it is definitely time to take a serious
stab at personal grooming. Besides, Danielle wants to look her best when she has
dinner with Tony tonight. She has a brief
consultation with Pearl, drops into a chair
and surrenders herself to the process.

The scissors are sweet as they slice
through her hair. So true, so simple. The
acrid solution on her head is shockingly
cold. Under the dryer, she falls into a
trance. Pregnant with Max, she sees him
through the translucent onionskin that is
her stomach. He is a tiny fetus, perfectly
formed, eyes closed. Red and blue veins in-
terlineate his little body. He curls around
them, waiting to come out. Wine-colored
blood and magenta amniotic fluid flow
seamlessly from mother to son in primal

grace. She rubs her stomach under the warm air.

Relaxed, she lets her mind wander to Tony and their dinner tonight. Will they make love again? A warm blush suffuses her body as she considers the possibility. She lets herself fantasize about a holiday with Tony — on a sandy beach somewhere in the Caribbean, the glistering azure of the waves lapping before them as they lie with their arms entwined like teenagers exploring a first love. After that, Tony will make regular trips to New York, where they will see plays, cook extravagant dinners and eat them in bed while watching old movies on television. Max will adore him, and Tony will happily be the father he has never had. She can almost see the glittering diamond on her finger and the look on Tony's face as he lifts her veil to kiss her . . .

"Done!" The redhead raps on her plastic helmet, takes her to the sink and rinses her hair. Plastic rollers plop into the bowl like hard rocks that clack against one another at the base of a waterfall. After a fierce blow-drying, she twirls Danielle around. "Terrific. You'll love it."

Danielle looks at the woman in the mirror. Her mouth forms a horrified O. She ignores the fact that her face is the color of powdered sugar and that exhaustion has worn deep ruts under her eyes. She squints at the new, close-cropped curls that have turned her head into a battleground. After a long moment, she decides they look like the crazy cockscomb of an electrocuted rooster.

"Don't you worry none, sugar," says Pearl. "Everybody thinks they're a little different-lookin' after a perm." She pulls an odd tool from her cart. It is some type of flat, metal comb with long spikes. She stabs and picks at the tight curls, her gum snapping nonstop until she reaches the desired effect. She hands the comb to Danielle. "A girl's best friend! Almost — if you know what I mean, honey!"

CHAPTER TEN

Danielle takes a deep breath. She barely caught the early flight out of Des Moines. E. Bartlett's secretary called her yesterday afternoon to inform her that the partners' meeting had been moved up a day. She saw Max before she left. He seemed a bit odd and flat, but stable. She also cancelled dinner with Tony by leaving a message at the front desk. She has to focus completely on her real life and, unfortunately, he doesn't fit into that category — yet.

Danielle hears the *ping* of her heels as they march across the marble floor. Her firm is in one of the oldest buildings on Wall Street, and its cool silence calms her. She takes the elevator upstairs. The receptionist smiles in greeting, her eyebrows rising suddenly as she stares at Danielle's hair. Nodding curtly, Danielle walks down the hallway and stops to collect herself. She takes a deep breath and opens the door. She takes in the large room on the forty-second floor and the thirty male partners of Blackwood & Price, an old-line bastion of the post–Second World War law firms. She studies the high gloss of the conference table, made of burled wood harvested from a special grove in South America. On top of the table is an impressive floral arrangement, an antique china and silver service for fifty, and a gourmet lunch catered by one of Manhattan's trendiest restaurants. At this point in the deliberations, stout coffee is being poured — a prerequisite for clear thinking after the wine that was served with the meal. There is a shuffling of papers and a few blurred coughs, the inevitable flotsam of decision making.

The partners around the table are not so different from those of any major law firm. There are the rainmakers, who expect routine ass-kissing and stupefying bonuses; the worker drones, who grind out hours on cases they are given; the young partners, who do the real work the senior partner has promised the client would be done only by him; the branch-office partners, bastard stepchildren; and the lazy remainder, a minority contingent with no major clients of their own who play resident sycophant to the powerful and, of course, who prostitute their votes on close decisions — like partnership.

A voice rumbles across the room. "Good afternoon, Danielle."

Danielle looks up and smiles despite her nervousness. It is Lowell Stratton Price III, the head of the executive committee. It is he who was mentored by the great admiralty and international lawyers — the ones who marched off to Europe and Scandinavia after the Second World War and cornered the shipping business. With silver hair and intelligent eyes, he commandeers the firm by virtue of the respect all accord him. Lowell Price will be fair.

"Hello, Mr. Price."

"Lowell, please." He gestures to the hot seat at the end of the massive table.

"Thank you, Lowell." In old-line New York firms, it is an unspoken rule that an associate may refer to a partner by his first name only when he or she has become a partner among the anointed. *Maybe it's a good sign,* she thinks. She crosses the room and sits, hands folded, as if she were in court, ready to jump and object. She glances at the partners around the room. They look neither pleased nor displeased. No one notices her strange hair. They're far too self-absorbed.

"Danielle, we have spent the morning discussing the fine associates who are up for partner this year," he says. "We have interviewed the other candidates and are now opening the floor to partners who have questions they would like to pose to you. I understand you've been somewhere in . . . Idaho, is it? On personal business?"

Danielle stifles a groan. "Iowa. And yes, I have taken a few weeks off to attend to a personal matter, but I plan to be back in the office shortly."

"Of course, of course," says Price. She knows he is trying to cushion the glare of white paper — the blank time entries of the past few weeks. She's had all she can handle just putting out fires on her cases. Even though she has worked as hard as she can, she knows that her concerns about Max have impacted her focus. Because of this, she did not feel justified in charging her clients for much of her time. She can almost read the other partners' minds. No time, no money. No money, no partnership. This is where E. Bartlett, if he had a shred of honesty secreted away in that monumental ego of his, should step in and sing her praises. She looks at him, but he doesn't meet her eye. In fact, he is flipping through a magazine. The message is clear: she's on her own. "I don't have your numbers in front of me, Danielle, but perhaps you could tell us what they are and some particulars about your practice."

God bless him, thinks Danielle. He's giving her an open door to toot her own horn. She sits up straight and puts on her game face. "Thank you, Lowell. I have billed thirty-two-hundred hours this year and believe I have shown sufficient drive and commitment to become a partner in this firm. In addition to my billable hours, my success in the *Baines* case resulted in a multimillion-dollar windfall to the firm. I have also generated new, significant clients whose collective billings represent an additional million dollars of the firm's gross revenue."

There is a rustling of paper. Danielle knows the partners are checking her figures.

"You are a very bright, young attorney, and your work ethic is extremely impressive," says Lowell. A murmur of what Danielle hopes is assent drones around the table. "Well, I am getting impatient looks from some of the other partners, so I'll let Ted Knox have the floor."

Danielle stiffens. Knox is a short man — with all of the attendant complexes — and a Lyman toady. Knox relies on Lyman to throw him the bulk of his cases. Without him, Knox couldn't get a job as a paralegal. What really worries her is that he's also a drinking buddy of E. Bartlett's. If Lyman and E. Bartlett are truly in cahoots, Knox is the perfect pit bull. E. Bartlett flips to another page in his magazine. Danielle feels a sharp pressure behind her eyes.

Knox clears his throat and squints at her with his pale, gray eyes. "Thank you for taking time to talk to us, Danielle. We regret that your personal problems — whatever they are — have kept you from the office for so long. Actually, some of us, many in fact, have reservations about your bid for partnership." He gives Lyman a sly grin. "Now, as Lowell mentioned, no one is knocking your hours. You're a good producer — a good associate. But I'm sure you agree that it takes more than long hours to be a partner at Blackwood & Price."

Danielle wants to ask him if the primary criteria include the presence of a penis. She holds her tongue.

"I'll just lay it out on the table." His voice is pedantic. "First, we don't typically consider associates who have been with us less than ten years. You're only in your sixth year. Second, most of us are not familiar with your work, a problem not of your own making, of course, but a problem nevertheless. Third, although you have demonstrated some marketing ability, the marketing in this firm is done by partners, and partners alone."

Danielle grips the side of her chair until her knuckles are white. She wants badly to respond, but has to make sure the little weasel is finished first.

Knox's voice is now syrup, as sticky as the outdated pomade he smears onto the three remaining hairs on his pate. "Let me move on to one of the most troubling aspects of your proposed partnership."

"And that would be?" she asks.

"Michael Sterns."

Danielle's mouth goes dry, but she manages to speak. "Michael Sterns is my client, as you know. I brought him into the firm three years ago, and the multi-jurisdictional class action I'm working on for him is, and will continue to be, extremely lucrative for the firm. In fact, that case alone has generated almost $350,000 in the past nine months."

Now heads come up and eyes fix upon hers. Nothing excites a partnership like talk of big fees. Knox leans back in his chair. "Yes, we're quite aware of what a good client Mr. Sterns is."

"Then I'm sure you can appreciate how thrilled I am to report that Mr. Stearns told me he intends for me to handle all of his future litigation — even though I'm only an associate." She can't resist that last dig. This guy is a card-carrying asshole, and if his clique manages to block a positive vote on her partnership, she wants everyone to know she won't take it lying down.

"Have you spoken to Michael lately?"

"Well, no —"

"Didn't he have a significant problem in New Orleans last week?"

Danielle chafes at his cross-examination. She could wring E. Bartlett's neck. He's cut her loose to hang in the breeze. Beneath her anger is a crushing panic. If she doesn't keep her job, if she doesn't make partner — how will she pay for Max? She looks at Knox with determination. He isn't going to take this away from her. "I wouldn't call it a problem. I'd call it a great case."

"But you refused to fly to New Orleans to accommodate him, despite the fact that his company has fee potential in the millions?" Knox's words are bullets. "Or that he has made it clear that he wants you — and you alone — to handle his cases?"

Danielle stops. What can she say? That she has neglected her work because she has to find out if her son is crazy? That, having been told that her son is receiving the best possible care, she still won't come back to work and take care of her clients? She is furious that she's given this mental-midget ammunition against her, particularly when the deck is stacked in the first place. She meets his cold stare head-on.

"Mr. Knox, as a parent, I'm sure you agree that some things in life take precedence. An emergency arose regarding my son. Michael Sterns had a vessel arrest in New Orleans. I arranged for a senior associate to fly down there and cover it for me. I was in constant touch by telephone. Believe me, Mr. Sterns is aware of the situation and has not complained about the handling of the matter at all."

"Not to you, perhaps," says Knox. "As it happens, Mr. Sterns flew up yesterday to let me know that he is, unfortunately, quite upset about your refusal to interrupt your little trip —"

"Ted, that's uncalled for," says Price. "Okay, fine." Knox's voice is brusque. "But you know as well as I do, Lowell, that this business is twenty-four hours a day. They need us; we go. If we don't, there are fourteen other law firms that'll jump to take our place. And if this girl doesn't have what it takes to make that commitment . . ."

A stunned silence fills the room. Danielle sits back, letting the gaffe sink in. "I'm a damned good lawyer, Mr. Knox," she says quietly. "And I've got the hours and the clients to prove it."

"Yes, yes, of course." Lowell's kind eyes match his reassuring voice.

"In fact," she says softly, "my billings are higher than yours were when you made partner."

Knox ignores the muffled laughter of a few of the other partners, who catch Danielle's eye and smile. "Be that as it may," he says stubbornly, "Sterns told me that he might be willing to let someone else in the firm handle his cases, given your . . . situation."

Danielle doesn't know what to say. Knox is humiliating her in front of the entire partnership, and not one partner has spoken in her defense. E. Bartlett abruptly excuses himself, apparently deciding to leave her to her own devices.

Knox's voice is cold. "I think it's obvious that your priorities have nothing to do with your clients or this firm —"

"That's enough." Lowell's voice is crackled frost. "I'm disappointed in you, Knox. We are not here to engage in personal attacks." He pauses a moment. "Does anyone else have something to say?"

Danielle looks around the table. Stony silence greets her.

"Well, thank you, Danielle," says Lowell. "Good luck."

"Thank you." Her voice is tight. Cinnabar stripes twin her cheeks as she pulls open the heavy, burled door and stalks out. "More like good riddance," she mutters.

CHAPTER ELEVEN

Danielle is breathless after her frantic drive back from the Des Moines airport to Maitland. The flight from New York had begun boarding when she received a hysterical call from the Fountainview night nurse, who told her of a crisis with Max. She said that Dr. Reyes-Moreno would meet Danielle at the hospital but that she was not at liberty to divulge any additional information. Danielle was terrified during the entire flight. When she finally lands in Des Moines, she drives as fast as she can to Plano; jams the car into a handicapped space; and dashes into the unit.

She catches sight of Reyes-Moreno in the hallway. She is in deep conversation with Fastow. He towers over her, his stick neck bent to catch her words. His black, frizzy hair is shot through with gray. They stop talking as soon as she reaches them. "What's wrong with Max?" she demands.

"Danielle," says Reyes-Moreno. "You remember Dr. Fastow. He is —"

"I know who he is," she interrupts. "Where's Max?"

Reyes-Moreno takes her arm and steers her into an empty office. Ichabod trails behind. "I'm afraid that Max seems to be dissociating," she says. "His behavior today — while not suicidal — has been highly erratic and disturbing."

Danielle tries to keep the panic out of her voice. "What do you mean, 'dissociating'?"

"He is losing touch with reality." Her olive eyes are rueful. "It could be the result of extreme anxiety, but we feel it needs to be addressed immediately. In addition to Max's continued perseveration upon suicidal ideations, he has had another . . . episode."

"What does that mean?"

Reyes-Moreno's eyes slide past Fastow before they fix on Danielle. "Max attacked Jonas. As you know, it isn't the first time."

Danielle's heart races. She flashes back to that horrible day when Max assaulted Jonas — the blood on his head and Marianne's stricken face. "Why didn't you tell me this? Did he . . . hurt him?"

"Unfortunately, we had to keep Jonas under observation all day yesterday." She touches Danielle's arm lightly. "He'll be fine. The fact remains, however, that Max punched Jonas in the nose, and the boy bled profusely. It also seems that Jonas has a cracked rib."

Danielle is shocked. "Where is Max now?"

"We put him in the quiet room —"

"How dare you?" Danielle has seen that room. It's solitary — that's what it is. A big white box with canvas padding all around and a slit of a window to shove food through. She stalks toward the door. Reyes-Moreno grasps her arm.

"Danielle — he isn't in there," she says. "We've had a bit of a . . . situation arise. Please, let's sit." Reyes-Moreno closes the door and continues. "As you know, we put Dr. Fastow on Max's team at the outset of his assessment. He has done a stellar job with Max's medications and is confident that he has found the right —"

"Cocktail," snaps Danielle. "What does that have to do with —"

"There simply isn't any other way to explain it, except to admit that an error has been made," says Fastow. "We are uncertain precisely how it happened, or who is responsible, but it appears that Max received a far higher dose of his current medications —"

"Oh, God," she says. "Is he all right?"

Fastow regards her calmly. "Of course."

Reyes-Moreno takes Danielle's trembling hands into her firm ones. "Max is resting comfortably in his room. He'll weather the overdose and be back to normal very soon."

Danielle yanks her arm free. "*Normal?* You think overdosing him is *normal?* I want to see him."

"There's nothing to see right now, Danielle." Reyes-Moreno's voice is salve on a burn. "He's asleep. I assure you that we'll call you the moment he wakes up."

Danielle stands rooted to the floor. It is all suddenly unbearable — her relinquishment of Max to this place; his terrifying displays of violence; the unspoken presumption that her insistence that she remain here with her own child is injurious to his treatment; and the even stronger undercurrent that somehow her son's very presence here must be her fault. The implication is that she, as his mother, should have seen the "signs" of the severity of Max's problems long before he wound up at Maitland. Her fear galvanizes into anger. "I've had about all of this I can stand. Why don't you tell me how such a thing could happen? You people are supposed to be running the foremost psychiatric hospital in the country — according to the pundits of your profession — and the minute I'm gone, you overdose my child!" She jerks her head toward Fastow. "And now we have his medicating physician, the famous psychopharmacologist, who has screwed up in colossal fashion —"

"Ms. Parkman, I must object to your accusations." Fastow's flat, liverish eyes fasten on hers. He leans forward in his chair, head and arms in praying-mantis pose. "This is very disturbing for you, I'm sure, but this was a staff error, not a prescribing error."

All of her pent-up frustration, fear and anger burst to the surface. "I don't care who fucked up — and that's the only word for it — but it's my boy in there. Who knows what an overdose like that will do to him?" She shakes her head when Fastow tries to respond. "Look — both of you — I've been more than patient and cooperative since we got here. When I tell you I want to stay here with my son, you tell me to go home. Then you put me on supervised visitation like I'm some kind of axe murderer. And now you tell me that Max has attacked a patient. It's absurd!"

Fastow folds his arms across his chest and stares at her, unperturbed. Reyes-Moreno's emerald eyes are kind. There is that pat on the arm again. Danielle fights the urge to shake it off. "Danielle," she says softly, "you have to keep in mind that we are dealing with a young man with serious issues — one who is obviously suicidal; who now appears to be having psychotic episodes; and who is becoming alarmingly violent. These things take time, which is why we don't like to meet with parents before we can give a true assessment."

Danielle feels the fury in her subside. Now she's just worried out of her mind. What is really wrong with Max? Is it possible that because he's been stripped of the old medications, this "psychotic" behavior — whatever it is — is the true Max coming out? She sighs. But this isn't a courtroom where she can use righteous indignation, however justified, to her advantage. She reminds herself that Maitland — and its doctors — are the very best in the country. It doesn't matter if she chafes at Fastow's arrogance. It's Max that matters. And if Max is exhibiting violent, psychotic behavior, he desperately needs their help, and she has to let them do their job. She turns to Fastow, her voice quivering as it always does when her anger gives way to fear. "I want a list of every medication Max is on — the milligrams, dose frequency and any known side effects."

Fastow gives her a bland look. "Of course. I'm sure most of the medications are known to you, although the combinations may be different."

An idea forms in her mind. She stares at him. "You don't have him on any experimental drugs, do you?"

Fastow's eyebrows — fat, ugly caterpillars — form upside-down U's and stay there. "Absolutely not. Surely you do not question my ethics —"

Reyes-Moreno steps between them, her voice poured oil. "When we have a collective diagnosis, I will schedule a meeting immediately."

"I'll be there." Danielle turns to Fastow. "Will you?"

He and Reyes-Moreno look at each other. Fastow uncoils his lean frame from the chair, a supercilious smile on his face. "I'm sure we'll have an opportunity to converse should Dr. Reyes-Moreno's explanation prove inadequate to address your concerns." He extends a bony hand to her, snake dry to the touch.

"I'll hold you to that."

Fastow gives her his hubristic stare and stalks out. Danielle wants to yank him back into the room and tell him what an arrogant son of a bitch he is, but doesn't. He isn't the first egomaniac in the medical profession who believes — no, knows — that he is God. Telling a deity that he is mortal is pointless. She starts to stand, when she has a revelation. Maybe she detests Fastow because she wants him to be the enemy. If he's giving Max some crazy medication — or overdosing him — then Reyes-Moreno's claim that Max is having psychotic episodes simply isn't true. Danielle knows enough about psychotropic medications to know that the risk of drug-drug interactions can be devastating. But if Fastow is on the up-and-up . . .

Danielle fights the black ice that grips her heart. Max can't be crazy. A slim hope surges in her. Maybe the hospital doesn't know all it should about Fastow, even if they think they did a good job screening him. She'll ask Georgia to run a background check on him. What could it hurt? She turns to Reyes-Moreno. "May I see Max?"

She shrugs. "I told you — he's fast asleep. But if you insist, please keep your visit brief. We don't want to upset him."

Danielle bites her tongue as Reyes-Moreno disappears down the hallway. "No," she mutters, "we certainly don't. A visit from his mother — now, that would upset anyone. But overdosing him is fine, just fine."

CHAPTER TWELVE

Today is the day.

Apparently the collective has finally arrived at a diagnosis. The last week has passed without incident — at least nothing that anyone saw fit to tell her. Max seems so much better. In so many ways, his sweet nature has returned. There have been no incidents of violence and he has shown no resistance to the completion of the assessment. His behavior has so improved that Reyes-Moreno has been able to complete her testing and conclude the evaluation. Even though he seems, at times, terribly sedated and somewhat disoriented, Danielle's guess is that Fastow has finally gotten his act together and fine-tuned Max's medication protocol. Georgia's background check on him turned up nothing at all. In fact, all she found was further evidence of his excellence and creativity in his field. Although Danielle's personal dislike of him has not abated, Fastow seems to have done a laudable job of straightening out Max's medications.

Danielle follows a path through the maze of white sidewalks to the administrative building. She looks up. The sky is a cobalt paint stroke, a piercing, hypnotic blue. The clear crispness of it slices straight through her. Her heart lifts.

"Ms. Parkman, will you come with me?" Reyes-Moreno's secretary, Celia, greets her with a brief handshake. She safeguards her boss like a trained Doberman, never saying whether Reyes-Moreno is there or not when Danielle calls — making it sound like she's always in the restroom or in session. Psychiatrists must have copyrighted employee-training software. They're all the same.

Danielle follows her down the hall that houses the psychiatrists' offices. Celia looks happy. She wouldn't be smiling if Danielle were about to get bad news, would she? She leads her into Reyes-Moreno's *sanctum sanctorum*. It is smaller than Danielle had imagined, especially with the obligatory couch and swivel chair. Toys are lined up on a series of shelves. Danielle turns one of them over gently in her hands, wondering if each represents something incredibly psychiatrically telling. She wonders what Max has said and done in this room.

Reyes-Moreno's diplomas and medical certifications hang in thick, black picture frames. An undergraduate degree from Pasadena, California. What is this? Doesn't everyone who reaches Mecca springboard from Stanford or Yale? At least UCLA? Her heart beats faster as she peers at the other squares of calligraphy displayed upon the wall. There it is — Harvard Medical School. She is relieved. Not that she has anything against Pasadena, but good God, if you're paying for top drawer, you damned well want a thoroughbred.

Danielle settles into one of the two wicker chairs that seem to be reserved specifically for parent consultations. Like her, they feel out of place. She thinks about Tony, wishing she had been able to see him again. After she cancelled their dinner, he left a note at the desk that said he had to go back to Des Moines. He wrote down his cell number, but she hasn't used it. Her life is far too uncertain right now to add him to the mix. The note is still in her purse, a hopeful talisman. She turns her mind to plane reservations. If they leave early tomorrow, she can get Max back to their apartment and still have time to unpack his things. Even the thought of doing his laundry makes her smile. Maybe Georgia, who has returned to Jonathan, can stop by Danielle's apartment tonight, open the windows, and get a few groceries in so it won't seem so deserted. Then maybe Max won't remember they've been gone so long.

Celia returns and hands her a lukewarm coffee. Reyes-Moreno is running a few minutes late. Probably still meeting with Max's team, she thinks. They work in packs here. No one shrink, neurologist, or psychiatrist — no one doctor responsible for anything. She takes a sip of the bitter brew. She'll have to try and square things at the office as soon as she gets home — big-time. She feels a fleeting panic and then pushes it out of her mind. First things first.

So, what will Reyes-Moreno tell her? She'll probably confirm all of the old diagnoses, tell her that the other doctors were mistaken, that they had him on the wrong medications. She smiles to herself. Max seems so much better. He looks more like, well, like Max.

The door opens and Celia comes in. Her eyes don't quite meet Danielle's. She is reminded of jurors who don't look her in the eye when they file back into the courtroom after deliberations. Reyes-Moreno walks in and closes the door. She gives Danielle a broad smile and squeezes her shoulder. The knot of tension Danielle has felt growing somewhere around her neck just as suddenly disappears.

"Good morning, Danielle." Her voice is soft and controlled. "How are you today?"

What appropriate niceties does one exchange with the person who holds your child's life in her hands? "Fine, Doctor. And you?"

"Let's sit, shall we?" She rolls the black swivel chair around until she faces Danielle, Celia slightly behind her. Danielle wonders what Celia is doing there, but doesn't want to ask. Instead, she crosses her legs and puts her hands on her lap. Ready.

Reyes-Moreno sits erect in her chair, eyes intent and focused. "Danielle, I know you've waited very patiently for us to have this meeting, and I'm happy to report that Max's team has reached a definite consensus on his diagnoses and treatment protocol."

Danielle discovers that she's been holding her breath. She forces oxygen into her lungs. Reyes-Moreno begins in a singsong voice. "It probably won't surprise you to learn that we are confirming a number of diagnoses Max has been given over the years."

Danielle relaxes back into her chair. Same

old stuff.

Dr. Reyes-Moreno continues, her rhythm unbroken. "We confirm that Max is autistic — Asperger's — and suffers from an unfortunately wide spectrum of learning disorders and disabilities," she continues in her soft, melodic voice. "He has both a receptive and expressive communication disorder, an auditory processing disorder . . ." Her voice drones on.

Nothing in the litany gets Danielle's attention. She has a legal pad in front of her. As Reyes-Moreno talks, she dutifully writes it all down, as if she's at a deposition getting boring background on an inconsequential witness. As the list of disorders wears on, though, she feels very sad — probably because all she wants to hear is that all the other well-meaning but misguided professionals not only made mistakes about the medications, but also about the autism diagnosis and underlying neurological differences. It would have been wonderful if Max didn't have to face all of these problems. Well, she thinks, as Reyes-Moreno ticks off the list — obsessive-compulsive disorder, fine motor difficulties, tactile defensiveness — she can deal with all of it.

"We recommend a new protocol of antidepressants to combat Max's suicidal tendencies," says Reyes-Moreno.

Danielle goes down a mental list of tricyclic antidepressants, SSRI's, SNRI's and their potential side effects, as well as those contained in the black box warnings. "What are you thinking of? Effexor? Cymbalta? Zoloft?"

Reyes-Moreno looks at Danielle, but doesn't say anything. Danielle turns abruptly and stares at Celia, who starts to say something, but catches a vague signal from Reyes-Moreno and looks away. Danielle's heart is beating too fast, a wild, caged thing struggling to get out.

Reyes-Moreno rolls her black chair closer, takes Danielle's hand and squeezes it. Her voice is baby-blanket soft. "There's more, I'm afraid."

Danielle pulls back. Reyes-Moreno's viridian eyes lock on hers. *If she smiles at me, it means he's all right.* Danielle smiles first — a small, desperate invitation.

Reyes-Moreno has no smile for her. "I'll just say it, and then I want you to know that we're all here for you."

Danielle has no body now. She is only her eyes, which see Reyes-Moreno and nothing else in the universe.

"Unfortunately, our testing has resulted in the diagnosis of a grave psychiatric illness.

Max has an extreme form of psychosis, called schizoaffective disorder." She pauses. "Fewer than one percent of all psychiatric patients fall into this category."

Danielle is stunned. "Max is schizo-phrenic?"

"In part. However, schizophrenia does not have the mood-disorder component that the schizoaffective label carries." She points to a stack of literature on her desk. "I've selected a series of articles that will better help you understand the challenges Max faces. Briefly, the onset of schizoaffective disorder peaks during adolescence and early adulthood. The severe disruptions to Max's social and emotional development — com-pounded by Asperger's — will continue over his lifetime. He will, in all probability, always pose a risk to himself and others, and involuntary hospitalizations will be frequent. Unfortunately, Max displays virtu-ally all of the symptoms under the DSM-IV-TR: delusions, hallucinations, frequently derailed speech, catatonic behavior, anhe-donia, avolition —"

Danielle forces herself to breathe. "This is crazy! He's never had any of the symptoms you're describing."

Reyes-Moreno shakes her head. "Perhaps not when he is with you. However, our daily charts clearly reflect Max's symptoms. You must have seen some of these signs. Parents often live in denial until, as here, the child breaks down completely."

"I do not live in denial." Danielle feels her cheeks flare. "Are you sure that these symptoms aren't a result of the overdose you gave him?"

"No." Reyes-Moreno shakes her head sadly. "These issues are far more pervasive and long-standing.

"What we don't know is if there is a history of psychosis or mood disorder in your family or his father's family." Reyes-Moreno's lips keep moving — like one of those Japanese cartoons where the red mouth looks like a real person's, but the rest of the body is a stiff, poorly drawn animation of a human being and the words come out long after the mouth has stopped. Danielle tries to absorb what Reyes-Moreno is saying, but her thoughts are a silent, deafening scream.

"As I mentioned, Max will require frequent, lengthy hospitalizations over the course of his lifetime due to recurrent psychotic breaks and the extreme incidents of violence we have observed and anticipate. I must tell you that with each successive break, Max's memory and his ability to assess reality will deteriorate exponentially, which unfortunately will compound the severity of his schizophrenia. It will most likely be impossible for him to hold a job or live independently as a result of these breaks. We must also be ever-vigilant with respect to the possibility of future suicide attempts. Unfortunately, Max is fully aware that his mind is compromised. We believe that this knowledge has driven him to consider suicide as the only option." She looks at Danielle. There seems to be real sadness in her eyes. "As such, we strongly recommend that Max be remitted to our residential facility for at least a year, probably longer. He will undergo extensive psychotherapy so we can help him accept his condition."

Danielle struggles to absorb what Reyes-Moreno is telling her, but it's like trying to process the news that you've got terminal cancer. Her mind is frozen, unavailable. She shakes her head.

"Danielle," Reyes-Moreno says softly, stretching out her hand. "Please let us help you deal with this."

She jerks back and stares bullets into Reyes-Moreno. "Leave me alone. I don't believe it. I'll never believe it."

Reyes-Moreno's gentle voice is relentless.

". . . so hard at first . . . terribly severe in his case . . . long-term residential options . . . some medications . . . Abilify, Saphris, Seroquel . . . new electroshock therapies . . ."

All she can think of is that she has to get out of there. She runs to the door without a backward glance, but can't find the knob. She needs the knob.

"Danielle, please listen —"

"Not to this, I won't," she snaps. She opens the door, strides into the hallway, finds a restroom, and slams the door. She grabs the thick, curled edge of the washbasin and sinks to her knees. The cold porcelain feels white and holy on her forehead. Her mind is in a wild panic. If she believes what they say, then everything black and horrible that has crept into her mind at the bleakest moments — and passionately denied — has come true. If she believes what they say, Max will have no life at all.

For one impossible moment, she lets herself feel that. What flows is a thick rush of hot lava, a keening that roils from her soul, dark and sick. She forces herself to stand up and stare at this woman with black tar under her eyes, this blotched face made ugly by knowledge and fear, this. . . . mother of a crazy child. Mother of a child with no hope. She curses God for the beautiful blue light He gave her this morning. She curses Him for what He's done to her boy. Stones, stones — all stones.

"Stop it," she hisses. She has to think, be clear, find a solution. She splashes cold water on her face and tries to breathe, but psychiatric hospitals are vacuums. You're not supposed to breathe fresh air or feel the sun on your face. You're supposed to be in a place where other people aren't. A place where you can be controlled every minute. Where you can be watched and drugged — kept away from normal people and the entire normal world. In a place that is always painted white. The color of a blank. The wiped slate. A place that reduces you, erases the sick part of you and, along with it, the part that makes you human and precious — the part that permits you to feel joy and give joy in return. A quiet, unchallenging world, hermetically sealed with a thick, black ring around it. A place that doesn't keep the dangers of the world from you, but your dangers from the world. A place where you can look at yourself in the mirror and see the truth — one that imprisons you for life.

She grasps the cool sink and stares once more into the mirror. She will not give in to this. She can't. Max needs her.

But the mirror tells her there's no way back. No way back to the time when she believed that someone could put it all back together and make it right. When she believed that even if everyone in the world told her it could never be made right, she would still find a way. No way back to the perfect, soft skin of his tiny, precious body, or the joy in his eyes when she first held him in her arms; his exquisitely gleeful gum smile; his obvious perfection in innocence — limitless in his possibilities. As the mirror blurs and blackens in front of her, the woman she is and the quintessence of that child disappear. The baby is shattered, splintered in the darkness. Cover the glass with a black shawl.

There's been a death in the family.

CHAPTER THIRTEEN

Danielle awakens from a deep, useless sleep — the kind that affords no rest and is punctured with grotesque forms and fractured events that have no link or purpose. When she opens her eyes, her heart beats erratically — a bird shot out of the sky. She feels an amorphous panic; wonders dully if someone is chasing her. The panic is quickly replaced with stark terror. They think Max is irretrievably mentally ill. Her first urge yesterday was to run to him and hold him in her arms. But she can't do that — not yet. If Max sees her eyes, he'll know what he fears is true — that she, too, thinks he's crazy. She never, ever, wants him to feel that.

She lay awake much of the night agonizing over every word Reyes-Moreno said. Danielle still doesn't believe what she told her, particularly the bizarre behaviors they attribute to Max — behaviors she's never seen. No matter how she slices it, there's no way Max could be what they say he is. But what if she's wrong? The right side of her brain tells her that denial is always the first response a parent has to devastating news about a special-needs child. She must do her best to divorce herself from either knee-jerk disbelief or the paralysis of emotional-ism. She has to get back into lawyer mode and uncover the core facts they've based their diagnosis upon. Once pointed in the right direction, she's a better fact finder than anyone she knows.

She jumps up and yanks on jeans and an old, gray sweatshirt. For the first time since they came to this dreadful place, she knows exactly where her compass is leading her.

Danielle crouches outside the rear wall of the Fountainview unit and swats mosquitoes from her neck. The night air is heavy, and tall grass forms a green nest around her. The steel back door stares at her, as if it knows of her intention.

She can't believe she's doing this. What if she gets caught? Even that begs the more basic question: What kind of a mother crawls around a psychiatric facility on her hands and knees in the pitch dark like some kind of card-carrying pervert? Danielle looks around. It would be just her luck if one of the security guards decides that now is the perfect time to make night rounds. She checks her watch. Ten fifty-two. There is only one night nurse on duty. At eleven, she usually sneaks a smoke in front of the unit until her maintenance man boyfriend arrives and enthusiastically feels her up in a dark corner. If Danielle is lucky, they will disappear into the woods for the fifteen minutes they apparently require to consummate their hot, savage passion. She knows this because she has often crept to Max's window late at night — just to watch him sleep. It took some of the sting out of the parsimonious visits allotted her by Maitland.

The locked door beckons, but Danielle is paralyzed. This feels like life or death. She can find out about Max or turn around; go back to her room; and never know why Maitland insists that her son is crazy. Yesterday, Danielle demanded — and Reyes-Moreno unequivocally refused to provide — the underlying data upon which they based Max's diagnosis. She knows that filing a lawsuit will get her nowhere. The hospital legal machine will find ways to hide the precise information Danielle needs. She has seen it happen far too many times. At that point, Danielle decided that she was entirely justified in getting it on her own.

Even so, she falters. She is desperate for information, but does her desperation justify breaking the law? But if she doesn't find out what they've really based Max's diagnosis on — the nuts and bolts of it — she'll never know if it has any merit. That is intolerable.

Danielle slips a plastic card with the Maitland logo on it from the back pocket of her jeans. She swiped a spare earlier today from the nurses' station. She takes a deep breath and inserts it into a shiny black box on the cold, metal door. She hears a distinct click.

She slips through the door like satin ribbon through a needle's eye. Now that she has crossed the line, what she is doing seems perfectly natural, as if she has been breaking and entering all of her life. The soft, eerie lights, dimmed for the slumbering patients, give her goose bumps. She feels as if she has stumbled into a psychic's murky parlor in an attempt to contact bodies long cold — a vain search for lost souls. She scans the silent hallway and darts into a small office. The first thing she does is to sidle underneath the security camera in the corner and point it skyward. She then places her flashlight on the computer desk and covers it with her red silk scarf. With a soft click, the flashlight's wide eye lights the room in a soft rose. Office supplies crowd a corner; textbooks queue up in military formation on metal shelves.

Danielle sits in front of the monitor — her nerves singing — and watches as a large, white *M* gyrates on the screen. After a few moments, a message box appears. *Maitland Psychiatric Hospital.* A smaller box forms. *Password, please.* The cursor stands waiting in the empty box. Danielle enters the system without a glitch. When Marianne had raised the issue of Maitland's security — she was unhappy with its laxness — Danielle was surprised to learn that the nurses on the Fountainview unit cavalierly scribble the daily password on a Post-it and stick it under the counter at the nurses' station. Marianne scoffed when she related how Maitland prided themselves on thinking that their security system was ironclad. She said they'd never get away with such carelessness in a big-city hospital.

Danielle smiles grimly as she types in the code. Hospital administrators, she is certain, worry about their employees mishandling the system, not the patients. Surely it had never occurred to them that a patient's mother would jimmy the system.

She gives the keyboard a few intent taps and tries to ignore the horrific consequences if she is apprehended. She is an officer of the court who is committing criminal acts (a few felonies like trespass and hacking) with full knowledge of the legal ramifications. If her law firm finds out, partnership will be the least of her problems. If she is convicted of a felony, the bar will take away her license. She'll be finished. There will be no way on earth to fund Max's care. She shakes off these terrifying thoughts. Her watch warns her that she has only ten minutes to complete her task — assuming the frantic coupling outside is still rattling the trees.

Her nails are castanets on the keys. Prompts flash on the screen in mad succession as she negotiates her way through them like a bayou dweller in the Louisiana backwater. The blue glow of the monitor washes her with a purplish cast, and the small room is now nest-egg warm. The screen before her looks like some kind of daily log. Max's name, unit and room number are at the top, as are his patient identification number and date of admission. Below are typewritten entries which, she surmises, are transcriptions from the handwritten notes of doctors, nurses and attendants. She makes out the initials of Fastow, Reyes-Moreno and Nurse Kreng. Unfamiliar names flash before her — probably other members of Max's "team." Danielle reads the first entry; sits back abruptly; and rubs her eyes. Something is very wrong. She checks the name at the top of the page. Max Parkman. She reads it again. Twice.

> *Day 6* Pt. violent; agg. w/staff. Threat. pt. with physical violence; had t/b restrained; continue new med protocol; paranoid delusions; psychosis; 20mg Valium Q.I.D. Focus on Mo-son relatnshp/rage/denial. JRF

Danielle waits until the shock passes. *Paranoid delusions? Psychosis?* How could they decide that he was psychotic only days into this nightmare? She saw absolutely no evidence of this during her daily visits with Max. And what about "Focus on mother-son relationship"? That Fastow should even suggest something harmful in her relationship with Max is devastating. Her mind races back to the day Max was admitted. How had they acted toward one another? Of course he was angry and anxious with her; of course he lashed out at Dwayne when he was forced to go into the unit. He was scared out of his wits. Surely that's

perfectly normal on admission day. She
reads on.

Day 12 Incident in cafeteria. Pt. lost control
in serving line. Strikes child; curses server;
throws tray. Restrained; taken back to unit;
destruction to rm; isolation/heavy sedation
Post: Pt. now episodically psychotic;
suspect schizoaffective disorder and/or
Cotard delusion (due to pt.'s depression
and derealization). Episodes occur only
late night. Pt. has no recollection following
day. Tricyclics/ SSRI's not effective; consider electroconvulsive therapy. R-M

Danielle gasps. *Cotard delusion? Electroconvulsive therapy?* No one has said a word
to her about any of this — not even Reyes-
Moreno when she delivered the death-knell
diagnosis. A wild thought flashes through
her brain: Are they making these things up?
She shakes her head. It's too crazy. But why
hasn't anyone told her the details of what
Max has been going through? How often
had they shot him up with sedatives —
other than the time they overdosed him?
And thrown him into "isolation"? Reyes-
Moreno only mentioned the one instance.
Danielle sees Max lying on the floor in a
padded room bleakly calling her name, his

131

hands and feet bound by white canvas strips — to prevent telltale ligature marks or bruises. This sounds more like a sinister clip straight out of *One Flew Over the Cuckoo's Nest* than the *modus operandi* of the most highly respected psychiatric hospital in the nation.

And why don't they even mention Asperger's? Does psychosis now trump autism? Danielle can't even begin to process the last sentence. Over her dead body will they strap Max down; put a piece of wood in his mouth; and electrify his brain. She shivers. She has to get him out of here — now.

Only a few minutes left. She quickly scrolls down to review a few more entries. Observations from play therapy. Educational and psychiatric testing attempted, but unsuccessfully completed due to soporific effect of sedatives and disordered thinking. Reiterations of Max's suicidal ideations. She flips to the entry for today.

Team Meeting. Pt. skilled at concealing symptoms fm Mo. Admits has not mentioned psychotic thoughts. Pt.'s violent tendencies real threat to himself/others; Pt. experiencing deep disturbances; auditory/visual/tactile hallucinations. Con-

tinues to threaten suicide. *Diagnosis:*
Schizoaffective disorder, psychosis —

The screen blips off and the room goes dark.

Danielle freezes, hands poised over the keyboard. Someone must have discovered that the card is gone and is trying to flush her out by scaring the hell out of her. She jumps up and rams her hip into the corner of the desk. "Damn!" She puts her ear to the door; opens it a crack; and peers outside. The hallway is crushed charcoal. Danielle hears and sees nothing. She closes the door softly and ducks under the desk. Even if her heart is in cardiac arrest, her brain has not entirely deserted her. She turns off the power switch to the CPU. She doesn't want someone to come in for a mop tomorrow and see Max's information on the screen. She snaps off the flashlight; grabs the scarf; and shoves the card back into her pocket. She ventures into the hallway — no one.

Danielle creeps down the dark corridor, using her hand on the wall as her guide. When she reaches the door, she pokes her head cautiously outside the metal door and scans the landscape. Apparently no one is out to get her. The lights all over Maitland are out. There must have been a massive power outage. It is pitch-black, except for a few buildings that give off a greenish glow. Must be the emergency generators. Danielle slips outside and tiptoes to the corner of the building. She hears voices. The nurse runs from the trees, her white skirt billowing behind her — a neon sheet hung in a high breeze. Her priapic Lothario is nowhere to be seen.

Danielle's heart beats so fast that she feels nauseated and terrified all at once. She is clearly not cut out for a life of crime. Time to surrender or flee. When the nurse is out of sight, she sprints across the grass at full speed. Flashlight beams bop up and down around her, like costumed children searching for candy on Halloween night. Her dark jeans and dirty gray sweatshirt aren't exactly camouflage, but they'll have to do.

"Damned deer," a voice growls from somewhere behind her. "Like rats. They're everywhere."

Danielle reaches a stand of trees and becomes one of them. The light bounces away, illuminating Fountainview. She clutches her chest and gasps. Even when it seems that the coast is clear, she clings to the tree and doesn't move for a solid hour. *Olly olly oxen free.*

CHAPTER FOURTEEN

Danielle waits in Maitland's main conference room — the one with the chalkboard
and the large U-shaped table. The meeting
can't start soon enough to suit her. This
time she'll be the one calling the shots.

Her first impulse after the bizarre discoveries last night was to march into the Fountainview unit and yank Max the hell out of
there, but deeper reflection convinced her
that this might be shortsighted. Her noctur-
nal felonies, while illuminating, now compound her confusion. She has no idea how
to assess observations of a Max she doesn't
know. When Reyes-Moreno left another
message this morning asking her if she had
made the decision to move Max to their
long-term residential facility, an idea flashed
through Danielle's brain. She told Reyes-
Moreno that before she could consider such
a step, she required a face-to-face discussion with the entire team.

Danielle looks at her watch. In a few minutes, she will have the chance to confront the entire collective. She has already decided that whatever they say, she will have Max discharged immediately and take him back to New York. Once there, she will contact Dr. Leonard and obtain a referral for a second opinion. There is no way she's leaving Max here indefinitely without external — and irrefutable — confirmation of Maitland's findings.

But what if the entries and Reyes-Moreno's diagnosis are true? Her superior ability to marshal the facts — which serves her so well as a lawyer — has completely deserted her. She tries again to order the conflicting scenarios that pummel her brain. If Max is truly psychotic, how is it possible that she never saw any of the signs? Surely Max would have said or done something of that ilk in her presence? Then she remembers the day she found Max's diary and his intricate plan to commit suicide — of which she had been completely oblivious. She also recalls the chilling question he asked her at the beginning of this nightmare: "What do we do if they say I'm really crazy?" Maybe Max, as his condition worsened, did his level best to appear normal to her in the frantic hope that her answer would not be

136

to condemn him to Maitland indefinitely. She flashes back to the entry that described Max's psychotic behavior as exhibiting itself at night, which would explain their claim that by morning — when Danielle saw him — he had no recollection of those events at all. Danielle had attributed his utter exhaustion to the soporific effect of the medications, but it could have been the result of his nightly . . . episodes.

Equally perplexing is that, notwithstanding the devastating diagnosis and damning entries, Max does seems to be improving — at least during the few moments they have together each morning. Danielle can only attribute this to one variable: Fastow. As requested, he sent her the list of Max's medications. They are all familiar to her, their side effects predictable. Maybe he is a psychopharmacological genius, as Marianne said.

She has picked up the telephone twenty times to tell Georgia about the diagnosis and to ask her to fly down again to give her moral support, but that would make it too real. She has an even stronger desire to talk to Marianne about everything, given the warmth of their growing friendship. But she is afraid that Marianne's medical education and psychiatric acumen — not to mention

Max's recent encounters with Jonas — will leave her friend no choice but to urge Danielle to accept Maitland's diagnosis. This she cannot bear. Most of all, she wants to explore these issues with Max, but that is impossible — at least for now. If Max's fear of losing his sanity has escalated so dramatically that he wants nothing other than to kill himself, then she cannot risk even a gentle probe into the darkness of his mind.

She tries to focus. The first order of business today is to find out how Maitland has the gall to demand that Max be surrendered for immediate, indefinite residential treatment — not the least of which is their intention to give him electroshock therapy without her knowledge, much less her consent. Her mind is already drafting the temporary restraining order to stop Maitland dead in their tracks on that one.

Danielle hastily researched ECT therapy on the Web last night. What she learned terrifies her: seizures are induced in the brain by brief bursts of high voltage and alternating current. This allegedly modifies neurotransmitters believed to cause severe mental illnesses. The risks include brain damage, seizures, cerebral hemorrhage, permanent memory loss — and death. The explanation concluded with the caveat that the use of this method — despite its return to popularity and the successes claimed — is still extremely controversial. *No shit,* she thinks.

"Ms. Parkman." Reyes-Moreno's kind smile is an oasis in the desert.

Danielle almost smiles back until she remembers the computer entry that questioned her emotional "lability" and her relationship with Max. Is she the one who wrote all that garbage, all those lies? "Hello, Doctor," she says coolly.

The rest of the entourage, including Dwayne, files into the room. As they take their places, Danielle reminds herself that there are all kinds of courtrooms in life, and all manner of adversaries.

Reyes-Moreno sits in the pole position at the head of the table. Fastow, on her left, regards Danielle with gelid, unpleasant eyes. His chair is not pulled up to the table, as if to broadcast his disengagement from and disdain for the proceedings. She still can't stand the guy — no matter what kind of genius he may be. The other doctors take their seats and stare thickly at their files, sheep mourning their wool after shearing.

"Shall we begin?" Reyes-Moreno doesn't ask the question as if she expects an answer.

"By all means."

"Danielle." Her green gaze is straight and true. "I understand that you have asked to meet because you have certain questions about the validity of our collective diagnosis." She raises her hand slightly before Danielle can say anything. "I also understand that you are reluctant to sign the necessary papers which would commit Max to our care for another year."

"That is correct." Her words are frozen bullets. "I want a detailed explanation of how the team concluded that my son is schizoaffective and psychotic."

Reyes-Moreno nods sympathetically. "Danielle, I've given you the reasons for our diagnosis. Perhaps you were too upset at the time to process it completely. Is there something you don't understand? We'll be happy to explain it to you."

"No, Doctor," she says. "What I want is a copy of Max's file — with every notation and observation upon which you base your diagnosis."

Reyes-Moreno's smile shrinks. "I'm afraid that won't be possible."

"Why not?"

"I hope you understand that we are not unwilling to accede to your request, but are simply unable to do so." Her eyes are calm, but firm. "As an attorney, surely you are aware that Max's file is protected by the physician-patient privilege. While we are required to explain Max's diagnosis to you, we are not at liberty to reveal our underlying observations. Of course, if you feel that you need documentation to confirm our diagnosis, I urge you to go through the appropriate legal channels."

Danielle's voice is lacquered lava. "I certainly will."

So they want to play hardball — fine. She'll file suit and obtain Max's documents — and more — through discovery. "Then what, if anything, will you and your 'team' now reveal to me that explains this extraordinary diagnosis of my son?"

"We are here to answer any questions relating to Max's medication protocol, future treatment possibilities or the nature of schizoaffective disorder." She gives Danielle a sharp look. "Frankly, we are very concerned about your reaction to Max's diagnosis. We want to help you accept it so that Max can begin long-term residential treatment. To that end, I would like to schedule a few sessions with you this week."

Danielle frowns. "With me? Why?"

Reyes-Moreno gives her those calm, green eyes again. "To ensure that before you go, you can help Max deal with his illness

141

within the context of your relationship."

Danielle ignores the intimation of her imminent departure. "Do you have a specific question about my relationship with Max?"

"It is something we believe requires further exploration."

"But you won't tell me why."

Reyes-Moreno shows the first break in her demeanor — a slight fissure in her countenance. "Not at this time. We can discuss it further when we present Max's treatment protocol in a few weeks."

Like hell we will, thinks Danielle. It is clear that she won't get anything more out of this tribe, not that she expected them to reveal their outrageous observations to her. She doesn't give a damn about Maitland's sterling reputation. It isn't enough. She will make a graceful departure so she can get Max out of this place. "Doctors, I want you to know that I am grateful for all you have done." Danielle nods at Reyes-Moreno and the others. All nod back, happy china dolls.

There, she's laid the groundwork. She is reasonable. She is grateful.

"I mean no disrespect when I tell you that I simply cannot agree with your conclusions," she says. "As such, Max and I will be leaving this afternoon." She places both palms on the table in front of her and stands. This indicates that the meeting is over and, although they have not reached a viable settlement, they will part on friendly terms.

"Danielle." Reyes-Moreno's voice is curt. "We know that you disagree with our diagnosis. What you do not seem to understand is that you are in denial of the gravity of Max's condition." Her unwavering gaze locks upon Danielle. "I simply cannot permit you to take Max out of this facility when we have concluded that he may well commit suicide the moment he walks out of these doors — not to mention his increasing psychosis and demonstration of serious violence with others. I will not expose this hospital to legal claims — which would be well-founded — arising out of the release of your son." She pauses. "Nor will I jeopardize Max's mental health and his life, or someone else's, by releasing him into your custody."

Danielle's eyes widen. "What are you saying — that I'm the one to blame here? That Max isn't safe with me?" Her voice is an invitation to battle, steely and removed. "Or maybe it's just that no one has had the mettle to question a diagnosis rendered by the superlative doctors of Maitland —" she looks pointedly at each face around the

143

table "— even when no basis for such a diagnosis exists."

There is silence. The eyes of the brain trust are glued to their folders. *Cowards,* she thinks. One of the interns starts to say something, but Reyes-Moreno inclines her head ever so slightly. He stops, a well-trained puppy.

"Ms. Parkman." Reyes-Moreno's green eyes are unrelenting; the voice a soft hammer. "We invite you to obtain a second opinion; however, I urge you to do so immediately. It is your refusal to accept what we are trying to tell you that is causing your son more damage, perhaps, than his underlying mental illness, which is grave enough in itself."

Danielle's anger ignites. "Are you telling me that I don't know my own child? That I'm so innately selfish that I would fail to admit the truth so I could cause my son additional harm?"

Reyes-Moreno looks at her as if she is a deadly virus just identified under her microscope. "Frankly, we find it extremely disturbing that you have failed to observe the warning signs. This is a progressive disorder, as you must be aware."

"What warning signs?" All she can think of are the lies in the entries — that she is a bad mother, that Max's "psychotic behavior" is something Danielle has blithely ignored. Red rises into her throat, but she manages to keep her voice level. "Max has been seen by reputable psychiatrists long before he came here. Not one of them has ever suggested that he might be violent in any way — much less schizoaffective. And no one — except you people — has conspired to strap my son down, shove a piece of plastic into his mouth and shoot 450 volts of electricity through his brain." She points her index finger at Reyes-Moreno. "Forget about lawsuits, Doctor. You're going to jail." She marches to the door.

"Max is not just suicidal. He is dangerous." Reyes-Moreno's words are black bullets.

Danielle turns and stares at her. The remainder of the team freezes. "What?"

The eyes are snapped whips. "Max has completely lost touch with reality. He is convinced that the Morrison boy has been torturing him. More specifically, he believes that there is a voice in his head that keeps him advised of Jonas's secret plot to harm him and, ultimately, to have him done away with."

"That's absurd!" Danielle strides across the room and stands directly in front of

Reyes-Moreno. "Do you people honestly expect me to buy this? What are you trying to accomplish with these monstrous lies?"

Reyes-Moreno's eyes are wide, alarmed. "I have no idea what —"

"You know exactly what I'm talking about." Danielle puts her hands on her hips. "So now Max believes that boy wants to kill him? Just how do you know that? Did he whisper it to you in a secret session? In a moment of some profound psychological breakthrough?" Her patience is gone. She leans forward and slams both of her open palms flat on the table directly in front of Reyes-Moreno. The crack of sound causes the doctor to recoil. Danielle leans so far forward that her face is inches from Reyes-Moreno's. "Why don't you tell me what in the hell is going on here, Doctor? I won't call it a conspiracy if you won't call it the truth."

Reyes-Moreno pulls back just as Dwayne stands up and grabs Danielle by the arms. The doctor stands, obviously shaken. "Danielle, you need immediate psychiatric treatment."

Danielle twists away with a harsh laugh. "Like hell, lady. By the time you people are through with me, I'd be foaming at the mouth and baying at the moon." Danielle shoots her a scathing look. "You have my son formally released from this execrable excuse of a hospital immediately, do you hear me? And if I don't have his goddamned records in one hour, I'll have an injunction slapped on you people so fast your heads will spin." Danielle then leans very close to Reyes-Moreno — so close she can see the lines on her lips. "Am I making myself clear?"

Reyes-Moreno doesn't flinch. "You won't reconsider?"

Danielle's voice is ice-blue. "No."

Reyes-Moreno sits down, pulls a document from her file, and hands it to her. "I'm sorry to say that we anticipated your reaction." Danielle snatches the paper from her and scans it. "Our temporary restraining order against you was granted by the judge this morning," the doctor says calmly. "I hope you understand how much we regret that your actions and attitude required that legal action be taken to protect Max."

Danielle shoots Reyes-Moreno a black stare; her voice is hardened tar. "What lies did you tell the court about me? Are you aware of the penalty for perjury, or do you people care as little for the truth as you do for the welfare of your patients?"

Reyes-Moreno shakes her head. "I don't know what you're talking about. In any event, that is for you to take up with the court."

"Don't worry about that," snaps Danielle. "I have every intention of pursuing Max's rights — and mine — in a court of law." She stands. "But right now I'm going to get my son the hell away from you people."

Reyes-Moreno raises an eyebrow. "In violation of the temporary restraining order?"

Danielle's legal mind races through the arguments and likelihood of success if she fights the T.R.O. She thinks of the schools; the principals; Maitland's psychiatrists; the scars on her arms — and now the team's damning reports of Max's deranged behavior and Danielle's abject refusal to accept the wretched facts. What judge in the world wouldn't summarily grant Maitland its remedy? The poor boy desperately needs the marvelous care of this impeccable institution and to be kept away from his lunatic mother. Danielle has no credible evidence to offer the court and, after her outburst today, no hope of getting any. She has no witnesses, except possibly Marianne, to call in her favor. Even if Marianne would testify that Danielle is a good mother —

and Danielle believes she would — she is afraid that if Marianne sees the entries, she might feel compelled to urge Danielle to accept Maitland's diagnosis. Not to mention the fact that Marianne would be compelled to recount Max's violent encounters with Jonas.

The restraining order will be in place for ten days, and then there will be a hearing on the temporary injunction, which will be in effect until a full-blown trial on the merits. Danielle will just have to wait. She will file her own lawsuit and present a well-reasoned explanation for violating the order. One thing she is damned sure of: she is not leaving Max in this place. The chips will have to fall where they may.

Danielle meets Reyes-Moreno's green gaze with her own. There's no point in bluffing. The old girl has poker eyes, and she's seen her hand. The reason Danielle's a really good lawyer is that she knows when to shut up. This is the battle, not the war. The immediate goal is to get Max out of here; hop on a plane; and get back to New York.

"Do I have your agreement?" Reyes-Moreno's words hang black in the air.

"Absolutely not," says Danielle. "I'm going to get a second opinion, and I want your written statement that you will fully co-operate with whomever I choose — including a summary of your diagnosis and all underlying observations that support it. And I want it today." She stalks past Reyes-Moreno. "Got it?"

She closes the door behind her. Hard.

CHAPTER FIFTEEN

Danielle's head is spinning. Despite her bravado in front of Reyes-Moreno and the others, a cold panic rises in her as she strides from the conference room and strikes a blind path away from the building. She must get control of herself. She can't give way to the fear and hopelessness they would have her feel. She has to think of a way to get Max out of here — and not get arrested doing it. She knows one truth: whatever they have done to him — whatever he is now — he's not the same Max she brought here. If he has indeed spiraled into madness, it happened here in this ghastly hospital. Any lingering doubts about her own judgment are gone. She stands stock-still and then marches toward the familiar white building.

She has to see Max. She doesn't care about the temporary restraining order or Maitland's decree that she not enter the unit unaccompanied. She's going to plant herself in his room and stay with him. If he's crazy, she isn't leaving until she sees it with her own eyes. Still, she thinks as she nears the building, there is no reason to invite further confrontation. She peers at her watch as she rounds the corner to the back entrance. It is almost eleven-thirty. That means that the nurses have lined up their charges and walked them the few hundred yards to the cafeteria for lunch. They won't be back for at least thirty minutes, maybe more. There is a chance that Max is with them, but she doubts it. She knows from the endless hours she has spent in the unit waiting room that some patients are routinely left in their rooms to sleep, particularly those undergoing heavy medication changes. Like Max.

She swings her purse over her shoulder and goes into the unit. The place is deserted. She walks down the cold hallway, her heels emitting a surreal sonar *ping* with each step. She opens Max's door just enough to slip in. The bed is mussed, but empty. She takes in the twisted sheets, the indention in the pillow — and then notices something new. Thick brown leather restraining straps hang unbuckled from the metal bed rails. The wide bands meant to enclose her son's wrists are open, as if awaiting his return. How long have they been restraining him? Is it only at night or also during the day? Her heart clutches. She takes a step toward the straps, touches one, shivers. She checks the bathroom. Empty. She races down the hall, her mind a wild vortex. The rooms blur as she hurtles past them. Every door is closed. Just before she reaches the lounge, she notices that the door to Jonas's room is ajar. She pushes it open and steps inside.

The sight that greets her is monstrous, unspeakable. She claps both hands to her mouth, trying to stifle the scream that tears at her throat. Wild spurts of red stab and soar at the ceiling; stripe the walls. Her eyes are pulled to the bed. There lies Jonas, his body laid open — full of bloody, gaping holes — his beautiful blue eyes open and staring wide-eyed at the ceiling, as if stunned by the psychotic artwork his life's blood has made. Danielle fights the over-whelming urge to vomit. She rushes to his side and grabs his wrist. A sickening smell fills her nostrils as the slick of fresh blood slides onto her fingers.

"Oh, God, Jonas, please . . ." she cries. There is no pulse. She grabs him by the shoulders and pulls him to her. "Breathe, Jonas. Please be alive." His body is warm, his sweet smell mixed with an acrid, sour odor. She slides her hand up to his neck, the carotid artery. There is no beat. She has to get help. Maybe there's still a chance. She spies the nurse's call button on the wall opposite the bed. She scrambles to reach it, her feet slipping in blood, so much blood. It is an eternity before she manages the few steps to the other side of the bed. Her red finger is just about to press the white button when she sees it.

He lies motionless in a slurry of blackened blood, his white T-shirt and underwear spattered with crazy, crimson spurts. His legs and arms are curled in the fetal position. His eyes are closed.

"No!" She slips and slides toward the form, finally rolling it over. Frantic hands cup his face. She shakes him. "Max! Max!" He lies listlessly in her arms. She searches desperately for a pulse. The strong, steady beat pierces her horror with joy. He is alive. Alive. She makes a frenzied search of his body for wounds. There are none. The blood is Jonas's, not his. She moans and starts to cradle him, to pick him up, to get him out of there, to get help — and then she sees it.

Clutched in her son's hand is something silver, sinister. It is her metal comb, coated in the ruby rage of the room. In a blind panic, she grabs Max and rips off his bloody T-shirt. Max rouses briefly; grabs her; and tries to speak, but then slides back onto the floor, unconscious. Danielle wrests the comb from his hand; wipes it; and stuffs it and the shirt into her purse. Moaning, she grabs Max's arms and drags his body across the bloody floor, his limbs leaving a trail of smeared, unholy red in their wake. The agonizing moments are almost at an end; they are steps away from the door — when it opens.

Nurse Kreng stands in the doorway. Her scream splits the silent death of the room, the stark white of her uniform shrieks murder to the unholy red on the walls.

■ ■ ■ ■

PART TWO

■ ■ ■ ■

Part Two

CHAPTER SIXTEEN

In the beginning there was blue. She felt it all around and above her as she was rushed from the jail to the courthouse for her arraignment and bond hearing, flanked by a court-appointed lawyer and a female guard. The color of the sky and the turn of the world have gone on, but her life is forever changed. Even her skin feels gray and tainted, unfamiliar to her. She has spent four tortured days in that cage without sky; without air; without Max. He must be wild by now. He has been charged with murder; she with a variety of lesser felony charges — accessory after the fact and obstruction of justice — to name but two.

Unbelievably, she made bond. At least now she can try to get Max out of Maitland, where the *ad litem* urged and the judge ordered that he remain until his competency hearing. She doesn't know which terrifies her most: the thought of Max still at Maitland or the knowledge that, at sixteen, he may be certified as an adult and thrown in the county jail until trial. If deemed a juvenile, at least he will not be surrounded by hardened criminals — she hopes. Everything hinges on his competency hearing in ten days. She cannot overcome her shock. Everything is an unspeakable nightmare.

Danielle's only telephone call on that terrible day was to Lowell Price, the kindly managing partner. He was, as she expected, stunned and horrified by the news that Max had been arrested for the murder of a young boy — a psychiatric patient, no less. Fortunately, she reached him before the *Times* picked up the story and flashed it across the wires. During their brief, tortured conversation, she asked for something she'd never asked for before — help. And help in the person of A. R. Sevillas is due to arrive at any moment. Danielle sits in his office in Des Moines, waiting. His secretary said he is running late — probably representing some other criminal. Her hands shake. She has to get Max — and herself — out of this hellish mess.

The door opens. Danielle turns and, for a brief, horrifying moment, stares into the brown eyes of a man she has not only met — but with whom she has shared passionate intimacies. Tony stands stock-still, the doorknob in his hand. "My God, Lauren?" His face lights up with a huge grin as he strides across the room. Before she knows it, she is in his arms. "How did you find me? I mean, I'm glad you did. When you cancelled dinner, I thought —"

"Oh, Tony!" Danielle bursts into tears and shakes her head. He holds her tighter and whispers wonderful, unintelligible things into her ear. She wraps her arms around his neck and buries her face into his crisp, white shirt. The now-familiar smell of him only makes her cry harder.

"It's all right, Lauren. Whatever it is, let me help you." He takes her by the shoulders and looks into her eyes. He exudes a quiet confidence that calms her enough to form the words she has to say.

She takes a deep breath. "My name isn't Lauren."

He misses a beat, but recovers quickly. "I see. That can't be what has you so upset."

"No, it isn't." She walks to the chair across from his dark, burled desk. "Please, Tony, sit down. I have a long story to tell you."

Sevillas glances at his watch. "I'm sorry, but I've got a client coming in. She'll be here in a few minutes."

Danielle shakes her head. "You don't

understand. She's already here."

Confusion fills his eyes, and then he blanches. "You don't mean —"

"I'm Danielle Parkman."

Tony falls into his chair, his eyes never leaving her face. "You can't be."

Shame fills her. "I'm afraid I am."

"Are you telling me that it's your son who is accused of murdering that boy at Maitland?"

Danielle resists the impulse to reach across the desk and touch his hand. Instead, she forces firmness into her voice. "Max didn't kill anyone, Tony. Please believe me."

He glances at the stack of pleadings on his desk and then looks at her, alarm and betrayal in his eyes. "I want to believe you, but Jesus Christ, Laur— Danielle." The intercom buzzes. His voice is harsh. "No interruptions. None."

"Tony —"

He raises his hand, visibly distressed. "The first thing I have to decide is whether or not I can represent you or your son at all, given our . . . relationship."

"Oh, Tony, please. You've got to help me." She hears the outright panic in her voice. "I'm so sorry — for all the lies, for everything —"

"I can't make a decision yet," he says

162

tersely. "My better judgment tells me to walk away."

"But you —"

He holds up his hand. "I'll let you know what I decide after I've heard all of the facts. So let's get the preliminaries out of the way." He opens a side drawer, from which he takes a creamy white envelope. He leans forward and hands it to her. Danielle grasps the envelope and slides her finger under the seal. "I take it you're a lawyer," he says dryly. "At least your firm is behind you."

"Yes," she murmurs. Lowell informed her that although the firm will pay for her bond and not fire her — for the moment — she has been placed on unpaid leave, which means they are waiting for the outcome of the trial to can her. Lowell also told her that the firm will make no statements to the press, and, for her own sake, he has instructed her not to contact any of her colleagues. She knows he wants to protect her from any incriminating statements she might make to Georgia or others who may be called to testify at trial. She also knows that he wants no one in the firm even remotely involved in a sordid murder trial. She looks at Tony. "Lowell Price is a good man."

He frowns. "Price? I wasn't contacted by

anyone named Price."

She slips the thick, embossed card from its envelope and takes in the square, black print and the familiar scrawl of the Mont Blanc signature.

Don't prove me wrong.

E.B.M.

"E. Bartlett?" That he should be the one to have intervened on her behalf is almost as incomprehensible as his ability to ramrod the partnership into standing behind her bond.

"Bartlett — that's who I talked to," he says. "Sharp guy."

Danielle gives him a wry look as she puts the card in her purse. "That he is."

"He also said that you are honest to a fault."

She stares him down. "I am."

"Of course you are . . . Lauren." His eyes are weary, as if he wishes she weren't like every defendant who reflexively proclaims innocence. His voice is all business. "Before we get into the facts, I want to take a moment to review the situation."

Danielle nods, stricken by his change of tone. The brown eyes now look cold, professional. He puts on a pair of glasses and

164

riffles through the papers on his desk. "Let's go over the terms of your bond. Maitland's temporary injunction prohibits you from going anywhere near Maitland or your son. In ten days, their lawyers will move to make it stick, at least until the trial is over."

She starts to speak, but he raises his hand again. "I know," he says. "You want to see your son — Sam, right?"

Crimson heat suffuses her face. "Max."

"Max?" His eyes regard her coldly. "Unfortunately, your violation of the order on the very day of its issuance and your status as the mother of the prime suspect in the murder of a psychiatric patient hardly leaves me with a compelling argument that you should be allowed access. Given that you were caught attempting to flee the scene with your son, I have no argument that you do not present a flight risk."

"I don't care what they do to me, but you have to find a way for me to see Max." Her voice cracks. "He must be terrified. He woke up with blood all over him; was arrested for murder; thrown in jail; arraigned; and then sent back to Maitland — all without knowing where I was or if I had abandoned him."

He shakes his head. "You know I can't do that."

"Tony, I'm begging you." Tears burn her raw eyes as panic laces her words. "Max has been very . . . ill. What if this pushes him over the edge? I'll never forgive myself." Her face crumples into her hands. When she is finally able to stop sobbing and look up, Tony's eyes soften for a moment.

"You're just going to have to wait," he says quietly. "I'll see him today and let you know how he is. After that, I'll try to push for daily telephone calls. Don't get your hopes up."

"Oh, Tony, thank you."

He glances at the pleadings on his desk. "I think we better focus on Max's murder charge."

Danielle feels her face burn. It is one thing to read the charges in the distancing language of the law and quite another to hear someone mention "Max" and "murder" in the same sentence. Her heart lurches as she realizes that though she's out, he isn't free — and unless she does something fast, he may never be. She can't even run to her boy and make sure he's all right or even talk to him about what happened on that horrible afternoon. By letting her out on bond, all they've done is given her a larger cage. She takes a deep breath. "Agreed."

"Before we address the murder charge, I want to be clear about the restrictions of your bond." Danielle does not remind him that she is a lawyer. Right now she's just a defendant, like her son. "We'll find you an apartment away from Maitland to avoid the press, but you're not to go farther afield than the fifty-mile radius stipulated in the court's order," he says. "Frankly, I was amazed you made bond at all given the nature of the crime and the fact that you were found at the scene attempting to flee with the murder suspect in your arms."

Danielle feels his eyes upon her. She glances down at her ankle and the carbon-fiber band that encloses it. The blue LED flashes ominously. The court-appointed lawyer offered up the device to the judge as an alternative when it became clear that he was on the verge of denying her bail. An experimental innovation, the bracelet comes with a computerized panel that the Plano sheriff will install in her new apartment. If she ventures beyond the fifty-mile limit, or tries to relocate the panel, the police station and the court will be simultaneously alerted. She is only in Des Moines because she is permitted to visit her attorney. The appointments must be phoned in by Tony in advance.

The order is clear. It's a one-time deal: if she violates it, she'll be thrown back in jail and her $500,000 bond, for which her firm is on the hook, will be revoked. She crosses her good ankle over the imprisoned one and tries to match his businesslike tone. He is her lawyer now, not her lover. "Can we talk about their case against Max? I'm eager to hear your strategy, and I have a few thoughts of my own."

Sevillas raises an eyebrow.

"Don't worry," she says quickly. "I know I'm ignorant about criminal law, but I'm a quick study and a good lawyer. Maybe you could think of me as a second chair."

He frowns. "I'm sorry, Danielle, but that's not how I work. I think you'd feel the same way if I were your client and tried to tell you how to run a civil case. It just isn't in Max's — or your — best interest. Besides, if I'm also going to represent you — and I haven't decided if you need separate counsel — it is critical that you not appear to be involved in his legal representation."

Danielle leans forward. "Tony, I'm asking you to make an exception. I promise to respect your role as chief strategist and our advocate in court. But it's Max's life we're talking about here, and I have to be involved."

His dark eyes are stone. "Look, I've been practicing a long time and, frankly, lawyers are my worst clients. They know it all, or worse, they know just enough to be dangerous." He shakes his head. "I have to call the shots or it's no deal."

"All right," she says quietly.

"Let's get to the facts, shall we?" He flips open a leather binder and draws a line down the middle of a page. He puts Max's name on the left side of the paper. She works the same way. One side for what the client says; one side for what the truth probably is.

"The D.A. has been only too happy to give me his version of what happened," he says. "The police report backs him up, as do the statements of various Maitland staff. He's sending over the black box tomorrow."

She gives him a quizzical look.

"That's their box of goodies. A list of the physical evidence, statements — everything they're required by law to disclose to the defense."

She nods.

"I'll summarize the State's case against both of you." Sevillas looks at a typewritten sheet and runs his finger down to a particular paragraph. "First, you and Max go to Maitland for a psychiatric assessment and you befriend the decedent and his mother. You repeatedly refuse to go back to New York while Maitland conducts its assessment and, on numerous occasions, interfere with the doctors and staff. These events are documented and reflect what Maitland *et al* term your increasingly 'erratic, labile and unbalanced' behavior."

He leans back in his chair and continues in a laconic voice. "They prohibit you from seeing your son more than once a day until the assessment is concluded. You still refuse to leave and spend your days hovering in the waiting room outside your son's unit. Much of this time is spent alone with the decedent and his mother."

He takes a breath and turns a page. "Now Max. When he arrives at Maitland, he is clearly suicidal; clinically depressed; and unresponsive to traditional psychiatric treatment. Thereafter, his mental state rapidly and profoundly deteriorates. He becomes increasingly psychotic; has auditory and visual hallucinations that the decedent wants to kill him; and is physically violent. Max's attacks upon the decedent escalate to the point that the boy requires significant medical attention on two separate occasions. Max's detachment from reality is so severe that the staff has no choice but to restrain him, particularly at night."

"Tony, let me explain —"

Sevillas holds up his stop-sign hand. "You

are then given your son's diagnosis of schizoaffective disorder — which you summarily dismiss — and then reject Maitland's strong recommendation that Max remain there so he may receive the intensive psychiatric treatment required to prevent him from committing suicide or assaulting third parties, particularly the decedent. The following day, you demand a meeting with the doctors on Max's team and, according to those at the meeting, you go berserk, complete with bizarre accusations and violent threats to one of the most well-respected adolescent psychiatrists in the nation, perhaps the world."

"That's not how it happened!"

Tony ignores her and continues, his voice completely devoid of emotion. "You march to the Fountainview unit in a rage, where you find the Morrison boy dead in his room. Your unconscious son is in the room, covered with the decedent's blood. A persuasive case is made that Max killed the boy by brutally stabbing him with a five-prong, eight-inch metal comb. In all, the coroner tallied three hundred and ten puncture wounds. Given the grouping of the wounds, this reflects sixty-two separate acts of stabbing. Of particular note is the wound to the boy's femoral artery, which is all but ripped open. When the head nurse arrives, she finds you dragging your bloodied son to the door, trying to escape with him, and all of the relevant physical evidence — the murder instrument and Max's bloody clothes — stuffed in your purse."

Sevillas closes the leather binder and raises his eyes. A world-weary look is in them. "I have to tell you that the facts are as bad as they come." He ticks them off on his fingers. "The murder weapon found in the room unquestionably caused the injuries and death of the decedent. Max's history of increasing violence with Jonas and his hallucinations that the boy was trying to kill him provide motive. There is no evidence of another suspect nor, in my opinion, is there likely to be. It is also unlikely that an Iowan jury will find an assertive New York female lawyer who has tried to flee with her son and the murder weapon sympathetic, let alone a young man who may have viciously murdered a patient of Maitland, the employer of over three hundred of the good citizens of Plano." He glances at her. "I'm sorry to be so blunt, but you need to know that we'll be swimming against the riptide from day one."

Danielle grips the arms of the chair so tightly that her knuckles blanch. She fights

172

a rolling wave of nausea. It's all wrong, so horribly wrong. How does she begin to explain Max, much less herself? It is critical that she divorce herself from fear and approach this like a lawyer. And she must somehow convince Tony that Max did not kill Jonas so that he presents a defense so compelling that no jury will convict him. She can't begin to think about the charges against her. Nothing matters but Max. But why should Tony believe her? All she has done from the moment they met is lie to him. And now she is going to lie again. She must use all of her powers of persuasion — all of her training — to convince Tony that someone else killed that boy.

And that the killer is not, in fact, her own son.

"Well?" Tony's gaze is direct.

Danielle leans forward, her voice eager. "Look, Tony, I can counter every allegation. But understand this: Max did not kill that boy. I know it looks awful, but I can explain what happened. Yes, I was angry when I left the meeting with Reyes-Moreno and went to Fountainview to see Max, but he wasn't in his room. I thought he was in the cafeteria with the other patients. As I was leaving, I noticed that Jonas's door was open, and I looked in on him." She looks up. "His mother and I are good friends. Did anyone tell you that?"

Tony shrugs. "Go on."

Danielle's voice trembles. "I can't even describe the horror of that room; all the blood; the hideous sight of poor Jonas." She struggles a moment, then goes on. "I grabbed him to see if he was still alive, but it was too late. I was just about to scream for help when I realized that Max was on the floor, covered in blood. I thought he was dead. I . . . dropped to the floor and checked his pulse. He was unconscious, but alive."

"Where was the comb?"

Danielle takes a deep breath. She has no choice. "It was across the room in a pool of blood."

Tony frowns. "What did you do then?"

"When I couldn't rouse Max, and none of the staff heard me scream, I tried to drag him out of the room to find help. With all that blood, I couldn't tell if Max had been stabbed, too."

"How did the comb wind up in your purse?"

Danielle is prepared for this. "I was convinced that the murderer had planned to kill Max as well, but I interrupted him. I grabbed the comb and shoved it into in my purse because I was afraid he'd come back and kill us both."

"What about Max's T-shirt?"

She looks at him earnestly. "I tore it off of him when I was trying to see if he had been stabbed. I don't remember putting it into my purse, but I guess I did. I was completely out of my mind."

He makes a few notes and then stops to look at her. "By the way, do you have any idea how your comb wound up in the Morrison boy's room?"

"I have no idea," she says. "It was always in my purse. Someone must have taken it, or I dropped it somewhere."

Sevillas's cross-examination is staccato, his gaze unwavering. "Did you leave your purse lying around?"

"No."

"Do you remember lending it to anyone?"

"No."

"Do you remember the last time you used it?"

"No."

"Could you have dropped it in the boy's room at some earlier time?"

"I could have," she says. "I was in and out of his room almost every day, visiting Marianne."

"But you don't recall losing it."

"No."

"Did Max regain consciousness from the time you found him until the nurse entered the room?"

"No."

"Did you see anyone else on the unit coming or going?"

She shakes her head. "It was lunchtime. The staff was usually in the cafeteria with the patients, as I said. As far as I know, only Max and Jonas were left behind. There could have been others — staff or patients. That's definitely something we need to investigate."

"Hmm," he says. "Why did they leave your son and the other boy behind?"

Danielle shrugs. "Max was undergoing an extensive medication change. He usually slept through lunch."

"And the decedent?"

"You'd have to ask the staff."

"Who won't talk to us until formal discovery starts. The D.A. will see to that. And certainly not in time for the hearing," he replies. "Did they leave these boys unattended? That seems irresponsible."

"There may have been a nurse somewhere on the floor. I don't know." She is careful to keep her next words measured and even.

"But they made sure they couldn't move around. They kept Max in restraints and there was a security camera inside his room. Someone disabled the camera, unfastened the restraints and dragged Max into Jonas's room."

Sevillas gives her a skeptical look. "Or the duty nurse forgot to put Max in restraints and he finagled the direction of the security camera, filched the comb from your purse, and stabbed Jonas to death." Danielle starts to speak, but Sevillas interrupts her. "And don't tell me he couldn't have disabled that camera. That's exactly what happened in Jonas's room."

She glares at him. "That is not what happened."

He leans slowly back in his chair. "I don't think you can make that statement given the fact that Max was repeatedly violent with Jonas and had vivid hallucinations that Jonas wanted to kill him. It seems much more plausible that Max acted out his psychotic hallucinations and killed Jonas before Jonas could kill him."

Her jaw tightens. "And he did this while unconscious?"

Tony shrugs. "We don't know when Max became unconscious. It could easily have happened after he killed Jonas."

She doesn't blink. "Or after the murderer dragged his unconscious body into Jonas's room, intending to kill Jonas and frame Max for the murder."

"We won't really know what happened until we have a chance to speak to Max," he says. "Although Maitland has documented that historically he is completely unaware, after the fact, of his actions during these psychotic fugues."

Danielle shakes her head. "I don't believe Maitland's entries."

"And why is that?"

She catches herself. This is no time to admit that she broke into Maitland's computer system and read legally privileged information from Max's file. "It's just a feeling I have."

He gives her a sharp glance. "Feelings aren't evidence." Danielle's cheeks flame. Tony crosses his arms and studies her carefully. "So, do you have any idea who might have done this? You've had some time to think about it."

Danielle feels her stomach constrict. She has thought of little else since that unspeakable moment when she found Max bloody and curled up on the floor — clutching the comb. All she could think of was that Max was alive, safe. And that is all she is thinking of now.

And it is possible that there is a viable suspect other than Max. She didn't spin this concept from whole cloth. In jail, as she replayed the hideous scene for the hundredth time, she suddenly recalled a form flitting by Jonas's window — just after she saw Max on the floor. Immediately after the turmoil and horror of finding Jonas dead and Max bloody and unconscious, only celluloid clips of those ghastly moments ran through her mind. It was not until later, after the arrest and jail, that she had sat quietly in her cell, closed her eyes and actually focused on the image. It swam into her mind's eye, an ephemeral eidolon that shimmered through blurred glass and then glistered away.

She asks herself the same question she did in jail: Did she really see this phantom, or is she simply desperate to have seen it? Even if she cannot believe that Max murdered Jonas, is she now sand-shifting the past to deny Maitland's contention that Max was not only psychotic, but apparently had repeated hallucinations that Jonas wanted to kill him? There is also no denying that she found Max gripping the comb covered in Jonas's blood.

She shakes her head. As his mother, she is

utterly incapable of believing that her son has murdered. She knows him better than any human on earth. They are warp and weft, fire and flame. There has to be another suspect — the real murderer. If there isn't, then all that is left is the unthinkable: Max will spend the rest of his life in a psychiatric institution — or prison — without her. No, she cannot go to that black place, no matter how unbalanced or violent Maitland claims he is. She sighs. If a client gave her such a story, she would never have bought it — and neither will Tony. No matter. Even if she is deluding herself and there is no other suspect, they must still build a defense sufficient to raise reasonable doubt in the minds of the jurors to acquit Max. This seems almost impossible given the damning physical evidence against him, even without the critical information she has concealed.

Her next thoughts are thorns. Every belief and value she has proclaimed immutable for herself now turn upon this one event, this one moment in her life. As an attorney and an officer of the court, she believes in the system, with all its frailties and foibles. As a human being, she believes in the dirt and clay of right and wrong. She is duty-bound to tell the truth, even if that truth leaves her son's entire life in jeopardy, in danger, in pieces.

Danielle fights off a sick feeling in her gut. There is another moral dilemma that she has refused to consider, the mere possibility of which fills her with self-loathing. If they are unable to find the real killer, she will be forced to decide whether or not to marshal evidence to cast suspicion upon innocents. She has convinced herself that, if it comes down to the wire, whatever evidence she will be able to uncover probably won't be enough to convict anyone — just enough to raise the requisite reasonable doubt to acquit Max. She can only pray that they find the real killer. If not, she doesn't trust herself to say that she will not cross over the line into what is, for her, a mortal sin. She would walk willingly into hell for Max. But will she forfeit her soul to save him?

Before Danielle can speak, the telephone rings. Tony murmurs a few words and hangs up. "Listen, before we go any further, there's someone I'd like to bring in on the case."

"Another lawyer?"

He smiles. "Not quite. His name is Doaks. He's a retired cop, now a private investigator. Since our position is that Max didn't do it, we're going to need someone top-

181

notch who knows where all the bones are buried. Someone with connections to the local constabulary."

Danielle notices his phrasing. Max's innocence is framed as a legal position, not verity. "That sounds like a good idea. You've used him before?"

Sevillas nods. "I've known him for thirty-five years. We grew up in Plano together. He's a little rough around the edges, but he's the absolute best and, frankly, exactly what we need."

"Then get him."

Sevillas stands and walks to the door. "Let me grab his number from my secretary and you can sit in on the call. I have to warn you, though. He calls it like he sees it."

She meets his probing gaze. "I can take it."

Sevillas points at a document on his desk. "Why don't you look this over? I'll be back in a minute."

Danielle stands quickly and walks over to him. She wants so badly to touch him, to have him know what she feels for him. He moves, as if to take her into his arms, and then stops himself.

"Tony, I —"

His brown eyes search hers as they both stand, immobile. "Danielle," he says quietly.

"I think we should focus on one thing — your and Max's defense. The rest is too . . . complicated."

"I know," she whispers. "But you have to know that our night together was real, that it was . . . true. I was just too afraid to let you in."

The brown eyes are warm again. He leans forward and kisses her gently on the forehead. "I believe you." He stands back and shakes his head. "This is insane. It might be the first time in my life that I've fallen so hard and so fast. And, of course, the woman turns out to be a defendant in a murder case with the absolutely worst facts I've ever seen." Sevillas sighs as he leans forward to embrace her. Danielle feels the warmth of his whisper against her neck. "I'm not sure how any of this is going to turn out, but I want you to know that I'm going to do the very best I can. As for the other," he pauses, "maybe it was just one wonderful night. If so, it's one I'll always cherish." With that, he strides to the door and disappears.

Drained, Danielle collapses into her chair as her forehead falls into her hands. Silent, treacherous tears slide down her face. Her universe is a vortex that has her in a pitiless grip. She struggles to quell her panic, now at an unprecedented height after Tony's rendition of the damning facts. She takes deep, ragged breaths. Max . . . she must think only of Max. She focuses on his smile; the light gray of his eyes; the curve of his cheek. Slowly, she comes to herself.

As she reaches for the document Tony asked her to read, she notices a law review article on the corner of the burled desk. "Update of Juvenile Criminal Law in Iowa: Too Young for Life?" She glances at the closed door and stashes the article into her purse. Just as quickly, she scans the pleading, which turns out to be Max's indictment. When she reads the style of the case — *The State of Iowa v. Defendant, Maxwell A. Parkman* — that numb, horrified feeling crawls over her again. She searches wildly through the indictment. Relief floods her as she realizes that there is no death-penalty demand.

A black thought slices through her brain. *It isn't that they won't ask a jury to kill him.*
They just haven't done it yet.

Sevillas brings her a cup of coffee and goes to his desk. "Ready?"

Danielle nods as she takes a sip of the hot liquid. "Absolutely."

"Here we go." He presses a button.

Danielle hears an enormous crash through

the speakerphone that has to involve shattered glass, followed by a loud "Goddammit!" The receiver on the other end of the line seems to be turning cartwheels as the invective continues. "Why in the fuck does a guy ever get married? Stinkin' knick-knacks. I shoulda tossed 'em when I threw her ass out!" There is the noise of something sweeping up shards from a wooden floor. "And that fuckin' pink wallpaper. What kinda FDS crap is that?" Another long moment passes, and then a sound that resembles the popping of the top of a beer can rattles through the line. Danielle raises her eyebrows. Sevillas shrugs.

There is another clatter, and the scratch of whiskers against the receiver. "Doaks," growls the voice. "And it better be damned good."

Sevillas smiles at Danielle and leans back in his chair. "What's up, buddy?"

"Christ, I knew I shoulda unplugged the phone." A noisy slurp follows. "Whatever it is, Taco Face, I ain't here."

"Whoa, Doaks." Sevillas uses his buttercream courtroom voice. "Can't an old friend call to see how life's treating Plano's finest?"

Doaks hoots. "You ain't got time, hotshot. I can't open the paper without lookin' at your ugly mug standin' on the courthouse steps after savin' some white-collar prince from the pen. Besides, if you're callin' me, it means those asswipes who pass for flatfoots at your shop can't be trusted not to screw somethin' up."

"Perceptive, as always," says Sevillas.

"No way," he says. "I'm out of it. Don't they teach you the word in law school? *R-E-T-I-R-E-D.*"

"Come on, Doaks."

"Blow me," he says. "I'm whatcha call an independent agent now. I don't gotta listen to squat."

"You don't even know why I'm calling."

"Don't take no genius," he says. "P.I. junk, that's what you're after."

"What if you're right?"

Doaks laughs. "I'd tell you to fuck off. Like I done a thousand times before."

"Come on, you know you miss it."

"Yeah, every morning I wake up wishin' I could stay up all night crammed in my car with cold coffee, chasin' some moron. Forget it."

"Just this once, pal," says Sevillas. "I need the best, and you're it."

"Yeah, sure." The unmistakable sound of someone crunching a can crackles through the line. Danielle can almost smell the beer.

"Let's reel in old Doaks one last time so he can do what those overpaid clods down in that fancy-shmancy office of yours ain't got the gray matter for. What do you think I am, fuckin' stupid?"

Sevillas sighs. "Did you hear about the Maitland murder?"

Doaks's voice is cautious. "You mean that whack-job who put about a thousand holes into some psycho kid?" Danielle closes her eyes. It sounds even worse when he says it than when Sevillas laid it out a few moments ago. Hot shame suffuses her face.

Sevillas casts an apologetic glance at Danielle. "Watch it, Doaks, you're referring to the son of our new client, Ms. Danielle Parkman, attorney-at-law, who also happens to be sitting across from me."

"Take me off that speakerphone, shit-for-brains."

Sevillas pretends to do precisely that. He winks at Danielle as he picks up the receiver and then puts it back in its cradle. "That better?"

"Yeah," he growls. "But I still ain't takin' no case."

"This one's different."

"Right," he scoffs. "How many times we played that forty-five?"

"The boy was killed with a metal comb."

187

"Interestin' choice of weapon," admits Doaks. "But not enough to get my blood goin'. So, you got any other suspects?"

"You're biting."

"No way."

"Look, John." The smooth voice is back. "I know you've got an axe to grind with Maitland."

There is a pause. "So?"

"I'm not calling to ask for repayment —"

"Sure as hell sounds like it."

"I'm just trying to help you out."

"Bullshit," says Doaks. "You need somebody who knows the joint inside and out."

"Of course I do." Sevillas lets the next words slide home. "How's Madeleine?"

Silence.

"Watch it, asshole." The voice is dark, angry.

Danielle raises her eyebrows, but says nothing. She makes a note to ask Sevillas about it later.

"So, you'll trot over to my office in the morning?" asks Sevillas mildly. "That's when we get the black box and start putting this defense together. And why don't you get the skinny from your buddies at Plano P.D. this afternoon?"

"Don't tell me how to run a stinkin' investigation," snarls Doaks. "I'm gonna watch Johnny Miller's chippin' lesson. No way this bullshit is gonna ruin my golf game."

Sevillas laughs. "Payback is murder, Doaks."

"Eat me," he grumbles. "You just took a perfectly good day and shot it all to hell."

CHAPTER SEVENTEEN

The next morning, Danielle smiles at Sevillas's secretary and takes the coffee and doughnut she offers. As the door closes, she settles into her chair and glances down at the navy pantsuit she put on this morning. She decides that, except for the ankle bracelet hidden beneath the folds of fabric, she feels more clearheaded than she has since this nightmare began. She is impatient to begin. At nine, Sevillas will be here, and they will plan the strategy that will comprise Max's defense — and her own.

But as the moments go by, black thoughts web her brain. If she is convicted, there will be no one to ensure that Max gets out of Maitland, or to financially fund his appeal. Even if Max is acquitted but she is in jail, who will take care of him? Georgia will do all she can, but Danielle knows she has neither the resources nor the ability to shoulder such a burden — nor would she ask her — and Danielle has no family to call upon. What if Max needs prolonged psychiatric care? She will have no income to fund it. And then there is the worst of scenarios: she is sent to prison, and Max is sentenced to life in prison. She refuses to even entertain the possibility that a jury would give him the death penalty. She shakes her head and wills the snarling hounds in her mind to flee.

Something catches her eye. It is a dark file box on the floor next to Tony's desk. She is about to make out the words scribbled on top when he walks in.

He looks crisp and professional in a gray pinstripe suit. He strides over to her and squeezes her shoulder. His touch is electric. "Good morning," he says. "You look like someone who had a good night's sleep."

"I did, actually. I was more tired than I thought."

He sits behind the desk and pours himself a coffee from a silver thermos. "As well you should be."

"Tony?" She tries to keep the desperation out of her voice. "Did you see Max? Is he all right? Can I see him?"

He nods. "Yes to the first two; no to the latter."

She is crestfallen. "First, tell me how he is."

"He seems well, but is understandably anxious about you and Jonas's death," he says. "I told him you were fine; that I was going to represent both of you; and that he could speak to you very soon. By the time I left, I think he felt much better."

"Can I talk to him?"

"I've arranged for you to have daily telephone conferences with him. The *ad litem* agreed that it was in Max's best interest."

Relief fills her. "Oh, Tony, I can't thank you enough. May I call him now?"

"This afternoon. And you've got to keep it short."

"How short?"

"The court ordered that the duty nurse has the discretion to terminate the conversation when she thinks it appropriate."

Danielle groans. "Nurse Kreng. She won't give me five minutes."

Tony shrugs. "We have no choice. Hopefully we'll be able to convince the *ad litem* to extend the phone conferences. And I'll try to get you a face-to-face visit — supervised, of course."

She takes a deep breath. "It isn't much, but I'll take it. Now, tell me all about your visit."

He tells her about Max's horrified reaction to the charges against both of them and the upcoming hearing. When questioned, Max was adamant that he had no memory of the event at all. He was in tears and terrified, but calmed down when Tony assured him that he would talk to him every day and that Danielle would be calling him very soon. Tony met with him for an hour, but Max couldn't stay alert. Tony stayed until he fell asleep. His voice softens. "He's a fine boy, Danielle. I'll do everything I can to bring him back to you."

Tears catch in her throat as she starts to rise to go to him. "Oh, Tony, how can I bear this?"

He points at her chair. "By keeping sharp and helping us build a strong defense." She sits back down. He smiles that wonderful, warm smile. "And by not coming over here and making it impossible for me to concentrate."

She smiles back. "Whatever you say, Counselor. Where do we start?"

Sevillas points to the box next to his desk. "Right there. As soon as I —"

The door opens, and a disheveled man wearing a dingy golf shirt and khakis with a large, dried coffee stain on the right thigh strolls in. His white hair stands on end. He

193

looks like he just stepped out of the shower and electrocuted himself. His voice is gravel crushed by a wooden wheel. "Mornin', all."

Danielle looks at Sevillas, expecting him to redirect the wanderer to the service elevator. Instead, Sevillas stands and smiles. "Doaks — good to see you. I'd like to introduce Danielle Parkman."

The man turns to Danielle and offers her a rough, brown hand. His wrinkled frown splits into a grin, as if his face is unaccustomed to it. "Glad to meet ya."

Shaking his hand is like grabbing a piece of sandpaper. "Good morning, Mr. Doaks."

"Just Doaks," he says. "That'll do fine." He plops himself on the chair next to hers, takes a look around the room, and gives a low whistle. Danielle follows his gaze. There is no question that power pervades the room with the inaudible but palpable white noise of wealth. Floor-to-ceiling windows provide a panoramic view of downtown Des Moines as the rumble of traffic below filters up. Mirrored windows from adjacent office buildings shoot light throughout the room, which falls on four canvases of modern art that fill it with brilliant color.

"Holy shit, big shot," he says. "What a dump you got here."

"Thanks, pal." Sevillas takes off his suit

jacket, tosses his cuff links into a crystal ashtray and rolls up the sleeves of his freshly starched shirt. He gives Doaks's trousers a wary look and winks at Danielle. "Appearances aren't everything."

"Fuck you." He turns to Danielle and gives her a sideways grin. "Sorry, ma'am. Sometimes the boy gets too big for his long pants, and I gotta take him down a notch or two." He turns to Sevillas. "Got any coffee in this hovel?"

Sevillas pushes a button on his phone and sits back. More coffee arrives on a platter loaded with Danish and coffee cake, smelling strongly of cinnamon and dripping with white icing. Within minutes, Doaks has waded through his first cup and spilled crumbs down the front of his shirt. He tips back in his chair. "Okay, clock's runnin'. Let's get started."

Sevillas turns to Danielle. "I've given Doaks a detailed rundown on where we are and what you and I discussed yesterday, but before we get to the black box, I'd like him to fill us in on what he's learned from the Plano Police Department. Doaks?"

"It was a rough conversation, if you know what I mean." He scratches his two-day-old whiskers and shoots a look at Danielle. "I kinda need to know the rules of the road here. You want the straight skinny or do I gotta water it down through big boy over there?"

Danielle looks back. "I want it straight. I'm a lawyer, Mr. Doaks, and I'm tougher than I look. I know that my son and I are in a terrible position and that we very much need your help and that of Mr. Sevillas. So fire away."

Doaks glances at Sevillas, who nods. His milky, blue eyes fasten upon hers. "I only got one rule."

"Which is?"

"Don't lie to me," he says quietly. "If you tell me the truth and don't bullshit me, we'll get on just fine."

Her voice is deadly serious. "I don't lie, Mr. Doaks. And my son is not a murderer."

Doaks swills down the last of his coffee and grins at her. "Then this ought to be as easy as greasin' a goose."

Danielle nods at the box. "Let's get to work."

"Okay. I had a brew over pool with my buddy Barnes last night."

"Who is Barnes?" asks Danielle.

"My partner when I was on the force," says Doaks. "He knows I'm a damned good dick and that whatever he's got, we'll wind up gettin' anyway. Bottom line, Barnes knows I'm comin' from the exact same place he is — as a cop. It's like bein' Catholic, ma'am. Once they get you, you're theirs forever." He flicks a fleck of pastry from his chin, kicks back and looks at the ceiling as if he is an altar boy reciting the catechism. "I ain't gonna rehash what you and Sevillas talked about yesterday. I'm just gonna lay out the scoop — the physical evidence. And it ain't good."

Danielle tenses. Doaks fixes rheumy eyes upon her. "As if it ain't bad enough that we got your boy all bloody in the dead kid's room and you tryin' to drag him outta the crime scene — with the murder weapon stuffed in your purse, no less, we got a few other strikes against us that I'd bet dollar to doughnuts are in that big box over there." He holds up a gnarled index finger. "First, they got tapes."

Danielle's mind flashes to the white cameras that stare down from each room in Maitland. *Oh, God.* That meant they already knew Max had the comb in his hand before she came into the room or, God forbid, that they have him on tape actually killing Jonas. But if Max didn't do it, then they must know who did. She tries to keep her voice calm. "What tapes?"

Doaks shrugs. "They got 'em in every

room and at the secured exits. Video feeds into the nurses' station and the main security post."

"Are you telling us they have the murder on video?" asks Sevillas.

Danielle holds her breath. Doaks takes another slug of coffee. "Them fuck-ups? Nah, it's one big blank — the whole thing."

Her heart pumps again. "Malfunctioned?"

"Disabled, more like." He gives her a look that she finds more than casually probing.

She doesn't care. Max is safe. And a blank is better than the jury seeing Max standing there with a bloody comb in his hand. At least he is no worse off than a few minutes ago. She pushes aside how quickly she had leapt to the possibility that the tape would show her son killing Jonas. And after all is said and done, this might well be the tragic truth. Maybe she's the crazy one, denying Max's guilt when the overwhelming evidence points directly at him.

Doaks sticks another stubby finger in the air. "But the tapes they do have are doozies, Barnes says. Max gunnin' for the decedent; him flippin' out at night; you denyin' stuff the docs are sayin'. You name it, they got it." He turns to Danielle. "We'll need to look at all of 'em together."

She nods. "Listen, I need to tell you both

198

something. I think I saw someone outside of Jonas's window while I was in the room."

Sevillas leans forward, his eyes eager. "Who was it?"

"I couldn't make out his face. It was just a flash of color, a blur." She shakes her head. "I'm sorry. All I could focus on in that horrible room were Jonas and Max."

Tony's brown eyes seem perplexed. "Why didn't you tell us this before?"

She flushes, but her voice is iron. "Because I wasn't sure."

"And now you are?"

"Sure enough to mention it."

Doaks and Sevillas exchange a look. Doaks heads for the coffee pot. "Well, that and a dime won't buy me this cup of coffee."

Danielle bristles. "It shows that someone else could have been in that room and then ran out when he heard me coming."

He walks back, sloshing coffee from cup to saucer. "Like who — the headless horseman?"

"Like the person who killed Jonas and was about to frame or kill Max." She gives him a sharp glance. "And who probably would have killed me if I'd walked in five minutes earlier."

Doaks lifts his cup and grins. "*Touché, Ms. P.*"

She can't help but smile back.

The phone buzzes. Sevillas punches a button and listens. "Put him on." There is a short pause. "This is counsel for Ms. Parkman. Just a moment."

Danielle's heart leaps as Sevillas motions for her to take the receiver, but to share it with him so he can listen. Hands shaking, she grasps the black receiver. "Max? Max, is it you, honey?"

"Mom!" The voice she loves as no other is so strong, so real, that she can almost reach out and touch it. If it weren't for the piteous, terrified tenor of his one word, Danielle has never been so thrilled to hear it. "Where are you? When will I see you?"

"Shh, sweetheart, don't worry." She forces calm into her voice. "It's going to be all right. I'm here in our lawyer's office, and we're working very hard to get you out of there."

"But I can't —" His voice cracks, an ice floe against the merciless hull of an arctic tanker. "I'm *scared,* Mom."

Her need to hold him close, to reach him with her eyes, is overwhelming. "I know, Max. Please believe me when I say it's going to be all right."

"But why do they think I killed Jonas?" His fear is palpable. "You know I didn't! I don't know how I woke up in all that blood!"

"Honey, listen to me." She takes a deep breath. "Do you remember anything at all about that day? You've got to calm down so we can figure this out."

A sob stabs through the receiver. She gives him time to collect himself. "All I remember is being out all morning. And before lunch, I think somebody put those goddamned things on my arms and legs. I passed out again. Then you came or the cop grabbed me and there was blood all over me . . ."

"You didn't see or hear anything at all before that? Do you remember how you wound up in Jonas's room?"

"No!" he cries. "I can't remember anything! They dope me up half the time, and then everything is all fucked up in my head. I get pissed off . . . crazy. I don't know what's wrong with me. You've got to come get me, Mom."

"I can't, sweetheart. They've got a restraining order against me."

"But when will I see you? Can't I even call you?"

"Not right now."

"Then I want my goddamned iPhone —

and my computer."

"Honey," she says. "If they made me take them away when you were admitted, there's no way they'll let you have them now."

"Just do it." His words are clipped. "I'll find a way to call you — and do a few other things they'll never figure out."

"Max —"

"Forget it, Mom."

She sighs. Like some people with Asperger's, Max is a computer savant. He could probably launch nuclear warheads with that iPhone. "I'll ask Tony to bring it the next time he sees you, but it won't do any good."

"Sevillas? He's a cool guy."

Tony smiles and takes the receiver. "Hey, hotshot. Forget about the computer *and* the iPhone. We're on thin ice with the judge as it is, and I'm not risking my behind so you can surf the Web."

"Well," says Max. "The iPhone is actually a computer, so I guess I don't really need the laptop." A slight pause. "Look, I've got my Game Boy. They're both black. We'll swap." There is a pause, and then a whisper. "Shit, here comes the Gestapo." A few moments elapse. "Okay, they're gone."

Danielle takes the receiver from Sevillas. "Max, I have to ask you this question again.

It's important. Why did you want to hurt Jonas?"

"I didn't!" he groans. "Look, the kid was weird, but I didn't give a shit about him."

"But we've talked about this before. Remember what happened on the unit that day? And when I was in New York? And the hospital has records of other . . . incidents." She draws a deep breath. "I need to know the truth."

"Why do you keep asking me these stupid questions?" Anger laces his words. "Has everybody gone nuts?"

"Calm down, sweetheart, I'm just trying —" There is a scuffling noise. "Max? *Max!*"

"Ms. Parkman." Danielle hears the stern voice of Nurse Kreng. "This conversation is concluded."

Fury overcomes her. "You put my son back on this phone — now."

The calm in Kreng's voice is maddening. "I have complete authority to terminate these telephone conferences when I determine the patient is overwrought. Goodbye, Ms. Parkman."

The line goes dead. Danielle turns to Sevillas. "She cut me off! Tony, Max —"

Tony replaces the receiver. She puts her hands over her eyes as sobs rack her body. The next thing she knows Tony's arms are around her, holding her tightly to him. She can't stop crying. She can't bear it — any of it. She presses her face against his chest until his heartbeat slows her cries. She looks up as Tony takes her face in his hands, his eyes steady and warm. Before she can say anything, he leans down and kisses her. Gently, lovingly.

"It'll be all right." He uses the same words she said to Max. "I'll take care of you. Both of you."

She nods. Words won't come. Tony leads her to her chair. Once there, she glances at Doaks. His raised eyebrow says: "So that's how it is."

"Okay," says Sevillas, "let's get started."

Danielle wipes her eyes. She has to put whatever she's feeling aside or she won't be able to help Max. She takes a deep breath and nods.

Sevillas's words are brisk. "Does he remember anything, Danielle?"

She shakes her head. "No."

Doaks gives her a crinkly smile. "This is where I come in. If somebody else did it, I'll find him."

She nods. "I appreciate that."

"Okay, so listen up," he says. "There's somethin' Barnes told me last night that don't figure for me. They tossed Max's room after the murder, and I got a few questions about what they found."

"Like what?" asks Sevillas.

Doaks turns to Danielle. "Like how come they find the dead kid's St. Christopher necklace under Max's pillow?"

Her heart lurches. She can't remember Jonas ever wearing a necklace. She takes a deep breath. "Someone must have put it there. Someone who was trying to frame Max."

Sevillas turns to Doaks. "Did it have fingerprints on it?"

"Don't know yet, but I'm sure they're gonna be real pleased to tell us if it does. And that ain't all." He pulls a crumpled scrap from his worn pocket and hands it to Danielle. Her hands tremble as she unfolds the paper and reads it. Impatience and disbelief rise in her throat.

Sevillas leans forward, curiosity on his face. "What is it, Doaks?"

He shrugs. "A page from Jonas's chart. They found it under Max's mattress."

"What does it say?" asks Sevillas.

"It's a copy of the dead kid's schedule — for the day of the murder."

CHAPTER EIGHTEEN

Danielle stares at the empty paper plates. Lunch has come and gone. She has done her best to tell Sevillas and Doaks everything that happened at Maitland. She has not minced words about her suspicion of the treatment Maitland provided Max and Jonas: Fastow's overdose of Max; their secret use of restraints; and their refusal to let her participate in the process, ultimately forbidding her access to her own son. She stressed that Max had been depressed, but not violent, and drastically deteriorated only after he was admitted to Maitland.

It is what she has not told them that troubles her.

She has excluded Max's violent behavior toward her and the damaging comments in the computer entries — not to mention her hacking into Maitland's computer to view that information. She has to constantly remind herself not to expose another indictable crime by revealing things she should have no way of knowing. The State already has enough rope to hang her.

The most critical omission, of course, is Max on the floor of Jonas's room, curled into a bloody ball, clutching the murder weapon. That she will take to her grave.

Sevillas and Doaks have returned from their bathroom break. She wonders why men seem to do their most important conversing while dangling their penises over a urinal. In this instance, there is little mystery why they have absented themselves. To go over her story. To see if they buy it. To see how they can build a defense around it.

Sevillas pours another cup of coffee before he joins her. Doaks slumps in his chair and pokes a fork at the remains of his pastry. The black box sits at the end of the conference table, waiting.

"So," says Sevillas, "we've laid out the bare bones of their case. We've heard your version. What we haven't discussed yet is whether or not you have some idea who could have done this thing."

Danielle feels their eyes upon her. She forces herself to forget about Max and to think like a lawyer. "I think we have to keep in mind that anyone could have done it. We have to explore every avenue, every staff member — from the janitor to the doctors, anyone with grudges or violent records who had an opportunity to be there, whether or not we think they had a motive."

"Good idea," says Sevillas.

"We should also subpoena the files of other patients on the unit who had violent tendencies," says Danielle. "Remember, I told you about that girl, Naomi, who was there when Max had the . . . altercation with Jonas and had to be dragged to her room. She is very bizarre and violent, not to mention the fact that she has at least a brown belt in karate. The orderlies can testify to that. And she also told me she cuts people. We need her records and background information. There's also a boy named Chris who had broken his mother's arm, but I've only seen him once on the unit. I'm not sure he's still there." She marshals her thoughts. "To be safe, I think we should subpoena the charts and histories of all of the patients on the unit. I'm sure they'll claim privilege, but we have a right to know the details of who was on the unit that day and if their psychiatric histories include physical violence of any kind."

Sevillas nods. "What about the boy's mother? Is there any evidence of her having violent tendencies toward her son?"

"No," she says and then stops. Nothing Danielle witnessed of their interactions even hints that Marianne harbored any ill will toward Jonas. In fact, her overwhelming impression is precisely the opposite. Even so, she has to find another suspect to shift the investigation away from Max. She hates what she is about to do, but she has no choice. "We can't rule anyone out at this point. I'd also like to talk about my taking a very active role in this investigation."

Doaks rips off a sheet of his legal pad. It looks like hamburger grease has been ground into it. He wads it up and shakes his head. "No offense, but I've been goin' down this road since before you started callin' your panties lingerie, and there ain't no way I'm gonna agree to somebody else callin' the shots on my part of the show."

Sevillas looks away and coughs, but not before Danielle sees his smile. She turns to Doaks. "I'm sure you understand that my son's life is at stake here. I won't interfere, but I have information you don't have, and there are a lot of people to track down and talk to."

Doaks waves a gnarled hand. "No way. I may not look like it, Ms. P., but I got everything I need — right up here." He taps his temple. "I ain't had any help in thirty years, and I'm way too old to start now."

"Come on, Doaks," says Sevillas. "For once you have a really smart defendant. She's the best source of information we've got. Maybe she can help you out. Besides, it'll keep her out of my hair on the legal side."

He flashes Sevillas a look that could slice boot leather. "You stay outta this."

Sevillas turns to Danielle. "Can you promise not to get in Doaks's way?"

"Absolutely," she says.

"Then get yourself another dick." Doaks grabs his legal pad and starts to rise.

"John, let's not forget why we're here." Sevillas gives him a meaningful glance.

"Don't push me, Tony. I don't care what you did to get Madeleine sprung from that place. You used up that card a long time ago." He falls back into his chair and turns to Danielle, who has silently observed this verbal volley that is fraught with a meaning she doesn't understand. "Look, Ms. P. . . ."

She smiles at him. "Danielle, please."

"Yeah, yeah, Danielle," he mutters. "If you're plantin' yourself in the middle of my mess kit, we gotta have, ya know, some serious boundaries. Lines you don't cross."

"You're absolutely right," she says. "What

would you suggest?"

Doaks scratches his white stubble. "There are some places you ain't gonna go," he says. "Some things I gotta do alone, like interviewin' important witnesses, without some broad trailing along behind me."

She nods.

"Nothin' personal," he says. "But I got connections you'd queer if anybody knew I was —"

"Listening to a woman?" She tries not to smile.

"No," he says irritably. "It ain't no male-pig thing. It's just that all my contacts know I fly solo. That's why they trust me."

Sevillas looks at Danielle. "I'm sure Ms. Parkman will respect the position of prominence you hold with your sources and will make every effort to preserve your sterling reputation."

Doaks shoots him a look of pure evil. "I ain't talkin' to you, asshole. You want to know what's goin' on, you're gonna have to ask your client."

Sevillas's eyes become serious as he looks at the black box. "Let's find out what they've got."

Danielle watches as Doaks pulls an old Swiss Army knife out of his pocket and slits

211

through the brown tape on the box. Sevillas turns to Danielle. "Nothing in this box is going to be good. As a lawyer, you might expect that it won't affect you as it would a layman. It just isn't true."

She feels her throat tighten. She nods.

Doaks pulls a sheaf of papers from the box. As he reviews them, he passes them to Sevillas who, in turn, hands them to Danielle. Doaks mutters as he scans the documents. "Not much here. The offense report is bare-bones. Got rough crime-scene diagrams, but no autopsy report; no lab report."

Danielle gets up and peers over Sevillas's shoulder. What she sees is what she has tried so hard to erase from her memory — ruby flashes of blood spatters; black, dusted walls; assorted views of the bloody bed. She closes her eyes. When she opens them, Jonas's vacant, dead eyes stare up at her like glazed marbles in a white bowl. Her stomach tightens. Danielle forces herself to study the series of close-ups. There are small but hideous stabs on both forearms. Different angles of the bloody corpse are shown: gaping holes on the tops of Jonas's thighs; dark, bloody craters on both sides of his genitals; gory rents near the femoral artery.

Doaks points at the last one. "Looks like

this is where most of the arterial spray came from." He shows them another photo of the spatters on the wall and the ceiling. He gives a low whistle.

Danielle feels revolted. She returns to her chair on the opposite side of the table, away from the box. After a few deep breaths, she concentrates on the papers in front of her, placing them into neat stacks. This calms her enough so that when Sevillas hands her the stack of bloody crime-scene photos, she is almost able to view them dispassionately.

She studies them one by one, wincing at the sight of the photographs of Max's bloody T-shirt and the contents of her purse. Something bothers her. Her eyes fly open. She flips through each photograph again, quickly this time. "It isn't there," she whispers. "Oh my God, it isn't there."

"What ain't there?" asks Doaks.

Sevillas walks around the conference table. "What is it, Danielle?"

She thrusts the photographs into his hand. "The comb."

Sevillas scans them, this time with Doaks looking over his shoulder. "I'll be damned."

"Holy shit," says Doaks. "There shoulda been a million pictures of that comb before anybody bagged or marked it for evidence — and way before they carted it downtown."

Sevillas shakes his head. "It's a fluke. Nobody could have missed that. We must not have all of the photographs."

"Yeah," says Doaks. "The photographer must've had his head up his ass or some idjit down at the D.A.'s office forgot to stick 'em in the stack before they got shipped out."

"What if it's not a mistake?" asks Danielle.

Doaks chortles. "It'd mean we'd have a helluva lot easier time gettin' proud of this defense. It'd mean that one of Barnes's guys fucked up to a fare-thee-well."

Sevillas hands her back the photographs. "Don't get your hopes up, Danielle. They've got the comb. Even if they forgot to photograph it, the cops will testify that they found it when they emptied your purse. Someone probably bagged it early on and ran it over to the evidence room."

"I think I'll hike on over to Plano P.D. later just to make sure," says Doaks. "You can't even guess at the weird shit that goes on in that joint."

"Sure, what could it hurt?" Sevillas's telephone rings. After a few quiet words, he looks at Danielle and then replaces the receiver.

"Tony, what is it?"

"The court clerk just called," he says. "The judge denied our motion. You can't see Max."

Her heart clutches. "For how long?"

"Until after the hearing."

Danielle turns away as tears flow down her face. Sevillas makes a hurried motion toward Doaks. "Let's move on."

Doaks picks up his ragged legal pad. "Right. We got Maitland's computer logs showin' Danielle's comings and goings, including the day of the murder. We got Max's unit logs — let's see what they look like." He rummages around and rattles off entries like a headmaster at roll call. *"Patient increasingly agitated and hallucinatory . . . Patient violent 2:00 a.m./required restraints . . ."*

Danielle takes a deep breath and turns to him. "Who made those notes?"

Doaks squints at the bottom of one of the pages. "Some nurse — Krang?"

"Kreng." She turns to Sevillas. "I can explain that."

Sevillas holds up his hand. "We'll get to it later."

They spend the next few hours going through the contents of the black box. Danielle grits her teeth as Doaks reads other chart entries by Reyes-Moreno listing

215

examples of Max's psychotic behavior, describing a Max unrecognizable to her. The D.A. must have had a field day at Maitland.

She stops short when she looks at a series of logs that describe various violent episodes between Max and Jonas. It isn't possible to tell from the entries who instigated the events, although the clear implication is that it was Max, with Jonas on the defensive. She doesn't believe it. Surely Marianne would have talked to her about it. She scans Max's chart. There is an entry made by the duty nurse on the day of the murder. *Patient in restraints. To remain in room during lunch hour.* Danielle sighs with relief. She turns her attention back to Doaks and Sevillas, who are discussing the items the police found in Max's room.

"Here's what I'm thinking," says Sevillas. "We'll draft a motion to suppress all of the evidence from Max's room. They had plenty of time to station a police officer outside of Max's room and obtain a warrant. They've claimed exigent circumstances, which we'll argue the court should reject." He shrugs. "It's worth a shot."

Sevillas stands and stretches. The first smudges of fatigue have appeared under his eyes, along with a shadow of beard along his jaw. He seems to be the only one who hasn't noticed that the orange sun is setting in the dusty Iowan sky. "Doaks, the M.E.'s report isn't here."

"I'm plannin' a trip to old Smythe first thing in the mornin'."

"Good," says Sevillas. "Then I want you to check out the police station and see what you can find out, especially about that comb."

"I already said I was gonna do that," he grumbles.

"I also want to demand Max's blood work," says Danielle. "I'm suspicious that the medications they gave him directly contributed to his decompensation at Maitland and, perhaps, his . . . violent behavior."

Sevillas gives her a long, studied look. Danielle stares at the floor. Her admission of Max's violent behavior — whatever the cause — implies that such violence could have led to murder. It is the first time she has even implicitly suggested that Max could have killed Jonas.

"I don't expect Maitland to cooperate," says Sevillas quietly, "but I'll include it in our subpoena. We probably won't get permission until the judge rules on it at the hearing."

"I asked a friend of mine to try to get

some information on Fastow, the psychopharmacologist who overdosed Max, but all she's been able to find out is that his last post was in Vienna, where he was doing some kind of new research in psychotropics. I think we need to do a thorough investigation into his past."

Sevillas gives her a look. "You think the overdose was intentional?"

"No. I can't put my finger on it, but there is something very wrong with Fastow."

"What makes you think that?"

"I told you before. Instinct."

"Anything more factual than that?"

"No."

Sevillas nods at Doaks, who sighs and makes a note. "Under the 'he's too squirrelly not to be guilty of somethin' theory,' right?"

Sevillas rubs his neck. "I also noticed that we only have excerpts of Max's chart and none of the victim's. If they're trying to create motive by introducing evidence of violence between Max and Jonas, we need both files in their entirety."

Danielle holds her tongue. If Sevillas gets Max's records by subpoena, she avoids having to admit that she hacked into Maitland's computer to support her claim that the hospital had to have something to do with

Jonas's death. Maybe when Tony sees the bizarre entries in Max's chart and compares them with the boy he has now met, he'll understand why she is so outraged by Maitland's treatment of him.

Doaks leans back in his chair. "I can think of a few things right off. If they have that comb, I want to see it for myself. I also want to pay a visit to that nurse — that Krang woman."

"Kreng," says Danielle. "I'll go with you. I have a lot of information you don't."

Doaks shoots Sevillas a poisonous glance and then turns to Danielle. "Remember how we talked about those things I gotta do alone? This ain't a good time for us to buddy up."

"Danielle, you obviously can't go onto Maitland property," says Sevillas. "I doubt the nurse will talk to Doaks, anyway. She certainly doesn't have to."

"She'll talk to me, all right." Doaks's smile splits his wrinkled face into a million pieces. "I got charm."

"But Danielle does have a point about prepping you," says Sevillas.

Doaks gazes skyward. "Why me, Lord?"

Danielle crosses her arms and waits. Doaks groans. "All right, all right. I'll pick you up at seven sharp and you can fill me

219

in on Kreng. I'm gonna park a ways down from Maitland, but then you gotta promise to stay in my sled until I'm done, *capish?*"

Danielle smiles. "Of course."

"I have some other bad news, I'm afraid." Sevillas points to a stack of papers on his desk. "The State has moved to have your bond raised to no bond. They've requested that it be considered at the hearing on the temporary restraining order."

"On what grounds?"

Sevillas shrugs. "Apparently they think they have information they didn't have at the time of the bond hearing."

Danielle's mind races. Could they have discovered her trespass and hacking? "How do we find out what they have?"

"Try not to think about it now, Danielle. I need you to stay in lawyer mode so we can lay out our game plan."

Danielle nods, but a dark panic blooms in her heart. She has to stay out of jail. If she is behind bars, how can she direct the investigation and, if necessary, find another suspect for the jury?

The icy truth of this last thought slices her soul. At some point, her absolute conviction of Max's innocence has faltered. She feels forced to accept that Max, whether driven by medication or something else, may have killed Jonas. She has plunged into the Cimmerian underworld of murk and damnation — into the black marrow of hell. She will do anything to set him free.

CHAPTER NINETEEN

"Okay," says Sevillas. "I think we've just about got it down."

"God, I hope so." Danielle rubs her neck after another morning of grueling preparation. Somewhere along the line, Sevillas has decided to let her participate in the legal aspects of the case. She doesn't ask why.

"Here's the game plan," says Sevillas. "We're going to find out everything we can before the hearing so we can go in swinging. We'll have torn apart every document the State has and since the purpose of a proof-evident hearing is for the judge to decide whether the State has sufficient basis to revoke your bond. The D.A. will have to put on key witnesses and experts — to show what color their underwear is, as our good friend John Doaks would say."

She nods. "This way we can cut away at the State's case before trial. The best part is that we'll have a terrific shot at free discovery."

"Not to mention the fact that all this will take place before trial," adds Sevillas. "The judge will hear it alone. There won't be a jury to worry about while we nail down the State's case and explore leads to exculpatory evidence."

"When do you think the judge will set the hearing?"

Sevillas shrugs. "Not for a while, I'd guess, but it wouldn't hurt to check the court's docket to see what we're looking at." He turns and murmurs into the telephone receiver.

The door opens, and Doaks marches in. He gives Danielle a cocky salute and tosses a white paper bag stained with heavy grease spots on top of Sevillas's burled wood conference table. "Good afternoon, all." He plops down into a plush, leather chair and lays out a napkin that looks as oily as the bag. With a loud smack, he pulls out a huge cheeseburger and squirts mustard from a plastic pouch onto his pants instead of the bun. Danielle hides a smile. She is beginning to see behind Doaks's rough façade. Her bet is that he's a soft touch who would rather take a bullet than admit it.

Sevillas takes in the pedestrian buffet

before him and looks at Danielle. "So, did you find anything at the police station?"

"Hold your water, Sevillas. I'm eatin' here." Doaks munches a dill pickle and smears a blob of mustard onto his khakis. His hair looks zany, as if he just stepped out of a tsunami. When he finally speaks, his mouth is full of unmasticated burger. The last fry finally disappears. "You're gonna kiss my feet for this one. They ain't got no pictures of the comb because the brain-dead sons-a-bitches lost it."

Sevillas leans forward. "Are you sure?"

Doaks grunts. "Hell, yes, I'm sure. Barnes is still reelin' from the chewin' out he caught from the chief this mornin'. Not to mention what the D.A.'s gonna do when he finds out."

Danielle feels a surge of excitement. "How did they lose it?"

"Some greenhorn handled the transfer of the evidence bags to the station." Doaks shrugs. "He lost it, plain and simple. My guess is that it fell outta his ride."

"But if it's gone, they can't meet their burden of proof, can they?"

"Don't get your hopes up," says Sevillas. "They'll find it. They always do."

"Yeah," mutters Doaks. "Still, it's great to march around shovin' it up the D.A.'s ass for a while." He walks over to the coffee pot and pours himself a cup of black coffee. "But however that plays out, I got some news that shows what a terrific dick I am." He turns and grins.

"Don't torture us," says Sevillas.

He strolls back to his seat and settles in. "So I'm walkin' down the hall at the P.D. mindin' my own business, when who do I run into? You remember Floyd J., don't you, Tony?" Sevillas shakes his head. "Sure you do — the janitor. The little guy with a gimped-out leg. Been there a thousand years."

"Oh, right."

"Well, Floyd J. and I are catchin' up and yakkin' away when I tell him I'm workin' the Maitland deal. All of a sudden he gets this funny look on his face. When I ask him what's up, he grabs his broom and takes me by the arm — secretlike — and walks me over to the conference room. You know, the one that's got the big window with the blinds on it."

"Right again." Sevillas gives Danielle a look that tells her to be patient. She turns back to Doaks, who is obviously warming to his story.

"So Floyd J. starts whisperin' about how some things just ain't right and how nobody

225

wants to listen to him, his bein' just a janitor and all," he says. "The next thing I know he's unlockin' the door and lettin' me in. Then he tells me he'll stand guard until I see what's goin' on in there." He pauses.

"Come on, Doaks," says Sevillas. "This isn't the sequel to *The Sopranos*, you know."

"That's what you think. So the minute the door closes, I flip on the light. You'll never guess what they're usin' that room for."

"No, I won't."

Doaks gives him a big grin. "A dryin' room, that's what." Sevillas's eyes widen. "Yeah, now you're startin' to get it," says Doaks. "Only you don't know what all I found."

"A drying room?" asks Danielle.

Doaks turns to her. "It's podunk Plano, ma'am. It never changes. See, evidence needs to be handled real careful. You can't just chuck it into a Ziploc and label it. You have to transport it from the crime scene quick — in paper bags so it won't mold — and then find some place to dry it out." He shrugs. "Hell, in big cities you got your official state-of-the-art dryin' room with exhaust fans and lots of high-tech shit to dry up blood, semen, urine, vomit — all of the ingredients that go into a really great crime scene. In dives like Plano, you hang crap up anywhere you can find a hook. Today it was the conference room. Tomorrow it'll be the john."

Sevillas comes around his desk. His eyes are earnest. "What did you see, John?"

"Now it's 'John,' ain't it?" he says. "Well, I'll tell you what I saw. Bloody sheets, towels and other stuff that couldn't have come from anywhere but the Maitland crime scene. It was layin' over chairs and hangin' from the walls." He winks at Sevillas. "Now for the good part. I start pawin' through the mess with my pencil and guess what's layin' around with all the bloody stuff?" He pauses dramatically. "The St. Christopher's medal, Jonas's bloody sheets, Max's clothes and other stuff from his room —"

"Jesus," breathes Sevillas.

"— Mary and Joseph, thank you very much," says Doaks.

"Cross-contamination to beat the band."

Danielle raises her hand. "Wait a minute. What does that mean legally?"

"It means we can move to have all of that evidence excluded," says Sevillas. "It's a colossal blunder."

Doaks smirks. "Nah, just Plano dumbshits bein' Plano dumbshits."

Sevillas frowns. "But we can't prove it. We can't very well say that you decided to

227

march into their evidence room and then put you on the stand to testify to what you saw."

Doaks gives them a wide, jubilant grin. "That's where my bein' a genius comes in." He fishes around in his pocket. "Just yesterday I decided I was gonna need some high-falutin' gadgets to get through this case. So I got myself a hot-shit cell phone and one of these." He holds up something that is razor thin and the size of a fat credit card.

"What's that?" asks Danielle.

"A camera, can you believe it?" He points it at Danielle, presses a button and a flash goes off. "Damndest thing you ever saw," he says. "So while I'm standin' there, I remember I got this beauty in my pocket, and I take a bunch of shots. The thing's digital, you know, so there ain't no film. Some lady at Walgreen's said she'd get me prints in an hour. She woulda e-mailed 'em to me, but I don't want nothin' to do with computers. They give me piles."

Danielle shakes her head. "You still can't get them into evidence."

"Hell, I hand you the Hope Diamond, and you tell me it ain't the shade of blue you like." He scratches the white whiskers on his chin. It sounds like someone scraping branches along a cedar fence. He stops and snaps his fingers. "I got it. Floyd J. can testify."

"And risk his job?" asks Sevillas.

"He's quittin'," he says. "Fed up. They won't give him benefits, not even a stinkin' pension. He'll testify if I ask him to."

Sevillas nods and makes a note on his legal pad. "It's terrific work, Doaks, but let's try not to break into any more government buildings than we have to, okay?"

"It was Floyd J.'s idea, not mine."

"What does it mean?" asks Danielle. "Will we get all of the evidence kicked out?"

"Unlikely," says Sevillas. "Let's wait and see the photos before we get too excited. Now, John, maybe you could tell us how your meeting with Smythe went."

"Who's that?" asks Danielle.

"The M.E. who doubles as the coroner. He would have been the first one to examine the body."

Doaks pulls out his grimy legal pad and sips his coffee. He passes on the good and the bad of his interview with Smythe: the conflicting evidence of cause of death, as Smythe found both petechial hemorrhaging (pinpoints of blood in the eyes), which indicates asphyxiation, and the lacerated femoral artery, which would have killed Jonas in minutes. He also relates Smythe's examination of a replica of the comb and his findings.

"But how could Max manage such an attack?" asks Danielle. "Jonas outweighed him by at least twenty pounds."

Doaks shakes his head. "Sorry, Ms. P., but you know how it's gonna play. They're gonna say that once a psycho blows his top . . ."

Sevillas catches Danielle's stricken eyes. "What Doaks means —"

"— is that he coulda lifted a damned freight train if he'd had to." Doaks shoots Sevillas a black look. "And don't fuckin' interrupt me."

Danielle goes on. "But why would the murderer — the real murderer — smother Jonas if he had already severed the femoral artery? Surely that would have killed him more quickly."

Doaks shrugs. "He chalks it up to how killers ain't always thinkin' straight when they're offin' somebody."

"What about defensive wounds?" asks Sevillas.

"Maybe, but the coroner's leaning toward them being self-inflicted. The kid has a history of it, you know."

Danielle is crestfallen. "Is there anything positive?"

230

"You never know what Smythe may have by the time he writes up his final report," says Sevillas.

"Oh, yeah," says Doaks. "Smythe was curious about somethin' else. He wants to run some more tests, because it looks like Jonas had some strange blood levels."

"What difference would that make?"

Doaks shrugs. "Probably nothin'. Just made him curious, is all."

Danielle feels a spear of hope. "Like I said, I want to know which psychopharmaceuticals Jonas and Max were taking. It could explain a lot."

"But whether or not the decedent was improperly medicated has nothing to do with how he was murdered," says Sevillas.

"Of course it does," says Danielle. "If the possibility exists that the wounds were self-inflicted, then Jonas's state of mind at the time of his death is critical. If he was under the influence of psychotropic medications, they could have directly affected his actions."

"A good point," says Sevillas. "But that doesn't help us with the evidence of asphyxiation."

"Ain't real easy to smother yourself," mutters Doaks.

Sevillas ignores him. "If, as Smythe posits,

Jonas died from lack of oxygen before he bled out and went into organ failure, then what is our argument? That Jonas stabbed himself repeatedly; lacerated his femoral artery; and then grabbed someone down the hall to smother him? And how does that explain Max's presence in his room without any defensive wounds, covered in Jonas's blood?"

Danielle tries not to let her frustration show. "Okay, okay."

Sevillas gives her a kindly look. "Let's wait until Smythe finishes his report. Don't get discouraged." He unscrews the top of his fountain pen and scratches out a note on his pad. The telephone rings, and he goes around to his desk to answer it. Head down, he murmurs into the receiver, his words inaudible.

Doaks stands, stretches and nods at Danielle. "I'm headin' out. Kreng's the first thing out of the box tomorrow."

"What time?"

Doaks groans. "You really gonna make me take you with me?"

"Just to ride along," says Danielle. "There are a few things I want to be sure you ask her."

Doaks shakes his head. "Man, you remind me of my daughter, you know that?"

Danielle gives him a surprised look, but then remembers Sevillas's mention of her when she first met Doaks. "She was at Maitland's?"

He frowns. "Yeah, nervous breakdown, and it didn't do her a damned bit of good. She's okay now. She's stubborn, just like you."

"I'll take that as a compliment."

He gives her a surprisingly tender glance. "It is."

Warmed by his words, she gives him a grateful smile. "I can't tell you how much that means to me. So I'll see you tomorrow morning?"

"You're just hell-bent on making my life miserable, ain't you?" he says gruffly. "I told you already you can ride shotgun, but leave me alone until tomorrow. Can you do that?"

She smiles. "I'll do my best."

Doaks stomps toward the door, muttering. "Women . . . Didn't God have nothin' better to do?"

CHAPTER TWENTY

Danielle watches from a distance as Doaks stumps toward the main entrance to Fountainview, a ragged legal pad in his hand. She pushes aside the empty soda cans, coffee cups and junk-food wrappers that carpet his old Nova. The glare of the sun compounds her headache. When she pulls down the visor of Doaks's car, the keys drop onto the driver's seat. She looks around the deserted lane where Doaks has parked her — safely, he thinks — far from Maitland.

Outrage and panic at the draconian measures the State has taken to threaten Max roil within her. She stares at the white, evil place where both she and Max began on a tortured road that may lead them both to prison — or death. Although she believes that Max will not get the death penalty due to his age, she has no idea what kind of prison sentence a jury would give him. After all, he was found lying on the floor next to

Jonas, covered in his blood. She knows that if she were on that jury, not knowing Max or Jonas, she would give a life sentence very serious consideration.

Danielle snaps the visor back into place. The hell with the restraining order. She can't stand being so close to Max and not seeing him. Their wretched, truncated calls have done nothing to quell Max's terror or hers.

She slides into the driver's seat and starts the car. That alone is a feat, not to mention jamming the antique gearshift into Reverse without killing the engine. She backs slowly out of the lane and onto the service road behind Maitland. When she gets to the unit, she puts the car into Park and leans back in the seat. The almost-cool air from the decrepit air conditioner blows over her face. The sun shines down on a bright, blue Iowa day. Which means that the visibility is perfect. Anyone on the grounds will remember her car. And anyone around the unit will be able to identify her: the slim woman in the black pantsuit — with the cumbersome ankle bracelet. At least they won't be able to track her. Thank God the anklet doesn't have GPS. Sevillas explained that GPS is expensive, and the county can't afford to use it. The anklet is activated only if she attempts to flee the jurisdiction, about a fifty-mile radius from her apartment. It doesn't keep her from going onto Maitland property — and Maitland is very much within the holy circle. Although it seems illogical, it is up to Maitland to be aware if she has violated the T.R.O. and then report it to the judge, who will revoke her bail and fine her.

It frightens her, this thing that compels her to put the car into Drive and cross the invisible border. Simply pressing the gas pedal could seal her fate. The State can slam her back into jail and revoke her bond — if they catch her. But, damn it, Max is in trouble. The layer of ice under her skin tells her that he needs her — only her.

The gravel crunches under the Nova's tires as she comes to a stop in the side parking lot. She has chosen this location hoping that the trees will partially camouflage her as she tries to sneak into the unit. This is stupid, she knows, terribly stupid. The duty nurse will see her and call security. She sits and tries to think clearly. She can't let her aching heart be the instrument of her imprisonment. What good can she do Max if she's in jail? Just before she turns around to back out of the lot, a movement catches her eye. She puts her foot on the brake and stares. One of the janitors has propped open a metal door with his foot. He grapples with an industrial trash can, which he uses to hold the door open. He yells something back into the building and disappears. The door stands open.

Danielle tries to think of the location of this door in terms of the unit's layout. It hits her. She parks, grabs her purse, and walks quickly but casually into the building. She ducks behind the door.

"Goddammit!" she hears a male voice yell. "I got to take out the trash. Tell Percy to do it!"

She hears footsteps recede from the door. She looks around. No one. She glides through the doorway and into the cool dimness of the storage room. She maneuvers around stacks of neatly organized linens, towels and bath soap, her sandals soundless on the concrete floor. The doorway to the unit is closed. She holds her breath and turns the knob. It releases and opens into the hallway one bedroom away from Max's — if they haven't moved him.

Blood thrums in her ears. Her adrenaline pumps so hard that every nerve is poised to flee or fight. She looks both ways down the hall and sees the back of one of the nurses headed in the opposite direction. The doors to the patient rooms are closed. She looks at her watch. Ten o'clock — time for the nurses to supervise the patients in their daily toilette: shower, brush teeth, dress. If the patient is unable to participate, the nurse simply changes the sheets and goes on to the next room. Danielle has no idea where they are in the cycle. Or when and if one of them will pop out of Max's room, assuming he's in his room. But it's too late to turn back now. She walks along the wall, head down, and stops. She peeks into the small window. He's there. And he's alone.

She glances up and down the hall once more and slips in. There's no way to lock the door from inside. Shit! She slides with her back along the wall, underneath the camera. She takes off her jacket and hooks it over the probing eye of the lens. Max is asleep, his arms and legs in the grip of leather restraints. He seems heavily sedated. She unbuckles the restraints and holds him to her, feeling his heart beat strong and clear. He does not stir. She lays him back on the bed and notices dark, purple marks on the inside of his right elbow. Needle marks. Her heart lurches. His thin arm has the tortured tracks of a heroin addict. What are they doing to him? She starts to panic and then forces herself to stay clearheaded.

She scans the counter. His chart is there, as well as two cobalt capsules she doesn't recognize. She puts them into her purse. Then she sees a sterile syringe packet, neatly enclosed in clear plastic, next to a glass test tube with a rubber stopper. Someone is coming to take his blood again. Why?

She doesn't have time to read the entire chart, but the scribbling on the cover catches her eye. It is a schedule of medications and blood drawings. She turns once again to the syringe, rips off the cellophane packaging, and removes the protective tip from the syringe. She takes a deep breath, knowing full well that watching nurses draw Max's blood for years is a far cry from doing it herself. But she has no choice — she has to know what they're doing to him.

Hands shaking, she gently lays out Max's left arm. She cannot bear to pierce the pathetically damaged right one. She tears a strip of cloth from the T-shirt he wears and wraps the makeshift tourniquet gently around his arm. When the vein is prominent, she carefully inserts the needle and then slowly loosens the binding. Max moans and looks straight into her eyes, but does not see her. As she watches the cardinal fluid gush into the test tube, Max's eyes flutter. She withdraws the needle; presses her finger against the tiny wound; and puts the tip back on the needle.

Frightened by the depth of Max's stupor, she shakes his shoulder. *"Max."* This time she sees recognition and joy in his clouded eyes. "Mom." He wraps his thin arms tightly around her neck and sobs, his rasps wretched and deep. Danielle hears footsteps far away. She holds Max's beautiful, pale face in her hands. "Sweetheart, I'm so, so sorry. I know this has been terrible for you, and I promise you won't be here long, but right now I have to go. Please don't worry."

"No!" Max struggles to embrace her again, his speech slurred. "Mom, they're drugging me. I don't know what they're giving me, but it makes me nuts and then knocks me out." He sits up and rubs his swollen, bloodshot eyes.

Danielle puts a hand on his arm and makes him look into her eyes. "Listen, sweetheart, I can't explain now, but if they find me here, they'll revoke my bond and I won't be free to try to save you."

Disbelief and horror flood his face. *"No way!* I'm getting dressed, and you're taking me with you." He swings his legs out of the bed and stands. He takes a few steps, but his legs crumple beneath him. He falls into her arms, his thin body a leaden weight.

"Mom, I —"

"I promise I'll get you out of here." She lays him back on the bed. "Where's your Game Boy?"

He points a shaking finger at the desk and seems confused until she pulls his iPhone out of her purse and slips the charger into a side drawer. He smiles faintly, clutching it as if it were the Holy Grail.

She bends down and gives him a last kiss, tears streaming down her face. "Use it to call me or text me. Just let me know you're all right."

He is clearly fighting to keep his eyes open, to hang on to her words, but she fears he is losing the battle. She shakes him again — hard. "Max, I need you to find out as much as you can about Fastow, the pills, anything you can. I don't know what's in them, but I think they have something to do with why you've been . . . behaving as you have."

His eyes widen. He starts to speak, but Danielle interrupts him. "And don't let them give you any more pills."

"How —"

She grasps his face and forces his eyes to focus on hers. "Hold them under your tongue. Flush them down the commode. They're making you sick; keeping you

241

drugged."

"But why, Mom? Why would they —"

"Just do it, Max. *Please.* And pretend to cooperate."

"What?"

She shakes her head. "If you don't fight them, they won't put you in restraints . . ." She can't trust her voice to finish the sentence.

His eyes fill with tears; his mouth quivers. "Don't leave me here all alone, Mom. I can't handle this — I really can't."

She puts her arms around him. "You won't be alone. Tony will see you every few days. His friend Doaks will come, too. I've already put their numbers in your phone. I'll try to get your aunt Georgia to fly down. You can see her as often as you like." A sob breaks from her as she holds him tighter. "I'll fix this — I promise. And I'll have my phone on every minute."

He nods, his eyes sick with resignation — worse even than when she first abandoned him to this hellish place. Max's eyes flutter again, but even as he falls back into a stupor, he grasps her arm as if it is a sailor's oar delivering him from an icy death. She buckles the four-point restraints, tears falling again — this time darkening the cracked, worn leather. She then gently unclasps his fingers and tucks the thin, blue blanket around him, the swirled emblem of Maitland emblazoned in bone white in the center. How can she possibly leave him?

"I've got to take care of the Parkman boy. Fastow's orders," says a voice down the hall.

Danielle freezes. She grabs her purse and jacket, drops to the floor, and creeps on hands and knees like a soldier in enemy territory — all well beneath the glaring, venomous eye of the security camera. After what seems like eons, she reaches the shower stall. The last thing she sees before she closes the shower curtain are the remains of the syringe packet and the test tube lying on top of Max's bed.

"Michelle is always running behind." The voice is loud now, but still outside the door. "You don't see anyone paying me double to do her job, do you?"

Danielle holds her breath. She hears the knob turn as someone enters the room. A bustle of activity and then angry muttering. "Look at that. She draws blood and leaves everything else lying around — on the patient's bed, no less! Kreng is going to have a fit."

A sudden silence convinces Danielle that she is gone. She rushes back to the bed and throws the needle and everything — even the torn T-shirt strip — into her purse. She creeps over to Max and presses her lips against his pale, moist forehead. She breathes deeply. He is still Max. He is still alive. And she will, so help her God, come back and get him out of this place. She slips to the wall, ducks beneath the camera, and removes her jacket. She leaves the same way she came in.

By some miracle, she manages to retrace her path to Doaks's car unobserved — she hopes. She crouches low in the seat as she slowly rolls the Nova through the Maitland gates and toward the small, wooded lane. Her heart pounds with the dreadful risk she has taken. From the ravages on Max's arms. From the knowledge that she has to leave him there. Sweat pours from her body for the next twenty minutes as her eyes fix on the rearview mirror, waiting for the police to arrest her and take her away.

Like the thief she is.

CHAPTER TWENTY-ONE

The next morning Sevillas takes his usual place at the head of the table. Doaks plops down somewhere in the middle and props his feet up on one of the leather chairs. Danielle sits next to Sevillas, trying not to let her nervousness show. Sevillas has called them together to tell them about his meeting with the D.A. His face is stern. "Here's the bottom line. I think the D.A.'s trying to force Danielle's hand."

"What do you mean?" she asks.

"They want Max to plead out."

"No shit?" asks Doaks.

Danielle's heart races. "Why would they do that? I thought they wanted a high-profile trial — especially because of Maitland."

Sevillas shakes his head. "It's because of Maitland that they want us to take a deal. Maitland is the biggest employer in Plano, Danielle. A mentally ill patient was brutally murdered in his room, with no one on the unit. Another patient, who was supposed to be in restraints, is found covered in blood with the murder weapon in the dead boy's room. The civil negligence suit, which I'm sure Mrs. Morrison's lawyer is preparing as we speak, will be in the millions. Given that the prime suspect is also a psychiatric patient with no criminal record won't help Maitland's standing in the community, its national reputation or its position in the Morrison lawsuit. Maitland has to limit its exposure — fast."

Doaks shrugs. "Makes sense to me."

"I can't believe this," says Danielle.

"The D.A.'s also using this threat to bolster their bond–no bond argument against you," says Sevillas. "With a murder charge, there's a good chance the judge will grant their motion and no bond you until trial."

Danielle gasps. She won't be able to try to find another suspect. She'll be in jail, help-less to speak to Max or even attend his trial. She locks frantic eyes on Sevillas and braces herself. "Tell me what they want."

"They'll give you deferred adjudication on the obstruction and accessory charges," he says.

"Sounds too good to be true." Danielle

gives him a piercing look. "What about Max?"

Sevillas reaches across the table and grasps her hand. "The State will agree to drop all charges against Max in return for a plea by reason of insanity and a joint motion to the court requesting an order to confine Max to an indefinite stay in a private or state institution until it is determined that he is competent."

"Christ," mutters Doaks.

Danielle no longer feels Sevillas's warm touch. All in her is ice. "You mean Maitland."

Sevillas clasps both of her hands in his and squeezes them. His brown eyes are solemn. "Yes. The D.A. made it clear that they will strongly urge the judge to keep Max at Maitland until they believe that he is well enough to be released into the general population. Maitland has agreed to treat Max without charge, but only if the terms of the plea are kept confidential."

Danielle pulls her hands free. "You want me to let them keep Max locked up in that lunatic asylum? They're the ones who made him crazy in the first place!" Her voice shakes. "What about the state institution?"

"It's in Des Moines and has the worst reputation there is," says Sevillas quietly.

"The judge will never send Max there."

Danielle stalks to the other side of the room. She turns, fists balled. "I will never agree to this. I don't care if they throw me in jail."

Sevillas sighs. "But are you willing to risk that Max may spend the rest of his life there? Even with good behavior, he'll serve fifteen years."

Danielle leans against the wall. Bile rises in her throat. *Thirty-one.* He'll be thirty-one when he gets out. His whole life will be forfeited. All he'll know is what he'll learn locked away with other . . . murderers. And if she violates the restraining order, they will try her for the obstruction and abetting charges. If convicted, she may not see him for years. She holds a cold hand to her forehead and then goes back to her chair. She puts steel into her voice. "I won't do it. It's too soon to even think about cutting a deal."

Sevillas shakes his head. "They want an answer before the hearing — two weeks from today. If not, they'll rescind the offer."

Danielle crosses her arms and looks Tony straight in the eyes. "That means we've got fourteen days to find a killer."

It is after lunch. Sevillas and Doaks are in

the conference-room office marshalling evidence for the hearing. Danielle has stepped into Tony's office to call Max. Now that Max has his iPhone, she can call him, but she knows it is dangerous. Kreng and the staff could easily catch him at it and confiscate the phone — not to mention what Sevillas would do if he finds out what she did yesterday. Even though it was only yesterday since she broke into Maitland, she simply has to hear his voice. She slips into Tony's office and shuts the door. Max answers immediately.

"Hi, Mom."

He sounds so normal that she is taken aback. "How are you, honey?"

"For being in this hellhole, I'm doing okay." She hears him tapping away. "I've found out some stuff you aren't going to believe."

"What is that noise?"

He sounds preoccupied. "Doing research."

"On what?"

There is a pause as the tapping ceases. "Fastow, what else?"

"How are you doing that?"

He groans. "On my iPhone."

"On the Web?"

There is a sound that is somewhere between a chortle and a laugh. "Come on,

Mom. Think outside the box."

She tries to keep her irritation at bay. "Max, tell me how you are. I worry about you constantly."

A sigh filters through the receiver. "I'm fine. I stopped taking the meds, and I act like a dumb cow every time they're around me."

"What about the blood draws? Is that all they're doing or are they also injecting you with something?"

"Neither one. I don't know why."

"Have you found out anything about Fastow?"

"Not much," he says. "Just stuff about how great he is. He's won all kinds of awards."

"What else did you find out. Anything about the meds?"

"I'm working on that," he says absently. "I took some photos of them with my phone, but I don't see anything that looks like the blue capsules in the Pharmacology Flash Cards, in Skyscape or Epocrates. The last one surprises me, because you can usually plug in any mystery pill and it comes up with a match in about three seconds."

Danielle sits down. "Max, what in the world are you talking about?"

Another exasperated sigh. "Let me make

it simple for you. The iPhone has access to lots of apps — applications. I downloaded the ones I thought I'd need, using your credit card number, of course. . . ."

She ignores the latter. "What applications?"

"Hmm, let's see." She can almost see him ticking off his fingers one at a time. "The Pharmacology Flash Cards are really cool. They keep up with the latest head drugs, clinical trials — all that kind of stuff."

"Max, how long have you been doing this?"

She hears a snort. "C'mon, Mom, what did you think? That you could feed me those lousy pills for years and I wouldn't find out what they are? Even a dumb-shit could tell they aren't aspirin."

Danielle blanches. So he knows he's been on antipsychotics.

"It's cool, Mom," he continues. "Skyscape is another drug program, like Epocrates, except that Epocrates has pictures."

"Of what?"

"Of the meds, Mom."

"Did you find out what they are?"

"No, that's the weird part. I've looked at every drug that could even be close to the ones Fastow gives me, and nothing matches — at least not any of the lunatic meds."

She doesn't touch that one, either. "This could be very important, Max. Were you able to do a visual comparison with —"

"Other atypical antipsychotics?"

Her heart stops. Oh, her son is no dummy. "Yes," she says weakly.

"None of them look like these. There's no imprint code, no nothing. I've even read the clinical studies and description of the conventional meds and compared the side effects and drug-drug interactions."

My God, how long has this been going on? He sounds like a Harvard Medical School graduate. "It must be experimental. Max, I don't want you taking a single one of the meds those people are giving you, even ones you've had before. And the more information you can collect, the better chance we'll have at the hearing to get you out of there."

"God, Mom, I hope so. I try not to think about it, but . . ."

"About what?"

The silence is knotted, fragile. If sadness were a color, it would be a blue stripe wound tightly around Max's voice. "Whether or not I'm crazy, even without that weird shit Fastow's been giving me."

Danielle puts a hand to her forehead and closes her eyes. At least she doesn't have to see him. She couldn't bear it.

252

"Mom?"

"Yes, honey." The pause lengthens. "I don't think you're psychotic, Max. I think they're wrong."

"But what if they're not? I pass out at night just like I did when they said I killed Jonas."

"Max, stop it."

He is quiet a moment. "Okay." Another pause. "Then let me tell you what else I found, and then I've got to go. It's time for the Dragon Lady to make sure I've done my 'personal hygiene.' "

Danielle laughs. "You don't do it at home. Why would you do it there?"

"Right. Okay, here's the scoop on Sylvius and Osirix." Danielle sighs. From experience, she knows she is about to get another Asperger's lecture, filled with minutiae she probably doesn't need. It seems as if psychopharmacology has been Max's obsession for a long time.

"I hacked into Maitland's database with my iPhone and then downloaded my MRIs using Osirix."

"How did you manage *that?*"

"Got lucky," he says. "The nurse's station is right outside my room. I snitched the password when no one was looking. Man, they're worthless."

Like mother, like son, she thinks.

"Anyway," says Max, "you can pan around it and see how your brain lights up when you take certain meds, and —"

"Max . . ."

"I know, I know, but this is important. With Sylvius, I sectioned through my own MRI, which I found in Maitland's database, to try to find out what's lighting up and what drugs might . . . Anyway, that's what I was doing when you called." He exhales deeply, as if his thoughts are racing ahead of his conclusions.

Danielle hears a noise. Sevillas opened the door and points a finger at the conference room. Danielle waits until Sevillas is gone and then whispers quickly into the phone. "Max, I have to go. You're doing amazing things. Send me everything you get, and I'll forward it on to Sevillas and Doaks so they can see if it's something we can use. I think it's clear that Fastow is hiding something."

"You really think he murdered Jonas?" Max's voice seems excited.

Danielle can't take any more. "Honey, I have to go. Call me later."

"Mom?"

"Yes?"

"If I can prove Fastow did it, then I'll know I didn't."

She puts her hand to her forehead, glad that he can't see her. "You didn't do it, Max," she says quietly.

He is silent for a long, painful moment. "I just don't know anymore, Mom," he whispers.

"Sweetheart, I know you better than anyone in the world, and I don't believe it."

The sad voice that comes through the line is that of an old man. "You're my mom. You have to say that."

"No, I don't," she says. "Now stop worrying about all of this for a while and try to rest." She utters a soft goodbye and sneaks out to the ladies' room. Where she cries as if her heart is breaking.

Back on the battlefield, they have spent the past few hours culling through the remainder of the State's documents.

"Not much there," says Sevillas.

"I didn't expect there to be." Danielle points to the tabs she has placed on a few of the documents the State has produced in response to their subpoena. "All I've found are a few minor discrepancies in Jonas's application to Maitland."

"What do you think, Doaks?"

"I always look at family first when you're talkin' about murder." He shrugs. "Most

255

people kill those they love."

"A rosy view of the world," says Sevillas, "but it doesn't seem to be the case here."

"No kiddin'," says Doaks. "According to Barnes and the boys down at the station, Jonas's mom is fuckin' Mother Teresa."

There is a knock, and Sevillas's secretary comes in with a manila envelope; hands it to Doaks; and leaves. He tears it open and pulls out a single piece of paper. He skims it and wads it into a ball. "Forget it. There ain't no angle on the mother. Damn, all we need is one stinkin' person who coulda, woulda, shoulda done it . . . and we ain't got jack."

"What was that?" asks Sevillas.

Doaks flops back into his chair. "Barnes sent it over. Told me he had a surprise for me. Man, just when you think those morons down there are dumber than stone, they turn around and do somethin' really smart."

"Fill us in, John."

He sighs. "The cops luminoled everyone at the hospital right after they got there. They all came out clean as a whistle."

"Luminoled?" asks Danielle. "What's that?"

Sevillas picks up his pen and makes a note. "Luminol is a chemical used to detect trace amounts of blood. When shown under a black light, the areas in which blood has adhered to a surface are identifiable. It's commonly used at a crime scene to see if and where a murderer might have tried to clean up after himself."

"Yeah," says Doaks, "but you'll never guess what those bozos did. They didn't just luminol everybody's clothes."

"What do you mean?" asks Sevillas.

"I mean they sprayed their hands, that's what." He shakes his head. "You ever heard of such bullshit?"

Sevillas stares at Doaks. "Their hands?"

"Yeah," he says. "I didn't even know the stuff worked on skin. You?"

"I've never had a case where they used it on the body."

"Doesn't matter," says Doaks. "They're all clean on that one, too."

"I'll have to do some research and find out if the results are reliable when used on human skin," says Sevillas. "It certainly wasn't the manufacturer's intended use."

"Well, don't get your hopes up." Doaks rubs his neck. "I'm strikin' out on a few other fronts, too. That girl — Naomi? She wasn't even on the unit the day of the murder. She was at the cafeteria eatin' fried chicken in front of about fifty witnesses." He shrugs. "Too bad about her. Just one

257

look at her, and a jury would love to put her away."

"Couldn't she have gotten in somehow?" asks Sevillas.

"Who knows?" grumbles Doaks. "All I know is that so far we got squat. At least it's early on."

Sevillas coughs and riffles through some papers. Doaks stares at him. "What's up? Why ain't you lookin' at me when I'm talkin' to you?"

Sevillas glances first at Doaks and then at Danielle. "Well, I'm afraid I have more bad news. I got a call from the court clerk late this morning. The judge has moved up the State's motion on the bond and proof-evident hearing for next Tuesday."

"What?" Doaks splutters. "Are you outta your ever-lovin' mind? I just got finished tellin' you we got *nada*. Do I gotta translate that for you?"

Sevillas shrugs. "It's Hempstead. You know what that means."

"Who is Hempstead?" asks Danielle. "The judge?"

Doaks rolls his eyes. "She's the judge, all right. Well, strike three and you're out."

Danielle feels a flare of panic. "What do you mean?"

Sevillas takes a deep breath. "The judge

who drew your case is Clarissa L. Hempstead, the youngest and toughest judge on the bench. She takes a very, shall we say, active role in her cases. Which means that if she wants a hearing on Tuesday, we'll have it on Tuesday. Don't worry, Danielle, we still have a few days to dig in and solidify our legal position."

Danielle gives him a worried look. "How much will it hurt us if we don't have at least one viable suspect?"

"We can still raise the specter of other patients and staff," he says. "She knows it's early in the case. Obviously it's not good that the only suspect is Max. I won't kid you, Danielle. The fact scenario is terrible. What worries me even more is that we don't have a single witness to call."

Danielle's heart sinks. The only one who can really tell them what happened is Max. And he doesn't remember a thing. Her heart quickens. They need exonerating evidence, and they need it fast. And, she prays, she has exactly that. "Tony, I think I have something that will help us."

"Saints preserve us," mutters Doaks.

Danielle picks up her purse and puts it on her lap. She had not planned to divulge the fruits of her foray into Maitland until she had a chance to send off the medication and blood sample to an independent lab and could present Tony with concrete evidence. But given the drastically shortened timetable, she has no choice. She pulls a small plastic bag from her purse and holds it up. The bright blue capsules catch the light.

Sevillas gives her a quizzical look. "What are those?"

"The medication Fastow has been giving my son," she says. "And probably to Jonas, as well. I believe this is what has caused Max's violent behavior. I don't know about Jonas or how it might have contributed to his death."

Doaks takes his feet off the chair and moves closer to inspect the contents of the bag. Wary gray eyes meet hers. "What makes you think that?"

"I know Max's behavior changed drastically after he came to Maitland."

Sevillas raises his eyebrows. "Where did you get those pills?"

Danielle thinks fast. "I took a few from the bottle when the nurse wasn't looking." She shrugs at Sevillas's quizzical look. "They didn't look like anything Max had taken before. I took some photos of them with my iPhone and sent them to one of Max's doctors in New York. He's never seen them before — either the color or the odd, asymmetrical shape." She hands him the Ziploc bag.

Sevillas stares at the pills. "So," he says slowly, "this has no bearing on the physical evidence against Max vis-à-vis the murder. It only has relevance to Max's allegedly erratic behavior at Maitland and your theory that Fastow, and supposedly Maitland as well, are using experimental drugs on their patients." He pauses. "And that's only if — and it's a big if — it turns out to be true that this is a medication not recommended by the FDA, which, I must say, is so unlikely as to be highly improbable."

Danielle fights the anger that wells up inside her. "I agree with you about the legal ramifications. I do not agree with you about the medication. That's why I need you to send it off to a lab to have it analyzed."

Sevillas and Doaks exchange a look. Doaks shrugs. "I think it's a waste of your money, but I'll do it."

"Before Tuesday?"

Sevillas shoots a look at Doaks.

"Yeah, yeah," he says. "I'll pull some strings."

"Fine," says Sevillas. "But how do we prove they were given to Max?"

Danielle chooses her words carefully. "I think I've solved that problem." She slowly extracts the vial of blood that she has kept in her refrigerator all night and packed in a freezer wrap she bought from the drugstore.

Doaks grunts. "What's that? You bringin' us Popsicles now?"

Danielle gently unwraps the test tube and hands it to Sevillas. "This needs to go to a lab, along with the medication."

Sevillas holds the test tube up to the light and then turns and stares at Danielle.

Doaks looks over Sevillas's shoulder. "Man, is that blood? Whose blood?"

Danielle clasps her hands. "Max's."

"How the fuck did you get Max's blood?" Doaks's eyes are narrow slits.

Sevillas holds the test tube as if it is nitroglycerin. His face is as grim as his voice. "Danielle, I think you better tell us what's going on."

She nods. "While Doaks was in with Nurse Kreng yesterday, I went into Max's room and found the pills and his medication chart. Max was practically unconscious and had needle tracks up and down his arms. I don't know if they're drawing his blood to take levels or injecting him with something. That's why we have to have the pills analyzed. Once we find out what's in his blood, we can go to court with our evidence and demand that the M.E. analyze a similar sample of Jonas's blood. We'll finally know what Fastow is up to." She takes a deep breath. "I don't think it's a far leap from there to legitimately suggest that Fastow was conducting some form of clinical trial with experimental psychotropics on Max and that they caused Max's violent behavior."

Doaks looks like a rocket about to explode. "Goddammit! I knew you were up to somethin'! Tellin' me the car was in a different place because the sun was in your eyes — my ass! Do you have any idea what kinda numbnut stunt that was? I oughtta pick up the phone and turn your ass in."

Sevillas places a hand on his arm. His words come out like bullets. "Stop it, Doaks. Sit down." Doaks does as he asks, muttering and gesticulating all the way.

Sevillas turns an angry gaze on her. "This is unbelievable. Do you realize you've jeopardized everything we've been working for? How am I supposed to keep you out of jail if you take insane risks like this?" He stops short. "How did you get the blood sample? Was it lying around in his room, too?"

Stung by his anger, she shakes her head. "I drew it. There was a syringe packet there and I —"

Doaks smacks himself on the side of the head. "Great! Hempstead's gonna love this. The murder suspect's loving mother sneaks into the hospital, flips up a middle finger at her bond and T.R.O., and then takes blood from her own kid — violatin' yet another court order to stay away from him! Could we be any more fucked?"

"I said stop it, Doaks," says Sevillas. "She knows exactly what she's done and what she's risked." Sevillas continues to stare at her. The silence between them is torturous.

"No one saw me," she says quietly.

"Right." Sevillas's voice could cut glass.

"What about the cameras?" asks Doaks. "You think of that, or are we gonna be lucky enough to have your felony on tape?"

"No," she says. "I disabled the camera."

"How?" asks Doaks.

"I put my jacket over it."

"Like the killer done on the day of the murder?" snaps Doaks.

"That's enough," says Sevillas.

Danielle takes the test tube from Sevillas and wraps it in its frozen nest. She hands it back to Sevillas with shaking hands. She knows she has betrayed his trust, but she also knows she is right. "I know you're upset with me, Tony, but you have to admit one thing. At least now we have a murder suspect."

Sevillas looks at her, his eyes filled with sadness. "I don't think you understand, Danielle. They've had one all along."

CHAPTER TWENTY-TWO

Danielle sits on the floor of the small, impersonal apartment Sevillas has rented for her. She wears her old gray sweat suit, and her feet are bare. Strewn around her are reams of paper from which she has culled three orderly stacks. She glances at her watch. It is 8:00 a.m. She rubs her eyes and sighs. She has worked all night.

When she left Sevillas's office yesterday, she took the accordion file of Jonas's records, an enormous stack of documents Maitland produced yesterday in response to Sevillas's subpoena, and the contents of the black box. She has pursued her quest for evidence to exonerate Max, but has ignored all documents relating to him. They lie in a heap underneath the cheap, laminated coffee table. Throughout the night, however, waves of doubt have plagued her. Without warning, they would grip her and rivet her bleary eyes to the pile of papers. Her heart tells her this morning that she is simply afraid to read them — afraid of what they might tell her that is worse than what she already knows.

So far the other documents have turned up nothing. Danielle stands and stretches. She should get some sleep. She has one more stack — a supplemental response by Maitland that Sevillas received just before she left his office yesterday. She walks over to the cheap Formica counter and pulls the even cheaper coffee pot from its coiled burner. As she pours herself a bitter cup, she tries not to think about Sevillas's last comments. He was adamant about one thing: that he and Doaks were going to continue to prepare for the hearing — which as of this morning is three days away — and she is to stay in her apartment. In other words, she is to let them do their job — and not commit any other felonies. She prays that when Max's blood and the pills are analyzed, they will confirm her claim that Max's behavior — whatever it was — had been beyond his control. Although Doaks told her it would take at least a week to get the results — particularly if the medication was experimental — she has little else to hang her hat on. She lifts the cup to her lips. It tastes like tar.

She picks up the last stack of documents provided by the State, which Sevillas has copied for her, and walks over to the small sofa that is covered in some kind of florid Navajo print. Her black reading glasses are perched on her nose. Slowly but surely she makes her way through the stack. A line in one of the application forms catches her eye. There it is again, the note about Jonas's referring doctor in Chicago. She flags it and reads Jonas's application to Maitland more closely. This one lists his place of residence as Reading, Pennsylvania. Danielle is almost positive that Marianne told her she had moved back to Texas before coming to Maitland. Even if that were not the case, why would Marianne live in Pennsylvania and have a referring physician for Jonas in Chicago?

The insignificance of the discrepancy reminds her that she has found nothing to disprove the overwhelming evidence that continues to stack up against Max. She studies the paper. Dr. Boris Jojanovich is probably some specialist Marianne took Jonas to. Maybe he can shed some light on whether or not Jonas was suicidal. The medical examiner did say that the angle of the wounds was such that they could have been caused by Jonas — even though it is an extremely remote possibility. If she can find some factual basis for this, perhaps it will counterbalance the preponderance of evidence against Max.

Her earlier excitement about Fastow as a primary murder suspect has waned. As it stands, it doesn't matter that when Max's blood is analyzed it will show that Fastow's strange blue capsules are in his system. Or that an outside expert might conclude that the meds have caused Max to have psychotic episodes. Even if Tony is satisfied with that defense, she is not. All it would prove is that Max had a *reason* for killing Jonas, not that he *didn't* kill him. It meant that Max will still be locked up somewhere for an untold period of time — in another kind of prison. But what if he is truly psychotic and the meds had nothing to do with it? *No.* She can't think about that. She grasps Jonas's application form tighter. It may be all she has.

She sighs, picks up her cell phone and calls Doaks. "Fuck off, whoever you are," growls the sleepy, familiar voice.

"It's me, Danielle. I've found something you need to check out." She explains about Jojanovich and gives him the doctor's Chicago address.

"Forget it," he mutters. "I'm up to my

elbows in alligators."

"But it's important."

His voice softens. "Come on, Ms. P., we're already trying to pull a zebra out of a Pekinese's ass. Don't be makin' any more waves right now."

"John, please, do it for me."

He sighs. "Baby, I would if I could. There just ain't time to check it out before the hearing."

"I know," she says sadly. "I just want to . . ."

"Do anything you can to help your kid," he says softly. "Just sit tight. You gotta trust us on this one."

She feels tears well up. "I'll try."

"Hang in there, kid," he says. "I'll call you if somethin' new kicks up."

She mumbles a few words and rings off. Frustrated, she paces the room. Now all she can think about is Max and whether or not he is all right. How *could* he be, given the last time she saw him, pale and practically unconscious? She hasn't been allowed another phone call and she hasn't heard from him, despite her text messages to him. They must be watching him very closely. It's as if all of the air to her lungs has been cut off.

She will keep her promise to get him out

of there. She has to follow every lead, no matter how improbable. She flips open her cell and calls Jojanovich's office. Given the early hour, she leaves her name and number on the answering machine with the message that she is a new patient who urgently needs to see Dr. Jojanovich.

Exhausted, she goes into the bathroom, takes off her clothes, and turns on the shower. Maybe this will relax her enough so she can get some sleep. As the hot water pounds on the back of her neck and the steam rises around her, she hears the brassy ring of her cell phone in the other room. She wraps a towel around her and rushes to the phone. She flips it open and punches the talk button again, but the call is gone. *"Damn."* Hair dripping, she waits until the icon appears on the tiny screen and goes through the machinations required to retrieve the message. She listens to it. Her mouth drops. She listens to it again. The tinny voice confirms that there has been a cancellation, and if she is available, Dr. Jojanovich will work her in sometime tomorrow.

Danielle snaps the phone shut and paces around the room. Her bare feet are soundless on the carpet, but the noise in her mind is deafening. What should she do? She can't call Sevillas. He will absolutely forbid her to go. Again. She looks at the ugly gray box on her ankle that holds her prisoner. She is no different than a lab rat with a microchip planted in its brain. She paces back and forth, her heart beating wildly. She has to do something.

She stops dead in her tracks. It could work. She flings the cell phone down on the sofa, races into the bedroom and yanks her laptop out of her briefcase. She sets it up on the coffee table and plops down on the floor, legs crossed. She scrolls through a list and highlights an icon in the appropriate directory. There it is: the *Reynolds* case file. She clicks it open and selects a document. The plaintiff, Sheila Reynolds, sued Danielle's client, Langston Manufacturing, Inc., for eight million dollars for design flaws involving a prosthetic device that malfunctioned when she fell down a flight of concrete stairs in her office building. She sustained serious brain injuries as a result of her fall, and the family had brought suit on her behalf.

"Come on, come on," mutters Danielle. She is searching for the affidavit of the partner of Langston Manufacturing, the small company that supplied component parts to Langston. She hits pay dirt. *Pros-*

thetics, Inc. "How original," she mutters.

The Plano telephone directory is about one-inch thick. She sits on the sofa and rifles through the negligible Yellow Pages section. She finds a likely candidate under Medical Supplies, a store about two blocks away from her. She checks her watch again. It's nine o'clock. Maybe they're open. She makes the call. They're open, all right. After a few seconds she flips the phone shut and sits back. Her heart is pounding.

She goes into the kitchen and takes her purse off the counter. Inside her wallet is the card she was given on the day she was released from jail. She squints at the number on the bottom of the card and punches it into her phone.

"Plano Sheriff's office," says a nasal female voice.

"Yes," she says. "My name is Danielle Parkman, and I'd like to speak to someone about my ankle bracelet."

"Identification number?"

"Excuse me?"

Her voice is weary. "Should be a seven-digit number on the back of your bond card."

Danielle searches the card, front and back. "There's nothing there."

"That can't be right," she says. "You sure?"

Danielle looks again. A thought strikes her. "Oh, wait. Mine is one of the new kind."

"One of them experimental jobs?"

"Right," she says, "and I'm having a problem. I'm sitting in my apartment, but the anklet beeps nonstop."

"Oh, hell, it's always something around here," she says. "Hold on a minute!" Danielle hears the receiver clatter down on the desk. "Otis?" Her voice is shrill enough to make Danielle hold the receiver slightly away from her ear. "You got to go fix one of those newfangled bracelets. Nobody else is here yet." There is a pause. "Okay, okay. I'll find out." Danielle hears another clatter, and then the woman is back on the line. "Otis — Officer Reever — says he'll be on over to bring you a new one this morning. You going to be there, or you want to come down here?"

Danielle's answer is quick and firm. "I'll be here. My address is —"

"It's 4578 Lilac Lane, Apartment 4S. Over by the new mall, right?"

"Yes, that's it," says Danielle. "Do you know when he might be here?"

"Saw him grab his keys off the hook, so I'd guess he's about to go have breakfast down at Ernie's. Knowing that crowd, I'd say he should be rolling into your place in about an hour and a half."

"Perfect."

"You have yourself a nice day, now," says the woman.

"Oh, I plan to," says Danielle.

After a lot of huffing and puffing, Officer Reever squats in front of her. His face is so red, she is afraid that myocardial infarction is but a labored breath away. She raises her foot with the anklet on it a bit higher so he won't have to bend over so far. He nods his thanks as he takes an unusual tool with a jagged blade from a plastic case and slices off the polyurethane band. "Now," he says, "I've already deactivated the doohickey on the box. Normally that'd raise six shades of hell down at the station, but Lily knows I'm over here replacing your anklet, so it's okay."

Danielle nods as she leans down to rub her freed ankle, which peeps out from under her slacks. It is enclosed in a thick cotton sock. "I wonder if it would be all right if you put the new one on my other ankle?"

Officer Reever grunts. "Yeah, I know them things wear on you a little."

Danielle raises her other foot. "Do you think you could put it on over my sock?"

He looks up at her, his wide expanse of belly between them. "No, ma'am. We're supposed to put it on right next to the skin, you know, so you can't take it off. I can give you about an inch and a half wiggle room, though. That ought to be a little more comfortable for you."

"Thank you, Officer," she says. "I'm always so cold that I wear socks every day, no matter how hot it gets outside."

He pushes down the sock on the other leg so that it pools at the top of her foot. After first approximating the amount of space he plans to leave between her leg and the device with his short, stubby thumb, he attaches the new ankle bracelet. When he finishes, he sits back on his heels and begins the grunting and puffing that finally elevates him to a standing position. He slaps his belly. "Well, ma'am, that should do it."

She lowers her pant leg and escorts him to the door. "Thank you again, Officer. You've been very helpful."

He tips his hat. "You be good, now. Don't do anything I wouldn't do."

She smiles at him. "Of course not, Officer. You've taken care of that."

After he leaves, Danielle walks swiftly into her bedroom. She pulls a slender cardboard box from under the bed. The white label marked *Prosthetics, Inc.* is torn where she ripped into the box this morning. She pulls off her shoes, pants and thick cotton socks. Her left leg, the one sporting the new ankle bracelet, looks markedly different from her right. She reaches down and slips off the anklet as easily as taking a halter from a horse's head. She hangs it on the hook on the back of the bedroom door. She then rips open the Velcro tabs that join behind her knee and slips off the lifelike covering, pulling away the special foam layer that clings to her leg. She throws everything into the cardboard box. She sees the insert that describes her purchases.

All prosthetic coverings are custom made from a unique blend of silicone polymers. This truly marvelous invention is a second skin. Silicone resists high and low temperatures and is well tolerated by the body. It is easy to repair and offers a translucent, specially pigmented appearance, which is colorfast and long-lasting. Custom veins and freckles are cast onto the wax. Only you will know it isn't real.

"How right you are," Danielle murmurs. She smiles as she recalls the quizzical look the saleswoman at the supply store gave her when she told her she only wanted to buy the prosthetic covering, not the prosthesis itself. She shoves the box back under the bed, puts on her pants and shoes, and goes to the hall closet. Inside are her packed bag, purse, laptop, papers, cell phone and her freshly printed, computerized plane ticket.

At best, she may find exactly what she needs to raise reasonable doubt in the jurors' minds: that Jonas was self-inflictive and suicidal before he went to Maitland. She can also find out why Dr. Jojanovich referred Jonas to Maitland — and why Marianne chose Jojanovich in Chicago if she lived in Pennsylvania. He may be aware of other psychiatrists who will be able to support her theory. At worst, she will be back tonight in time for the hearing tomorrow, with no one the wiser. Her cell phone will not reveal her whereabouts should Sevillas or Doaks try to call her, and if they want to see her, she can plead illness. She makes a quick call to Georgia and begs her to fly down from New York that evening. Georgia tries to make Danielle explain why she needs to come and what is so urgent, but Danielle puts her off, telling her that she can't explain now, and that Georgia just has to trust her that her presence is crucial. Apparently the desperation in Danielle's voice convinces Georgia. She agrees to catch the next flight.

She takes the key to her apartment off of her key ring, opens the door and slips it under the mat. Georgia will be here tonight. Danielle is flooded with relief. She could never leave Max — even for a night — without knowing that someone who loves him as much as she does will be there in her stead.

Before she can change her mind, she takes a last look around the apartment. When she slams the door, the lock clicks with an ominous finality.

CHAPTER TWENTY-THREE

Danielle paces as the morning sun spills onto the thick carpet of her Chicago hotel room. She stands at the window and thinks of the last time she was here. Two years ago, a sexy corporate embezzlement case brought her to this very hotel. The Whitehall reminds her of what she used to be, of the intellectual sparring during the day and the long dinners with clients in trendy restaurants at night. It has the old-world luxury absent in most American hotels — the penned note on the pillow of her turned-down bed; the thick white robe hanging on the back of the bathroom door; a glass of her favorite cognac poured just so on the side table, remembered from her last visit. Nestled off of Michigan Avenue in the Gold Coast, it speaks to her of times past and of times that may never come again.

She resists the strong urge to answer Tony's frantic calls. She knows he will hit the roof if he finds out that she has violated the terms of her bond . . . yet again. With any luck, she will be back in Plano tonight with at least one piece of information that will keep the hearing from being a disaster. She is a desperate woman, grasping for a ray of light in the dark. She cannot leave a single stone unturned.

Late last night, when she was certain he would be asleep, Danielle left a message on Sevillas's cell phone, informing him about Georgia and that she was to be put on Max's visitation list as co-counsel for the defense. She instructed him to let Georgia visit Max whenever she likes, and whenever Max needs her. Danielle winces even now to think of Tony's reaction to her unilateral directive. She is grateful she won't be there when he finds out where she is — and what she's doing. If all goes according to plan, he won't know anything. She made Georgia swear only to tell Tony that she is sick in bed.

Just as she sits down with a cup of coffee, her cell phone rings. She grabs it and taps the screen: *Max.* Her heart is seized with panic. "Sweetheart, are you all right?"

His voice is riddled with anger and panic. "What are you doing in Chicago? How could you leave me here and take off without telling me?"

"Max, it's all right. Wait, how did you know I was in Chicago? Did Tony tell you?"

"Sevillas?" He snorts. "I tracked you with my GPS."

"What GPS?"

"We've both got GPS — on our iPhones, remember?" His voice is grim. "Now would you quit stalling and tell me what you're up to?"

Danielle shakes her head. "I'm looking for evidence. For the hearing."

"Why Chicago?" he asks. "Sevillas told me about that creep, Fastow, and I've been checking up on him."

She spends the next half hour trying to convince Max that she will be back in time for the hearing, that it is important that she follow this lead on Marianne, and that he should line up all his information and e-mail it to Sevillas. Then, if she doesn't come up with anything, there's no harm done and they can go after Fastow full bore, which she promises they will do in any event. She urges him to continue his research and to keep his eyes open, particularly with regard to Fastow. She hopes that this will provide a major distraction that will lessen his terror about the hearing and the possibility that she won't be there. She also makes a mental note to call Georgia and ask her to stay with him as much as possible today. If he can't have his mother, at least he'll have the next best thing.

Now she paces around the room, waiting for word that her felony flight has not been in vain. Her rumpled bed is a fair reflection of another sleepless night. She forces herself to sit on the smooth leather sofa and light a cigarette. The smoke tastes bitter. Just as she closes her eyes and begins to relax, her cell phone rings. She glances at caller ID and flips open the phone. "Hello?"

"Ms. Talbert?"

"Speaking."

"This is Marcia, Dr. Jojanovich's nurse?"

"Yes, Marcia," she says. "Thank you for calling back so promptly."

"Well," she says. "Because you said your case is urgent, the doctor says he can give you a few minutes around twelve-thirty."

"That will be just fine." She picks up the pen and pad from the glass coffee table. "If you could just give me directions."

"Go to 5896 Polanski Avenue. It's on the northwest side on the fourth floor," she says. "Oh, and the doctor said to bring whatever records you have, since you're a new patient. He'll want to go over them after he looks at his file."

"Of course," says Danielle. "I'll bring everything I've got."

Danielle looks out of the back of the taxi. They pass quickly from the glittering stores of Michigan Avenue into Chicago's more depressing neighborhoods until they reach a narrow, dilapidated building. The brass plate above the doorbell is tarnished, the lettering barely legible. *Boris Jojanovich, M.D.* She pushes a tarnished intercom button. The tinny voice scratches through like an old seventy-eight. "May I help you?"

"Ms. Talbert to see the doctor."

"Oh, yes," the voice says. "Buzzing through."

A sound like an electric razor gone bad comes from somewhere around the doorknob. Danielle pushes hard. The door moves grudgingly, then slams behind her. A list of tenants is stuck to the wall with yellowed Scotch tape. The typewriting looks like the product of a Royal manual, circa 1950, badly in need of a new ribbon. Danielle runs her index finger down to the *J*'s and finds the suite number on the fourth floor. She sighs when she sees the out-of-service sign on the elevator. By the time she climbs the stairs to the designated floor, she is out of breath, but she is no longer nervous. She smooths her hair and walks to the reception desk.

"Good afternoon, Ms. Talbert." Marcia, a twentysomething whose mellifluous voice belies her solid frame and sensible navy dress, stands and pours her a glass of water. "Everyone needs this after climbing those stairs. Here you go."

Danielle takes a long drink. "Thank you."

"You're right on time. Just take a seat and I'll let the doctor know you're here."

The walk to the three empty wooden chairs is short. Danielle is barely seated when a side door opens and an elderly man in a white coat appears. His bespectacled face is stern. Impressive folds of flesh hang between his eyes and form bulldog jowls at his collar.

She stands and extends her hand. "Dr. Jojanovich?"

"Yes. Ms. Talbert, is it?" His voice is a deep baritone. "I'm not quite sure how I can help you, but come in. Hold my calls, Marcia."

"Yes, Doctor."

The office Danielle enters is surprisingly large. A dusty computer sits on top of an old desk, a thick cord wrapped around its base like an umbilicus. Dr. Jojanovich points to a sagging club chair, and, after she is seated, he settles into an ancient leather affair. It produces a *whooshing* noise as he descends. Intent brown eyes study her carefully. "Well, Ms. Talbert, what can I do for you? Marcia said you needed to see me immediately."

Danielle takes a deep breath and gives him her most confident smile. "Actually, Dr. Jojanovich, I'm not the patient. I'm a lawyer. My name is Danielle Parkman."

The eyebrows rise. "A lawyer?"

"Yes," she says. "I find myself in an odd position, Dr. Jojanovich. If you'll let me explain."

He rests his gnarled hands on the worn desk. "Please do. I'm not overly fond of attorneys."

She smiles. "Most people aren't. I represent a client who has run into problems in Plano, Iowa."

He shakes his head. "I have never practiced in Iowa, Ms. Parkman."

"Well," she says, "the problem is in the form of a homicide, I'm sorry to say, involving one of your former patients."

Jojanovich's eyes open wide enough for some white to show. "Homicide?"

"Possibly suicide."

"Let me be certain I understand you, Ms. Parkman," he says slowly. "You make an emergency appointment under false pretenses, when in fact you wish to discuss a possible murder or suicide in Iowa, where I have never practiced and, God willing, never will. As a lawyer, you must know that I cannot discuss one of my patients with you without violating the doctor-patient privilege." He shakes his head again and stands. "I'm afraid I can't help you. Now, if you'll excuse me —"

Danielle steps quickly into his path. "Please, Doctor. My client could be facing the death penalty for the murder of your patient. The State may be successful if I don't get the information I need right away." She goes back to her seat, trying not to let him see how terrified she is just saying those words. Maybe if she sits, he will.

The doctor remains standing. "Which patient?"

"His name is Jonas Morrison." There is no recognition in Jojanovich's eyes. "He was seventeen years old. He was admitted into a psychiatric hospital in Iowa this summer and died of . . . severe wounds. The autopsy is inconclusive, so we don't know whether the wounds were self-inflicted or the result of a homicide. My client has been accused of killing him." She meets his eyes. "I'm trying to find out anything you know that might shed light on the situation."

Jojanovich looks at his chair as if noticing it for the first time. He sits. "What in the world led you to me?"

Danielle pulls a piece of paper out of her purse. "I've been trying to track down some background information on the boy, but all I've found is this document with your signature on it as the referring physician to a psychiatric hospital — Maitland."

"Hmm." Jojanovich takes the paper from her. He lights a half-smoked cigar that rests on an old tin ashtray. After a few ruminative puffs, he studies what she has given him. When he is finished, he looks up. "I think you've made a mistake, Ms. Parkman."

"Doctor, if you're worried about privilege —"

"No."

"Because if it is, the patient is dead and the privilege does not supersede —"

"No, Ms. Parkman," he says. "That is not the issue."

Danielle leans forward. "Then what is? If you would like confirmation that I'm an attorney . . ."

He shakes his head. "You don't understand. I have no patient by the name of Jonas Morrison."

Danielle stares at him.

He leans back in his chair. "Besides, I'm not a psychiatrist, nor do I have a pediatric or adolescent practice. Never have."

Bewildered, Danielle studies the paper he hands back to her. It is right there in black and white. "Doctor, please bear with me. This simply doesn't make sense. Isn't this your name and address listed as the primary referral source for Jonas's admission to Maitland Psychiatric Asylum in Plano, Iowa?"

Jojanovich stands. "I'm sorry, Ms. Parkman. I'd like to help you, but I don't have any idea where this came from and I've never had a patient by that name. Now, if you'll excuse me." He walks toward the door.

Danielle slowly folds the piece of paper and puts it inside her purse. "Doctor, perhaps you remember his mother, Marianne Morrison?"

"No, I'm sorry."

The black well of doubt about Max that has followed her from Iowa grows larger. Sevillas and Doaks are right. She is just another desperate defendant off on a wild-goose chase. All she has accomplished is to ensure that the moment she steps off the plane, she'll be handcuffed and thrown back into jail. She has made a fool of herself, and this time the price will be her freedom — and Max's. *Stop it,* she tells herself. She has to keep trying. "Let me describe her for you. She's about five-one or five-two, blond hair, blue eyes, early forties . . ."

"No, I've told you —"

"Maybe if you thought about it for just a moment."

Jojanovich's opaque eyes are patient. "What did you say her name was?"

"Marianne Morrison."

The doctor returns to his desk. The deep crevice between his eyes threatens to sew both brows into a single, furry line. She can tell he is trying to humor her so she will finally give up and leave. He is obviously of the generation of men who are not accustomed to throwing a woman out of his office. "How does she talk? Dress?"

Danielle's mind races. "She's Southern, from Texas originally. Her clothes are very expensive and elegant, but . . . colorful. She tends to wear tailored suits and a lot of jewelry." She searches Jojanovich's face for any sign of recognition from the pathetic portrait she has sketched. The older man's face is a blank. She decides to toss out any detail she can remember. Maybe something will click. "She is a widow who was educated to be a physician, but became a nurse instead. Oh, I understand that she's very good with computers. She used them a lot when she was a nurse. Her son, Jonas, had severe psychiatric problems. He was born in Pennsylvania." Her voice trails off.

Jojanovich's eye wattle recedes to reveal a sad glance. "I'm genuinely sorry, Ms. Parkman. I wish I could help."

Danielle sighs. Wordlessly, she walks over and shakes his hand. As she says a dispirited goodbye to Marcia and begins the long descent to the street, her mind whirls. What now? All she has left is a barely legible Chicago address that she found scrawled in the margin of some document Maitland produced. She doesn't even know if it has anything to do with Jonas. If her visit to Jojanovich is any indication, it's just another dead end. Why would Marianne have faked a referral for Jonas? God knows there is no question that he needed to be at Maitland. The doctor must be lying. Or he just doesn't want to get involved. But if all he did was refer Jonas to Maitland, why would he be worried about malpractice? Danielle knows the answer before the question fully forms in her mind. Because anyone can sue anyone for anything. This is America.

She hails a cab and pulls her raincoat around her. Dark clouds gather in the distance. As she directs the driver back to the Whitehall, her cell phone rings. She looks at the caller ID. It's Doaks. He must believe that she is in her apartment doing precisely as she has been instructed: leaving them alone to do their jobs. She ignores the call.

She can't go back empty-handed.

CHAPTER TWENTY-FOUR

Danielle runs into the hotel lobby just as the skies open. At the front desk, the clerk hands her the brass room key with a quiet smile and a polite inquiry about her day. She mumbles some response and, out of habit, asks for her messages. There is one from Max. "Call me." How does he know what hotel she is in? She shakes her head. She can't talk to him right now, not without a shred of evidence that would justify her impulsive flight to Chicago, and certainly not when weighed against the fact that her folly may send her to prison, where she will never be able to save him. She also can't tell him why trying to blame Fastow for the murder isn't good enough or that his best shot may be accepting a plea that will result in his being virtually imprisoned at Maitland — possibly for years. Georgia called yesterday and Danielle filled her in on why she is in Chicago. Georgia was terrified that Danielle had taken such a risk, but promised to keep mum about her whereabouts. She assured Danielle that Max is all right, but Danielle can tell from the tone in her voice that Max's mind-set isn't the best. She knows that he must be frantic that she is gone. She sends him a text telling him she loves him and will call him soon.

All she wants to do is go upstairs, draw a hot bath, and forget the hopelessness that is now her life. The elevator is empty. The quiet thrum of well-oiled machinery acts as a metronome upon her nerves. By the time she reaches her floor, she is exhausted. She puts the key in the door, turns it, and goes inside. The curtains are drawn. She takes off her shoes and her jacket. The combination of the dusky afternoon and the thick carpet under her feet make her suddenly sleepy. Too weary to even run a bath, she heads for the bedroom. Before she can reach it, she hears something. It seems to come from the living area. She stops. She listens. Nothing. She starts once more toward the bedroom, but hears it again. She tiptoes slowly into the living room. It is dark.

A figure is seated on the leather couch — a man. His feet are propped up on the glass coffee table. "Do you have any idea how fuckin' stupid you are?"

She flips on the light. "Doaks!"

"Yeah, Doaks — who'd you expect?" he asks. "The Feds?"

"How did you —"

"I'm a detective, remember? I talked the girl at the desk into giving me an extra card to your room. Told her I was your stinkin' husband, of all things." He grins. "Besides it's what I do — find nutballs like you who pull boneheaded stunts that wind 'em up back in the slammer where they belong. Didn't hurt none that your boy is trackin' your ass and kinda trusts me now, at least enough to tell us where you were." He shakes his head. "He's a whiz with that gadget, ain't no doubt about that. And man, he got a bad case of the red-ass when he found out where you were."

So much for keeping her crazy trip on the Q.T.

Doaks wears an oily raincoat and an old felt hat that looks like it was trampled by a herd of elk. "Do you have any idea how pissed off Sevillas is at you? You better be good and glad I talked him into lettin' me come up here and drag you home. If he had his way, he woulda flown some cop here on a jet to slap you in irons and take you back to Plano." He pulls an envelope out of his raincoat. "From Tony."

The cream-colored page has but a few, hastily scrawled words.

Danielle,
Please come back — now. You know how I feel about you, but I can't protect you or Max this way. Everything will work out, but you have to listen to me. It's the only way you can help Max.

Tony

Danielle sits in the chair opposite Doaks. All she feels is tired — bone tired. "I don't see any point in defending myself."

"Nah, I just bet you don't," he says. "What in Sam Hill you doin' up here, anyway? Not to get off the subject of how you finagled your way outta that fancy bracelet of yours." He chuckles. "I gotta hand it to you. If they figure it out before I get back, which I doubt, old Reever's gonna be the laughin'-stock of the force. When I saw the box under your bed, I thought about tyin' it up in a red bow and givin' it to him for Christmas."

"How did you get into my apartment?"

He just looks at her.

"Okay, okay." She sighs.

"You shoulda answered your cell phone," he says mildly. "Told us you was havin' female problems or some such. We woulda backed off for a few days."

"I had a lead," she says. "I asked you to look into it, but you wouldn't."

"A lead, huh?" He rolls his eyes. "You sound like god-damned Perry Mason. So, is that where you been all day, followin' your 'lead'?"

She nods.

"Did it pan out?"

She shakes her head.

"Uh-huh." He kicks his dusty feet on top of the glass coffee table and surveys the room. "Say, you got somethin' to drink around here? I'm parched."

She gets up and takes a variety of small bottles of alcohol out of the minibar. He points at two of them. She puts out the glasses and he pours one for both of them. After the first, long swallow, Doaks glances at the papers on the desk and her suitcase. He points to the latter. "Okay, Ms. P., drink up and get packed. We're outta here on a six o'clock flight. If I can sneak you back into your apartment without those dipshits down at the station figurin' it out, maybe we'll both get out of this with our asses intact."

Danielle takes a healthy sip of her drink. "I'm not going back. I have one more thing to check out."

Doaks shakes his finger at her like a father who has caught his teenaged daughter sneaking into the back door after midnight. "Don't go gettin' horsy with me, missy. You're gonna get your kit and come with me. We're goin' back to that one-horse town and get ready for that hearing. I ain't got time to keep runnin' around haulin' your ass outta trouble."

She puts her glass on the coffee table and forces conviction into her voice. "Look, John, I appreciate what you're trying to do, but I have to follow up on this one last thing. Then I'll go with you — I promise."

He empties his glass and reaches for hers. Before she hands it to him, she squeezes his outstretched hand. "I'm so glad you're here. I can't think of anyone else I'd rather be with right now."

His voice is gruff, but his eyes soften. "Okay, cookie, you better fill me in." He holds up his right hand. "I ain't sayin' I'm goin' for it. I'm just sayin' you got five minutes before I throw you over my shoulder and drag you home. Shoot."

She shows him the paper and the address penned in under Jonas's name. She emphasizes her concerns about the incongruity between the Jojanovich referral, her meeting with the doctor, and what the Maitland admission papers reflect. He studies it for a moment. "This ain't diddly. You know that."

She sighs. "I know it doesn't look like much, but it's all I've got. There has to be some information somewhere about whether or not Jonas has ever been suicidal."

He stares at her. "That don't prove Max wasn't lying there or that you weren't standin' next to him with the murder weapon in your purse." He tosses the papers on the coffee table. "And just what're you plannin' to do now, Miss James Bond? Break into some house you don't even know has anythin' to do with the dead kid? I been doin' this my whole life, and this is a waste of time."

"It may be. But it's my time." She stands and puts on her shoes. "And I'm going to check it out before I go back to Iowa."

"Don't you want to know what we've come up with since you flew the coop?"

Danielle pauses. "What?"

Doaks settles back into the couch and puts his hands behind his head. "Been doin' a little research on our boy Fastow. He ain't as squeaky clean as that old-bat nurse thinks he is."

Danielle sits down. "What did you find out?"

"Wasn't me — it was that brainiac kid of

yours. He used that phone thing of his and Googled the dweeb — not that I have a clue what that means. Ain't never had a computer, ya know." He takes a grimy notepad out of his pocket and flips a few pages. "Looks like you were right. He's knee-deep in some kinda newfangled research."

"We already know that he's doing psychotropic research. Isn't there anything more specific?"

"How am I supposed to know?" he grumbles. "I'm right in the middle of it and I gotta hop a bird and tend to another one of your grand mal fuckups."

"Have you gotten Max's blood analyzed?"

He looks at her with weary eyes. "I pulled some strings. Oughtta have it tomorrow. I still ain't figured out how you're gonna use it."

"I'll just have to tell the court how I got it. The court will revoke my bond, but Tony will make a motion that they order another blood test to confirm the results of the one I took."

"You think the court will do that?"

"I hope so. If it shows what I hope it will, the blood results will be offered to the court as evidence that whatever Max did, he did it because of the meds Fastow had him on. We'll claim that there isn't any other explanation for Max's increased aggressiveness and other odd behaviors. It will go to intent, motive and Max's state of mind at the time of the murder."

Doaks waves a dismissive hand. "Whatever."

"What about the pills?" asks Danielle.

"Same."

"In time for the hearing?"

"That's the theory." He stands up. "And another reason we gotta get the hell outta here and catch that plane." He points at her suitcase. "Let's go."

She doesn't move.

"I ain't askin' twice, Danielle." It is the first time he has called her by her first name.

She stands. "I'll come back. After I check out that address."

"Goddammit. Dames." He picks up his hat and reaches for the paper in her hand. "Give it to me."

"No."

He strides over to her. "I said hand it over."

She gives him the paper. "It doesn't matter. I have the address memorized."

"Ain't you a wonder." He stuffs it into the pocket of his raincoat. "If we didn't have time to kill, I wouldn't be doin' this at all. Now, you park your ass on that sofa and keep it there until I get back."

Danielle starts to argue with him, but takes one look at his set jaw and reconsiders. He heads for the door. She follows him, feeling useless. "Are you sure you don't want me to go with you?"

He gives her a look.

"Doaks, I . . ." The words stick in her throat.

"Yeah, you owe me one, all right, big-time." His voice is gruff, but she sees real affection in his eyes. "Do me a favor, huh?"

"Of course."

"Keep your goddamned cell phone on and answer it when I call you." He chucks her on the chin, gives her a wink, and stomps down the hall. She closes the door. And waits.

CHAPTER TWENTY-FIVE

The sky is as dark as Doaks's mood. A heavy rain drives against the windshield and covers it like a second sheet of blurred glass. The cab winds its way through unkempt streets. The tires jolt through deep potholes and spray water that joins a dirty stream that flows down the side of the curb. The driver studies his street map every few stop signs and peers through the deluge to stay his course. Row houses stare out from behind buckled sidewalks and full garbage cans. Here, mold is a smell and a color. It rises out of the ground and creeps up to the rafters.

Doaks knows these houses, these people. They're hardworking folks afraid to hope things will get better and more afraid that no amount of hoping will make it so. The driver finally pulls up curbside and points. Doaks tells him to beat it for a while. He grabs his raincoat; yanks at the collar; and runs onto the porch of an old brick house that looks like all the others. He shakes off like a wet Lab, then bangs on the door. No answer.

He peers through a grimy window with cupped hands. As he rubs it with his sleeve to get a better view, he realizes the dirt isn't on the outside. Squinting harder, he makes out a dim light in the front hall. He pushes the doorbell. While he waits, he looks at the porches of the adjacent houses, but sees no one. Probably at work. If it weren't raining so hard, there would be kids in the streets or old people on chairs smoking — somebody for him to talk to.

After five minutes of pounding, Doaks curses. He feels the cold in his bones. He grinds an old cigarette butt into the porch with his heel. It breaks and smears. He crams down hard on the buzzer for another long, irritating minute. There, he's done it. A dead end, just like he told her. He checks his watch. He's got plenty of time to pick her up and head for the airport.

He starts down the rickety stairs when he hears a noise behind him. He sees the blurred outline of a figure behind the filthy window. A pink palm bangs against the glass. He walks to the door and makes out a small female form whose mouth is moving.

The door opens a crack. A harsh, smoky voice speaks. "What in the hell do you want?"

"Good afternoon, ma'am." Doaks holds his old hat in front of him. "I'm —"

"Trying to sell something?" Her voice snaps as the door opens an inch. "Well, you can turn right around and get out."

He catches a slice of a short, gray-haired woman with steel eyes. As the door closes, Doaks does his classic toe move, so fast it makes the door bounce back instead of slam shut. Before she can react, he's talking. "I'm really sorry to bother you, but I'm lookin' for a woman who lives here — or used to live here." He holds up the scrap of paper with Marianne's address on it. "If you could take a minute to help me out, I'd really appreciate it."

The old woman starts to close the door again. "I don't talk to nobody in this neighborhood, mister. Get your head blown off that way."

"Please, lady, it's my wife," he says. "She's taken off, and you're the only one who can help me."

The door remains open a few inches. The old woman gives him a hard once-over through the chain's half-moon arc.

Doaks puts on his lost-my-last-buddy-in-

Nam look. "Hey, I'll stand right out here in the rain. I'm just a guy lookin' for his kid, that's all."

Bingo.

The door opens wide and she appears in full view. He figures her for seventy-five, maybe eighty. She wears a chenille robe so worn out even the pockets look tired. A threadbare nightgown shows where the robe gapes open. Her breasts hang low and sad, almost flat to her stomach, like dead birds strung up by their claws. "You got a name?"

"Yes, ma'am," he says. "Edwin Johnson. Pipe fitter from Norman, Oklahoma."

"Who you looking for?"

"A lady — my ex-wife."

"She got a name?"

"Marianne Morrison. About so high . . ." He holds his hand up to his chest. "Blond hair, blue eyes. Forty or so."

"Nobody like that here." Her eyes are hard.

He can tell she's getting ready to bolt. He moves closer. "Yes, ma'am, I know, but she lived here a while back. She put this address on a medical form for my son."

"No blondes in this house. Brunette, maybe," she says. "How old's your boy?"

"Seventeen."

Her eyes flash. The door opens a little

wider. He starts to walk in. She steps out onto the porch and forces him back into the full brunt of the rain. He smiles again. His wet, pathetic attempt to be adopted and taken in is ignored.

"Got a question for you," she says.

"Yes, ma'am?"

Her cold eyes search his like a spotlight. "Anything special about that kid of yours?"

"There sure is," he replies. "His name is Jonas and he's got some — problems. He's autistic and acts a little strange . . ."

"You willing to pay her debts?" Her eyes are sharp and clear. "You being her husband and all?"

"Sure might be, ma'am." He clasps his hands like a Baptist preacher. "I don't have two nickels to rub together, but I've always paid my family's obligations."

She glares at him, but waves him in with an impatient hand. "Bitch left owing two months' rent. Ain't no big trick for brunettes to be blondes or vicey-versey, I guess."

Doaks can't believe Danielle might actually have stumbled upon something, even if it probably won't mean much. He starts to follow when he sees something out of the corner of his eye. The cabdriver has pulled up in front of the house next door. He glances quickly at the old lady to make sure she hasn't seen. Just what he needs — for her to get a gander at the poor Okie who's riding around Chicago in a metered sled. There'll be no end to the cash he'll have to slip her. Once she disappears into the house, he makes a circular motion with his hand, telling the driver to cruise awhile. Shouldn't take long. He'll either be onto something or she'll have thrown him back out into the wet.

She waits in the narrow hallway and makes him wipe his shoes on an old towel she uses as a doormat. He hangs up his dripping raincoat and sopping hat on a rickety stand and follows her into a cramped living room. She sits in a recliner that was new when Eisenhower was president. The stuffing hangs out and the seat is caved in over the springs. On a spindly table are an ashtray and a pack of Lucky Strikes — filterless. She pulls one out and lights up. She inhales deeply and closes her eyes, not reacting at all to the first punch of pure tobacco. He feels around in his pocket for his Marlboro Lights. No real man would smoke such pantywaist crap. She'll think he's a pussy. They sit and smoke, eyeing each other.

The living room is stifling. The dim glow that filters through the one overhead fixture outlines the bodies of fifty years' worth of moths, their corpses illuminated grotesquely against the bottom of the glass. Brown water spots dominate plaster walls that have been patched to hell and back. A plastic crate supports a small television set. It looks so old that he wonders if it even gets color. He tips his chair back and tries to see more of the downstairs.

"Stop that!" the old woman says. "Don't try to snoop around here. This ain't your goddamned house, mister. It's mine."

Doaks assumes the pose of a penitent. "Sorry, ma'am. It's just that I'm trying to imagine my wife and son here. How they lived; where they might have gone . . ." He lets his voice trail as he gazes ruminatively into space.

Her look is forged steel. "Bullshit."

"Excuse me?"

"I said 'bullshit.' Let's cut the crap, shall we, Mr. Johnson?" Her jagged smile shows good dental work gone bad. The old bird's already smoked her cigarette down to her stained fingers. She gives a quick snort and stubs it into the overflowing ashtray. "Come on, whoever-the-hell-you-are. You're not bad, but I'm better. You don't know a goddamned thing about that woman and her kid, do you?"

Doaks is silent.

She jerks her head toward the street with a sly grin. "You belong in that cab out front as much as I do. You got private dick written all over you."

Doaks smiles. He doesn't mind being found out if she'll talk. He drops all pretense at charm. "Yeah, I know about 'em, but you're right, they don't belong to me."

She nods as if he has passed a test. "So what are you bothering an old lady about?" She catches his eye and motions to a fifth of whiskey and a smeared glass on top of the television set. He brings them to her. She pours a healthy shot — at least two man-size fingers — and then offers the glass to Doaks.

"That's okay. You go on."

She shakes her head. "Take it."

"Want me to fetch another glass?" He can get a better look around if she'll let him go into the kitchen.

"Nah, I like it straight from the horse's mouth." She tips her head and lets the cheap, brown liquid run down her throat. Her lips purse in a satisfied smack as her eyes narrow. "Let's get down to business."

"Look," he says. "Here's the deal — no bullshit. A seventeen-year-old autistic kid was murdered or committed suicide in a

310

mental hospital in Iowa. The kid used to live here. I'm tryin' to track down the mother."

She looks up, a parrot poised for a cracker. "Why do you care?"

"I represent another boy who was in the same hospital, and they're tryin' him for the murder," he says. "I don't think he did it. I'm just tryin' to dig up some information about the dead kid so I can help prove he offed himself. So, what can you tell me? How long did she live here? She leave anything behind?"

The old lady grins. "What's in it for me?"

The surprise is that she hasn't asked sooner. "What do you think would be fair?" He holds up a hand. "Not crazy — fair."

She holds out thin arms. "Look around, mister. I'm an old woman with no money, no family, no nothing." She taps a finger on her temple. "Except for what I got up here and the few bucks I get to rent these lousy properties for some big shot downtown. Now, what the hell is fair about that?"

"Twenty bucks." He stopped paying real money for the sad songs of old ladies a long time ago. Whatever he gives her will be burnin' a hole in her liver by the time he's out of the door.

"Fifty," she counters, eyes gleaming.

"Done." He fishes out two wadded twenties and a torn ten and places them in her palm.

She sticks the bills under the strap of her ratty nightgown. "I'd put 'em here —" indicating where her cleavage used to be "— but they'd be on the floor the minute I stand up."

"Let's have it."

"Bad news, that's what she was," she says. "Lived here with that crazy kid of hers about two years ago. Had brown hair ratted to the nines; fancy clothes; lots of makeup. Always late with the rent. I was stupid enough to let her get away with it." She shrugs. "The kid, you know. I felt sorry for him. Anyway, she had church people here all hours of the day and night. They took care of the kid while she worked someplace downtown. That kid was a mess. Always making weird noises and scratching himself up all the time. After about a year, she up and left."

"Know where she went?"

"Nope." She pours Doaks another shot. "Don't know and don't care. Caught holy hell from the owner, I can tell you that."

"Leave any personal belongings?"

The old woman hoots. "Ha! She left me with a pile of crap — that's what she left

312

me. The place was a wreck."

He sighs. "She leave anything with her name on it? Check stubs, bills, notepads?"

Her eyes narrow like a cat eyeing its prey. He can almost feel his wallet burning. He'll have to pay again to play, but he doesn't have to make it easy on her. He pulls another twenty from his wallet. "No ticky, no laundry. You don't see this unless you get me somethin' I can take outta here. And I don't mean an old boot and some bobby pins. I mean somethin' with her name on it — somethin' I can use."

"There ain't much," she admits.

"Much what?"

"I told you," she says. "She left the place in a hell of a mess: dirty clothes, food in the kitchen, all her garbage for me to clean up." She waves her hand, indicating everything and nothing. "I threw most of it out for the trashman — old papers, bills, stuff like that. But I still got a box of her junk up there in the attic." She points upstairs, eyes hungry for the cash in his hand.

"Not so fast, sister." He puts the twenty back in his pocket and stands. "Show me first. If it ain't worth a damn, you keep your fifty bucks and I'm on my way. *Capish?*"

The old lady glares at him, but rises unsteadily from her chair. Scotch and old bones don't help when she tries to put it into gear. Once on her feet, she shuffles slowly as Doaks follows her upstairs into a bedroom large enough to accommodate a mattress and not much else. She points at the closet. He opens the door, looks in. It's crammed full of clothes that smell like that stinky lavender shit old ladies like. Doaks kicks away at the mess on the floor.

"You got a ladder?" He's already sweating like a stevedore. The air in that room hasn't moved since 1928. She points at the corner. He stomps over and places a wobbly chair under the opening to the closet ceiling, which is so low he can poke his head into the attic just by standing. It's pitch-black except for slats of light that come through a few roof holes. He groans as he grapples to hoist his sadly neglected body through the attic opening. After many unattractive attempts and copious cursing, he finally succeeds. The smell that greets his nostrils is a mix of rodent feces, mold and rot. "Terrific."

"There's a light switch up there somewhere," the old woman calls. "Don't sit on it."

"Now she tells me," he mutters. He feels around to the right and left, but hits only dirt and rotted wood. His fingers go a little farther afield and happen upon a switch that protrudes from an old beam. He flips it. Nothing. "Got a flashlight?"

Apparently the old lady didn't have much faith in the switch, either. While he's up there clawing through rat shit, she's managed to find a decent flashlight. Her third toss makes it up to his knees, and he grabs it. He's sweating so hard dank rivulets pour down his chest.

"First the fuckin' rain and now a damned inferno," he mutters. He'd like to see Sevillas up here on his hands and knees, covered in bat guano or whatever kind of offal he's wading through. Everything has a wild smell. As he flicks the light around, ugly silhouettes of a few rats and a moving wall of roaches appear and then scuttle into the darkness. There's something about the sound of vermin scrabbling and whirring around a person in the dark.

His cell phone rings. "Fuck me, Rachel," he mutters. He fishes it out of his pocket and flips it open. "What?"

"It's me, Danielle."

"Thought it was the Queen of Sheba," he growls. "I'm knee-deep in rat shit here."

"Have you found anything?"

"Nope, just like I told you. Hope you got

your shit packed, because we split in an hour."

"Please, Doaks, keep trying," she pleads. "It's the only lead we've got."

"Then quit botherin' me," he says. "I'll give it two more minutes, and then I'm outta here." He snaps the phone shut and sticks it back into his pocket. He plays the light over the floor and makes out three cardboard boxes. He shines the light into the first box. Old photographs of a younger version of the woman downstairs. Age sure did a number on her. The second box crumbles when he tries to open it. He moves on to the last box and pulls back the flap. Inside is a weird collection of odds and ends. Old purses, shoes without mates, an umbrella with most of its spokes gone. He finds a red leather collar with a small black box attached to it and holds it up to the light. It's one of those fancy dog-shock collars.

Doaks's frustration mounts. There's nothing here but a bunch of leftover crap anybody would ditch if they decided to split without ponying up the rent. "Why did the old bat drag my fifty-six-year-old ass up here if all I was gonna get was a handful of wet rat turds?" he mutters. "Just tryin' to bone me for a few more bucks." He leans over the attic opening and yells down. "There isn't a damned thing up here!"

"Yes, there is!" Her voice is impatient. "Look in the box."

"Why don't you haul your scrawny ass up here and look in the stinkin' box?" he mutters. He takes a last look in the third box and finally turns the whole thing upside down. Dried roach shells and dust fill the air. A piece of paper floats down. Doaks grabs it and sticks it under the flashlight.

Dear Ms. Morrison,
We are pleased you have contacted American Home Mortgage with respect to your potential purchase at 2808 Leek Street, Phoenix, Arizona, Plat 51, Lot 6. We regret to inform you that we are unable to assist you in the financing of this property . . .

Doaks flips over the envelope to look at the date. April 7, 2009. A few months before Marianne took Jonas to Maitland. He turns it over.

As requested, we are providing a copy of this letter to both your Chicago and Arizona residences in the event you are in transit . . . cc: Desert Bloom Apartments, Unit 411, 6948 E. Ranch Road, Phoenix, AZ 85006.

He snaps off the flashlight. He stuffs the piece of paper into his pocket and quickly descends. In the light of the bedroom, he sees he's covered with black. Dirt, grunge, roach wings — you name it. He smells like he's rolled in elephant manure. The old lady is waiting for him. She wrinkles her nose.

"Ain't my attic, lady." He pulls the paper from his pocket. "What'd you say her name was?"

"Sharon Miller."

"Ever see any ID to that effect?"

She gives him a bitter look and waves a hand. "What does this look like — the goddamned Ritz?"

Doaks shrugs and turns to go. He looks at his watch. Almost five. So much for that six o'clock flight. He needs to get back to the hotel and tell Danielle what he's found. Then they need to call Sevillas. The old lady grabs his arm with bony fingers that are surprisingly strong. She wears a triumphant grin. "I want my money."

"For what? One stinkin' piece of paper?" He shakes his head. "Fat chance."

She gets right up in his face, her breath like black tar on a bar floor after a Saturday night. "We had a deal. You give me my money!" She cusses him all the way downstairs. In the front hallway, Doaks grabs his raincoat and hat. She plants her hands on her hips and blocks his path. "If you didn't find anything, why're you taking that paper with you?"

He reaches into his pocket; pulls out the twenty; and lays it in her palm. He takes a deep bow. "And madam," he says with a twinkle in his eye, "we thank you for your hospitality and wish you a long, happy life." Before she can say anything, Doaks is back in the cab, speeding toward the hotel. "I hate old women," he says to no one in particular.

"Young ones ain't so great, either," replies the driver.

"Yeah," says Doaks. "At least when the young ones screw you, it don't make you feel so bad."

CHAPTER TWENTY-SIX

Danielle zips up her traveling bag and looks at her watch. It's almost five. She just got a text message from Max. He's doing more research and he wants her back, *now.* Where is Doaks? She hopes he's late because something good has finally happened. He's probably bogged down in Chicago traffic. Just as she is about to try him on his cell phone again, there is a knock on the door. She opens it. What she sees is not what she expects.

Standing, hat in hand, is none other than Dr. Jojanovich. His face is white-bread pale. "Ms. Parkman."

"Dr. Jojanovich," she says. "What a . . . surprise."

He points his hat weakly at the living room. "May I come in?"

Danielle steps back. "Of course. Please."

The doctor moves slowly forward. Danielle watches as he eases himself into a chair.

"Doctor, I hope you don't mind my saying so, but you don't look well."

"What is wrong with me, Ms. Parkman, has nothing to do with my health."

"May I take your coat or offer you something to drink?"

"I'm fine," he says. "Although I wouldn't turn down a whiskey if you have one."

Danielle splashes some Scotch into a glass and hands it to him. He grips it like the anointed knight who has found the Holy Grail. After the first, deep swallow, some color returns to his face. "I hope you don't mind my coming without calling first. My secretary wrote your hotel and room number on my message pad this morning." He glances at her suitcase. "So, you are leaving Chicago?"

"I was supposed to be on a six o'clock flight," she says, "but I'm afraid I've been delayed."

Jojanovich stares at the floor. When he finally looks up, his eyes are leaden. "I am sure you would like to know why I have come here."

Danielle tries to keep her face impassive. She nods.

"I have no idea whether anything I say may be of benefit to your client," he says. "But I was unable to withhold certain information I have if it may in any way tend to make the difference between the life and death of a human being."

The doctor has the look of a witness who wants to tell his story. The less intrusive she is, the better. "I want to hear anything you'd like to tell me."

Jojanovich clasps and unclasps his hands. "Two years ago, Ms. Parkman, I hired a woman to work in my office. This woman was a highly skilled nurse. I'd never had better. In fact, she was so talented at her job that I often wondered how I could be so fortunate to have her when my practice is not what you would call . . . cutting-edge." His shoulders sag. "After a period of months, she suggested that she could easily handle the administrative side of my practice, as well as perform her nursing duties. I agreed immediately." His eyes are suddenly animated.

"I had never met anyone like her. She was a . . . dynamo. My patients loved her, and she kept the place running smooth as a top. That went on for about a year." He sinks back into his chair, eyes hooded. "Her name was Sharon — Sharon Miller. I am afraid she may be the same person you were inquiring about in my office today."

Danielle forces herself to stay in lawyer

mode. "Why do you think that?"

"Because she fits the description you gave me."

"Blond hair?"

"No," he says, "but everything else matches up. The height, her voice, very computer savvy."

"In what way?"

"Look, Ms. Parkman, within two months that woman had the entire place set up on computer. She was a whiz. I had no idea how to even run the damned thing." He smiles ruefully. "She was supposed to get around to teaching me someday."

"Exactly how did she set up your office?"

He shrugs. "Ordered some medical software. Input patient lists and records, appointments, lab reports, correspondence. You name it, she took care of everything."

"All on the computer?"

"Yes," he says. "She thought my way of keeping charts was old-fashioned. She was probably right."

Danielle studies him. "Why did she leave, Doctor?"

Jojanovich pulls out a large cigar. "Do you mind?"

"Not at all."

Jojanovich puffs on his cigar, exhaling small, dark clouds. His eyes recede deeply into their folds, wary crabs. "She left . . . for a variety of reasons."

Danielle feels something, a tingle at the back of her neck. "Did you fire her?"

"No," he says. "But I suppose I would have had to."

"Why?"

He avoids her eyes. "Miss Miller left my employ without giving notice. One day things were fine, and the next — she was gone."

"I'm confused, Doctor," she says. "You say she left for a number of reasons. Then you say she disappeared."

The doctor looks up, a miserable expression on his face. "I only discovered the reasons after she left."

Danielle reaches over and touches his arm. "It's all right. Just tell me what happened."

He squares his shoulders. "Very well. But before I tell you, I must have your word that you will not use this information to pursue her legally."

Danielle pauses. "Why?"

"What I mean is that even if you use this information to help your client, you must promise me that no relevant legal authorities will be alerted to her activities here." His voice is the strongest it has been all evening. "I do not want her facing charges. Do you understand?"

Danielle's mind runs the traps. Whatever this woman has done in Illinois — even if she is Marianne — is of no relevance to her. What she needs is information. Now. Her words are carefully chosen. "As you know, I have no control over what the authorities in Illinois may or may not do, but I have no intention of contacting them. Is that satisfactory?"

"Fine." He seems relieved. When he speaks again, it is quickly, as if now that the honey has started dripping from the bottle, he can't stop the flow. "When Miss Miller left, I was shocked. Here was this woman who had run everything so smoothly that I had no idea what to do when she was gone. You saw the computer on my desk?" Danielle nods and remembers how odd she found it that the computer was not even plugged in.

"Well, after she left I couldn't even find out when I had an appointment, much less what bills to pay or how to access my patients' records. When Sharon was there, I wrote down my comments on the patient's chart during the office visit, and she transcribed and entered it into the computer." He shrugs. "I don't know. I always thought it was fine just to keep the chart in a manila folder, but Sharon wanted it all on the system. After she left, I had to call a computer company in just to figure out how to run my own office." His eyes have heat in them for the first time.

"It took weeks to get the whole thing straightened out so I could conduct my practice in anything approaching normalcy. I hired a new nurse and went back to having a receptionist in the front office." His large hands hang helplessly over the sides of the chair. "I wanted everything switched back to paper — paper I could see. I had the new girl bring up all the old charts and files from the basement, where Sharon had put them after she programmed everything into the computer."

"What happened then?"

The man sighs. "The new girl brought the files into my office. She asked me to look them over because they confused her. Well, I took them home and read them cover to cover. Every single file had been changed."

"What do you mean, changed?"

He looks away. "When I reviewed the patient's chart and the notations I made during an office visit, I noticed that the computer version of the same account was . . . different."

Danielle leans forward. "Different how?"

Jojanovich shakes his head. "The computer version — the one that became the official patient file — didn't match the comments I made when I saw the patient. The changes were subtle in some cases and not so subtle in others." His jaw tightens. "In some cases, even if the patient's condition was correctly described, the treatment or medication I ordered was not."

Danielle cannot help her sharp intake of breath. She flashes on Marianne's knowledge of the nurses' password and hospital-security procedures. She imagines Marianne's fingers flying over the keys of the Maitland computer. Changing Jonas's entries? Changing Max's entries?

Jojanovich does not notice her reaction. "Many of the medications prescribed in the computer version were in fact contraindicated for the specific condition I had diagnosed." His voice drops to a whisper. "In some cases, the medications she wrote down would have either seriously compromised the patient — or done terrible damage."

Oh, my God, she thinks. *Jonas. Max.* She turns to Jojanovich. "Why would she do something like that, Doctor?"

His face darkens. "I'll get to that in a moment. I also discovered that Sharon had created her own medical forms with my name on them. Apparently, she would enter a patient's name, medical history, the date of the visit, that sort of thing. These were then scanned into the computer after they had my signature on them." Danielle gives him a quizzical look.

"Sharon had a stamp made of my signature," he explains, "so I wouldn't be bothered to sign routine correspondence. In other words, she fabricated symptoms and treatment protocols. I didn't believe it at first, but when it became clear that at least twenty of my patients' files were falsified, I had no choice." He takes a sip of his now-watery drink.

"Did you actually write prescriptions for the medications she noted on the falsified charts?"

"Honestly, Ms. Parkman," he says miserably. "I don't know. Every doctor with a competent nurse lets them write prescriptions onto a signed pad. She was an excellent nurse. I had no reason to mistrust her." He pauses. "Until later."

"Did any of your patients complain of unusual symptoms or problems?" She thinks of Max, in a drugged stupor, acting out violently, killing Jonas? She shudders.

"After she left, a few of them reported irregular symptoms when compared to what I would have expected, but I called all of them in for free consultations," says Jojanovich. "I had to change a number of the medications that Sharon had 'prescribed' without my knowledge. Fortunately, none of the patients were seriously affected. I was able to correct the problem in each case." He looks up, a whipping boy ready to take his beating.

"But why would she do that?" asks Danielle. "What possible reason could she have for prescribing the wrong medication to your patients?"

"Of course," he says softly, "it all sounds very strange until a woman walks into your office and wants to know about a patient you've never seen — one who has been murdered — and shows you a document with your signature on it."

Danielle considers what he has said. The same question troubles her. Why did Marianne have to fake a referral for Jonas to get into Maitland? And why, of all people, did she select a doctor whose practice she had brought to the very brink of ruin? It was a stupid thing to do. And Marianne is anything but stupid. "Why would . . . Sharon . . . use you as a reference for her son when she knew you would discover what she had done after she left?"

Waste and dread fill the old man's face. "This is very difficult for me, Ms. Parkman. There is another aspect to this matter I have been . . . reluctant to discuss."

"Like what?"

"Blackmail," he says simply.

Danielle moves to the edge of the couch. Jojanovich gives her a warning glance. "You must promise me again that nothing I tell you will result in any criminal charges against Miss Miller."

She meets his glance squarely. "I have given you my word, Doctor. You can rely upon it."

He nods. "After Miss Miller had been in my employ for approximately six months, our relationship . . . changed. I attribute a good deal of my inability to detect some of the activities I told you about earlier to this lapse of judgment on my part."

"You had an affair with her."

The doctor nods, his face full of pain and longing.

"And she fabricated the documents and wrote fake prescriptions in order to black-mail you in the event you didn't stand behind Jonas's referral to Maitland."

He shakes his head. "No, I never knew she had a son."

"She never mentioned Jonas?"

"Never." A reddening starts at the base of the old man's neck and spreads in a sickly way toward his cheeks. "She wanted me to divorce my wife and move away with her to Florida. She told me I was the love of her life. That she never dreamed . . ."

"Where does the blackmail come in?"

"Oh, yes." He reaches into his jacket pocket and pulls out a piece of paper. Danielle takes it and reads. It is a Xerox copy on Jojanovich's letterhead.

My dearest Sharon,
I am overwhelmed with emotion as I write this letter. As I have told you so often during our stolen time together, I have loved you from the moment I saw you. It wasn't that you were the best nurse I have ever had the pleasure to employ; it was everything about you — your beauty, compassion, personality and obvious intelligence.

I am sending this letter because I am too weak to leave my wife. It is with great despair and regret that I write these words that must set you free. I am an old man and you are young and beautiful. You can have any man you choose.

I must confess something else. I am mortified to admit that, because of my obsession with you, I have not given my patients the attention they deserve. In fact, I live in fear that I may have committed diagnostic and treatment errors that rise to the level of medical malpractice.

I know that this letter will devastate you — not only emotionally, but financially. I want you to be able to pursue your new life free of worry, so I am enclosing the sum of $175,000. I am providing this amount in cash — as a gift — as it is not my intent that you pay taxes upon it. It is yours to do with as you please. Please do not contact me. The result would only be disastrous for us both.

Boris

Danielle finds the medical record she brought from Plano and compares the doctor's signature to the one on the letter. They are identical. She looks at Jojanovich, who stares at the floor. "You didn't write this."

He smiles bitterly. "Of course not, Ms. Parkman. After she left, I received a large envelope in the mail with no return address."

"Always the efficient secretary."

He nods sadly. "The letterhead and signature line were the same as the hundreds she routinely prepared for me to sign for correspondence purposes. She always typed in the text to the patient."

Danielle shakes her head. "So she has the original of this letter somewhere. And if anyone asks her, she will say you sent it to her."

"Correct."

"Did you send her the money?"

"Yes," he replies stiffly. "I had to make a substantial withdrawal from my retirement fund, but I sent her the money."

"Did you ever try to go to her house in Chicago?"

"Once," he says. "She had already moved out."

"Has she contacted you since?"

"No." He gives her a hopeless look. "Why?"

Danielle can't think of anything else to ask. She holds the letter in her hand. "May I keep this?"

"I wish you would, actually. I never want to see it again." He sighs. "Anyway, Ms. Parkman, that is my story. A sad and pitiful tale from a stupid old man who was deceived. Not a novel one, to be sure."

Danielle nods. Jojanovich struggles out of his chair, as if giving the account of his downfall has made him older than when he started. Danielle takes his elbow as he walks to the door. He lets her. She opens the door as he puts on his hat and belts his raincoat.

"Doctor," she says. "I can't thank you enough. It took a lot of courage to come here today. You did the right thing."

"Not soon enough, Ms. Parkman," he says sadly. "Not nearly soon enough."

The door closes behind him. Danielle turns and walks to the window. Everything Jojanovich has told her swims in her head as she tries to match it to Marianne at Maitland, Jonas's death and Max's meds. She glances at her suitcase. She isn't going anywhere until she figures out how all of this fits together. She turns back and gazes at the glittering city below, not seeing any of it. A tingle courses up her neck. She is electric.

CHAPTER TWENTY-SEVEN

Danielle stares out as the city lights flash by. She and Doaks are on their way to the Chicago airport. She stops typing on her laptop and puts the computer back in her bag. The drive has passed silently. They are at an impasse. Despite the information they have collectively uncovered about Marianne, Doaks insists that they call Sevillas before pursuing the investigation further. Danielle demands that they go on to Phoenix. The traffic is murderous.

Doaks tosses her his cell phone. "Make the call."

She looks at him. "Why? You know what he's going to say."

"And you know he's right." He takes the phone from her and punches in a number. There is a pause. "Yeah, yeah, I know. Hey, don't ream me out, hotshot. She's your client, remember?" There is another pause. "Well, we found some good stuff." Doaks paraphrases what he and Danielle have uncovered about Marianne: her affair and successful blackmailing of Jojanovich, the falsification of Jonas's records and Doaks's discovery of Marianne's Phoenix address. There is another long silence. "Yeah, I hear you. I ain't deaf, ya know. No way. I ain't your messenger boy. You tell her." He holds the cell phone out to Danielle.

She sighs and holds it to her ear. She imagines the set of Sevillas's jaw, his controlled anger. "Hello."

"That's it?" The words are spit bullets. "That's all you have to say to me?"

"Tony, look, I'm sorry —"

"Don't go there with me, Danielle." Frustration and anxiety lace his voice. "Get on that plane. I don't want excuses; I don't want explanations. You simply have to show up in the courtroom for this hearing tomorrow. Do you have any idea what position you'll put me in with the court if you're not there at your own bond hearing? I will not behave unethically or ruin my professional reputation so you can go off on some ridiculous witch hunt."

"I know I've put you in a terrible position, but —"

"Forget about me," he says. "Think about yourself. Think about Max."

"That's exactly who I'm thinking of."

His words are hammer chinks on frozen metal. "Right now your son is so beside himself that you've left him that he's driving himself crazy trying to prove that Fastow did it just so you'll come back. Even with Georgia here, I don't think he can take much more."

"But he's all right, isn't he?" she asks anxiously.

"So far he is," he says. "Georgia is here with me. She's seen him. Since she's your oldest friend, maybe you'll listen to her."

Danielle hears a rustling and then Georgia's mellifluous voice. "Danny, Max is fine. I just left him. But you know how he gets this monomaniacal focus on something when he's really scared or nervous? That's what he's doing now."

Danielle closes her eyes. Dread fills her. "Do you think he's on the verge of a break? Tell me right now, and I'll come back."

"No," she says slowly, as if to mask what she and Danielle are discussing for Sevillas's sake. "Max is managing to hide most of the pills, and I haven't noticed anything that indicates he's losing touch with reality. Even so, you do need to be back for the hearing."

"But you think as long as I do that, I

should follow up on what I'm doing if it means possibly getting Max free?"

"I would say that's true," she says slowly.

"You know why I don't think going after Fastow is the answer?"

"Yes, I do, and I would have to agree with you. It's a temporary fix."

"I'll be back for the hearing. I love you, Georgia. Take care of my boy for me until tomorrow."

"Will do. I'm going to be with him until he falls asleep tonight, and then I'm taking him to the hearing with us."

Danielle's relief is overwhelming. "Bless you, Georgia."

"Love you, too, Danny."

Another rustle and then Tony. "I don't know what that was about, but I don't think Georgia appreciates how very serious your situation is."

"Tony, please understand," she says. "I have to go to Phoenix. I'll be back in time for the hearing."

She can almost hear his temperature rise. If he could spit bullets instead of words, she believes he would. "Listen to me, Danielle. You've jumped bond. You're now a wanted felon who is at large. The sheriff's office is in an uproar. They can tell your monitor isn't moving. Do you think that just because

338

they're from Iowa, they're stupid? All your son had to do was turn on his damned cell phone."

She hears him take a deep breath. A moment passes. "All I care about is what happens to you and Max. And unless you show up at the hearing in the morning, they're going to get a warrant to search your apartment. When they find out you're missing, they're going to scope out the Des Moines airport and slap you in cuffs the minute you walk up the jetway."

She is terrified. "What did you tell them?"

"That you're sick in bed." His voice is curt. "That you're so seriously ill that you haven't moved for forty-eight hours. That I'm planning to produce a doctor's affidavit to that effect if the judge asks for it. That the damned bracelet is acting up again."

"Tony, I truly am sorry, but we're onto something here. Marianne —"

"Forget Marianne," he says. "You're a lawyer — act like one. So what if she blackmailed some old man she was screwing? So what if she falsified some records? We're talking about murder here, Danielle, not monetary felonies. We're talking about you standing there with the bloody comb in your purse — with Max covered in Jonas's blood!"

Danielle presses the phone closer to her ear and uses her most persuasive voice. "But I am certain that she was involved in Jonas's murder."

"Why?"

"Because she's a liar and an extortionist," she says. "Because she submitted false information to ensure that Jonas was admitted to Maitland when it was completely unnecessary."

"You're grabbing at straws, Danielle," he says wearily. "I'm trying to help you — to save Max, dammit — and you're doing everything you can to screw it up."

"Tony, please listen to me," she says. "I hope you know how much I . . . care for you."

"And I for you," he says sadly. "But we can't go anywhere if you keep this up. Listen, the whole deal with Fastow has split wide open. He did it."

"What do you mean?"

"I mean that we finally have a real suspect — other than Max." His voice is firm. "You can stop this wild-goose chase and trying to pin the murder on the mother, which doesn't wash, anyway, as you would realize if you weren't so scared and could look at the evidence clearly." He pauses a moment. She hears the rustle of papers. "Smythe's toxicology report is back. So is Max's blood sample and the chemical breakdown of the pills."

Danielle's heart races. "What do they say?"

"You were on the right track," he says. "Fastow's dismissal from the Viennese hospital was hushed up. He had developed a psychotropic 'wonder drug' which, while amazing in many respects, also had terrible side effects. It seems that Fastow was suspected of falsifying data during clinical trials, but apparently the hospital couldn't prove it and so they fired him. When Fastow figured out that he was busted, he probably threatened to sue them for breach of his employment contract, knowing that they couldn't prove anything. It looks like they gave him a good reference just to get him out of there.

"Anyway, it's pretty clear that Fastow has been hell-bent on making a name for himself for some time. Max found out that he has close ties with a certain Swiss pharmaceutical company to patent a new drug. That kid — he's amazing."

The blue capsules flash in her mind's eye. "What kind of drug?"

Another rustle of papers. "Smythe's final report and the toxicology results we've got concur. The labs don't have a clue what the chemicals are in Max's blood. They've been sent off to a specialty lab in New York for further analysis. No one knows what this stuff is."

She closes her eyes. "Max," she whispers. Her eyes fly open. "Tony, you've got to get a T.R.O. against Fastow and Maitland. Max is still in there taking that medication — except for what he's been able to hide under his tongue and flush away. They've got to be stopped. God knows how many other patients he's poisoned."

"My plan, which you'd know if you'd been here, is to put Fastow and Smythe on the stand tomorrow and move immediately for a T.R.O. on Max's behalf. That'll be the quickest way to have the court grant it," he says. "I'm tracking down the patent lawyer on the medication so I can subpoena his records. I probably won't get them in time for the hearing, but we'll get them, all right." He pauses. "Where exactly are you?"

Danielle looks outside. The traffic is now moving. "We're about ten minutes away from O'Hare."

"On your way back." His words do not form a question.

She is silent. Danielle can't deny his logic. Still . . .

"Sweetheart." The word is awkward, but somehow feels right. "Please. You know I'm right."

Her heart leaps at his endearment, but her head takes over. "I'm sorry, Tony. I know what I'm doing seems preposterous in light of the risks. But I have to follow up on this lead about Marianne."

"They're gonna lock you up and eat the key," mutters Doaks.

An exasperated noise comes through the receiver. "We'll reassess our defense once Fastow testifies."

Danielle looks at Doaks. She can tell that Sevillas convinced him of this path before he handed her the phone. He shrugs.

She pauses for a moment. "All right," she says slowly. "I'll come back. But you have to promise me you'll file that T.R.O. for Max first thing in the morning."

"Done."

"And that Doaks will leave when the hearing is over and go straight to Phoenix."

"Fine."

Danielle sighs. "I'll see you tomorrow."

"Safe home."

She rings off and hands the cell phone back to Doaks.

He shoots her a look. "What he's sayin' makes sense, ya know."

She doesn't answer. The cabdriver finally enters the ramp and pulls up to the curb. She and Doaks grab their bags, pay the fare and get in line. Doaks rummages around in his pocket and pulls out his ticket. "We got a few minutes. I'm gonna hit the head."

"Go on," she says. "Give me your bag. I'll check in and meet you at the gate. Could you get me a cup of coffee on the way back?"

"Sure, sure," he grumbles. "I'll mop the floors while I'm at it."

She takes his overnight bag and watches him walk away. As soon as he is out of sight, she yanks out her laptop and checks her e-mail. The confirmation is there. She grabs both bags and heads for the opposite end of the terminal, where she has booked a flight to Phoenix, Arizona.

CHAPTER TWENTY-EIGHT

Danielle looks out of her window seat. The flight from Chicago to Phoenix will give her an opportunity to at least try to think calmly about what she is going to do. She is not ignorant of the gravity of her situation. Tony is absolutely correct. He has taken a seemingly hopeless murder case and developed a viable suspect. He will put that suspect on the stand tomorrow and most likely glean even more information helpful to an otherwise lame defense. He will advocate strenuously, and most likely persuasively, for her bond to remain intact.

She, on the other hand, has gone nuts, possibly destroying every brick he has laid in place on her behalf. She is a loose cannon who has committed felony after felony in direct contravention of his sound advice. And why?

Because she knows that, as the State's star witness, Marianne will crucify Max when she takes the stand. She will be enormously sympathetic as a perfect mother shattered by her autistic son's brutal murder. Her tearful recounting of Max's violent behavior will go uncontroverted. Danielle has to find something — anything — to impeach her.

If not, Danielle is terrified that the jury, with the Court's blessing, will have no choice but to convict Max. Given that, she must pursue all leads, no matter how far-fetched. Just one thread, if followed painstakingly, could provide that evidence. And right now that thread is Phoenix. If Tony weren't so worried about her own legal situation, she knows he would agree.

After Chicago, she knows that Marianne is a con artist and an extortionist, but Jojanovich won't testify against her. Yet a strange, strong instinct tells her that Marianne must have conned others. Perhaps she is even a suspect in other crimes. Danielle has to go where Marianne lives, think as she thinks, and tear her place apart if she has to.

She also doesn't believe that Fastow would kill Jonas and Max — at Maitland, no less — to conceal the fact that he was using experimental drugs on his patients. His only plausible motivation would be to avoid detection, and Tony's theory that he killed to accomplish that end, no matter how well crafted, is painfully thin. It strains credulity that brutally murdering one of his patients would lessen suspicion of him. The opposite is true. The bodies would be autopsied, and the blood analyzed. All roads would lead to him. And although a bastard, Fastow is no fool.

Another reason Danielle is convinced that going to Phoenix now is the right thing to do is that she will still get back to Plano in time for the hearing. If the 5:00 a.m. flight to Des Moines is on time and the moon and planets are properly aligned, she will make it to the courthouse well before the preliminary motions are argued. Before the sheriff gets his search warrant.

She shakes her head at the stewardess. A lifeless sandwich of stale bread, limp lettuce and salt-riddled luncheon meat is not what she needs. She points at a small bottle of gin. Rocks, no tonic. Dutch courage, isn't that what they call it? Thankfully, she has the entire row of seats to herself. She pulls Doaks's overnight bag from under the seat and roots through it. She knows the damned thing is in there.

Danielle extracts a worn golf shirt, a wrinkled pair of khakis, socks, underwear, assorted lint and detritus. She piles it all on the seat next to her and peers into the bag. Empty. *Damn.* He must have it on him. He said he never goes anywhere without it. He told her with pride that he had a police buddy of his build a special lead tube around the instrument, which fitted neatly into the frame of his carry-on. If only she can find it. She spies four zippers and yanks on each one, inspecting the exteriors of the black round frame pieces that hold the bag together. There is nothing until she gets to the last one. She slides it open. Inside is a cylindrical leather case. She takes it out, opens it and smiles at the strange instrument. It looks like a small metal toothbrush with a little ball on one end. Certainly nothing that would alert security. She puts everything back into the bag, reinserts the tool into the round piece of black framing and slides it shut. The warmth of the gin floods her. It almost makes her believe her plan will work.

She stands on the sidewalk in front of the Desert Bloom Apartments. The dark blue cool of the Arizona night takes her by surprise. She knows that in the daylight, the low humidity would evaporate her sweat before it forms on her skin. Now, though, she shivers — not from the night — but in preparation for yet another performance. And another felony. She tousles her hair, picks up her bags and walks toward the mud-colored adobe kiosk that stands between her and the entrance. This place is nothing like the house Doaks described in Chicago. Behind the gate, elaborate fountains spill over volcanic rock and into intricate botanical gardens. The apartments seem to be newly constructed, tri-level townhomes, each with its own yard and pool.

She stops in front of the kiosk and puts down her bags. She taps on the window, which slides to reveal a young man in a stiff, blue uniform. On the pocket of his jacket is a name tag. "Brett" gives her an uncertain look. "Can I help you?"

Danielle tries to look weary and world-worn. "Morrison, Marianne Morrison."

"Uh, just a minute." He pulls out a laminated sheet. His index finger leaves a sweaty smear in its wake as it stops somewhere near the end of the list. He looks up. "What unit?"

She gazes skyward and sighs. "Four-one-one. Look, would you buzz me through? It's almost one in the morning and I just got in from the airport after a very long flight from New York. All I want to do is get into my house, feed my cat and go to bed."

He pores over the list. "I'm sorry, but I'm new here. Chuck is sick —"

"Well, Chuck most assuredly knows who I am." She points at the gate. "Now, let me in. I don't have time for this. I have two hip replacements tomorrow morning, and if I get into the O.R. even half an hour late, it'll throw off my schedule for the rest of the day."

He stares at her. "You're a doctor?"

She groans. "No, I'm a yardman. Now, are you going to let me in?"

"Do you have some ID?"

"Good God." She drops her bags and pulls furiously on the zipper of her purse. She yanks out her cell phone and flips it open. "What is your last name, Brett?"

He turns white. "Oh, hey, what are you doing?"

"Calling management," she says calmly. "Once Carl Mortenson hears that you've kept me waiting —"

He holds up his hand. His voice shakes. "Hey, I'm sorry, okay? I told you. I'm just doing Chuck a favor." A buzzing sound comes from the door on the side of the gate. "Go on in, Dr. Morrison. Sorry about the confusion."

She picks up her bags, wheels around and

marches through the gate. She kicks it closed behind her. She doesn't look back.

The antique grandfather clock that stands on the plush carpet of the lobby entrance bongs. By the time it has stopped, Danielle's heart has almost stopped with it. She takes a few steps into the hall. It is deserted. On the wall is a framed, colored map of the complex, complete with unit lots and numbers. Danielle winds her way around the communal areas until she locates Marianne's unit. She hides her bags in a concrete niche. The front door is solid and locked. No surprise there.

She swings open the teak gate and enters the backyard. The pool glistens in the desert moonlight as small waves lap against its concrete lips. She tiptoes to the back door. Luck has found her once more. She stands in front of a large, glass door. Her reflection stares at her. She reaches into Doaks's bag and removes the small, leather case. She pulls out the four-inch glass cutter. In the dark, she can't make out how to use it. She curses and fumbles in her purse until she finds her key ring. On the end is a tiny flashlight. She presses the button and illuminates the tool. The name Fletcher appears on the thin metal shaft. On the toothbrush end, she finally spies it — an impossibly small wheel. That must be how it works. Just like pizza.

She turns her attention back to the glass door. With the aid of the narrow beam from her key ring, she estimates the path the tool is to take. She presses the pizza wheel against the glass — harder than she thought she would have to — and scores a neat square directly next to the handle of the sliding door. She's not really sure how to do the next part, but she'll have to wing it. Further examination of the bottom of Doaks's bag reveals a modest red rubber suction cup. She licks its bitter edges and affixes it to the section of glass she has scored. After a silent prayer that there is no burglar alarm, Danielle flips the instrument in her hand and, using the golden ball on its end, lightly taps the glass. As she hoped, the tap breaks the tensile strength of the glass at the point of fracture.

She puts the glass cutter back into the secret hiding place in Doaks's bag and pulls gently on the suction cup. The glass comes out in one piece. She spies a large flowerpot outside by the pool. She puts the glass underneath it and tosses the suction cup into her purse. With trembling hands, she unlatches the switch and slides open the door.

An unbearable stench stops her dead in her tracks. She covers her nose as she tries to locate the source, but it takes a few moments for her eyes to adjust to the darkness. She feels her way to a floor lamp and slides the switch until an eerie halogen glow fills the room. She moves cautiously forward.

"Hey, you!" A loud voice comes from somewhere outside by the pool. Danielle freezes and then moves swiftly across the room and down the hall. She crouches in front of what looks like a spare room. She spies a closet, ready to provide temporary shelter if need be. The odor she smelled when she first entered the house is horrific here.

"Come on, Barry, we don't have all night!" The voice sounds like it is two feet away. She stands very still, her back against the wall.

"I'm in the water, asshole," shouts another voice.

"You sure they're not here?"

"Nah, been gone for weeks."

Danielle slips into the living room and peers, unseen, from the side of the sliding door. Teenagers. She sees the blurred outline of two nude boys in the dimly lit pool. She feels her breath come a bit more slowly. She reaches out, unobserved, and locks the latch on the door. After a few moments, she returns to the spare room, draws the curtains, and turns on a desk lamp, which sends out a slim halo of yellow light. A computer and monitor are on the table.

Wedged into the opposite corner is a wooden desk. Odd green lights shine dully from a bookcase onto the desktop. They make a strange, buzzing noise. The table is completely covered with small plastic disks and glass containers of varying shapes and colors. She leans over them and sniffs. The foul odor does not emanate from them. Danielle flicks on her tiny flashlight and passes it slowly over each item. Petri dishes nestle against one another, a neat white label affixed to each. Angry puffs of mold in all shades of the color wheel fill each container to bursting — as if what is inside wants out. She comes closer. *Stachybotrys atra. Aspergillus. Fusarium. Claviceps purpurea.*

"Oh, my God," she whispers.

It looks like a Level 4 lab at the Center for Disease Control in Atlanta. She flashes the light around and finds a large sky-blue binder. It is very heavy. Inside, detailed charts and logs fill hundreds of pages. The sections are tabbed with more strange names. *Aflatoxins. Ergotism. Mycotoxins.* Danielle shuts the book and searches the rest of the room. All she finds is a stack of bills. Nothing else — no postcards, no personal correspondence, nothing that reveals any more about Marianne or Jonas than she knew before she left for Chicago. What can she bring back to Sevillas and the judge? Evidence that Marianne does odd scientific experiments in her guest room? Maybe she has a research job in a lab and does part of her work at home. Whatever it is, it doesn't spell murder.

She turns off the lamp and feels her way into another room. The curtains are drawn here as well. It has the stale, unused odor of an abandoned space. She turns on a table lamp. Marianne's bedroom. The king-size bed has a lace coverlet that is barely visible under a sea of pillows that suffocate the bed. Everything is covered in a cloying, flowered fabric. The room overflows with knick-knacks. China dolls crowd tables and fill bookcases. The curtains bloom from the window in strangled floral patterns of soft pink and vibrant red. Out of place amid the *Southern Home* décor are wooden bookcases crammed with thick medical and pharmaceutical texts.

A perfunctory inventory of Marianne's closet reveals nothing unusual. She quickly searches the drawers, but her curious fingers find only a plethora of lacy undergarments. In the last drawer, under a pile of garter belts, she finds a tiny key. She searches the room for a jewelry box that might hold its contents. Nothing.

She walks to another room at the end of the hall. It is weakly illuminated by two night-lights. At least here the stench is less horrific. This must be Jonas's room, although nothing indicates it belongs to a teenager. The bed is neatly made and covered with a cheerful red-and-blue throw. On the wall is an embroidered scene of a small boy kneeling at the feet of his mother, while she sits in a chair with her hand on his head. Underneath, in painstaking cross-stitch, are the somehow ominous words: *Every good boy does fine.* The room has no window. On top of the dresser is one photograph — Marianne holding Jonas as a baby. He is wrapped tightly in a blue blanket. She clutches him to her chest and looks straight into the camera. Her smile stretches beyond pride.

The only other furniture is a small wooden desk that looks as if it were used long ago in an elementary school. It's marred with pencil gouges. The corners are chewed. Danielle opens the closet door to a neat row of shirts and pants. In plastic cubes on shelves are underwear, socks and shorts — arranged as sternly as the contents of an army footlocker.

Danielle pulls back the bedcovers. A thick metal ring catches her eye. Leather restraining cuffs are tethered to either side. Danielle feels her pulse quicken. She holds one in her hands. The buckles are made of cast metal, heavy and menacing. The leather is lighter and cracked at the point where the cuffs meet the straps that fasten them to the bed. They look worn and weary — beyond broken in.

Perspiring now, she gets down on her knees and shines the light under the bed. She pushes a tennis shoe out of the way and hits something. Twisting her arm, she pulls out an object covered with dust. Danielle stands, fingering the small black box connected to red nylon. It is an electronic dog collar.

She makes a quick inspection of the kitchen. No dog bowl on the floor; no dog food in the pantry. She thinks of the crude holes that were punched in the neoprene collar to make it smaller — small enough to fit around a boy's neck. Danielle feels sick.

She puts the collar back under the bed. The glowing hands of her watch show that she has been here almost an hour. The noise outside has stopped. She slips out of the room and stands in the living room. Silence. The boys must be gone. A quick inspection of the bathroom reveals nothing other than a medicine cabinet and everyday toiletries.

She walks back to the spare room and opens the closet. A stench so vile hits her that she fights an overwhelming urge to vomit. This is the source of the putrid, stifling odor that emanates throughout the house. She clamps her hand to her mouth and flips on the wall switch. Everything touched by the light has an odd, bluish glow. Winter clothes hang from the racks, bathed in the foul smell. Could a rat have died in the walls? She starts to flick off the light when something catches her eye, something on the corner shelf. It seems to have a light source all its own. Danielle pushes aside the hanging clothes that hide it.

Swimming in surreal light is what appears to be a glass receptacle. A pink, quilted cloth partially covers it. She looks closer. A tea cozy. She takes a deep breath and slides it off. Underneath is a laboratory specimen jar, its lid askew as if someone forgot to secure it. The reek almost blinds her. She shrinks back and drops the quilted cozy onto the floor.

It is what is inside the jar that confounds her. It looks like a dark shape suspended in a viscous, colored fluid. The blue cast of the overhead bulb lends a strange shadow to the form. The interplay of light and a soft humming noise give the entire corner an otherworldly, eerie appearance. Danielle blinks. The form in the jar appears to move, barely, like a lava lamp that has just been turned on and is slowly responding to the heat that causes its contents to twist and rise. She stares, mesmerized. Some primitive part of her brain goes on alert. An irrational fear overwhelms her with the conviction that any sudden movement on her part will cause the form to spring from its container and attack her.

Hypnotized, she moves closer. Each inch brings the form more clearly into focus. One minute it is a coiled mass of scales and fur — the next nothing more than a smooth, shiny piece of protoplasm suspended in midair. When Danielle finally brings her face level with it, she makes out bulging folds of a shape in the murkiness. The thing seems to be twisted upon itself. Almost too frightened to breathe, she points her tiny flashlight at the jar. What stares back makes her recoil as if it had leapt out of the jar and struck her.

They are the dead, translucent eyes of a fetus. It hangs, paralyzed and grotesque, in an opaque, curdling fluid. She fights down the bile that closes her throat and forces herself to look once more. Its eyes, in shadow, seem alive. They implore her, entreat her.

For what?

After the longest moment, it comes to her. The tiny eyes beg for mercy, justice, retribution. But above all — they scream for their mother.

CHAPTER TWENTY-NINE

Danielle sits on a bar stool in the kitchen, as far from the specter in the closet as possible. Her mind whirls as she tries to assimilate these bizarre discoveries. She fumbles in her purse for a cigarette. Her hands shake. Before she has a chance to exhale, her cell phone rings. It is earsplitting in the silence of the house. She digs in her purse again and looks at the screen. Doaks. The miracle is that he hasn't called sooner. She lets four rings shrill before she decides to answer. "Hello?"

"Don't you fuckin' 'hello' me!" he snaps. "Where the hell are you?"

"In Arizona."

"As if I didn't know. It's one thing you duckin' out on Sevillas, but now you're screwin' with me. Are you off your nut?"

She is silent.

"Well?" The gravel voice is harsh. "You comin' back, or are you plannin' to wait till

Tony sics the Feds on you? Don't think he won't, girlie, and I'll be right behind 'em."

She takes a substantial drag on her cigarette. Exhaustion and severe jitters hit her all at once. "Are you finished?"

"Finished? I ain't even gotten started."

"Have you told Sevillas?"

He snorts. "That I'm stupid enough to let you give me the slip? No way. Now, spill it — are you comin' back or not?"

"Doaks, you can't imagine what I've found here."

"Sure I do." His words sound like shots from a Gatling gun. "The bloody comb? A written confession?"

"Cut it out," she says curtly. "I don't have time for this. It's almost three, and I have to catch the early flight out of here to make it back for the hearing."

"Assumin' you don't decide to ride the magic carpet to some other planet," he mutters. "You're lucky I like you, kiddo, or you'd be dead. All right, I'm in. Tell me what you got."

She takes a deep breath and tells him about the strange scientific experiments, the collection of molds and toxins, the pharmaceutical and medical texts in Marianne's bedroom. Before she can continue, he makes an exasperated noise on the other end of the line. "So what?"

Danielle hears him chomping on something with nuts in it. He goes on. "All we got in Chicago is that the broad humped and blackmailed some old coot and took off with his dough. And now you're tellin' me she does some kinda mad-scientist shit instead of buyin' junk off the Home Shopping Channel. She's a doctor, for chrissakes — they do that kind of crap. It don't get us down the road none."

"John," she blurts. "She's got a dead fetus in her closet."

The chomping stops. "She's got a what in her what?"

"You heard me."

There is a silence.

"God, it's all too bizarre to put into words. There is real evil in this house. I can feel it."

Doaks groans. "Listen, honey, so we show that the broad's got a bat in her belfry and a fetus in her closet. Where the hell does that get us? You gonna march into that courtroom tomorrow and hoist that thing up in front of the judge, and yell 'Murder'?" A short pause and then muttering. "Lord, why do I get all the friggin' whack-jobs? Ain't it somebody else's turn?" A cough. "Look, Danny, you know you got nothin' that connects the dots between that broad and her boy. You're pissin' in the wind."

"Like hell I am." Anger rises red inside her. "I found an electronic dog collar. She had to be abusing Jonas with it. There's no sign of a dog here."

"Hold the phone." There is a short silence. "Yeah, I found the same thing in that attic. But maybe she boarded the dog. And even if it's true, that don't mean murder, Danielle. You know it, I know it and the jury's sure gonna know it."

"Child abuse never leads to murder?"

"There ain't no pattern, no evidence," he says. "Nothin' in the records; nothin' in her past."

"That we know of."

"That we can prove right now." His voice is tired. "C'mon, missy, head back here, would ya? I told you I'd go back and scope it out after the hearing, and you know I will. I'm not sayin' she ain't mental — no question she is. What I'm sayin' is that you're screwin' yourself to the wall if you don't get your ass in court by nine tomorrow morning."

"I can't. I'm not finished." She feels as strong-willed as she sounds.

Her feet have brought her back to the spare room. She has to focus. There must be something else, something she's missed. She glances at the table with its petri dishes and the closet with its private horrors. This is where Marianne must keep her secrets, she feels certain. But what has she missed? Danielle turns to the other desk. Of course, the computer. How could she be so blind? Marianne and computers. "John? Listen, I just found something. I'll call you back." Before he can say anything, she snaps the phone shut.

Danielle yanks out the swivel chair and sits. As the computer boots up, she opens the first drawer and claws through an assortment of pens, paper clips and pads. The drawer on the other side is full of CDs labeled in strange number and letter codes Danielle doesn't understand. The cabinet beneath is locked. "Finally," she whispers. A locked door means there is something to hide. Her breath quickens as she fumbles in her pocket. She has it — the small key she found in Marianne's lingerie drawer. She takes a deep breath and inserts it into the lock. The door springs open. She sees a few photo albums and some cloth-covered books. Then, front and center, a box of CDs. She counts them. Five.

She reminds herself to breathe as she turns to the computer monitor. She inserts the first CD. The desktop has the typical icons. She clicks on the document file and opens it. A quick review reveals nothing unusual. She notices a folder named "TGRFT" on the desktop. She opens it. It is a summary of some kind of tissue-graft study. Other files with similar acronyms seem to be the coded results of experiments involving various infections and bacteria. The last series includes notes on organic brain damage, psychiatric and behavioral disorders — including clinical trials of relevant medications — complete with Web sites and links. The file entitled "Maitland" has a neatly organized set of articles about the place, but nothing else. Danielle sighs. If someone broke into her computer, they'd find much of the same psychiatric research she has done on Max. It's what mothers of damaged children do.

Danielle looks at her watch. Thirty minutes to get to the airport. She cannot miss that flight. She quickly opens the remaining files, but finds nothing related to Marianne's blackmail of Jojanovich or the phony documents he said she created. Marianne is not stupid. She would never leave incriminating data on her computer. She picks up the first of the CDs from her lap, inserts it and groans. The box that appears has one word and then a blank space. *Password,* it demands. She tries to bypass it, but the computer denies her access. "Damn."

Think, think. "Birthdays, anniversaries, nicknames," she mutters. She pulls Jonas's application to Maitland out of her purse. It has Marianne's birth date, Jonas's birth date and Social Security number. Danielle tries every combination of these she can think of. *Access denied.*

Danielle studies the application again. She looks at the fake Pennsylvania address. *5724 Piedmont Lane.* She flips the form over. The telephone number of one of Jonas's general physicians, whom Maitland would have had no reason to contact, catches her eye. 555-4600. Surely this is too coincidental. She punches in groupings of these numbers, with no success. Exasperated, Danielle stands up and paces around the house. In Jonas's room, she sits on the bed. Marianne and Jonas stare accusingly at her from the photograph on the wall. She stands up to leave when her eye catches the needlepoint of mother and child. *Every good boy does fine.* Her mind races as she rushes back and types the words into the computer. Nothing. Then she remembers a game she used to play with the neighborhood kids — transposing the letters of the alphabet into numbers to send coded messages their parents couldn't understand. She punches in the numbers for the first letter of each word. *57246.* Nothing. "Damn!" She slams her fist on the table. She's getting nowhere and the clock is ticking. One more try. She grabs a pad and a pen, scribbles furiously and types in "EGBDF."

The password box disappears, and a series of files cascades across the screen. She feels an electric tingle rise on the nape of her neck. Marianne must never have thought anyone else would use this computer. The files are untitled, but appear to be arranged chronologically. A quick scan shows that the first entry is dated shortly before Marianne's departure for Maitland. Danielle's fingers shake as she clicks on the document.

Dear Dr. Joyce,
All I've ever wanted is the unconditional love a child has for its mother — the kind Joyce Brothers understands. That's why I'm dedicating my thoughts to her. I'm a very special mother — no mean feat, given the delicate state of my health. I've had sixty-eight operations, each more thrilling than the last. Not in the same hospital, of course, that would be unwise. All babies are quite sweet in the beginning — at least

right after they're born. But after all the oohs and aahs, you're left alone with ugly little monkey face. All it does is eat, defecate, cry, and cause trouble. It simply isn't an acceptable situation.

So I put a stop to it.

Horrified, Danielle skips down the page.

The diagnosis of a tiny infant is a fluid, beautiful thing, but elusive. You must carefully select the diagnosis you want and stick with the basics. Cyanosis and bacterial infections are my building blocks, if you will, but cyanosis is tricky. Honestly, how many times can you go through the same exercise — with your child turning blue — and not expect to arouse suspicion? The key to success is to achieve the proper level of distress, but avoid strangulation. By the time Ashley was born, it was a snap.

Ashley? Who is *Ashley?* Danielle scrolls to the end of the entry.

It is, of course, very difficult to be masterful in these matters after a youngster reaches a certain age. Children will talk. Of course, you can introduce foreign bacteria, rat droppings, or fungus, and achieve a fairly satisfactory result. But a child's immune system is as strong as a horse. And when you walk that line between creating the effect you desire and not being too obvious, their little bodies fight you every step of the way.

Isn't that just like children?

■ ■ ■ ■

PART THREE

■ ■ ■ ■

CHAPTER THIRTY

Sevillas walks into the courtroom. He is dressed in a simple navy blue suit, a starched white shirt and a conservative tie. He believes that all lawyers should wear blue to court. To him it's the color of sincerity. Today he fervently hopes that it will mask the variety of untruths he may be required to tell the court in defense of his client. He looks at his watch. Eight-forty. He scans the courtroom. No sign of Danielle or Doaks. He feels perspiration begin to form at the base of his neck. The bailiff brings in a white, terrified Max and seats him next to Sevillas at the defense table. Max's entire body seems to tremble. Sevillas has developed a good relationship with Max during his visits to Maitland. Although Sevillas is somewhat more confident that the boy is innocent, the evidence against him is so damning that a jury conviction is not just a possibility — it's a probability. He puts his arm around his shoulders as Max looks wildly around the courtroom.

"Where's my mom?" His voice is a high, frightened plea. He twists his head around the room again, frantically searching. Sevillas grips him closer and tries to quell his trembling. "She'll be here in a minute, buddy, don't worry." Max closes his eyes a moment; stifles a sob; and turns to Georgia, who squeezes his shoulder from behind the railing. "It's all right, Max. Don't worry about your mom. She'll be here." She murmurs more comforting words. Max seems to calm down. Tony hands Max a list of exhibits and asks him to check and make sure that each document matches its description. It's busywork, to be sure, but he thinks that is exactly what Max needs right now.

Sevillas looks up at the judge's bench. Neither Judge Hempstead nor her clerk is present. The court stenographer, a level beneath the throne, is setting up. She gives him a smile. He manages a friendly nod and then hears footsteps behind him. Relief floods him until he realizes that it is not Danielle, but his adversary.

Oliver Alton Langley struts down the aisle. Two younger D.A.'s and a paralegal trail behind him. He has a military bearing, probably from his stint in the Marines. Every corner of him is crisp and pressed. In the current fashion, his scalp is shaved bald, although he is only fortysomething. Oddly out of place are dark, bushy eyebrows that meet in the middle and pale, gray eyes that dart from underneath them. He makes a direct line to the defense table and sticks out his hand. "Good morning, Counselor."

Sevillas rises and briefly shakes hands. "Langley."

Max raises terrified eyes at the D.A. Langley leans on the table and locks eyes with the boy. "So you're Max Parkman?" He sticks out his hand. "I'm Mr. Langley — the District Attorney. I represent the State on behalf of Jonas Morrison."

Max raises a thin, trembling arm. Langley encompasses his hand and shakes it — hard. "Let's make sure everybody tells the truth today, shall we?" Max shrinks back and moves his chair closer to Sevillas. Georgia glares at Langley and pats Max's hand.

Sevillas stands and breaks the grip Langley's eyes have on the boy. "That's enough, Langley. Keep away from my client."

The D.A. shrugs and points at the pile of papers on Sevillas's table. "Last-minute details?" Before Sevillas can answer, Langley glances at the State's table, where his minions are busily arranging orderly stacks of files and exhibits. He gives Sevillas a smug sneer, a general proud of his troops.

Sevillas's smile is cool. "You know what they say, Alton. If you think you're ready, you're not."

Langley gives him a short salute. "Good luck."

Sevillas sees Doaks rush in from the back of the courtroom. "Excuse me," he says as he motions at Doaks to meet him outside.

As Sevillas heads for the hallway, Max's terrified eyes track every step he takes. He walks back. "Max," he whispers.

"Yes?" His eyes are eager, hungry.

"Can you do something for me?"

"Sure."

"Why don't you organize all the evidence against Fastow you have? It would be a big help."

"No problem." He immediately dives into a stack of documents. Georgia gives Sevillas a thumbs-up sign. He squeezes her shoulder and leaves the courtroom.

Langley joins his entourage, jostling against the wave of reporters who barrel in with their cameras and chatter. Doaks stands outside near the men's room. He looks like shit. The obligatory khaki pants are grimier than usual, although he has thrown on a frayed jacket over his yellow golf shirt. His white, kinky hair seems more psychotic than ever before, and the dark circles under his eyes tell Sevillas that Doaks has been up when he should've slept. He cranes his neck through the flow of humanity in the hallway and grabs Doaks by the arm. "Where is she?"

Doaks pulls him into a small niche near the john. "She's on her way."

Sevillas stands with his fists on his hips, his voice crushed concrete. "From where?"

Doaks shrugs. He gives Sevillas a nonchalant look. "Probably puttin' on her panty hose. You know how broads are."

Sevillas's eyes narrow as he glares at Doaks. "You better be telling me the truth, Doaks, because if you're not, I'm going to have your ass."

Doaks points at the clock on the wall. "Shouldn't you be gettin' in there? It's showtime, buddy. Remember, she's sick and runnin' a little late."

"I'm going," he says tightly. "I'll try to stall until she shows up. Max is in there, and he's petrified. And you —" he thrusts an angry finger in Doaks's face "— you get her here."

"Yes, sir, boss."

Sevillas turns and stalks back into the

courtroom. It is packed. Not a seat remains. Just as he reaches the defense table, the bailiff stands. "All rise!"

Everyone complies in unison. Judge Hempstead strides to the bench, climbs the five stairs that elevate her above the commoners and takes her seat in a high-backed chair. She nods at the bailiff.

"All those present are called to this court to hear and be heard," he bawls. "This is the 158th Precinct, Plano District Court, Honorable Judge Clarissa Hempstead presiding. Calling Cause Number 14-33698."

The judge smacks her gavel and dons steely half-lens glasses. She motions to the court reporter, whose hands are poised over her machine, to begin the formal record. She flips open a file and speaks sternly, without looking up. "For purposes of the record, this is both a proof-evident hearing to determine if the defendant was properly granted bail and an evidentiary hearing to determine if probable cause existed to charge the defendant, Max Parkman, in this case. The Court will consider evidence pertaining only to whether or not there is sufficient evidence to support the indictment against the defendants." She gives an imperious look around the courtroom. The lawyers nod respectfully. "Also for the record," she adds, "defendant's motion to suppress on the ground of cross-contamination is denied."

Max clutches his arm. "What does it mean, Tony? Is it bad?" Sevillas squeezes Max's shoulder and stares straight ahead. It's bad, all right. It's all coming in: the bloody comb, if they find it; the bloody clothing; Jonas's St. Christopher's medal — all the damning physical evidence. He lowers his head and writes on his legal pad. He does not look at Langley.

Hempstead ends what appears to be a conference between her law clerk and court coordinator and turns to the audience. "The Court sees that members of the press have decided to grace us with their presence." She gives them a withering glance. "I will say this once and only once. There will be no photographs taken in this courtroom and no disturbances from the press. You will check your cameras at the door. Unless you plan to stay until the Court declares a recess, don't come at all. I will not have people jumping up and down or trailing in and out of my courtroom, distracting counsel and witnesses." She peers out over her glasses. "Mr. Neville?"

A man with slick gray sideburns and an expensive suit stands. "Yes, Your Honor?"

"I wouldn't want to name anyone in particular, but I will say that anyone caught in my courtroom with any kind of recording device will be charged with contempt." The man sits quickly. Hempstead turns back to counsel. "Now, gentlemen," she says. "Let the games begin."

Langley speaks softly to his associates and points at a sheaf of papers in front of him. He pulls a document from the stack and studies it.

The judge drums her manicured nails on top of the bench. "Mr. Langley?"

He looks up. "Yes, Judge?"

"Are you planning to start, or shall I let the defendant's bond stay right where it is?"

"Absolutely not, Your Honor." He speaks at warp speed. "The State is ready to proceed."

"Praise be. Call your first witness." The judge holds up her hand as the bailiff whispers something in her ear. She looks at the defense table. "Mr. Sevillas?"

He stands. "Yes, Your Honor?"

"Would it be impertinent of me to ask where the other defendant might be?"

Sevillas clears his throat. "Of course not, Your Honor. I'm afraid Ms. Parkman has been very ill for the past week. She is confined to her bed under doctor's orders.

She has assured me that, if at all possible, she will be here today."

"Does that mean she's coming or not?" The brown eyes magnified by the half-moon lenses are displeased. "You are aware, Mr. Sevillas, that I have a trial beginning this afternoon. I have no intention of asking my coordinator to change that setting."

"Yes, Your Honor."

"Mr. Langley?"

Langley shoots to his feet. Before he can speak, Hempstead does. "Does the State intend to question Ms. Parkman today?"

His head bobs up and down. "Absolutely, Your Honor."

She turns back to Sevillas. "Before Mr. Langley calls his first witness, you go out in the hall and call your client. Tell her I have ordered her to attend this hearing. And —" she points her pen at him "— I will not postpone Mr. Langley's direct. This hearing will be over today, come hell or high water."

"Yes, Your Honor." Sevillas nods reassuringly at Max and then turns and walks out. The hall is deserted. He turns the corner and sees Doaks standing next to the elevators with his cell phone glued to his ear. As soon as he sees Sevillas, he snaps it shut. "What's up?"

"The judge told me to get Danielle in

there — now." He takes Doaks by the arm and looks him straight in the eyes. "You were just on the phone. Is she on her way?"

"Yeah, you could say that." Doaks pulls his arm away. "Why don't you try to buy a little time —"

"Are you crazy? Hempstead's already royally pissed off, Langley's licking his lips, and Max is about to lose it. Now, when will she be here?"

Doaks looks at his watch. "Before lunch, I think."

Sevillas glares at him. "You drag her out of bed and tell her if she isn't here in ten minutes, I quit."

"I can't do that."

"Why the hell not?"

"Because she ain't there," he says slowly. "She's comin' back, but she got . . . delayed."

"Wait a minute." Sevillas puts his face very close to Doaks's. "Are you telling me she didn't come back from Chicago when you did? That she isn't in her apartment?"

Doaks steps back and gives him a shrug. "Okay, okay, I ain't been totally straight with you. Truth is, she gave me the slip in Chicago."

Sevillas groans. "To do what?"

"To go to Arizona, where the Morrison

broad lives. She found some wild stuff —"

"Oh, Christ, don't give me that tired line again." He shakes his head. "She has completely fucked herself, does she know that? Jumped bond to fly around to two different states chasing nothing. We know who did it. She just won't face it." Sevillas glances at his watch and then at the courtroom door. "I've got to get back in there."

"What're you gonna say?"

Sevillas gives him a hard look. "If anyone expects me to lie to the Court and lose my license — guess again. And if she thinks I'm going to be able to keep her out of jail, she's nuts." He takes a deep breath and straightens his suit jacket.

Doaks grips Sevillas's shoulder. "Come on, Tony, hang tough. She'll show up."

Sevillas shrugs free and opens the door. He looks back. "By the time she gets here, the judge will throw us all in jail."

Doaks winks at him. "Won't be my first time."

CHAPTER THIRTY-ONE

Danielle clutches her purse. It contains the computer discs and two cloth diaries from Marianne's desk. She has compelling evidence, but is losing hope that she can deliver it in time to save Max.

She is at Gate 21 in the Phoenix airport, where her flight should have been pushing away from the gate. She sits in the crowded waiting area and looks at red blinking dots: "Flight 4831 — Delayed — Mechanical difficulties." Desperate, she fears she has exhausted the capabilities of the hapless check-in girl, whom Danielle has charged to find another flight to Des Moines that will get her to the hearing — before it's over. No luck yet, but she's still trying. Her smoking gun won't matter a damn if she isn't there. She'll just have to wait it out.

Exhausted, she senses that her thoughts are no longer linear. The mental discipline that has carried her through this nightmare is unraveling. Marianne's diaries have made her throw up twice, but she forces herself to pull another from her bag. It is covered in pink, sweetheart roses. The first entry blooms on the page in elaborate, feminine handwriting.

Dear Dr. Joyce,
Kevin was my special boy. It was so much fun at the hospital — a constant stream of visitors. I wore an absolutely stunning bed jacket — the palest little-girl pink with flaming red edging. Then we went home and, as usual, the trouble started.

Danielle skips over the revolting description of the myriad of tests and torment she put the poor child through.

One day I had a brilliant idea. I'd heard about succinylcholine when I was a nurse. It's used as a muscle relaxant in surgery. Since my boy was in such awful pain, what would happen if I gave him just the teeniest dose? Besides, I'm only human — all that crying got on my nerves. So I injected him behind his knee (remember what I said about needle marks?) and it worked like a charm until he had a seizure. I had to bag him to get some oxygen into him.

For those crucial minutes, he hovered between life and death. I've never felt so alive — terrified and thrilled — just like a roller-coaster ride.

Danielle shuts the diary as another wave of nausea washes over her. Who will believe such a monster exists if they can't read these entries with their own eyes? Her watch tells her it is now 10:00 a.m. in the Plano courtroom. Tony must be completely untethered by now. God, she has to tell him what she's found so he'll know how to question Marianne if she doesn't get there in time. She digs in her purse for her cell phone, but realizes that Sevillas is incommunicado. Doaks. She punches in the number.

"Where are you?"

"In the airport."

"I'm comin' to get you," he says. "You're up shit creek."

"John, I'm in Phoenix. The flight is delayed."

"Oh, Christ," he groans. "For how long?"

"Until they fix the plane. Listen, Doaks, I need you to —"

"Look, Sevillas is so pissed at you that he's in there right now suckin' wind. That old sack Kreng's on the stand callin' Max a

386

violent psycho and you a world-class whack-job. And Max is totally freakin' out. I don't know how long Georgia can prop him up. Get your behind on another flight and get here, Danny, or this whole thing's goin' right down the tubes."

"Doaks, please just listen to me." She summons her most confident voice. "I'll be there as soon as I can, but Sevillas can handle it until then. I've hit pay dirt, and I'm bringing it with me."

"Not again." He mutters something she can't hear. "Look, I know the mother's nuts, but you ain't —"

"Nuts isn't what I have," she says. "Murder is what I have."

She hears a sharp intake of breath. "Better tell me quick."

"I've got cold, hard evidence that shows without a doubt that Marianne had other children, that she killed them in abominable, unthinkable ways —"

"Jesus, Mary and Joseph. How many kids did she have?"

"I don't know. At least two before Jonas."

"Got anything that links her directly to Jonas?"

"Not yet, but I'll scan all of the entries before I land."

"Just get here quick," he says. "Sevillas

ain't got that many card tricks left."

"I know, but you've got to find some way to get into her hotel room. She must have entries on her computer that relate to Jonas. All I have are diaries from years ago. She also probably travels with at least some trophies from her earlier murders, as many serial killers do. Each time she looks at them, they would remind her of her brilliance. Besides, it's clear that Marianne is too arrogant to believe that she'd ever be caught. I'll e-mail you her password from my cell."

"This ain't gonna be easy, ya know."

"Without that evidence, we've got nothing to link her to Jonas's murder."

"Yeah, yeah," he mutters. "Christ, pile another fuckin' felony onto the stack."

"Put Sevillas on the phone."

"Can't. He's in the courtroom dealin' with Kreng."

"Who's the next witness?"

"Don't know."

"Tell him to try to keep Marianne off the stand until I get back."

"And if he can't?"

"It's not an option."

"Right." His voice is battery acid. "Tony'll love it when I lay that on him."

"Now get going and call me back when

you've tossed her room." Her words are cut steel.

"Jesus, you're startin' to sound like a fuckin' cop."

"You haven't seen anything yet."

CHAPTER THIRTY-TWO

Nurse Kreng perches on the witness stand. She looks like a piece of petrified wood in her conventional whites, her hair yanked back from her face as tightly as a hundred-pack of bobby pins permits. Langley has taken her through every incident Doaks related to Sevillas from her interview: Max Parkman uncontrollably violent shortly after he was admitted to Maitland; Max Parkman psychotic and requiring almost nightly physical restraint; Max Parkman threatening Jonas Morrison's life on numerous occasions. The list seems endless. All the while, Langley casts sidelong, sly grins at Sevillas as if letting him know he's just getting warmed up. Then Kreng's vivid description of the murder scene. For the first time, Judge Hempstead blanched and looked sharply at the defense table.

Sevillas looks at Max. He sat very still during Kreng's direct, trying to keep Sevillas and Georgia from seeing the tears he rubbed furiously from his face. Georgia kept whispering encouragements to him from behind the bar. Thank God, because the poor kid looked as if he might just crumble into a heap right there in the courtroom.

He looks at the clock. Kreng's direct has taken an hour. Langley is winding up. Sevillas glances at the note Doaks just slipped him. Scrawled in his inimitable handwriting, Danielle's instructions are precise. He is not to mention Max. He is to stall if Marianne takes the stand. Danielle has critical evidence that implicates Marianne in Jonas's murder.

Max sits up when he sees Doaks pass the note to Sevillas. "Is it from my mom?" he whispers. "Is she coming?"

Sevillas leans over. "She's on her way. Don't worry, son."

Max gives him a grateful look and manages a half smile for Georgia.

"A quick question, Nurse Kreng." Langley's voice is as slick as canola oil sliding into a glass bowl. "Does your log indicate that the victim's mother, Marianne Morrison, was present on the day of the murder?"

"No, it does not."

Sevillas stands. "Objection. There is no evidence, either documentary or through witness testimony, that establishes Jonas Morrison was murdered by anyone."

"Do you doubt the boy is dead, Tony?" asks Langley.

"Mr. Langley!" the judge barks. "I respond to objections in this court, not counsel. Take your seat." He goes to his chair like a whipped puppy. "Now, Mr. Sevillas, would you care to enlighten me as to the nature of your objection?"

"Your Honor." His voice booms with new confidence. "We will be introducing evidence about the specific nature of the decedent's injuries and whether they were self-inflicted or caused by a third party." He looks at Langley. "Or both."

Langley's confusion is written on his face. The judge looks keenly at Sevillas. "Are you telling me it is the defense's contention that this boy caused his own death?"

Sevillas folds his hands. "Your Honor, we prefer to introduce our evidence at the appropriate time. Our objection is limited to the extent that there is no foundation at this time for the State to characterize the decedent's death."

The judge regards him thoughtfully, then shrugs. "Well, Mr. Sevillas, it's your defense. Run it any way you want. But don't think you're going to spring some cockamamie forensic theory on me today. I'm not in the mood." She turns to Langley. "Objection sustained. Rephrase."

Langley shakes his head, as if Sevillas's last statement is too absurd to warrant reflection. "Nurse Kreng, did you or your staff contact Ms. Morrison on the day Jonas Morrison . . . died?"

Kreng purses her thin, colorless lips together. "She was called, of course, after we found the boy. She viewed the body and became hysterical. We administered some medication, and she rested for a while. Then I believe she was interviewed briefly by one of the police officers and taken to the police station for further questioning."

"Thank you, Nurse, but if you try to testify about what Ms. Morrison said, that would be hearsay." A small smile lights the D.A.'s lips. "We will hear from the bereaved mother directly, in any event."

Sevillas turns around to see Marianne looking straight at him. Whatever Danielle thinks she's found, it better be good. Langley's star witness may well be a candidate for sainthood after she takes the stand.

"Nurse Kreng, can you tell us if you ever viewed Maitland security footage of Max Parkman attempting to harm Jonas Morrison or, in fact, screaming that he wanted to kill him —"

"Objection, Your Honor!" says Sevillas. "There has been absolutely no foundation laid for the existence of such security recordings, who took the video and whether or not it has been tampered with — not to mention the fact that no such tapes were provided to the defense prior to this hearing."

Langley strides forward. "Judge, critical to the question of whether or not Max Parkman murdered Jonas Morrison is the twisted relationship the defendant had with the deceased."

Sevillas stands. "Your Honor, the question is completely inappropriate. The State's sole intention is to harass and prejudice my client."

"Approach!"

Sevillas and Langley walk in unison, trained seals angling for the same fish. They reach the bench in time to hear Hempstead's angry whisper. "Look, boys, this is not a trial. There is no jury. There'll be no grandstanding here today. You've got reporters out there just waiting to write down every word potential jurors will read in the paper tomorrow. And believe me, you don't want them to hear what I'd like to say right now." Her voice sears cleanly through them, a machete through grass. "I'm going to give each of you ample latitude in your questioning." She shakes a warning finger at them. "But don't trip each other up on technical objections. And don't try to sneak in evidence that isn't in the record." Her eyes shoot spears at Langley. "You have something you want me to consider, get a witness who can properly introduce it. Otherwise, I'll make one or both of you a laughingstock by lunchtime." She gives them a stony look over her wire rims. "Got it?"

Both quickly say "Yes, Your Honor" as if only too pleased to get their judicial asschewing. Any other reaction will not serve either of them well when the case goes to trial.

"Mr. Langley," the judge says, her voice loud for the benefit of the court reporter. "Proceed."

Sevillas's lips are tight as he walks back to the defense table. He stares at his legal pad while Langley walks Kreng through the rest of her testimony. He establishes her independent observations of Max's violent, psychotic demeanor and the obscenities and fears he expressed about Jonas. Hempstead's expression is impassive, but Sevillas can tell she is riveted, evidenced by her constant note taking. When it is over, she stares at Max with sharp curiosity. Sevillas sees another wave of panic go through Max and looks at the empty chair next to him. Where the hell is she?

Langley smiles and pitches his last ball. "Nurse Kreng, we know that Max Parkman was found unconscious on the floor in the room where Jonas was murdered, covered in blood. What was Ms. Parkman doing when you entered the room?"

Kreng draws herself up, an ironing board in white. "She was half carrying, half dragging her son through pools of blood, trying to sneak him out of the room —"

"Objection!" Sevillas jumps to his feet. "Any attempt on the part of the witness to ascribe motive to the defendant —"

Hempstead holds up her hand. "Sustained."

Unperturbed, Langley continues. "Nurse Kreng, how would you describe Ms. Parkman's affect when you personally observed her?"

Kreng gives Sevillas a defiant look. "I would have to describe it as the reaction of an unbalanced, hysterical woman."

Sevillas starts to rise to his feet, but Langley jumps in. "That's fine, Nurse Kreng. Thank you very much."

Sevillas hesitates, but the cow is already out of the barn and there is no jury to be tainted — only the judge, who has already absorbed the damaging testimony. Objecting now would only draw more attention to it. He sits down.

Langley grins at Sevillas. "Pass the witness."

Tony walks to the witness stand and keeps his voice calm.

"Nurse Kreng, you have recounted a number of episodes and personal observations of both Max Parkman and his mother at Maitland, including their emotional and psychological states. Is that correct?"

"Yes."

"Are you a licensed psychiatrist?"

She gives him an annoyed look. "Of course not."

"I didn't think so." His voice is kind. "So you would agree with me that whatever personal observations you have shared with us today involving Max or his mother are simply your subjective opinion — nothing more."

"No, Mr. Sevillas," she replies stiffly. "My observations are those of a professional who has observed patient and parental behavior in all of the facets one would experience after thirty years as a highly qualified psychiatric nurse and administrative manager of a psychiatric facility with an impeccable, worldwide reputation."

"Are you qualified to diagnose Ms. Parkman?"

"No."

"Are you qualified to diagnose Max Parkman?"

"No."

Sevillas smiles. "Other than following the doctor's orders, was it your job to speculate upon either Max Parkman's diagnosis or Ms. Parkman's emotional state in your capacity as a nurse?"

Kreng glares at Sevillas as the words barely escape her mouth — a furious ventriloquist. "No."

"Is there any question in your mind that Max Parkman's mother is devoted to him?"

Her face softens ever so slightly. "No, there isn't."

"Given your thirty years as a psychiatric nurse, and as an observer of, I am sure, hundreds of parents' reactions over those years, has it been your experience that parents of children who are admitted to a psychiatric facility often suffer denial and intense emotional pressure?"

"Of course," she says. "Whenever a parent watches his or her own child suffer a mental disturbance that requires treatment of that magnitude, there is always considerable emotional pain and stress."

"Do all parents of these children express that kind of emotional pain and stress in an identical fashion?"

"Of course not."

"By the way, Ms. Kreng, you also had ample opportunity to observe Mrs. Morrison, the decedent's mother, did you not?"

"Yes."

"Did you find her behavior to be atypical?"

Langley rolls his eyes. "Your Honor, is there anything relevant about this line of questioning? Other than a diversionary tactic by defense counsel to try to distract us from the actions of his own clients?"

Hempstead peers over her glasses. "Not an unwarranted inquiry, Mr. Sevillas."

"We'll drop it for now, Your Honor." He'd have to wait to see if Danielle can come up with something to implicate Marianne. At least he's laid some sort of foundation, however flimsy.

He walks slowly in front of the witness box and catches Max's eye. The poor kid is hanging on to every word. Sevillas nods in what he hopes is a comforting way. Max remains stone-faced. Sevillas turns back to the witness. "Nurse Kreng, when you entered the room on the day of Jonas's death and established that there were numerous puncture wounds on the body, did you see the implement which might have been used to cause these injuries?"

"Yes."

"You did?" He shows surprise.

"I most certainly did." She smacks her lips slightly, a lizard that has just flicked out its tongue and likes the feel of the fly in its mouth, struggling.

"Where was it?"

"The police pulled it out of Ms. Parkman's purse."

Hempstead leans forward a bit, intent.

Sevillas smiles and turns back to the witness. "And what was this object?"

"Objection, Your Honor!" Langley is on his feet. "The question exceeds the scope of my direct examination of this witness."

The judge looks at Sevillas.

"Judge, counsel opened the door when he had Nurse Kreng describe what she saw when she entered the boy's room. I am merely asking a follow-up question into the very area he introduced."

She gives Langley a disdainful glance. "Overruled."

"Exception," Langley responds.

Hempstead doesn't even bother to look at him. "Noted. Proceed."

Sevillas nods. "What was the object you saw in the room?"

"It was a . . . comb of some sort."

"What did it look like?"

She holds both hands up, palms facing one another. "I would guess it was about this size — six or eight inches — with long metal spikes."

"Did you touch the comb when you saw it?"

She gives him an offended look. "Of course not, Mr. Sevillas. One of the policemen pulled it from Ms. Parkman's purse and held it up."

"Did you happen to see what he did with the comb at that point?"

She sniffs. "No, I did not. I was extremely busy contacting Ms. Morrison and Dr. Hauptmann and ensuring the whereabouts and safety of the other patients on the unit."

"Are you aware if anyone besides the police entered the room that afternoon?"

"The medical examiner, of course." She gives him a stern look. "You would be better served to ask the police about the comb, Mr. Sevillas."

He looks at Langley and then turns and smiles at the judge. "Yes, indeed, Nurse

Kreng. We've done that, of course, but it seems that the comb has mysteriously disappeared. Do you have any idea where it might have gone?"

"Objection!" Langley stomps toward the bench. "Your Honor! Asked and answered. This witness has already told us she has no idea what happened to the comb and —"

"And she's told us that the police took possession of the comb."

Langley lifts his hands. "Your Honor, we're going to put on witnesses about the comb."

"And how they never had it long enough to even test it for prints," Sevillas says with a flourish.

Hempstead's thin eyebrows rise and stay there. "Mr. Langley, counsel seems to be saying that the alleged murder weapon disappeared from the crime scene and has not been located. Is that true, Mr. Prosecutor?"

Langley fiddles with his tie, as if the knot is too tight for his neck. "Well, Your Honor, it's like this. Yes, the murder weapon was at the scene, but we're still working on locating it."

"What do you mean, 'working' on it?" she asks curtly. "Do you or don't you have possession of the comb?"

"Not right this second, Judge, but —"

"No buts, Mr. Langley." She turns to Sevillas. "Well, it seems that the defense has something going for it after all. However, I would remind you, Mr. Sevillas, that this is a limited hearing set for very narrow purposes. Don't put on your entire defense today. We will all wait with bated breath to watch it unfold at trial."

"Thank you, Your Honor."

"Be seated, Mr. District Attorney." Langley sits like a well-trained dog. She turns to Sevillas. "Proceed, counsel."

Sevillas catches Max giving him a proud grin. "Two points for our side," he seemed to say. He turns to the witness. "Nurse Kreng, you were in charge of the Fountainview unit, which housed both Jonas Morrison and Max Parkman?"

"Yes."

Sevillas walks to within two feet of the witness stand and looks Kreng in the eyes. "Was Max Parkman on the unit the day Jonas died?"

She glares at him. "Yes, he was."

"Am I correct in stating that it is your position that he was in his bed down the hall?"

"Yes, as reflected by the logs," she says. "Which also state that he was restrained."

"By leather straps?"

"Yes."

Sevillas smiles at her. "Now, Nurse Kreng, perhaps you can enlighten me, because there is something about this I simply don't understand. How could Max Parkman have removed thick, leather restraining straps on both his hands and feet by himself?"

Her eyes are black spears. "It is our belief that the entry in the log was erroneous."

Sevillas feigns surprise. "Did you make that entry, Nurse Kreng?"

A blue vein pulses near her forehead as Kreng spits out words like bullets spit from an automatic. "Absolutely not."

"That would be the duty nurse on that shift — Nurse Grodin?"

"Yes."

Sevillas places his hands on the witness stand. "Come now, Nurse Kreng, are you telling us everything?" Before Langley can object, he continues. "Nurse Grodin is no longer in Maitland's employ, is she?"

Kreng fixes her flat eyes straight ahead. "No, she is not."

"She was fired, wasn't she?"

"Yes."

"Please tell us why she was discharged."

Her voice is a slice of crisp, burnt toast. "Because she did not fulfill her duties in accordance with the standards of our facility."

"You found out that she refused to say that she failed to put Max Parkman in restraints that day, didn't you?"

Kreng draws up. "I believe that she lied to cover her malfeasance."

Sevillas rocks back on his heels. "In fact, there was not a single Maitland staff person on duty on the Fountainview unit during that fatal lunch hour, was there, Nurse Kreng?"

She glares at him. "There was no real need for a staff person, Mr. Sevillas. The only two patients on the unit were Jonas Morrison and Max Parkman — and both were in restraints."

"If that were the case, Nurse Kreng," he says softly, "then how in the world do you explain how both of them were out of restraints at the time of the murder?"

Kreng is silent.

"If there wasn't a single staff member on that unit, Nurse Kreng, can you or anyone from Maitland say — under oath — who took off the restraints the duty nurse swears she put on Max Parkman?"

"Objection," says Langley.

"Overruled," says the judge.

Sevillas strides to the defense table and picks up a piece of paper. "So this log is worthless. Anyone could have been on that unit during the lunch hour. For all we know, both Max and Jonas were wandering around loose."

Kreng's head snaps up. "Absolutely not."

Sevillas puts a finger alongside his nose. "Come now, Nurse Kreng. You're in no position to give such a response. You weren't there."

She does not respond. Sevillas moves close to the witness box and waits until she meets his eyes. "In fact, there could easily have been a third party — another patient, another staff member — who drugged Max Parkman, dragged him into Jonas's room, killed Jonas, and was on the verge of killing Max Parkman when his mother scared the murderer off before he could complete that task."

Kreng's eyes are the size of half-dollars. "That is preposterous!"

"Your Honor!" Langley looks as if he is on the verge of an aneurism. "This witness is being asked to comment upon the defense's absurd fairy tale of events so he can plant a murder theory that there is absolutely no foundation for in the facts of this case!"

Hempstead studies Sevillas over her wire rims. "Very creative, Mr. Sevillas." She turns to Langley. "I am, however, eminently capable of comprehending and applying the facts to whatever theory either of you chooses to put before me."

"But Judge —"

She shakes her head. "Overruled."

Sevillas turns back to Kreng. "Isn't it also possible, Nurse Kreng, that a staff member could have taken the comb used to stab Jonas Morrison from Ms. Parkman's purse while it was on the unit unattended?"

"Objection!" Langley marches up to the judge's bench. "Judge, Ms. Parkman was found in Jonas's room with the comb in her purse."

"The comb he can't produce," says Sevillas calmly.

"Your Honor, this is outrageous!"

"Outrageous is not an objection of which I am aware," says Hempstead. "It seems to me that Mr. Sevillas is doing what any good defense lawyer would do. He's coming up with another murder suspect. Not to mention the fact that you don't have the murder weapon, Mr. Langley. If you could show me a print on that comb, or even the comb," she says dryly, "I might feel differently. Overruled."

Sevillas turns back to Kreng. "One last question. Are you aware if anyone from Maitland checked any other patient's room for traces of blood or other physical evidence on that day?"

Kreng is as white as her uniform. "No, they did not."

"So we don't know whether or not another patient or third party either committed the murder or was responsible for planting incriminating evidence in Max Parkman's room."

Sevillas turns to the judge. "No further questions, Your Honor." He nods at the witness box. "Thank you very much, Nurse Kreng."

"All rise!" the bailiff wails.

"Twenty-minute recess." The judge stands, collects her robes and leaves the bench without a backward glance.

CHAPTER THIRTY-THREE

Danielle fastens her seat belt as the airplane finally begins its ascent: the only flight she could get from Phoenix to Des Moines has a brief stopover in Dallas. And after that, she still has the damned drive to Plano. She has tried and tried to reach Max, but if he is in the courtroom, she knows he can't leave his iPhone on. He must be frantically awaiting her arrival. If she doesn't get back in time, her boy will be the one to suffer.

She's had no further calls from Doaks. She hopes he has broken into Marianne's room by now and found something, anything, to link her to Jonas's death. The second sweetheart-rose diary lies in her lap. If she reads from now until the moment she lands in Des Moines, she will get through it and the remaining computer disks. And she must not cave in and cry about the horrors she is reading. She is a lawyer — a lawyer looking for evidence to exonerate her son and herself. She opens the book to the next entry.

Dear Dr. Joyce,
Ashley's funeral was so gratifying. All eyes were riveted on me as I floated down the aisle in my mourning black. I had on my dark veil that let me see out, but didn't let them see in — just like Mata Hari. I picked out a darling off-white coffin with a hint of a pink cast to it. The flowers required more sensitivity. Lilies are too depressing for a four-year-old girl, so I chose daisies — so fresh and innocent. The service was closed-coffin. I don't think everyone needs to see everything.

The highlight of the day, though, was Ashley's pediatrician, who told everyone what a wonderful, caring mother I am. When he left, he clasped both of my hands and told me he had never seen a mother show such strength and courage in the face of two losses so close together. It's time for the wake, and I'm exhausted.

A mother's work is never done.

Danielle requests a coffee from the stewardess and then flips to the end of the diary. Two dead children and who knew how many "miscarriages" so far. She has clipped the pages she will attempt to enter into evidence — assuming the judge will even let her stand up in court and question a witness. And then she can compare Marianne's handwriting to the sprawling cursive in her diaries. She's desperate to know what tack Sevillas has taken so far. She refuses to think about how her disappearance may have ruined his ability to protect Max — and her. She scans down to the last entry.

Dear Dr. Joyce,

I can barely hold the pen to write, my poor heart is fluttering so. My Raymond is gone — just like that. Last night he wasn't feeling well, so I fluffed up his pillows and we went to sleep like two teaspoons. I woke up in the middle of the night and felt something cold and clammy. I turned on the light and — oh, my God — there he was, lying with his eyes wide open. I could tell right away that he'd had a stroke. He lay there looking at me, but he couldn't move. I didn't call an ambulance. Frankly, I needed a moment to consider my options. After about fifteen minutes, he had another stroke and was still. I checked his vitals and there's just no sugarcoating it — he was stone-cold dead.

After I called the ambulance, I covered

411

Raymond with an old blanket (he was messy) and went downstairs to dig into his papers. I had to review the state of my finances. He didn't leave me much, but it's enough to get by on for a few years. I'm not interested in finding another man just yet. I have to get this funeral over with and start a new life.

Besides, I have a real problem to consider. I was planning to tell Raymond this weekend, but it looks like I'm in the family way again. If it's a boy, I think I'll call him Jonas. It isn't the most favorable of circumstances, despite the sympathy it will generate. I think I'll just move away and start a new life. Yes, that's ex-act-ly what I'll do. First I'll dye my hair blond.

They have more fun, don't they?

CHAPTER THIRTY-FOUR

Sevillas glances at the witness list he has compiled. He's arranged them in the order he thinks Langley will put them on. His bet this morning was that Langley would put on the M.E., Kreng and then Marianne Morrison. When the bailiff calls out the next name, he's glad he didn't put any money on the table.

He glances over at Max. The poor kid is barely hanging on as it is. He turns to look at Georgia over Max's bowed head. He can tell that she is also skeptical that Danielle will arrive in time to save them.

Reyes-Moreno has been on the stand for about fifteen minutes. Langley is making his ponderous way through a laundry list of credentials that would impress Freud. President of the Board of Directors of the American Psychiatric Association; first in her class at Harvard Medical School; practicing psychiatrist for twenty-five years, fifteen at Maitland; worldwide lecturer on myriad psychiatric and neurological disorders in adolescent patients. Sevillas would have welcomed this delay, but doesn't want the judge to hear a complete laundry list of what a great expert Reyes-Moreno is.

"Your Honor?" He rises halfway out of his seat. "If it please the Court, the defense accepts that the witness's credentials the District Attorney so liberally provides are accurate. As we are not in trial and there is no jury to consider, could we get on with questioning pertinent to the issues at hand?"

Hempstead gives Sevillas a small smile. "Objection sustained. The court will accept a written résumé of the witness, Mr. Langley. Let's get on with it, shall we?"

Langley looks annoyed, but nods and turns to his witness. "Dr. Reyes-Moreno, do you know the defendant, Max Parkman?" Langley then points at Max. The doctor smiles at Max and directs her gaze at Langley.

"Yes." Her voice is clear and melodic. Dressed in a soft gray suit that contrasts with her white hair, her manner appears thoughtful and professional.

"Your basic witness nightmare," Sevillas mutters to himself. He knows that if a woman is smart and presents herself well,

414

the judge will think she is a credit to the sex — someone who's fought hard to get to the top, just like her. If she's stupid, the judge won't be able to imagine how she got there and will resent an undeserved climb up the professional ladder. If she's smart — but also a smart-ass — the judge will feel obliged to take her down a peg or two, lest she discredit the sisterhood.

"How often did you interact with Max Parkman after he was admitted?"

"I saw Max on a daily basis." The doctor folds her hands calmly in her lap and looks at the judge with clear, emerald eyes. "The Maitland concept of psychiatric treatment is to create a 'team' for each patient. We select a specific group of psychiatrists, neurologists and educational psychologists who we feel are most qualified to work together on the diagnostic aspects of the case, as well as to devise the best long-term solution for the whole child. Each team is as different as each child." The judge nods, obviously impressed.

"Were you on Max's team?" asks Langley.

"Yes, I was Max's primary psychiatrist and thus had the responsibility for overseeing his team and treatment plan. I attended all staffings related to Max and conducted all psychiatric sessions with him."

Langley rustles through his notes and then looks up. "I assume that you were ultimately able to diagnose Max's psychiatric problems?"

She takes off her silver glasses and rubs her eyes. "It was not solely my diagnosis, but the conclusion reached by each member of Max's team."

"And what was that diagnosis, Doctor?"

Sevillas jumps to his feet. "Objection, Your Honor."

"Yes, Mr. Sevillas?"

"The defendant's diagnosis is protected by the doctor-patient privilege."

Langley approaches the bench. "Judge, it is the State's position that the diagnosis of Max Parkman and his erratic and increasingly violent behavior are intrinsically related to the murder of Jonas Morrison by the defendant. This witness will testify as to both. It is imperative that she be allowed to explain the diagnosis and her observations of the effect this had on the defendant's state of mind prior to the murder."

"Your Honor," says Sevillas. "If you permit this witness to testify in open court about the actual diagnosis of Max Parkman, you will be subjecting that boy to extreme prejudice, especially once the press gets it. This diagnosis was made in a private facility which keeps patient information strictly confidential unless the patient or his legal guardian permits disclosure to a third party." He draws a breath. "And I can assure you, Judge, no such permission has been given in this case, either by the patient or his mother."

"Now, Mr. Sevillas, if we were sitting here in front of a jury, I would agree with you," she says. "However, there is no harm in having the bench hear this testimony, and I believe you have to admit it is relevant to the State's case." Sevillas starts to object further, but Hempstead raises her hand. "To avoid any potential prejudice to Max Parkman and to preclude any future jury pool contamination, I now order that the courtroom be cleared."

The bailiff rises. "Clear the courtroom."

After a few moments of grumbling and shuffling feet, the disappointed observers and press corps make their exit. Sevillas gives Georgia a quick glance that says Max doesn't need to hear what Reyes-Moreno has to say about his mental or emotional problems. She nods and touches Max's shoulder. With a terrified look at Sevillas, Max follows Georgia and the bailiff out of the courtroom.

Langley smiles at Reyes-Moreno. "Now,

Doctor, please tell the judge the purpose of the June 20 meeting and what you observed on that date with respect to the defendant."

Reyes-Moreno faces the judge. "I actually orchestrated the meeting. Everyone on the team had substantial . . . concerns . . . and I determined it would be productive to the patient for Ms. Parkman to meet with us."

"What 'concerns' are you referring to?"

"As you mentioned, Max was experiencing increasing volatility, paranoid delusions and violent tendencies. The purpose of the meeting was to more thoroughly explain the basis for our collective diagnosis and to give Ms. Parkman an opportunity to question the entire team."

Langley smiles. "And what exactly was that diagnosis, Dr. Reyes-Moreno?"

"Schizoaffective disorder and psychosis N.O.S."

"What does 'psychosis N.O.S.' mean?"

"It means that the patient has experienced a break with reality — on at least one occasion — and the appellation in Max's case was 'not otherwise specified.' " She folds her hands. "It is a more general category, given his age and the observations we made during the short time he has been with us."

"Mr. Langley," says the judge. "If there will be no more specific mention of the diagnosis, I would like to open the court-room to the masses once again."

"Of course, Your Honor." As the bailiff opens the door and the observers file in, Langley turns and shoots Sevillas a sly grin. When all are settled, he turns back to the witness. "Do you schedule such meetings with every parent after such a diagnosis is revealed?"

"No," the doctor says. "In this particular case, Ms. Parkman was unusually reactive. Despite my overtures, she refused to discuss the diagnosis further. I knew that Ms. Park-man's adamant state of denial would nega-tively impact Max's ability to ultimately come to terms with his disease. It is impera-tive, of course, that the parents of such a child fully support the medical team. If a parent refuses to accept the facts, they can-not help the child cope with the reality of the situation."

"Please tell us what happened during the conference."

"Certainly." She speaks in a professional, yet caring voice. Her demeanor is one of ultimate credibility. The judge takes notes. It is clear that she takes Reyes-Moreno's testimony seriously. "I began by telling Ms. Parkman that I understood her level of concern about the seriousness of Max's diagnosis. I assured her that we had not come to our conclusions lightly and that all of our testing clearly indicated that the diagnosis was correct. At that point, Ms. Parkman became upset and told me that she would not accept our diagnosis, regardless of what our tests showed."

"What happened next?"

Reyes-Moreno looks at the judge. "I informed Ms. Parkman that her refusal to accept the diagnosis was extremely detrimental to Max's well-being and that she needed to face it for his sake. She continued to disagree vehemently."

"Was there any discussion of a second opinion?"

"Absolutely," she says. "I told her that she was welcome to have any professional she chose review our results. I urged her to do it quickly, however, given the gravity of the situation."

"And then?"

"I informed Ms. Parkman that Max believed that Jonas was plotting to hurt him or kill him —"

Sevillas stands. "Your Honor, this is dangerously close to violating the court's order not to discuss Max Parkman's diagnosis in public."

"Mr. Langley, I warned you not to cross

the line." She looks sharply at the D.A. "Proceed with caution."

He nods. "How did Ms. Parkman react to your telling her of Max's fears?"

Reyes-Moreno takes a deep breath. "She flew into a rage. She accused us not only of having fabricated his symptoms, but of falsifying entries we made into Max's chart that clearly exhibited his violent behavior."

"What happened then?"

The doctor shakes her head. "Ms. Parkman jumped up from the conference table, and it appeared that she intended to attack me. An orderly was forced to restrain her."

Langley smacks his lips, as if he has just polished off a crème brûlée. "Is this a common response?"

She shakes her head sadly. "Not at all, I'm afraid."

"Go on, Doctor."

She clears her throat. "At that time, I felt it imperative that we calm Ms. Parkman down. I then attempted to convince her that we had no 'secret agenda' and that our diagnosis was based upon clinical facts and observations, with the conclusion that Max was clearly psychotic."

Sevillas leaps across the room. "Your Honor! This flies completely in the face of the Court's order! Why did we bother to clear the courtroom? Counsel is flagrantly attempting to introduce details of that boy's diagnosis in open court by sliding it in as a question to the witness!"

"Sustained."

Sevillas's face is flushed. "Your Honor, the defense requests that the District Attorney be cited with contempt for deliberately disobeying this court's order."

The judge shakes her head. "You certainly deserve it, Mr. Langley. I will take the defense's motion under advisement and will rule on it at the end of the day."

Langley gives the judge a short bow. "I apologize, Your Honor. I assure you, it was just a slip."

Sevillas curses under his breath. The damage is done. Langley will happily risk a contempt citation because he's gotten exactly what he wanted. By this evening, every reporter in the courtroom will turn in copy about how Max is dangerously psychotic and was convinced that Jonas wanted to kill him. Sevillas is sure that it will hit the wires before the evening news. Even worse, any jury pool that might have kept an objective view of Max's innocence will be tainted. If he doesn't get a change of venue for the trial, Max will buy it for sure.

Langley turns to the witness. "What was

Ms. Parkman's reaction to her son's diagnosis?"

"She became highly agitated. She accused me and the entire team of fabricating and doctoring Max's entries solely for the purpose of substantiating our diagnosis." She pauses for breath. "She then began cursing and demanding the release of her son."

"What was your response?"

"I told Ms. Parkman that it would be extremely detrimental to Max's treatment and his rapidly dissociative behavior to remove him from Maitland."

"What did Ms. Parkman say?"

"To the best of my recollection, and please understand that I wrote these notes after our meeting, I believe she said: 'Like hell, lady. By the time you people are through with me, I'd be foaming at the mouth and baying at the moon.' "

"And then?"

The doctor looks down at her notes. "Then she stood up and told me to get Max's — excuse me for the language, Your Honor — 'fucking records' copied and sent to her hotel immediately."

"Did she say anything else?"

"Yes." Her eyes are sad as she skims the piece of paper in her hand. "She said that she was planning to take Max out of our 'execrable excuse for a hospital' — despite our insistence that this would harm Max — and told me that I better 'fucking well' send Max's entire chart to her hotel immediately."

The judge looks at her. "Doctor, did you believe at that time that Ms. Parkman intended to leave the jurisdiction with her son?"

"Yes, Judge, I must say that there was — and is — no question in my mind that, given the opportunity, Ms. Parkman would immediately leave Plano with Max and return to New York."

"And do you believe that Max Parkman would continue to suffer serious deterioration of his psychiatric condition if this occurred?"

"I'm afraid so," she finishes softly. "It is also my professional opinion that the violence he has exhibited will escalate."

Sevillas tries not to let his emotions show. Any chance Danielle had to stay out on bond after this highly credible testimony is now zero. Langley grins at Sevillas. "Pass the witness."

Sevillas moves as far away from Langley as he can and still be within hearing distance of the bailiff, who stands close to Max until the courtroom reconvenes.

"Where's Mom?" asks Max anxiously. "She should be here by now."

"She sent me a text message," lies Georgia. "She's coming just as fast as she can. Her plane was delayed a little."

Max gives her a wary look. "Where's my iPhone? I can find out exactly where she is."

Max frowns and turns to Sevillas, who punches a speed dial on his cell phone — for the third time. He's going to keep trying until he gets the son of a bitch. On the eighth ring, he hears the familiar gravel of Doaks's voice.

"Yeah?"

"Where the hell are you?"

"C'mon, Tony, grab your dick and take a deep breath," he says. "I'm busy right now."

"Busy?" Sevillas snaps. "Doing what, for God's sake?"

"Look, I told you Danielle is on to somethin' about that Marianne broad. She's got some diaries that have all kinds of abuse shit in it, and not only that —"

"Damn it, Doaks!" he says. "Do you have any idea how impossible it is for me to operate this way? How can I present a proper defense when the only fact witness Max has is his mother and she's off somewhere taking a flier." He pauses for breath. "And do you realize that Langley is ripping me a new asshole with every witness? Reyes-Moreno just leveled Max — and Danielle — on direct, and now I get to cross her without one single piece of Danielle's so-called evidence. Even if you two are convinced that Marianne is the killer, I can't even raise her behavior with Jonas because there's no credible factual basis for it. Do you hear anything I'm saying?"

"Listen, dickhead." Doaks's voice is red around the edges. "Let's not forget whose brilliant idea it was to let the judge cram this hearing down our throats barely a week after the kid's iced. I've been bustin' my hump 24/7. I'm gonna yank your sorry ass out of the fire, but you gotta give me more time."

Langley comes down the hall. Sevillas turns the other way and lowers his voice to a hiss. "Listen, you geriatric piece of shit. You fly halfway across the country with Danielle on some half-assed hunch, and I'm supposed to completely change my whole M.O. for this defense? I'm sitting here with nothing — not even one of the goddamned defendants — thanks to you."

"Back off, Tony. You just have to trust her.

Look, she's convinced she's got more than enough to get Max off — and she ain't no dummy."

"Christ, Doaks, I hope you're right." The anger melts from his voice, leaving an undercurrent of fear. "Just get her here as fast as you can."

"Tony, look, I gotta go. Barnes just got here."

"What does Barnes have to do with it?"

"You don't wanna know, and I ain't gonna tell you."

Sevillas hears the bailiff's cry. "How in the hell am I going to drag this out before Hempstead throws me in jail for contempt?"

"For what?" asks Doaks.

He sighs. "For lying to the court. I promised her Danielle was on the way."

Doaks chuckles. "Well, she is. You just keep that Morrison broad on the stand if she shows up," says Doaks, "and we'll fuckin' cover you in evidence."

"And pigs will fly." Sevillas snaps the phone shut.

CHAPTER THIRTY-FIVE

Danielle checks her watch. They have made good time to Dallas and she is waiting to board the plane to Des Moines. If only she knew which witnesses have already taken the stand and how Sevillas has handled them. Her phone rings, and she grabs it. "Georgia? How is Max? Is he all right?"

"God, Danielle, where are you?" There is a frantic note in her voice. "I'm in the ladies' room. He's okay — just scared and very anxious that you aren't here yet."

"I've sent him text messages. Has he gotten any of them?"

"No," says Georgia. "I had to leave his cell phone in the car. He isn't allowed to have it in the courtroom."

"Right. Well, my flight was delayed out of Phoenix and I'll be there as soon as I can," she says. "Who is on the stand? Has he kept Marianne off?"

"The D.A. hasn't put her on yet," says

Georgia. "Kreng and Reyes-Moreno have testified. They've established, as you might guess, a fairly airtight case against Max. Sevillas is treading water and trying to stall, but you really need to get here."

"Just tell him I know that Marianne did it," she says. "And that he has to try to hold on until I can get the evidence to him."

"I've got to go," says Georgia. "Max needs me."

"Are you sure he's okay?" Danielle feels almost frantic. "Can I talk to him?"

"No way. The bailiff won't let him out of his sight, much less out of the courtroom."

They sign off, but Danielle's concern for Max consumes her. She imagines him sitting next to Tony at the defense table, petrified that she isn't there and not understanding the legal posturing between the D.A. and Sevillas. She can't let herself panic. The only thing she can do now is to get through as many of Marianne's entries as possible, and to flag those she intends to introduce — assuming the judge doesn't throw her in jail the minute she walks into the courtroom.

During the flight, she exhausts the earlier diaries and slogs her way through the CDs from the computer cabinet. At long last there is a mention of Jonas. Given what she absorbed from the earlier entries, she shudders to learn what befell Jonas as a child. She shakes her head. She cannot afford sentiment. She reads an entry about Jonas dated shortly before they went to Maitland.

Dear Dr. Joyce,
I have to come out and admit it. Jonas has turned out to be a true disappointment. When he was a baby, he was so sweet and never complained — no matter how many times we wound up in the emergency room. Unfortunately, after one of his seizures, he went without oxygen for too long — a bit ambitious on my part, I'm afraid — and mental retardation was the result. I was dismayed at first, but I soon realized that it made him infinitely easier to handle. Everything in life is a trade-off.

Now, Dr. Joyce, pay careful attention to what I describe, because I have conducted a brilliant scientific experiment with unprecedented results. I have created autism where none existed. First I tackled the basic fact that many autistics are incapable of intelligible speech. Everyone thinks Jonas can't speak, but they're dead wrong. The behaviors I taught him allow him to communicate perfectly well with me — and it was obviously to my advantage that he not converse with anyone else.

Then came the challenge of self-infliction. I taught Jonas to slap his face whenever I said "no" or "bad." Then I would give him lots of praise and a big hug. (It's so important to provide positive feedback with children.) By the time he was six, Jonas knew that he was allowed to use anything he wanted to discipline himself and that I, in turn, would shower him with affection. Eventually, all I had to do was give him a look and he knew exactly what to do. The restraints and electric collar were useful training tools. The most inspired plans are simple ones, but they don't fall out of the sky. It requires a tremendous commitment and a lifetime of sacrifice.

Not many women have that kind of character.

CHAPTER THIRTY-SIX

Sevillas walks back into the courtroom. He has left Georgia and Max in a conference room adjacent to the courtroom and told them to stay there until he calls them. Georgia promised to calm Max down and get him something to drink. The poor kid can't take much more. Neither, Sevillas admits, can he.

As he nears the defense table, he sees a tense gathering at the judge's bench. Hempstead stands in deep conversation with her law clerk and the sheriff. His back is to Sevillas, but there is obviously something in his hands that is the subject of this *ad hoc* discussion. Langley's head is bowed as he studies documents his baby attorneys feed him.

Hempstead looks up and sees Sevillas. The sheriff turns around, arms behind his back. "Mr. Sevillas." Her voice is charged, edgy. "I took the opportunity during your absence to ask Sheriff Wollensky to ascertain the whereabouts of your client, as it appears that you have forgotten my order to produce her here today."

Sevillas approaches the bench. "Your Honor, I did try —"

She holds up her hand. "Don't bother, Counsel. Sheriff Wollensky has been to Ms. Parkman's apartment, with a warrant signed by yours truly, and — wonder of wonders — she is nowhere to be found." Her pale eyes through the steel rims shoot bullets at him. "Do you have any possible explanation as to where she might be?"

Langley has stopped looking at his documents and sits back with a smug grin on his face. Sevillas clasps his hands in front of him and summons his most sincere expression. "I have no idea, Your Honor. As instructed this morning, I tried repeatedly to reach Ms. Parkman by telephone, but was unsuccessful. As I related, my client has been seriously ill this week. It is highly likely that she has gone to the doctor. If the court likes, I could step into the hall and attempt again to reach her —"

Hempstead shakes her head impatiently. "Mr. Sevillas, I recommend that you not toy with me. If you know where your client is, you better tell me — now."

Sevillas shrugs and raises his hands. "I honestly have no idea, Judge."

She scowls at him. "I find it odd indeed that such a sick woman would leave her bed. At least I found it odd until Sheriff Wollensky came back during the break and showed me this." She motions to the sheriff, who holds up what seems to be a long, rubbery stocking.

Sevillas tries to keep his expression impassive as his mind races to figure out what stunt Danielle has pulled now. "I'm sorry, Your Honor, what is that?"

"You have no idea?"

"I do not," he says firmly.

"Approach," she says. "You, too, Mr. Langley."

Sevillas and Langley move toward the bench as the sheriff hands the thing to Hempstead. She holds it on high as if it is a malodorous lab specimen. "Sheriff Wollensky found this . . . thing . . . under your client's bed, along with a box labeled *Prosthetics, Inc.*" Sevillas gives the judge a puzzled look. "It took us a while to figure it out, too, Counselor, but it appears that this is a synthetic covering for a prosthetic leg which your client apparently padded and placed over her own leg to dupe one of the other sheriffs into switching out her ankle

434

bracelet."

"Jesus Christ," he mutters. "Your Honor, I hope you know that I had no part in whatever Ms. Parkman has —"

"Let me finish. Your client then slipped off the ankle bracelet and hung it on the back of her bedroom door. The sheriff has ascertained that her suitcase and most of her items of clothing are missing. Now." Her eyes are steel slits. "Do you have anything productive to say?"

Sevillas sighs. "I have no explanation, Judge. As far as I knew, she was ill and in bed."

"That's your story, and you're sticking to it, I suppose." She gives him a harsh look. "Well, I've put out an APB for your client. If she's left the jurisdiction, which I have to assume is the case, this entire hearing vis-à-vis the bond issue is moot. Ms. Parkman will have the pleasure of enjoying our county jail until the date of her trial. And I better not learn, Counselor, that you had any knowledge of this whatsoever. If I do —" she points a long finger at him "— you will have the opportunity to join her."

Sevillas nods his head.

Hempstead leans forward. "The moment you hear from her, you will so advise this Court."

"Yes, Your Honor."

"Be seated."

Sevillas, perspiring now, takes his seat. He never thought to ask Doaks how in the hell Danielle ditched that anklet. He was so upset about her jumping bond that he didn't think to ask how she pulled it off. Well, Hempstead won't need to throw her in jail — he'll throttle her the minute she walks into the courtroom.

He watches as Georgia and Max take their seats. Max looks better. Sevillas leans over the rail and whispers to Georgia. "You work miracles with that boy."

She smiles.

"It's because he's as much mine as Danielle's."

For the next half hour, they sit through Langley's direct of Smythe, the courtly medical examiner. Although Sevillas follows the questioning with one ear, inwardly he is fuming. Maybe he should just file a motion to withdraw. Now Danielle hasn't just screwed up her case, she's put him in the worst possible light with one of the best judges in Iowa. This could ruin his hard-won reputation. Besides, he has wondered from the outset if his personal feelings for Danielle have prevented him from being as effective as her counsel — and Max's — as

436

he should be. He glances at Max, who seems wrought with hopelessness and fear, but who sits next to him quietly, occasionally looking up at Sevillas for assurance. Sevillas leans over to him and squeezes his shoulder. "Hang in there, champ."

Max looks at him gratefully as his body seems to unwind just a hair. "I'm trying," he whispers.

Langley suddenly poses a question that takes Sevillas's brain off automatic pilot.

"Can you describe the instrument used on Jonas Morrison's body on the day of his death?"

"Objection," says Sevillas. "Your Honor, again, the State has failed to produce any instrument they can claim is the alleged murder weapon. Any description by the witness would be mere speculation."

The judge casts a dark look from the bench. "Mr. Langley, I am in no mood to traverse this ground again. Has the State recovered the comb?"

A cranberry flush crawls up Langley's neck. "Your Honor, we are planning to put Officer Dougherty on the stand soon. He was the first officer on the scene, and he can clearly describe what the murder weapon looked like. Dr. Smythe, in any event, can describe the murder weapon based upon the nature and extent of the injuries he observed during the autopsy —"

The judge holds up her hand. Her face is a thundercloud. "Mr. Langley, you obviously did not hear my question. Do you or don't you have a murder weapon to show me?"

"N-not this instant, Judge," he stammers. "But —"

The judge shakes her head. "Unbelievable. No, Mr. Langley, I will not permit you to ask specific questions about a murder weapon you can't produce." She turns to the witness. "Dr. Smythe, you are free to testify as to your observations during the autopsy of the decedent. However —" she casts a sharp look at Langley "— there will be no reference by you to an item that has not been physically produced into evidence nor, it seems, is likely to be produced." She glares at both Sevillas and Langley. "This is not your finest hour, gentlemen."

"But Judge —" Langley begins.

"The witness may testify as to his opinion of what type of instrument might have caused the injuries he found, but that's it. If you want to go any further, find the evidence or put the proper witness on to testify to what he or she saw. You can't do it through this witness. Are we clear?"

"Yes, Your Honor." Langley sighs.

The judge motions for her court clerk. "And release the jury for the case this afternoon. It's clear we won't be hearing anything else today." She turns back to Langley. "Proceed."

"Dr. Smythe, would you please describe the injuries you observed on the body of Jonas Morrison when he was presented for autopsy?"

Smythe, in a black pinstripe suit with a white, starched shirt and a gray tie, lends an air of quiet authority. He adjusts his glasses and peers briefly at the report on his lap. "Late on the afternoon of June 20, I conducted the autopsy of Jonas James Morrison, a seventeen-year-old male. The first injuries I examined were numerous puncture wounds on the forearms, upper arms and thighs, and in the groin area of the decedent. There was bleeding from the nose and mouth, as well as petechial hemorrhaging in the whites of the eyes. The femoral artery and the femoral vein were both punctured."

Langley strides to the witness box. "Doctor, were you able to make a count of the number of puncture marks on the boy's body?"

Smythe looks up. "I counted approximately three hundred and fifty such marks."

A gasp goes through the courtroom. Sevillas turns to gauge the reaction. Marianne, in a somber suit, sobs. The reporters who have fought hard to win seats next to her have their arms around her, offering comfort. Mascara runs down her face like dark icing dripping down a white cake. When he turns back around, Judge Hempstead gives him a hard look.

Langley pauses to gaze at her sympathetically as he lets Smythe's comment sit for a moment. "How large would you say each puncture mark was, Doctor?"

Smythe takes off his glasses and rubs his eyes as if the mere act of counting all the wounds has given him eyestrain. "The punctures occurred in series of fives and were approximately one-eighth of an inch wide at the most narrow to one-fourth of an inch at the widest of the wounds."

"What do you mean, 'in series of fives'?"

"I mean that whatever object was used to puncture the flesh contained five prongs, and each prong was approximately one-eighth to one-fourth of an inch wide." He demonstrates by creating a space between each of his fingers. "Like so."

"So each time the instrument was thrust into the skin," Langley says slowly, "it left five wounds in a row?"

"That is correct."

Langley leans against the witness box. "Doctor, are you able to tell us anything more about the physical attributes of the object that caused these wounds?" Hempstead's eyes narrow as she listens for the response. Sevillas leans forward in his chair.

"I can say that it was at least four inches wide and was probably made of some kind of metal, given the clean cuts it made," says Smythe. "Also, given the depth of the wounds, I would say that it was probably six to eight inches long."

"Objection, Your Honor." Sevillas half rises. "That is more speculative than factual."

"True, but I'll allow it," she says. "I'm not the jury, Mr. Sevillas, and it seems to be a reasonable conclusion for the M.E. to draw from his observations. Proceed, Mr. Langley."

"Doctor, what did you determine was the cause of Jonas Morrison's death?"

"Many of the puncture wounds were superficial in nature. They alone would not have caused the boy's death. Unfortunately," he adds, "both the femoral artery and vein were punctured. Anatomically speaking, they are side by side in the groin.

Once these two were severed —" he makes a slicing motion with his hand "— there would have been a tremendous arterial spray. Just severing the femoral artery would have killed him, but certainly the combination of both the artery and vein being punctured are the primary causes of death."

There is a muffled moan from the front row of the courtroom. Marianne covers her face with her hands.

Langley pauses a moment, gives her a sympathetic glance and continues.

"Are these injuries you would commonly expect if the decedent had attempted to commit suicide?"

Smythe pauses. "No."

"And how long would it have taken for Jonas to die from these wounds?"

"Between five to ten minutes, given the severity of the femoral injuries."

Langley goes back to his table and picks up a stack of eight-by-ten glossy color photographs. With his back to the judge so the press corps is treated to a good, long look, he takes a moment to flip through the lurid photos of Jonas's partially nude, bloody body and the grotesque spray that covered the floor, walls and ceiling. Langley selects a few and hands them to Smythe. "Are these the photographs you took of the decedent at the crime scene?"

"Yes."

"We'd like to have these marked as State's Exhibit 1." Langley hands them to the clerk, who then hands them to the judge. She studies them, her mouth grim. Langley smiles at Sevillas as he walks over and places copies of the photographs on the defense table. "The State passes the witness."

Sevillas is surprised, and his face shows it. He had hoped Langley would do his usual ponderous job of leading the medical examiner through all the gory details of the autopsy. Then again, Langley doesn't have the time for it. The judge has told him he has to wrap up today, and Langley needs every minute so he can put on more damaging witnesses.

"Your Honor?" Sevillas stands. "May we have a fifteen-minute recess?"

The judge looks over her glasses at him. "I would prefer to press on at this juncture. We've had a number of breaks this morning."

"If you'll give me just a moment, I'll begin."

"Certainly, Mr. Sevillas."

He races through the notes he took on direct and decides on a course of action. Maybe he can drag this out long enough so the hearing has to go into tomorrow. He approaches the witness with a friendly smile. "Dr. Smythe."

The doctor returns his smile. "Good morning, Mr. Sevillas. It's nice to see you again."

"And you. Let's talk about these injuries for a moment," he says. "There are a number of points I'd like you to clarify for me."

"Of course."

"Were you able to observe the angle of the injuries on Jonas Morrison's body?"

"Yes, I was."

"Now, Doctor, is it possible that Jonas could have caused those injuries to himself?" He raises his hand. "Before you answer, I want you to understand something of this boy's psychiatric history, about which I believe we are all in agreement." He walks to the bench and looks up at the judge. "Jonas Morrison had a lifetime of psychiatric and behavioral problems. This young man was mentally retarded, autistic and had severe speech and language problems. Further, he had been engaged since early childhood in an established pattern of self-infliction of physical harm, which was a component of his psychiatric and cognitive disorders." Langley squints, as if this might help him formulate an appropriate objection. Sevillas goes on. "Jonas Morrison also had an established pattern of causing physical harm to himself by using various objects — including his own teeth and fingernails — which resulted in bloody wounds and numerous scars."

A murmur starts in the crowd. The judge casts a warning look, and silence falls once again.

"Given the decedent's history, Doctor," says Sevillas, "is it possible that the puncture wounds you observed could have been self-inflicted?" Sevillas takes the crime photos from a folder on the desk, but forgets that Max is sitting next to him. He rushes to the witness stand and hands them to Smythe, but not soon enough to evade Max's notice. The stricken look on the boy's face is almost more than he can bear.

Smythe studies the photographs. "I was informed that the decedent had these tendencies for self-abuse. And I must admit that I have considered at great length what impact this may have had on the wounds I observed after his death." He pauses. "I would like to preface what I say by noting that I have carefully studied the pertinent photographs and my autopsy notes on this issue. My answer is that yes, although it is highly unlikely, these wounds could have been self-inflicted. It is possible."

"Thank you, Doctor," Sevillas says quickly, avoiding the asphyxiation issue for the moment. "Now, onto another area. I see here that you admit you have never seen the alleged murder weapon Counsel has referred to — is that correct?"

"Yes."

"And if the police had managed to retain the object, a lab would have been able to identify whatever prints were on it. In turn, they could have confirmed whether those fingerprints matched those of the decedent and helped you ascertain if the comb was used by the decedent to cause his own death. Is that correct?"

Langley jumps up. "Your Honor! Objection — talk about calling for speculation. 'If he saw, he might . . .' "

"Withdrawn." Sevillas turns to the witness. "Doctor, isn't it true that if the alleged object were on the scene when you arrived, you would have been able to observe a ridge, or latent — if either were present — which the police could then compare to fingerprints of Jonas, my client or another third party?"

"It is, of course, possible to obtain fingerprints from a metal object under the proper circumstances."

"Let me ask you something else," says Sevillas. "Given that there was no object provided you by the police to compare to the wounds you observed, you did not have a means of determining if my client's fingerprints were present on such an object, did you?"

Smythe gives him a smile. "Of course not, Mr. Sevillas."

"And you found no latent fingerprints on the body?"

"No. That is very rare under the best of circumstances, and we are simply not equipped for that kind of analysis."

"Fine," says Sevillas. "Let me look at my notes. It says here that you established the primary cause of death as the severing of both the femoral artery and the femoral vein, correct?"

"Yes."

"Can you tell us why death would occur more quickly if both the artery and vein are punctured simultaneously?"

"Certainly," he says. "As I mentioned previously, puncturing the femoral artery causes a massive arterial spray, which would have resulted in death within about ten to fifteen minutes. However, by also puncturing the femoral vein, air then enters the vein from the outside and causes an embolism, which causes death to occur in mere minutes."

"I see. And what happens when an embolism occurs?"

Smythe leans back. "When both are punctured in the way I have described, the victim goes into shock and becomes unconscious. Although it is not possible to pinpoint the exact moment any given person will become unconscious by virtue of an autopsy, it is certain that death would take only a few minutes at most."

Sevillas walks the length of the judge's bench. "And what happens physically to the body after a person is unconscious and death occurs?"

"The lungs fail and the heart, although it is beating extremely fast, has no blood to pump because it all flows out of the wounds I mentioned earlier. This results in oxygen starvation and, usually, cardiac arrest and failure."

The courtroom is silent.

"Doctor, you also mentioned that the decedent had petechial hemorrhaging," says Sevillas. "What does that mean?"

The doctor shrugs. "It means that the autopsy revealed that the decedent had ruptured blood vessels in the eyes — and actually, in his face as well."

"Is this common?"

"Yes. It is evidence that someone has experienced a heart attack prior to death."

"So, it is your opinion that Jonas Morrison also sustained a heart attack before he died?"

"Yes."

"Doctor, would you expect to encounter petechial hemorrhaging in any other situation?"

Smythe looks up. "I'm not sure I understand what you are asking."

"Is petechial hemorrhaging invariably present when a decedent has been, let's say, asphyxiated?"

"Yes, of course."

"Let me ask you this," says Sevillas. "Since petechial hemorrhaging is typical of a strangulation victim and is also, according to you, a sign in this case that the Morrison boy suffered a heart attack as a result of an air embolism —" he pauses a moment "— how are we to know which caused the death of Jonas Morrison?"

Smythe raises an eyebrow. "An interesting question."

"In fact, Doctor, do you not agree with me that, given the angle of the wounds and other observations you have made — including that of extensive petechial hemorrhaging — you cannot tell us with absolute certainty whether the decedent's actual death was caused by his own self-inflicted wounds or whether he was killed by someone who might have severed the arteries, as well as asphyxiated him simultaneously?"

Smythe takes a deep breath. He then answers slowly and resolutely. "I cannot be absolutely certain whether the young man was killed only by the severing of the femoral artery and vein — which I said earlier could have been self-inflicted — but which now, as you so rightly explain, does not rule out the possibility of concomitant asphyxiation." He pauses. "It is possible that the death could also have resulted from the killer administrating the fatal puncture wounds in conjunction with the asphyxiation."

Sevillas sighs. "Thank you, Doctor. I have one more area of questioning, and then we'll let you go." He walks back to the defense table and picks up a stapled set of papers, which he then hands to Smythe. "Please take a look at these for me, would you?" While Smythe studies the documents, Sevillas takes a copy over to Langley.

He turns back to the witness. "Now, Dr. Smythe, do you recognize what has been put before you?"

Smythe flips the page over and looks up. "Yes, although I have not seen this document before."

"What is it?"

"It appears to be a toxicology report performed on a blood sample of one Max Parkman."

"Objection, Your Honor!" Langley is on his feet. "This has absolutely no relevance to this case and certainly should not be put in through this witness."

Hempstead motions impatiently for Sevillas's copy of the document. As she reads it, her expression is skeptical. "All right, Mr. Sevillas. I'm intensely curious to see how you purport to link this up."

Sevillas clasps his hands in front of him. "Your Honor, it has been suggested by other witnesses that Max Parkman had a history of violent behavior with the decedent and that he was increasingly labile during his stay at Maitland." He takes a deep breath. "Dr. Smythe is fully qualified to look at the toxicology report issued pursuant to Jonas Morrison's autopsy and to compare those results with what was in Max Parkman's blood, which we believe will give an entirely new meaning to the facts of this case."

"Keep talking, Mr. Sevillas," she says. "You're not there yet."

"It is the defense's contention that another suspect exists in this case — Maitland."

The courtroom is still. Langley is on his feet again. "Your Honor — this is preposterous!"

She waves him away. "Continue."

"We issued a subpoena for one Dr. Fastow of Maitland, the psychopharmacologist who gave Max Parkman and Jonas Morrison the same medication. And —" he pauses dramatically "— we will put on witnesses and show that this medication was experimental in nature and had graveside effects, which may explain many, if not all, of the behaviors of Max Parkman. In addition, we believe that it is entirely possible that Dr. Fastow had ample motive and opportunity to murder Jonas Morrison for fear that his actions would be discovered. It also would explain why Max was found in Jonas's room. Fastow was trying to set up Max to take the blame — or worse. It is entirely plausible that he planned to kill Max, too, but was scared off when he heard Ms. Parkman coming down the hallway."

The judge makes a note and then stares at him. "All that may be true, Mr. Sevillas, but you know very well that it isn't the M.E.'s specific area of expertise. If you want to introduce that report, you had better get

Dr. Fastow down here and quick. Mr. Langley has informed me that he has one final witness to put on today, and then you're up."

Sevillas shakes his head. "I can't do that, Judge."

"And why is that?"

"Because I subpoenaed him to appear this morning, and I just received word that he will not be coming to the courtroom."

The judge rubs her temples. "And why would that be, Mr. Sevillas?"

"It appears that Dr. Fastow has left the country. We believe that his flight bolsters our claim that he could well have been the murderer of Jonas Morrison. In fact, we are in the process of having criminal charges brought against him. This may be moot now that he has left the country, but if he is found, we will have him brought to justice."

Hempstead snaps her head toward the bailiff. "Get someone over to that hospital and find Dr. Fastow. Until then, this court is recessed. Dr. Smythe, stay close. It won't be long."

Chapter Thirty-Seven

As the airplane makes its approach into Des Moines, Danielle's nerves thrum. She is finally at the end of Marianne's CDs — a good thing, because her laptop is almost out of juice.

Dear Dr. Joyce,
Yesterday I was flipping through one of my psychiatric magazines and came across an article about the Maitland psychiatric hospital in Iowa. It's the *crème de la crème.* Eminent doctors from all over the world go there to explore cutting-edge methods of treating psychiatric and neurological disorders. Imagine conferring with that caliber of specialist — just thinking about it gives me goose bumps!

The application arrived today. Even though they asked for all of Jonas's medical and psychiatric records, I was selective. They don't need to know everything.

Here's where the rubber meets the road, as they say. All my years of research, experimentation and creation are culminating in this flash of brilliance. It's high time my intelligence is recognized. This will be my finest moment.

Carpe diem!

Danielle inserts the final CD into her laptop with trembling hands. This is Marianne's last record before she and Jonas went to Maitland. She hopes that Doaks has found additional evidence in Marianne's hotel room. What she has is damning, but it isn't murder. Not yet.

Dear Dr. Joyce,
Jonas is in! I couldn't be prouder than if he had been accepted at Harvard. It hasn't happened a moment too soon. Jonas has gone from rebellion to physical violence. Last night I sat down at my vanity table, looked myself in the mirror and admitted the simple fact that he's becoming a man. It certainly isn't anything I ever intended, because my other babies were taken from me so young. Now I'm forced to find a more creative solution. I have to give up any soft, motherly notions and get down to brass tacks. There's really only one

question: What kind of life will Jonas have when I'm gone? It's clear — none at all. I am also driven by the stark financial reality of the situation. If I am to live comfortably, I can't have Jonas continually draining my reserves. So I have planned everything down to the last detail. I'll be matching wits with the best minds in the world, and everything must be perfectly choreographed.

Maitland is my moment. I'll do what must be done.

CHAPTER THIRTY-EIGHT

"All rise!"

Shuffling feet scrape the linoleum floor like the rumblings of a dawn cattle call. The courtroom is packed to capacity now that word has leaked from the D.A.'s office that Marianne Morrison will be taking the stand. Langley organizes his notes as Marianne sits calmly in her front-row seat. Sevillas has given up on either Danielle or Doaks showing up in time. After the beating Sevillas has taken today, he is fed up with Langley's snide smirks.

Max and Georgia are back in the courtroom. Sevillas hopes that Georgia has managed to calm Max down. He leans over and puts an arm around the boy's thin shoulders. "Don't worry, son. I'll handle things until she gets here. I'm not bad at this, you know."

Max gives him a half smile. It's better than nothing. Georgia squeezes Max's hand from the other side. Sandwiched between them, he seems to be comforted.

"Counsel, please approach," says Hempstead. They stride to the bench. The judge looks at them over her steel-gray glasses. "Welcome back, gentlemen. By my watch, it is now two twenty-five. Mr. Langley, do you have an educated guess when we might conclude the festivities today?"

Langley bobs his head. "Yes, Your Honor. The State plans to call no more witnesses after Ms. Morrison, which will conclude our testimony on the proof-evident and bail aspects of the case." He casts a sly glance at Sevillas. "Of course, we can't speak for the defense."

"Counselor?"

Sevillas clears his throat. "Judge, as the District Attorney has managed to spend the entire day putting on his version of the evidence, it appears that the defense will not have the opportunity to put on its case until tomorrow."

Hempstead gives him an edgy look. "I don't see it that way at all, Mr. Sevillas. Now that I've been forced to postpone my other trial until tomorrow morning, I'm perfectly willing to go late into the evening. It seems to me that what you lack here is one of your defendants to put on the stand.

458

Or perhaps you would like to swear in young Mr. Parkman?"

Sevillas turns to look at Max. His eyes beg like those of a hungry child on a street corner. Sevillas walks back to the defense table. Max grabs his arm. "Tony, no!" he hisses. "I can't!" Sevillas gives him a comforting nod and turns to the judge. "We will not be putting Max Parkman on the stand."

"Very well, then. Mr. Langley, let's speed this up."

Langley shifts uncomfortably. "Your Honor, we're making every effort to be as brief and succinct as possible."

The judge taps her fingernails, as if the concept of a lawyer being succinct is as likely as her levitating from the bench and flying around the room. She nods dismissively. Both men return to their battle stations. "Let's play ball. Call your next witness."

Langley springs up. "The State calls Marianne Morrison to the stand." Max blanches. Sevillas watches as Langley makes a production out of helping her out of her chair and wrapping his arm around her shoulder, as if she lacks sufficient motor ability to propel herself forward. He leads her slowly to the witness stand. Marianne wears a black-and-white hounds-tooth suit, her hair sprayed into a severe helmet. Her white blouse is simple and professional. She stands before the bailiff, Bible in hand.

"Do you promise to tell the truth, the whole truth and nothing but the truth, so help you God?"

She looks at the judge. "I do." Her voice is clear. With that, she clasps her hands and mounts the steps to the witness stand.

"Ms. Morrison, could you give us some general information about yourself?"

Marianne smoothes her pageboy, which has not a hair out of place. "I'd be happy to. I was born in Pennsylvania. My father was a sergeant in the United States Army and my mother was a homemaker — just like me." She glances at the judge. "Once I married, I devoted my life to making a happy home for my husband and, after that, for Jonas. My husband was a physician until he passed away."

"Now, Ms. Morrison, was Jonas your only child?"

Marianne's eyes look as if someone has poured thimblefuls of water into them. Whole droplets glide down her cheeks. She pulls a simple lace square from her skirt and dabs at each eye. "Yes, Mr. Langley." Her voice quivers. "Jonas was the only baby I ever had. He was the light of my life, my only reason for living after my husband was taken from me."

Langley heaves a theatrical sigh. Sevillas's stomach threatens to drop low in his gut.

"Ms. Morrison," asks Langley, "could you give us a thumbnail sketch of your life with Jonas?"

Marianne clasps her handkerchief. "Well, after my husband passed away, I raised Jonas all by myself. God knows it wasn't easy — it never is for any widow — but I suppose you could say that my situation was a bit more . . . involved. My poor boy had his share of difficulties. He was mentally challenged, autistic, and did not speak well." She manages a small smile. "But somehow we muddled through, just the two of us."

"Would you call yourself a devoted mother?"

Marianne raises sad, blue eyes. "I don't customarily engage in self-aggrandizement, Mr. Langley. But I have to say that if there's one thing I've done well, it's to be the best mother I could be. Children are a gift, not a burden. Even with all of Jonas's problems, I can honestly say that being his mother has been the greatest honor and blessing of my life." Eyes brimming, she casts a pained glance at Hempstead, who gives her a

461

sympathetic nod and hands her a box of tissues.

Langley gives her a few moments to collect herself. "Now, Ms. Morrison, could you
tell us the circumstances which led you and
Jonas to Maitland?"

Marianne draws a deep breath. "Certainly.
As you may know, I attended Johns Hopkins
and am a medical doctor myself. I think
every mother of a special-needs child owes
it to that child to remain at the forefront of
all possible treatment and medication protocols." She continues in an earnest voice. "I
also made a point of identifying those doctors who specialize in autism and other
neurological disorders. During my studies, I
came across Maitland and decided that if
anyone could help my boy, it would be
them."

"Ms. Morrison," says Langley. "I know
that the rest of our discussion today will be
extremely painful for you, but I want to
begin at the point when you and Jonas arrived at Maitland."

Marianne sets her mouth. The judge's face
mirrors her expression. Not a sound comes
from the courtroom, as if the spectators
have voted on collective silence. Sevillas
picks up his pen.

"What was your impression of Maitland

when you first arrived?" asks Langley.

"I was introduced to Dr. Ebhart Hauptmann, the chief psychiatrist. We discussed Jonas's problems, and I felt certain he was in good hands." She leans toward the judge, a confused look on her face. "Your Honor?"

"Yes, Ms. Morrison?"

"I am reluctant to discuss whether the hospital adequately cared for Jonas, because my lawyer advised me not to."

"That's fine, Ms. Morrison." Hempstead turns to Langley. "I believe the witness has answered the question, hasn't she, Mr. Langley? Perhaps you could move on to something else."

Langley nods. "Certainly, Your Honor. Ms. Morrison, did you spend much time with Jonas after he was admitted to Maitland?"

"Of course I did. I only left the hospital to eat and sleep." She turns to the judge. "I couldn't stand to leave my baby alone."

"And would you say you spent more time with Jonas than any other mother with a child on the unit?"

"I certainly did."

"And during Jonas's stay, did you have occasion to meet the defendant, Ms. Parkman?"

"Yes."

"Can you explain the circumstances of your first meeting with Ms. Parkman and how your relationship, if any, developed from that point on?"

"Well, I noticed that Ms. Parkman and I were staying at the same hotel and that our children were on the same unit, so I introduced myself. You know," she says in a confidential tone, "there is a certain bond between mothers who have children with special needs. We understand each other's pain and are uniquely situated to comfort and support one another."

"Please go on, Ms. Morrison."

"I was naive, I suppose. I always look for the good in people, and I thought Danielle was such a wonderful woman." She looks earnestly at the judge. "She seemed devoted to her son — as I was — and I made a concerted effort to befriend her and Max."

Langley moves forward. "What do you mean by that?"

Sevillas freezes. Here it comes.

Marianne shakes her head. "It was just so obvious the poor woman had so much to bear. Max was severely psychotic and violent —"

Max jumps to his feet. "You're a liar!"

Sevillas shoves Max down into his chair and jumps up. "Objection! Are we now going to let the mother of the decedent give an expert opinion on my client's mental health?" He gives Marianne a warning look. She smiles back politely.

"Counsel, control your client. And Ms. Morrison," says the judge gently. "Our rules of evidence do not permit you to comment upon the psychiatric condition of the defendant. Perhaps you could just tell us what you observed."

"Well," Marianne says, "I do think I'm qualified to provide an opinion, given my background, but, of course, Your Honor, I'll do whatever you tell me to." She turns back to Langley, who is poised to rephrase his question.

"Ms. Morrison, how often did you see Ms. Parkman once you made her acquaintance?"

"We spent a considerable amount of time together on a daily basis. We often went to lunch or dinner together. Of course, I was very busy with Dr. Hauptmann and the other doctors, orienting them to Jonas's various disorders."

"Would you say that the two of you became friends?"

Marianne looks at Hempstead, who peers at her over her glasses. "In my opinion, we became very good friends in a short period of time." Her blue eyes appear open and honest. "Here was this woman, so sweet, caring and intelligent — and also a lawyer — that I trusted her implicitly. When Max became so psychotic, Danielle really began to unravel —"

Max jumps to his feet. "That's not true!"

The judge raps her gavel sharply. "Bailiff, remove Mr. Parkman from the courtroom. I've had enough of his outbursts."

"But Your Honor!" says Sevillas.

Hempstead holds up her hand as Max is escorted by the bailiff outside the courtroom. Georgia follows them. The judge then turns to Marianne. "And Mrs. Morrison, please try to limit your testimony to the facts, not your opinion of the defendant's psychiatric problems."

"Please forgive me, Your Honor," she says quickly. "It won't happen again."

Hempstead nods at Langley to continue.

"Could you describe a typical day at Maitland for us?"

Marianne holds a water glass to her pink lips and takes a sip. "Well, I arrived every day at seven o'clock. That way, I could catch Dr. Hauptmann on his morning rounds and get an update on Jonas. After we conferred, I would take Jonas to the cafeteria for breakfast. Then we'd come back, sit on the couch and visit." She looks at the judge.

"Typically, Danielle would not arrive until after nine. Then I would bring her up to date on what was going on with Max. . . ."

Langley looks at her in mock surprise. "You would bring Ms. Parkman up to date on her own son?"

Marianne nods. "Well, of course. For whatever reason, the doctors had banned Danielle from seeing her son except for short visits twice a day, while I had free access to Jonas. So when she finally came in, I'd let her know how Max looked, what he was doing — that kind of thing."

Sevillas stares at his legal pad.

"And then?"

"Then Danielle and I would sit and have a cup of coffee."

"Where was Jonas during this time?"

"Next to me, of course."

"And Max Parkman?"

"In the beginning, he sat across from Danielle, but later he was almost always in his room." She turns to the judge. "I won't say what kind of psychiatric problems that child has, because you told me not to, but just let me say that he was on enormous amounts of psychotropic medication."

Hempstead waves Sevillas off. "Go on, Ms. Morrison."

"Max slept a lot during the day," she says.

"My understanding from the nurses is that he was up all night ranting and then required sedation. I'm sure that's why he was so tired —"

"Objection again, Your Honor!" Sevillas stands. "Is it possible for the witness to tell us only what she observed instead of relying on hearsay to speculate upon Max Parkman's activities?"

"Judge," says Langley, the word dripping in innocence, "please forgive Mrs. Morrison. She's just trying to answer as fulsomely as possible." He turns to Marianne. "Only your actual observations, please, Mrs. Morrison."

Marianne nods, chastened. "I'm so sorry."

"Let's move on to something else." Langley's eyes remind Sevillas of a cockroach scuttling across the floor. "Please relate your specific observations of the interactions between Max Parkman and your son."

Marianne straightens her skirt. "Let's see. Given the amount of time they spent with us, Jonas naturally tried to befriend them." Her face brightens. "Jonas was such a warm, loving boy, a true innocent. He loved people. Just a heart of gold, that's all." Hempstead gives her a commiserating look. "Jonas actually became quite attached to Max." She sighs. "From the beginning, Max was very unkind in the way he rejected Jonas's overtures. I could tell that for some unknown reason, Max hated Jonas."

"Judge, this is preposterous." Sevillas stalks toward the bench. "Now she's testifying about how my client felt!"

Langley's voice is as mild as milk. "No, Tony, she's testifying about what she thought your client was feeling."

The judge rolls her eyes. "That's enough. Mr. Langley, help the witness by asking more specific questions. And Mr. Sevillas," she says equably, "understand that I'm going to allow the State considerable latitude with this witness. Remember that I am perfectly capable of sifting out proper from improper testimony. You're just going to have to trust me on that."

Sevillas would rather hand over his newborn to the antichrist. "Yes, Judge."

She turns again to Sevillas. "And I'd like to remind you, Counselor, that if your other client were here, she would be able to give us her own observations about the relationship between her son and the decedent, now wouldn't she?"

Sevillas gives a curt nod and sits down. *Goddammit.* Danielle is lucky she isn't here right now. He'd like nothing better than to feed her whole to Hempstead. There is a slight rustle as Georgia guides Max back to his seat. Sevillas is so intent upon the questioning that he barely notices.

"Ms. Morrison," Langley intones, "is it true that Max Parkman was in regular contact with your son?"

Marianne nods. "That is correct. Danielle and I spent so much of our time together, of course I trusted her to monitor Max and Jonas." Her eyes begin to tear again as she turns to Hempstead. "You don't know how many times every day now I wish I hadn't been so trusting."

Langley's face emotes practiced concern. "And what did you actually observe take place between Max and Jonas during the times they were together?"

"In the beginning," she says, "Max seemed to ignore Jonas's overtures to be friendly. As Max became progressively psy—" She turns to Hempstead. "I'm sorry, Your Honor. Max became increasingly hostile toward Jonas."

"In what way?"

She gives him a sorrowful look. "I personally witnessed a few such events, each more troubling than the last. It all started with Jonas trying to be friendly with Max — you know, sitting beside him, showing him a toy, that kind of thing. As the days progressed,

Max grew increasingly irritated and slapped Jonas when he thought no one was looking. I told Danielle about it, but she denied that Max would do such a thing." A ragged sob breaks from her. "If only I had believed my son instead of Danielle. But how was I to know that she was so terribly frightened of the change in Max's behavior that she would lie to protect him?"

Langley nods sympathetically and hands her another tissue. "And what was the worst of these episodes?"

Marianne daubs at streaks of mascara that slide down her cheeks. "It's so hard for me to talk about. One morning, Jonas, Danielle, Max and I were in the TV room. It was very peaceful. I was knitting, and Jonas was holding my yarn for me. As usual, Max was asleep on the sofa. At some point, Danielle stepped out to smoke a cigarette, something she did quite often. Jonas went over to Max and gently woke him up. When Jonas tried to give him a simple hug, Max went berserk. He jumped up, screamed at Jonas, and then bashed his head against the top of the coffee table. . . ." Her voice catches. After a moment's struggle, she continues. "Of course, there wasn't a single nurse or orderly there . . ."

Sevillas makes a note. *Building her civil*

case against hospital.

". . . so I rushed over to Jonas, and there he was — screaming on the floor with his head split wide open and blood everywhere, while Max beat him until he broke his ribs." She breaks down, her head in her hands.

Max shoots to his feet, his face a mottled red. "She's a liar! That's not how it happened!"

Sevillas yanks him back, but not before the judge spears him with a look as black as ground charcoal. "Mr. Sevillas! You will control your client or I'll have him taken into custody. We are dealing with a grieving mother here. If you want to put Mr. Parkman on the stand, I'll be happy to question him myself." She peers down at Max. "And you will remain completely silent for the rest of this proceeding, or I will have you removed again. Is that clear?"

Max's eyes widen, and he nods furiously. "Yes, Your Honor."

Sevillas half stands. "No, Your Honor, that won't be necessary." He sits down and places a very firm hand on Max's arm. Max still looks as if he's ready to explode. Sevillas leans over and whispers in his ear. "*Be quiet.* Do you want them to think you're the lunatic they say you are?" Max scowls at Sevillas. He crosses his arms and slides down in his seat.

Langley walks up to the witness stand, puts his arm around Marianne's shoulder and pats it gently. When she finally rallies, he walks back to the podium. "Mrs. Morrison, can you tell us what happened then?"

She nods. "I'll try. After that, nurses and orderlies came from everywhere. They pulled Max off of Jonas — with Max ranting about Jonas wanting to kill him. That horrible Naomi girl was there, too, egging Max on. A staff member had to drag her away. Dwayne, the strongest orderly, was the only one who could handle Max. He was screaming and cursing, kicking and biting. It was as if he had gone completely mad. I honestly don't know how Dwayne managed to get him back into his room." She draws a deep breath. "Only then did the nurse try to treat my poor Jonas for his wounds, but they were so serious that he had to go to the hospital for stitches and X-rays of his ribs." She raises her eyes to the sympathetic audience. "The only reason I permitted Jonas to stay on the same ward with that boy is because they assured me that Max would never come in contact with Jonas again — and because Danielle promised me she would do everything in her power to have Max moved to another ward."

Max shoves Sevillas a hastily scribbled note: *She's nuts!* Sevillas shakes his head in amazement. Marianne is just making it up as she goes along.

Langley preens to the press and then turns back to Marianne. "Are you aware of any other violent episodes between Max and Jonas?"

"Not that I saw." She looks down. "But later, well, after I spoke with the nurses, and they told me something I wasn't aware of."

"Such as?"

Sevillas stands. "Objection — hearsay."

The judge barely gives him a glance. "You may cross-examine. Go on, Ms. Morrison."

"Well, apparently Max had broken his mother's compact and threatened Jonas with one of the glass shards."

Sevillas grips Max's shoulder — hard. "Don't even think about it," he hisses. Max gives him a malevolent look, but stays in his seat.

"Anything else, Ms. Morrison?"

"One of the nurses told me she could tell what a difference a good mother made when she looked at Jonas and how she couldn't understand how Danielle could remain in denial of her own son's terrible mental problems —"

"Fine." Langley cuts her off as he glances nervously at Sevillas. "Did you personally observe any behavior on the part of Ms. Parkman that you would call unusual?"

"Yes, I'm afraid I did."

"Can you describe such an instance for us?"

"I'll do my best." She turns toward the judge as if they're having coffee and biscotti at Starbucks. "One day, Danielle and I were sitting outside. Out of the blue, she asked me the oddest question." The judge's gaze is rapt. "She said, 'Marianne, do you have any experience with hospital computer systems?' I told her that during my years of residency and nursing, I became quite proficient at working with computers. She asked me a lot of questions about firewalls, passwords, security — that kind of thing. I thought she was just making conversation. Then she sat very still for a moment; looked me straight in the eyes; and said: 'What do you know about Maitland's computer system?' I said, 'What do you mean?' She got this very strange look in her eyes, and I felt the hair stand straight up on the back of my neck. Then she told me she wanted to break into Maitland's computer system."

The judge's eyes widen. Langley is Sylvester the Cat with Tweety's tail feathers dangling out of his mouth. "Why did she want to do that?"

"Objection — hearsay." Sevillas's voice is rote. He knows Hempstead will overrule him. She does so with a wave of her hand.

Marianne's eyes are clear blue. "She was desperate to retrieve whatever logs or notes the staff had recorded about Max. She was convinced that the entire hospital staff was fabricating his symptoms." She shakes her head sadly. "Of course, I told her not only no, but absolutely no. I'm afraid I was a bit harsh with her, Judge. I informed her that, for better or worse, I have a very strong moral code and could never be party to such a thing."

Sevillas closes his eyes and wonders if it will ever end.

"What happened then?"

Marianne shrugs. "She told me she intended to have those records and that if I wouldn't help her, she'd do it herself."

"And to your knowledge, did Ms. Parkman in fact hack into the Maitland computer system?"

"I have to assume she did," Marianne says calmly. "Later that week, she told me that she had looked at Max's records and just knew that the hospital, for whatever reason, was falsifying them."

476

Hempstead raises her eyebrows and casts a glance Sevillas's way. He does not react. Langley presses on. "Did you learn anything else?"

Marianne looks directly at Hempstead. "She told me that after she read the reports, she got furious. Then she told me that she went back to his records — and changed them."

Sevillas shakes his head. She's lying through her teeth — he's sure of that — but he doesn't have a witness, much less a client, to rebut her. It makes his skin crawl. He glances at Georgia, who seems to be having as difficult a time remaining silent as Max is. She gives him a sympathetic look. She knows that when you get slammed, you get slammed and go on.

Langley walks slowly in front of the judge. "She altered professional psychiatric records of her son?"

"That's certainly what she told me."

"Did you ask her why she would do such a thing?"

Marianne looks at him with troubled eyes. "Frankly, Mr. Langley, I was a bit afraid to delve into it too deeply. She seemed so, well, disturbed."

Langley casts a warning look, and Marianne stops. "Thank you, Mrs. Morrison."

Sevillas watches as Langley pulls something from a large, brown envelope. Before he realizes it, he is standing, an objection on his lips. Before he can speak, Langley yanks something made of metal the rest of the way out of the envelope and holds it above his head, right in front of Marianne. She recoils and gasps as Sevillas leaps forward.

"Judge!" he yells. "Objection! Whatever that is, it has not been properly introduced as evidence. The State has produced no murder weapon, and they're not entitled to start waving things around the courtroom without prior disclosure —"

"Judge, we have no intention of doing anything that violates the court's order."

A tropical disturbance forms on Hempstead's face. "Approach." When they stand before her, she leans forward and says in a stage whisper, "Just what are you trying to pull here, Mr. Langley?"

"Nothing, Your Honor. We have no intention of asking Ms. Morrison whether or not this is the murder weapon. We merely want to establish that she has seen a comb like this in the possession of the defendants at one time or another."

Sevillas barks out a short laugh. "Oh, right, Judge." He holds out his arms expansively. "Let's just wave it around — whatever it is — without laying any foundation or establishing a chain of custody. He hasn't even shown it to the M.E. to ascertain if it even remotely resembles their alleged murder weapon. In the meantime, he's prejudicing the hell out of my clients."

Hempstead looks keenly at Langley. "Are you claiming that this object is in fact the murder weapon you say was found at the scene?"

"No, Your Honor, we're not."

"Have you found the object you're claiming was used in the alleged murder?"

Langley shakes his head. "We haven't exactly located it yet, but this comb is just like the one in Ms. Parkman's possession."

"And how do we know that?"

"Because we went to the same beauty parlor where Ms. Parkman got her hair done, and the stylist gave us this comb and told us it was exactly the same one she sold to the defendant." He stops for breath.

Sevillas slaps a palm on the bench. "Your Honor, so what if he says this one is supposed to 'look like' whatever comb they say they found at the scene? The fact remains that they've produced no comb, and now they're trying to prejudice my client by introducing this one into evidence through the back door. Our objection stands."

Hempstead looks at the comb and clears her throat. "Mr. Sevillas, ordinarily I would sustain your objection as well-founded. If we were in front of a jury, I would agree that the possibility of prejudice is high indeed." She turns to Langley. "However, we are not involved in a trial, but in an evidentiary proceeding. I am, as I have repeatedly stated, very capable of separating wheat from chaff without danger of prejudice. I will permit you to follow this line of questioning." Langley's face breaks into an expression of relief. "However, I will terminate this entire inquiry if you attempt — even once — to imply that the comb you have in your hand is in any way related to the injuries of Jonas Morrison." She shakes a warning finger at him. "Are we clear?"

He nods vigorously. "Of course, Judge."

Sevillas turns on his heel without even bothering to acknowledge the judge's ruling. He stalks back and throws his pen on top of his legal pad. Max's face is still the same shade of powder white it was when Langley dropped the murder weapon. This time when Sevillas sits down it is Max who grasps his hand.

Langley returns to the witness box and thrusts the comb in front of her. "Ms. Morrison, I have here an object marked as Exhibit C, which I would appreciate your identifying."

Marianne sees the comb at close range and clutches her throat. A small cry escapes from her. "Oh!" she gasps. "Is that — ?"

Langley interrupts her quickly and firmly. "I must ask you not to make any comments unrelated to my specific questions about this object. Can you do that?"

Marianne flushes a pretty shade of pink. "Yes, well, I'll try . . ."

"Ms. Morrison, what do you see before you?"

"Why, it's a comb, Mr. Langley."

"Have you ever seen a comb like this before?"

"I most certainly have."

"Where?"

"I've seen one exactly like that at Maitland."

"And whose was it, to your knowledge?"

"It was Danielle's."

"How do you know that?"

"Well, she kept it in her purse, and I saw her use it on numerous occasions." She turns to the judge. "She got a permanent wave right after she put Max in Maitland, Your Honor." She pauses. "I saw her use it all the time."

Langley walks slowly toward the defense table. He stops there and crosses his arms. "Ms. Morrison, I want to thank you for coming here today and giving us testimony that was difficult and painful for you. I just have one more question. Are you aware that part of the reason we're here today is because Ms. Parkman has requested that she remain out on bail before her trial?"

Sevillas starts to his feet, but Hempstead is way ahead of him. "Mr. Langley, given that the defendant has clearly violated the terms of her bond, I hardly think that is still at issue here."

"I have another reason for asking the question, Your Honor."

Hempstead looks at Marianne and then at the lawyers. "Mr. Langley, this is where I draw the line. If the witness is planning to testify to facts about the alleged murder which are not in evidence in order to provide an opinion on bail — which Mr. Sevillas has correctly pointed out is not her decision to make — I can't see how any opinion she would give is relevant."

"Your Honor, this testimony has nothing to do with that. It relates to an event personally experienced by the witness which bears directly upon the proof-evident portion of this hearing."

The judge gives him a skeptical look. "All right, I'll let you begin, but the minute you try to slip anything under the door, I'll cut you off so fast it'll make your head spin. Understood?"

Sevillas shakes his head and sits down. *Is there anything she won't let in?*

Langley takes a deep breath and turns to Marianne. "Now, Ms. Morrison, can you explain to the judge what you told me for the first time this morning?"

Marianne has been glued to this exchange like a tennis fan at the U.S. Open. "Yes, I certainly can. I hate to bring this up, Your Honor, but other than what has befallen my son — which is the tragedy of my life — Ms. Parkman has also said and done things to me that make me certain she is a dangerous and violent person."

"Objection, Your Honor!" Sevillas bellows. "This is rank speculation, not fact. This line of questioning should be terminated immediately. It's nothing but a gratuitous attempt to let the mother of the deceased get in another jab —"

"Mr. Sevillas!" Hempstead's voice is harsh. "I hardly think it appropriate to characterize Ms. Morrison's testimony as 'getting jabs in.' Don't forget that she has recently lost her son in a most heinous fashion."

"I know, Judge, but —"

"No buts." She turns to Marianne and speaks in a kindly voice. "Ms. Morrison, I'd like to ask you about the underlying facts you are referring to, not the opinion you formed from them. Perhaps you can explain it to me, as the State seems incapable of clarifying that for you."

"Well," she says. "One day, right before the murder, Danielle and I were having dinner. She drank far too much vodka, so I offered to drive her home. When we got back to the hotel, she got out of the car and stumbled. She seemed disoriented and then, for no reason, she flew into a rage and started accusing me of lying about Max. She even had her arm raised to hit me —"

"Your Honor!" Sevillas can't take any more. Furious, he strides to the bench. His voice is cold, measured. "This witness is lying!"

"Mr. Sevillas, stop immediately!" Hempstead cracks her gavel and gives him a livid glare. "There will be no testifying by counsel in my courtroom! You wait until cross — or until that elusive day when you can produce your other client — or I'll hold you in contempt right now."

Sevillas is beyond caring. The case is in

484

the ditch. He turns to Marianne, his voice ice shards. "I will, Your Honor, but it is unconscionable that this woman would so blatantly lie and turn on a woman who did nothing but show her the kindness of a friend —"

Marianne's eyes blaze. "I never lie." She turns to the judge and bursts into tears. "Her son killed my baby, Your Honor. Murdered him right in his own hospital bed. It's too late for Jonas, but I know now — without a shadow of a doubt — that Max didn't fall far from his mother's tree." She casts a beseeching look at the onlookers. "Oh, dear Lord, won't someone help me?"

The judge's face is contorted with wrath. She points her gavel at Sevillas. "You are now officially in contempt of this court. I will decide what happens to you after the hearing."

Sevillas says nothing. He takes his seat and glares at Marianne.

"Now." Hempstead puts her gavel down. "I am going to take over the questioning. Mrs. Morrison, I'd like you to tell me if Max Parkman ever threatened you with bodily harm."

Marianne looks directly at the reporters in the front row. She turns back to the judge, her eyes a midnight blue. "One day, a week before the murder, I was on the sofa knitting a sweater for Jonas, and Max suddenly pulled something that glinted like metal from his pocket."

The onlookers gasp and gape at Max. Tony clasps Max's wrist until he sees his fist unclench. The judge nods soberly. "And then?"

Marianne's eyes are as wide as plates. "Then he brandished it over my head."

The judge tries to hide her shock. "Were you alone with Mr. Parkman when this happened?"

"Unfortunately, yes." Marianne shakes her head. "By the time I recovered from my shock, Max had run to a different part of the unit."

"Surely you reported this."

"Of course I did," she says. "But apparently the video monitors were malfunctioning that day, and I had no real evidence to offer the staff. It was his word against mine."

Hempstead's eyes cloud. "Surely they believed you over a psychiatric patient?"

She shrugs sadly. "They searched throughout the unit, including Max's room and his clothing. The item was nowhere to be found."

"Did you tell his mother?"

"Of course I did." Her white hand touches

her forehead as if to quell a throbbing headache. "She said that I must have been mistaken."

"Did you ask the staff to take additional precautions after this incident?"

"Yes, Your Honor, I did, but I don't think they took me seriously."

Hempstead nods and writes something slowly on her legal pad. She looks up at Marianne. "And after that?"

"After that," Marianne says simply, "Max wasn't violent with Jonas." She gives the press another pained glance. "Until he murdered my son, that is."

Langley jumps up before Sevillas can object. "Pass the witness."

CHAPTER THIRTY-NINE

Judge Hempstead turns to Sevillas. "Do you wish to cross-examine?"

Sevillas takes a last backward glance at the courtroom door. Max's terrified eyes meet his. There's no doubt now. Sevillas is on his own. "I certainly do, Your Honor."

She looks at her watch. "I have four forty-seven. As it appears that this is taking much longer than anticipated, let me clarify the state of events for the record." She turns to Langley. "The State has completed calling witnesses for today, correct?"

"Yes, Your Honor."

"Proceed, Mr. Sevillas."

Sevillas approaches the witness. As he opens his mouth to ask his first question, there is a commotion behind him. All eyes turn as Danielle, dressed in an elegant suit, walks down the aisle. Doaks and Lieutenant Barnes — Doaks's former partner on the force — follow in her wake. Max jumps up from the defense table and runs the few short steps to her. Danielle embraces him tightly. The joy in his face is electric, his eyes liquid with relief. "I'm here, honey," she whispers. "I love you."

"I love you, too, Mom." Max doesn't bother to wipe the tears from his face as he sits down. Danielle bends for a brief kiss on Georgia's cheek and meets Sevillas's eyes. He looks angry but relieved. She walks toward the bench, but before she makes it to the bar, Judge Hempstead cracks her gavel. "Silence!" She regards Danielle and her entourage with ire. "And who might we have here?"

"Your Honor, I am Danielle Parkman." She glances at Sevillas. His expression is somewhere between fury and relief.

Hempstead's mouth is a razor slice. "Well, well, the phantom defendant. Approach, Ms. Parkman."

"Yes, Your Honor."

"Bailiff," Hempstead says curtly, "place Ms. Parkman in custody."

"Judge," protests Danielle, "please let me explain . . ."

Hempstead points the gavel at her. "I will do no such thing, Ms. Parkman. You are a criminal defendant in my court who has committed a felony by violating every

489

condition of bond. You are hereby remitted to the county jail." She turns to the bailiff. "Cuff her."

Danielle catches Marianne's satisfied look as the bailiff approaches, handcuffs in hand. "Your Honor, I understand your perfectly justifiable response to my actions, but I must move that I be permitted to cross-examine this witness. I have crucial evidence that goes directly to —"

Hempstead leans over her bench as the bailiff snaps the handcuffs on Danielle's wrists. "I don't care if you have evidence that the world is flat, Ms. Parkman. You are hereby remanded to be incarcerated until your trial. As an attorney and an officer of this court, you had full knowledge that your actions would lead to immediate revocation of your bond. What you do not appear to comprehend is that you, in addition to your son, are now also an accused felon who has flouted the laws of this state and the express orders of this Court." There is steel in her voice. "You are not in New York, Ms. Parkman. You are in *my* courtroom under *my* jurisdiction."

Sevillas casts her a look that says he is powerless. Max stares at her, petrified. The bailiff puts his hand on her shoulder. Danielle pulls back. "Judge, I move that I be allowed to appear before this court in my own defense."

Hempstead gives her a poisonous look. "You are already represented by counsel." She points at Sevillas. "Any questions posed on your behalf will be through your designated attorney."

The bailiff grasps her arm. Danielle takes another step toward the bench, her voice firm. "Your Honor, I believe my counsel has a motion to make."

Sevillas glances up in alarm. Danielle meets his eyes. After a moment he shakes his head.

"Apparently your counsel disagrees, Ms. Parkman." She nods at the bailiff.

Danielle draws herself up. "Mr. Sevillas makes a motion to withdraw as my counsel, Your Honor."

Hempstead looks at Sevillas with surprise. "Is that so, Mr. Sevillas?"

Sevillas stares bullets at Doaks, who nods vigorously from the front row. He locks eyes with Danielle. There it is — they click. Sevillas turns to Hempstead. "Your Honor, I respectfully move to withdraw as counsel for Ms. Parkman."

A nanosecond elapses. "Motion denied."

Sevillas and Danielle exchange a quick look before he turns back to the judge.

"With all due respect, Your Honor, I'm afraid I must withdraw in any event."

Hempstead's eyes blaze. "Must I remind you that you are already in contempt of this court?"

"No, Your Honor."

She turns to Danielle, her lips tight with fury. "I cannot force you to retain counsel, Ms. Parkman, but get one thing straight. The remainder of this hearing will be conducted in strict accordance with the law and the rules. The minute you cross the line, I'm going to shut this thing down. And don't bother attempting to convince me you are worthy of bond. When the hearing is concluded, you go straight to jail. Your bond is hereby revoked."

She turns to the bailiff. "Remove the handcuffs from Ms. Parkman." The bailiff quickly inserts his key. Danielle rubs her wrists. "Now, place them on Mr. Sevillas and take him to the holding cell."

"Your Honor —" says Danielle.

"Prepare to cross-examine the witness, Ms. Parkman."

Danielle watches helplessly as Sevillas holds up his wrists to be shackled and is led away. As she turns to the defense table, she catches another glimpse of Max. The fear in his eyes as Sevillas is marched away is not something she can do anything about — not yet.

"Ms. Parkman." Hempstead's voice is crisp, cold. "Proceed."

Danielle turns and motions to Doaks, who struggles to the defense table with a large file box. Danielle removes the lid, extracts a sheaf of papers, takes a deep breath, and turns to the witness. "Ms. Morrison, I have a few background questions for you."

Marianne eyes her confidently, her voice cool. "Of course, Ms. Parkman."

"Where were you born?"

"In Pennsylvania."

"Not Texas?"

"No." Her eyes are clear.

"Where were you raised?"

She sighs. "My father was in the military. I was raised all over the United States."

"Have you ever lived in Vermont?"

"No."

"Florida?"

"No."

"Illinois?"

The slightest beat of hesitation. "No."

"Thank you." Danielle flips through the documents. "Now, Ms. Morrison, how many times did you say you were married?"

She folds her hands primly. "Once."

"To whom?"

"Raymond Morrison."

"Never married before?"

"No."

"Ever have other children?"

Her gaze is clear. "No."

Danielle walks slowly to the witness box. "No other children, is that right?"

"Your Honor," Langley whines. "Asked and answered. I do think Ms. Morrison would remember if she had any other children." A titter ripples through the courtroom.

"I'll be happy to move on, Judge," she says. "Ms. Morrison, have you ever experienced any chronic physical conditions?"

Marianne fixes the judge with a pained look. "I've suffered from a variety of illnesses in my life. I haven't spoken about it here because I think it's inappropriate."

"Perhaps you could give us a brief summary?" asks Danielle.

Marianne colors. "I wouldn't know where to begin."

"Have you been hospitalized for these conditions?"

"Oh, yes."

"How many times?"

"Too many to count."

"Would you say sixty-eight is an accurate number?"

A gasp comes from the crowd. Before Langley can intervene, Marianne laughs. "That is ridiculous."

"Do you have evidence of this assertion, Ms. Parkman?" asks Hempstead.

"I'm getting there, Your Honor."

"Not that I can see."

Danielle walks to the defense table. Doaks has taken Sevillas's chair and hands her a notepad he has pulled from his battered briefcase. "Have you ever been diagnosed as having any psychological problems?"

"Your Honor," says Langley. "The mental condition of this poor woman is completely irrelevant to the murder charges brought against the defendant. We strongly object to any attempt on the part of the defense to impugn this woman's character."

The judge gives Danielle a disapproving look. "Ms. Parkman, I intend to give you the same latitude I have afforded the State all day — which you obviously were not here to observe — but I agree that the physical and mental condition of the witness is irrelevant to the charges leveled against your son — and you." She points her gavel at Langley. "The State has a running objection to all questions posed by Ms. Parkman. I will ensure that her questions are appropriate. Save us time, Mr. Langley, and keep your seat."

Danielle's voice is calm. "Judge, as I am certain that both my mental state and that of my son have been put into question on direct, I believe it only fair that this witness, the mother of a disturbed child, be subjected to the same line of inquiry."

Hempstead frowns. "It's your time, Ms. Parkman, but if you choose to waste it, I will shut you down. Understood?"

"Yes, Your Honor."

Langley makes a big show of turning to the reporters and shaking his head. They scribble on their pads. Danielle turns back to Marianne. "Could you answer the question, please?"

"I have never had any psychological problems."

"Have you ever been told that you suffer from a psychological condition?"

"Absolutely not," she replies haughtily. "I bear my troubles privately and rely upon the grace of the good Lord to get me through." She gives the judge an offended look and fingers the cross that hangs from her neck in a pointed fashion.

"Ms. Morrison, when was Jonas first diagnosed with any kind of problem?"

"If I am totally honest, I have to admit that I knew something was wrong with

Jonas long before any of the doctors did."
She turns to the judge. "A mother knows these things. He had apnea problems as an infant. He would just stop breathing, for no reason at all."

"How was this treated?"

"Well." She leans forward, as if warming to the subject. "It was absolutely the most terrifying thing for a new mother. I had to watch him day and night. When he stopped breathing, he turned this hideous shade of blue. I would have to call an ambulance or rush him to the emergency room." Tears fill her eyes. She takes another tissue from the box the judge has provided and gently dabs her eyes.

"What did they do for him?" asks Danielle.

Marianne looks up with a pained expression. "They 'bagged' him — forced oxygen into his lungs so he could breathe properly."

"How often did this happen?"

Marianne twists the tissue around her fingers. "I don't think more than two weeks went by without my having to rush that poor baby to the hospital. Then they gave me an apnea machine. It set off an alarm when the baby stopped breathing. It was horrible."

"Did anyone at the hospital ever tell you

that they suspected Jonas did not have apnea at all?"

Marianne gives her a confused look. "I don't understand the question."

Danielle takes a step closer. "Did any of the doctors tell you that they suspected you were smothering Jonas?"

Langley jumps to his feet with a roar. "Your Honor! This is outrageous!"

"Save yourself the trouble, Mr. Langley." Hempstead points an angry finger at Danielle. "You will stop this line of questioning immediately, Counselor. You have laid absolutely no foundation of any abuse on the part of this witness. Maybe this is how they conduct cross-examinations in New York, but I will not have it."

Danielle shrugs. "Yes, Your Honor."

"Move on."

Danielle shifts her unperturbed gaze to Marianne. "Who told you that Jonas was autistic or mentally retarded for the first time?"

Marianne's look is full of hate. "I will never forget that day as long as I live. Jonas was four, and we were living in Pittsburgh. A specialist was traveling through." She turns to the judge. "I wasn't terribly satisfied with the care Jonas had been receiving. Anyway, the doctor tested Jonas for hours and then called me into the waiting room." She sniffles into her tissue. The judge closes her eyes for a moment, clearly moved.

"He sat me down and told me that my poor baby would never be normal. That his brain was — damaged — that's all. That he was retarded and showed every sign of being autistic." She wipes away the rest of her tears as she looks at Hempstead. "At that moment I decided to become an advocate for my child. I spent the next fourteen years of his life making sure he received the best care and all the love I could possibly give him. I never remarried or cared about anything again — except my son."

Danielle walks back to the defense table. A few of the spectators look at her as if she has just defiled a statue of the Virgin Mary. Langley gives her a gleeful smirk. She continues. "Ms. Morrison, did any of the doctors who examined Jonas imply that there might be some other cause for Jonas's disorders?"

"What do you mean?"

"You've told us Jonas's problems started at birth," she says. "Did anyone ever tell you that these disorders in fact developed much later and what they suspected caused them?"

"No, they did not."

"No one ever suggested that there was some intervening event that might have led to damage to his brain?"

Marianne shoots her a smug look. "I don't know what you're trying to trick me into saying, Ms. Parkman. No one ever told me such a thing. I took excellent care of my child."

Hempstead fixes Danielle with a harsh look. "Ms. Parkman, the care given by the mother of the decedent during his childhood and later years is not at issue in this case."

"Perhaps it should be, Your Honor."

Hempstead arches her eyebrows. "If you have evidence of what you claim, produce it. If not, there must be some area of inquiry relevant to your defense. Find it."

"Of course, Your Honor." She puts her hand on the witness stand and looks directly into Marianne's eyes. "Ms. Morrison, you were educated as a physician and were a nurse for many years, isn't that true?"

Marianne's face relaxes. "Indeed, I was. Nursing provided me with the flexibility to give Jonas the care he needed."

"What area of nursing did you specialize in?"

Marianne smiles. "Pediatrics."

Danielle leans closer. "And isn't it also

true that in the course of your work you became very familiar with the computer systems of a number of hospitals and pediatric facilities?"

"Of course."

Danielle's voice is soft. "Isn't it also true, Ms. Morrison, that you broke into other computer systems long before you told me how to obtain the password into the Maitland system?"

It is as if a tidal wave hits the room. The judge slams her gavel on the block so hard it jumps. Langley bounds to his feet and throws his hands into the air. "Objection! We ask that the question be stricken and that Counsel be severely admonished."

Fury darkens Hempstead's face. Her voice is ice and fire. "Counselor, are you perfect-ly aware of what you are doing?"

Danielle walks to the bench and stands there, hands behind her back. "Your Honor, I promise you, I am not engaging in idle character assassination. If the Court will permit me some latitude —"

"Latitude!" Langley roars. "Your Honor!"

Danielle takes a deep breath. "It was Marianne Morrison who broke into the Maitland computer system and manipulated Max's entries —"

"Stop." Hempstead's voice is harsh. "You

501

may not proceed with this area of inquiry. Move on — immediately." Before Danielle can speak, the judge continues. "And Ms. Parkman?"

"Yes, Your Honor?"

"If you have an overweening desire to join your former counsel, just keep going down this path. This is your last warning," she says. "Knock it off."

Danielle turns and walks to the defense table. She pulls back the top flap of the box, looks inside, and turns to the witness. "Ms. Morrison, did you keep any kind of record of your life with Jonas?"

"What do you mean?"

Danielle peers further into the box and then straightens. "Oh, you know — photo albums, records, that sort of thing."

"Of course I did." She turns to the judge with a sorrowful look. "Every mother keeps pictures of their baby. I must have hundreds."

Danielle nods thoughtfully. "Did you keep any other kind of record?"

This time Marianne pauses. Her eyes fix on the box. When she speaks, her voice is measured and precise. "I'm sure I don't know what you mean."

Danielle shrugs. "Let me clarify. Did you keep what you might call a diary or a

502

journal —"

Marianne's face is implacable.

"— and write in it every day?" Danielle smiles.

A chair scrapes behind the prosecution table, and Langley is on his feet again. "Objection. Whether Ms. Morrison keeps a diary has no bearing on whether Max Parkman killed her son. Counsel is harassing the witness."

"Sustained," says Hempstead. "Move on, Ms. Parkman."

Danielle walks slowly past the witness box and then turns. "Ms. Morrison, where were you on the morning of your son's death?"

Marianne holds her hand up weakly. "At the hotel."

"I thought you visited Jonas every morning, rain or shine?"

"Oh, I did. It was just that on that morning — of all mornings — I wasn't feeling well and decided it was better if I stayed at the hotel instead of running the risk that I'd give Jonas my cold." Tears shine brightly as she breaks down. "If only I'd known what would happen! I'd never have left him for a single minute!"

Danielle continues calmly. "So you had not been on the unit until someone called and told you what happened?"

Her sobs are fresh as she struggles to answer. "That's right — yes."

"Is it possible that you're mistaken?"

Marianne glares at her. "No, it's not possible."

Danielle walks slowly to the witness stand, places both hands on the wooden rail, and looks Marianne in the eyes. "Does the name Kevin ring a bell, Ms. Morrison?"

Marianne stiffens slightly, but otherwise shows no reaction. "I have no idea what you're talking about."

Danielle leans over the bar and gives her a small smile. "Oh, I think you do."

Marianne shakes her head.

"How about the name Ashley?" she whispers. "I think it's such a marvelous name for a little girl, don't you?"

Marianne looks imploringly at the judge.

"Judge!" Langley slams his hand down on the desk. "She's harassing the witness with inane questions in an attempt to intimidate her!"

Hempstead's face is a sight to behold. "Sustained. Ms. Parkman, stand back from that witness box." Danielle steps back. "I've given you so much rope, you've obviously decided to hang yourself with it." Her voice is brittle. "You will ask a relevant question of this witness, or I will excuse her."

"Of course, Judge." Danielle pulls a blank piece of paper from her pad and hands it to Marianne, along with her pen. "Ms. Morrison, will you please write the following words — Maitland Psychiatric Asylum?"

"Ms. Parkman, you have two minutes to connect all of this, after which I plan to terminate this hearing and put you in jail."

Danielle nods. Marianne flashes her a look of disgust before she writes the words in what appears to be an expansive script. She hands the paper back to Danielle.

"Thank you." Danielle pulls one of the rose diaries from the box. As she turns, she pauses to look at Marianne. Her mouth opens and, as quickly, closes. Her blue eyes turn to slits. Danielle hands the diary to Marianne. "I've marked this item as defense Exhibit A. Can you identify it, Ms. Morrison?"

Marianne holds it a moment and then gives it back. "I've never seen this before in my life," she says icily.

"I'd like you to turn to the tabbed page and read it into the record," says Danielle.

"Objection! Lack of foundation," says Langley. "The witness has just said she can't identify it."

Danielle hands Marianne's handwriting sample and the diary to the judge. "Your

Honor, I'd like the Court to recognize that the witness's handwriting is the same as that in the diary." After a cursory glance, Hempstead shakes her head.

"I'm surprised at you, Ms. Parkman," she says dryly. "This is a tactic I would expect from a layman, not a reputable New York attorney such as yourself. You have put on no handwriting expert, nor have you laid any foundation to establish the chain of custody of this piece of evidence."

"Your Honor, I respectfully request that the cross-examination of Ms. Morrison be briefly postponed while I call Lieutenant Barnes of the Plano police force to the stand."

Hempstead's face is stone. "I have no intention of permitting you to disrupt Ms. Morrison's cross."

"But Judge," she protests, "you won't let me question the witness to establish a foundation. Once you read even part of this diary, you will know the truth."

"And what truth might that be?"

Danielle takes a deep breath and points her index finger at Marianne, who now sobs uncontrollably in the witness box. "That this woman is not what she appears. She is no mother. She is a consummate liar, a blackmailer, a cheat and a murderer —"

"Ms. Parkman — stop this instant!" The judge stands, her face dark, livid red. "Bailiff, take Ms. Parkman into custody." The bailiff moves so fast his shoes squeak. Langley has made his way to the witness box and wrapped his arms around a hysterical Marianne.

Hempstead's eyes blaze. "Counselor, your behavior in this courtroom is contemptible." She bites off each word. "Your attempt to malign and fling bizarre accusations at a mother whose child has been brutally murdered is not only wholly unprofessional, but morally appalling."

"Judge, if you would simply allow me —"

"I do not intend to permit you to do anything to further traumatize this witness or make a farce of this proceeding." She turns to the bailiff. "Escort Ms. Parkman to the county jail."

"Your Honor." Danielle shakes off the bailiff and takes a quick step toward the bench. "I haven't had an opportunity to respond to your ruling that I not be permitted to continue my cross-examination of Ms. Morrison."

Hempstead shakes her head in disbelief. "This is neither the time nor the place for you to lodge complaints about anything."

"Judge," says Danielle. "I know you're going to put me in jail. I accept that. But first I have to insist that you permit me to respond to the Court's ruling. If not, the appellate court won't be happy with either of us."

Hempstead gives her a wary look. "Fine, Ms. Parkman. Let's go through the motions. The Court sustains the State's objection. Your response?"

Danielle's voice is clear. "The defense wishes to file a bill of exception."

The judge's eyes widen. "You what?"

"The defense wishes to put on a bill of exception."

Hempstead's face is now unbridled in its fury. "Ms. Parkman, I'm warning you. Think very carefully before you push me into this corner."

Danielle knows that Hempstead cannot refuse to permit the defense to file the bill. This age-old legal device allows the party who feels that the judge's ruling is wrong to put on the very evidence that is being precluded. This evidence is incorporated into the record so that the appellate court can review precisely what is being excluded and determine if the evidence should have been admitted. But Hempstead knows what it really is. It's a backdoor way to let Danielle do precisely what she wants — whether the judge likes it or not. If Danielle had simply stood in front of her and raised her middle finger, it would have communicated the same message.

Hempstead crosses her arms and leans back. Her look says *touché.* "Please, Ms. Parkman. Put on your bill. The Court welcomes it."

Danielle makes a quick decision to put on only the evidence Doaks found in Marianne's hotel room, which she reviewed on the courthouse steps. The judge can still shut her down if she varies even an inch from the relevant path. She glances at Marianne, who has recovered somewhat, but looks pale and pitiful as makeup sluices down her face. Danielle picks up the diary and walks to the witness stand. "Ms. Morrison, what is your room number at the hotel?"

Her pinprick eyes stab at Danielle's. Her voice is strong. "Twenty-three."

Danielle hands her the diary again. "And you claim that this journal does not belong to you and was not in your room this morning?"

Marianne straightens. "That is correct."

"This is not your handwriting?"

Her eyes narrow as she looks at the page Danielle has laid before her. She turns to the judge. "That is not my handwriting."

"Your Honor, we would like to dim the lights and ask the bailiff to pull down the projection screen in order to show the witness excerpts taken from some of the documents."

"Documents which she has not identified."

"Yes, Your Honor."

Marianne turns to the judge, sobbing hysterically. "Your Honor, if I could just have a moment to collect myself —"

"Of course, Ms. Morrison," she says. "You may step down from the stand and take your place in the courtroom."

Langley jumps up and escorts Marianne to the bar. She sits a few rows back and wipes her eyes.

"Go on, Ms. Parkman," says Hempstead tersely.

Danielle nods at the bailiff, who goes to the other side of the courtroom and pulls down a white projector screen. On his way back, he turns off the lights. The darkness is almost palpable. The only real light emanates from the screen of Danielle's laptop that Doaks has placed on top of the defense table. In Arizona, Danielle had used her digital camera to photograph various pages of Marianne's diaries and then uploaded them to her computer. She now leans over the laptop and presses a button.

A hush falls over the courtroom. The darkness lends a surreal aura to the words as they shimmer on the screen. The handwriting flows and moves with feminine curlicues and flowery exclamation points. It is a living thing unto itself.

Dear Dr. Joyce,
Maitland has been the defining experience of my life! Every day has been filled with twists and turns, just like improvisation on Broadway. Interfacing with this caliber of medical genius thrills me, although it's no more than my due. There is only one small seed of disappointment. It is all coming to an end. It's sad to be alone at the mountaintop. No one will ever realize how truly brilliant I am, because disclosure of that simple fact would ruin everything. Still, what's important is that I've passed every test, bested them all. Just wait until I've executed my final plan. That will be my finest moment. Like eating that special chocolate from a Valentine box.

It's a shame about Jonas. I suppose it's been selfish of me to keep him with me as long as I have. I made sure that Kevin, Ashley and Raymond left this world when they needed to, and now it's clear to me that the Lord wants to bring Jonas home. To everything there is a season, you know. The exhilaration of proving to the doctors that Jonas is precisely what he appears to be — just as I have created him — has completed the cycle. I must now focus on the loving plan ahead.

Since the good Lord put Max right in my path, it is clear to me that his ultimate purpose in life is to help me ease Jonas to the next world and stop his suffering forever. I'm sure Danielle will miss Max, but God will know that she has made the ultimate sacrifice. Besides, when a higher purpose is involved, life is invariably cruel. Look at Jesus. I often reflect on the fact that righteous deeds in this life are always rewarded in the next.

Both Danielle and I will have a safe place in heaven.

There is a collective gasp from the crowd. Max clutches Danielle's hand. "It's all right," she whispers. She nods at the bailiff, who turns up the lights just enough so that the judge's face is illuminated. It is as white as the projection screen. She looks at Danielle, who extracts another item from the box. In the dim light, a blue velvet case takes shape. Danielle walks to the bench and hands it to the judge. Hempstead opens it, blanches and closes her eyes. Danielle silently takes it from her and walks over to the prosecution table. What Langley sees makes his mouth go slack in one horrified movement.

Hempstead's voice trembles. "Ms. Parkman, please identify what you have just shown me."

"Your Honor, Lieutenant Barnes obtained a warrant to search Ms. Morrison's hotel room early this morning. He discovered this diary, various ampoules and syringes — and this." She borrows Doaks's handkerchief and opens the velvet box. She holds the item on high. "This is my comb, Judge, which was found in Ms. Morrison's closet, covered in Jonas's dried blood and pieces of human tissue which preliminary testing has identified as belonging to the decedent."

The courtroom is hushed. Hempstead looks at Danielle, her face a mixture of horror, confusion and — yes — a brief glint of apology. "Have you ascertained how the comb came into Mrs. Morrison's possession?"

"Yes, Your Honor," she says. "After Mrs. Morrison was taken to the police station, Sergeant Barnes will testify that she was left for a short time in the drying room so that she could avoid the reporters swarming the station. It is then, he believes, that Mrs. Morrison took the comb."

The judge gives Danielle a confused look. "But why would she take the comb? It was the one piece of damning evidence against Max."

Danielle nods. "The diaries are clear that she kept trophies of all of her murders. She even kept the poison ampoules that she used on her other children. Marianne was obviously convinced that she would never be caught. She had outsmarted the best and the brightest." Hempstead nods numbly, mute in shocked silence.

Danielle steps forward. "This concludes the bill of exception on the part of the defense. We recall Marianne Morrison to the stand."

Doaks hits the switch, and the room is suddenly awash in light. Everyone, including the judge, takes a few moments to blink and adjust their eyes.

"Marianne Morrison to the stand!" the bailiff cries.

A murmur begins as a small wave in the courtroom and rises to a swell. The judge finds the gavel and her voice. "Order!" She bangs it again. "Order, I said!"

"Ms. Marianne Morrison to the stand!" the bailiff cries again.

A silence falls over the room.

Marianne has vanished.

CHAPTER FORTY

The courtroom is in pandemonium. The judge stands at her bench in earnest conversation with her bailiff. Langley sits in his chair in a state of shock.

Danielle wastes no time. "Doaks!"

"I'm on it. If she's anywhere in this stinkin' town, I'll find her." He dashes through the crowd and slips out of the side door. Danielle rushes over to Max, who crumples in her arms. "It's almost over, sweetheart," she whispers. "Be strong — just a little while longer." She holds him for a long moment and then walks back to the judge's bench.

Hempstead bangs her gavel, and the room falls into an uneasy quiet. "Counsel? Approach." When they reach the bench, she nods briskly at both lawyers. "Mr. Langley, where is the State's chief witness?"

Langley looks wildly around the room. "I don't know, Judge. One minute she was

516

here, and the next — well, she wasn't."

"Don't you think you better find her?" He stares at her. She holds up her hand. "Never mind. I've sent my bailiff out to look for her. You better hope she's in the building, or the State is going to have even more to answer for." She turns to Danielle. "I'm not terribly pleased with you, either, Ms. Parkman. Don't you think it would have been more appropriate if you had made the State and the bench aware of this new evidence before making a spectacle in open court?"

"I certainly tried, Your Honor," says Danielle.

"Never mind, never mind." For the first time, she lets her emotions show. "Can either one of you explain what happened to this poor child?"

"Judge, the defense has one more witness to call," says Danielle. "I believe she will be able to answer all your questions."

The bailiff returns. "Can't . . . find . . . her . . . Judge," he gasps, his face red with exertion.

"Try again," she hisses. She turns to Danielle and raises her voice. "Ms. Parkman, do you have a witness you wish to call?"

"The defense recalls Dr. Reyes-Moreno to the stand," she says. "And Judge?"

"Yes?"

"May we request that Mr. Sevillas be permitted to rejoin the defense team?"

Hempstead nods at the sheriff. "Retrieve Mr. Sevillas."

"Thank you, Your Honor." Danielle waits nervously until Tony has taken his place at the defense table. Their eyes meet. Love is a blue jolt that crackles between them. Danielle forces herself to turn to the bench.

In response to the bailiff's cattle call, Dr. Reyes-Moreno walks up the aisle holding two cloth-covered diaries and an accordion file. The bailiff holds out the Bible to her. She takes the oath. Her mouth is set, eyes grim.

Danielle paces in front of her. "Doctor, have you reviewed the documentation we provided to you and the evidence obtained from Ms. Morrison's hotel room?"

"Most if it," she says.

"Enough to establish a diagnosis?"

"I'm afraid so." She shakes her head sadly. "Every piece fits perfectly — now that it is too late."

Danielle nods. "Please tell the court what the diagnosis of Jonas Morrison is — and has always been."

"Jonas Morrison suffered from Munchausen syndrome by proxy."

Hempstead leans toward the witness.

"Doctor, isn't this just a horrific case of child abuse? That's what I see."

The doctor shakes her head. "Perhaps I should explain the difference between Munchausen and Munchausen syndrome by proxy."

"Of course."

"Women with Munchausen syndrome, which is now well-known, fabricate illnesses to get attention. One of the most startling cases involves a woman who had two hundred procedures performed in over eighty different hospitals by the time she was sixty. Her mental illness went undetected until her final hospitalization."

The judge's face is white. "Go on."

Reyes-Moreno takes off her glasses. "Munchausen syndrome by proxy is a similar but separate disorder. Instead of the deception being perpetrated by the adult with respect to her own health, the deception relates to the child. The essential features involve pathological lying, peregrination — constant moving to avoid detection — and recurrent, feigned illnesses that are inflicted by the mother upon the child. It is rarely seen in a child past the age of four."

"Why is that?"

Reyes-Moreno shakes her head. "Most children who are victims of MSBP are untrustworthy as they get older and communicate their pain — which is why most victims are infants or toddlers."

Danielle takes a deep breath. "Please continue."

"The mother usually has antisocial personality traits, accompanied by an odd lack of concern for the child — particularly with respect to painful surgical procedures she has elected for the child to undergo. She has extensive knowledge of the medical field and derives intense pleasure from manipulating the various physicians involved, as well as creating the 'illnesses' which bring her child to the attention of doctors and hospitals."

"Anything else about the mother?"

"Yes," she says. "As with Ms. Morrison, the mother is often intelligent and appears to be wonderfully devoted to the child — often too devoted."

"What physical symptoms are present with such children?"

Reyes-Moreno shakes her head. "That's the problem. The range of feigned illnesses covers the entire spectrum of the human body. Anything from respiratory, feeding and thriving difficulties to complex blood diseases or systemic infections can be induced. There are cases of mothers giving their children nitroglycerine over long periods of time; putting acid into their food; or cutting their children and bathing the wounds in toilet water. That is what makes it so very difficult for the treating physician. He sees a child in an emergency room with inexplicable symptoms, and he wants to fix him. If he can't find anything wrong, the number of exploratory tests and surgeries are overwhelming."

Hempstead's shoulders sag as Danielle walks toward the witness. "Why aren't they caught more often?"

The doctor fixes her with a weary look. "Who wants to believe that a mother could purposely sicken her child or even kill him?" She shakes her head. "As a society, we've had exposure to horrific incidences of child abuse. I believe what makes MSBP so incomprehensible is that the mother derives such intense pleasure from the attention she garners in harming or killing her children."

"Dr. Reyes-Moreno, have you discovered any link between Max Parkman's violent behavior and the medication he took while at Maitland?"

The doctor takes a deep breath. "Yes, I'm afraid I have." She turns to the judge. "The hospital recently hired a Dr. Fastow, a psychopharmacologist who had, so everyone thought, impeccable credentials. My understanding is that the Maitland board screened him very carefully. The hospital in Vienna where he worked prior to coming to Maitland had no reservations about recommending him to us. In fact, they gave him the highest of praise.

"He was to consult on our most difficult cases and to continue his research into various psychotropic medications, some of which were very exciting." She shakes her head. "What we didn't know, and what seems apparent now, is that Dr. Fastow — instead of running a formal clinical trial with the appropriate controls — was experimenting with a new drug protocol on some of our patients. As you know, he has disappeared. When Lieutenant Barnes showed us the toxicology report of a sample of Max Parkman's blood, we were appalled to learn that the medications he gave both Max and Jonas had serious side effects."

Danielle feels her throat tighten. "And what were those?"

Reyes-Moreno looks at her. "All of the patients on Dr. Fastow's medication protocol exhibited significant spikes in bizarre and violent behavior during their assessments. Although some parents claimed that these behaviors were not present at the time of admission, the psychiatrists treating those patients — including me, I'm sorry to say — observed them firsthand and discounted such claims as denial."

Danielle sees the apology in her eyes. "And such behaviors were the basis for erroneous diagnoses of some of the patients, were they not?"

The doctor clasps her hands. "Yes."

"Including Max Parkman?"

"Yes."

Danielle nods, satisfied. A quick glance at Max reveals a look of overwhelming relief on his face. Tears brim and fall unashamedly down his cheeks. Danielle turns back to Reyes-Moreno. "Let's get back to Ms. Morrison. What do the entries reveal about her intentions toward Jonas?"

"She had deceived the entire Maitland staff, while basking in the attention and pity she craved. In her mind, there was nothing else to achieve — no accolade Jonas could still be instrumental in affording her." She shakes her head. "She decided to get rid of him."

"And where did Max come in, Doctor?"

"Oh," she says simply. "He was the perfect foil. The diaries are clear that once she ascertained that Max exhibited violent behavior, her plan was to set him up for

Jonas's murder. We have no evidence that indicates that Ms. Morrison knew that Dr. Fastow's medication had made Max violent. In that respect, she just got lucky."

Danielle turns to the defense table. The warmth and relief in Tony's brown eyes say it all. She takes a deep breath and turns back to the witness. "Is that all?"

Reyes-Moreno looks uncomfortable. "I'm afraid not. I have never heard of a case like this."

"In what way?"

The doctor stares at her hands. "Jonas Morrison was not born autistic, retarded, obsessive-compulsive or self-inflictive. Autism is a spectrum disorder — a psychological and neurological disorder," she says. "Ms. Morrison succeeded in actually creating a profound, tragic psychiatric illness in a normal child. It is clear that Jonas was trying in whatever way he could to break free from his mother and his life of pain."

"Why didn't Marianne just poison or overdose Jonas instead of exposing herself to the risk of discovery?" asks the judge.

Reyes-Moreno shakes her head. "One must understand the core nature of this disorder, Your Honor. Ms. Morrison craved the attention. Tell me, would you rather be the mother of a horribly disabled child who dies from an unintentional overdose —" she looks at the judge "— or the center of national attention from the press and a sympathetic world?"

The judge bows her head. Not a word is heard anywhere in the courtroom. The bailiff trails in from the back of the courtroom. Hempstead looks up. "Bailiff, have you located Ms. Morrison?"

"She's gone, Your Honor. Disappeared into thin air."

CHAPTER FORTY-ONE

The sun has set. The rectangular windows of the courtroom show the flicker of street-lights. Judge Hempstead has returned after a short break, leaving reporters and observers milling about the courtroom, many on their cell phones sending in last-minute details of the hearing.

"All rise!"

All shuffle to their feet until the judge is seated. Her face shows the wear and tear of the day, but her voice is resolute. "Ms. Parkman?"

Danielle stands, never letting go of Max's hand. "Yes, Your Honor?"

"I am advised by the police department and the sheriff that all current efforts to locate Ms. Morrison have been unsuccessful. Do you have anything else you wish to offer the Court at this time?"

"In fact, I do, Judge." She reaches into the file box and pulls out a videotape.

"There is one more piece of evidence I would like to show the Court. It was found in Ms. Morrison's room. I would be happy to put on Lieutenant Barnes to establish the chain of custody if you wish."

Hempstead waves a weary hand. "That won't be necessary. I believe all of this evidence will be properly submitted to the judge who is assigned to the trial of Ms. Morrison — if she is ever found."

"May I proceed, Your Honor?"

"Yes, please do."

Danielle whispers something to Max and then nods at Georgia, who takes him gently by the hand and leads him from the courtroom. Danielle signals to Doaks, who has returned with only the news that Marianne left everything in her hotel room and that law enforcement is scrambling to track her down. He pulls down the projection screen and dims the lights. She inserts the tape and turns to the judge. "I'm afraid this will tie up all unanswered questions, Your Honor. This video was found in Ms. Morrison's closet and appears to have been taken from the Fountainview unit on the day Jonas died." She presses the play button. There is a whirring noise and a blank screen. After a few moments, it begins.

Marianne enters the room and drags a form out of view of the camera. It does not move. She closes the door, takes a rubber doorstop and wedges it tightly under the door. She slips on a pair of thin latex gloves and crouches down, only white nurse shoes visible under her dress. She inches her way to the bed.

Jonas is turned with his face against the wall, knees drawn up tightly into his body. His angle of repose makes him look even more childlike, hauntingly vulnerable. Sandy hair is swept back from his face. Eyes closed, he looks peaceful, angelic.

She sits on the bed next to him. She places a large shopping bag on the floor beside the bed and puts her hand softly on his shoulder. One can almost sense the warmth of his body against her palm. Gently, she loosens and then removes the restraints in place around his wrists and legs. Without taking her right hand from his body, she gropes in the bag. She caresses the cool metal of the comb as if it is inviting to her fingertips. She places the instrument on the side of the bed.

It is so quiet.

As she shakes his shoulder, his eyes flutter, then focus on hers. He pulls himself into a sitting position and hugs his knees to his chest, watching her carefully. "Go ahead, Jonas, do it now," she urges. He immediately begins banging his head against the wall — first the back, one side, then the back, then the other side. He does it in a continuous rhythm, a drumming with eyes closed, following the ritual. Four bangs in back, four left, four back, four right. Four, four, four, four. When the requisite number of raps has been accomplished, he begins slapping his face, first with the right hand, then the left — right, left, right, left. His hands move faster and faster in staccato syncopation. The strokes are harder and harder. The skin mottles.

Jonas opens his eyes and searches her face, as if looking for confirmation that this is what she wants. She shakes her head no. He starts biting the top of his right hand — bite, bite, bite, bite. She leans over and picks up the metal comb with the long, sharp prongs and begins tapping it against her palm. Slap, slap, slap, slap. It is a metronome, keeping time with his methodic inflictions.

Alerted by the new sound, he looks up and sees the comb. It flashes in the light. His eyes fix upon it like a parrot watching the sun glint off the mirror in his cage. He bites his hands ever harder. It takes a long time for them to bleed, misshapen as they are with calluses from years of earlier assaults.

She nods and taps, watching as the curiosity flickers in his eyes. "Yes, baby, yes," she whispers, smiling at him. "You can touch it in a minute, my love, and you're going to feel so much better." Her voice is a croon, her eye applause.

The left hand is bleeding strongly now — on top, where he has found a vein. He moves to the right and begins again, further renting the skin each time with smaller, angrier bites. His head rocks slowly up and down, up and down, his eyes never moving from the sight of the rhythmic slapping of the metal comb in her hands. He no longer looks for her eyes. It is as if he knows what she wants. His eyes are glazed, hypnotic.

Once she sees that he has successfully penetrated the skin of the right hand and is biting hard, she moves ever so carefully closer, the metal comb keeping time with their dance. Holding the instrument in her left hand, she gently taps the side of the bed with it, the soft, muffled beat uninterrupted. With her right hand, she strokes his head as his eyes track the vertical bobbing of the comb. Her face surges with love.

"There, there," she murmurs. She leans down and kisses the top of his head, loving him, as the comb taps against the sheet. He rocks with her. "Isn't that a pretty thing? So shiny, so new." He bobs more rapidly and reaches for the comb with his ruined left hand. "Oh, no, my love, not yet, not yet," she whispers. She pulls back the covers to expose his bare legs. He stops biting and grunts softly, reaching for the comb in earnest. She places the comb in his right hand and wraps his left hand tightly around it.

Raising their linked hands, she helps him press the sharp prongs against his skin — just hard enough to leave five red impressions on his right thigh after the pressure is released. He stares at the comb in his hands, transfixed. She raises their hands again and croons softly, a mother teaching her child to raise a baby spoon to his lips for the first time. Slowly, she continues to lift his hands high above his face, and together they come down upon his thigh, this time with more force.

He does not whisper or moan, but stares with fascination as this effort produces bright red droplets where the prongs

531

pierce the skin. Now he automatically raises his hands on his own, this time so high at the peak that they are actually behind his head. She stands close by, tenderly cupping her hand around the back of his neck.

"You're such a good boy, Jonas, such a good boy." Her chant is low and satisfied.

He is monomaniacal in his focus now. He swings his head back roughly and pushes her away. She moves silently to the corner of the room and observes. It is as if she knows what he will do. She glances at her watch. "Twenty-two minutes," she whispers.

He swings his legs over the side of the bed, the metal comb clasped tightly in his right hand. With the left, he pinches the top of each thigh. He stabs the right, then the left, the right, the left. Awkward at first, he finds a shorter arc better suited to his purpose. He switches seamlessly from one leg to the other. He moans softly now, eyes glassy. Soon both legs are flowing blood. His stabs become faster and deeper. He doesn't stop, but looks up at her.

Where now, where now? his eyes ask.

"Nomomah, Jonas, nomomah?" she whispers. "Are you ready? If you are, if you really are, baby, I'm going to give you nomomah and let you stop." She takes a few steps back, puts her arms around herself and begins to rock.

"Nomomah, nomomah, nomomah." His chant is psalm.

She walks across the room and sits in the armchair, first covering it with a sheet. "Look at me, baby, and I'll show you how to do it, I'll show you how to fix it all." She stretches her legs straight out and points her index finger at the soft vein in her groin. Calmly and purposefully, she raises her hands together and clasps them high above her head. She then viciously drives her balled fist into the area of her femoral artery.

She smiles dreamily and nestles back into the chair. "It will be quiet, and there will be no more pain, my darling, no more at all." She closes her eyes, still smiling — as if to show him the glory and peace of it all. He has eyes only for her. After a moment, she stands and goes to him. She takes one of his white socks from the floor and stuffs it into his mouth. He doesn't react, as if it isn't the first time.

She looks again at her watch. "Fourteen minutes."

His eyes follow her as she takes her seat

across the room once more. The comb dangles in his hands. He doesn't seem to see the red holes that stare up at him from his thighs, doesn't see the blood running down his legs. He grasps the comb more tightly. It is wet with gore. He clutches the handle and, with interlocked fingers, holds it high above his head.

He gives her one last look, a gaze filled with bruises, trust, betrayal, torture and finally — damnation. He turns his head upward, as if in prayer. Without a sound, he uses all his force to plunge the iron prongs directly into his lifeline. Even with the muffling of the sock in his mouth, his scream is crazed and awful. His neck arcs and bends, inhumanly rigid, his throat a parallel line to the ceiling. He is paralyzed, lightning-struck in that position for what seems like an impossible moment before he collapses back onto the bed.

A spurt of blood so violent and forceful shoots from his groin that she seems both revolted and gratified at its height, its breadth. She is there in a flash, running around and behind him, placing the pillow over his mouth. He struggles against her for a few moments, but the horrific beauty of the red geyser seems to have lent her inhuman strength and power.

Blue eyes stare into the camera's eye. It is the gaze of a righteous woman.

She turns back to him and forces him down, strong as a man. When minutes have passed and he is finally still, she lifts the pillow and places it neatly on top of the bed. She takes the sock out of his mouth, carefully removes the comb from his hands and places it purposefully into the hand of an unidentifiable form lying next to the bed.

Blood is everywhere — on the bed, the floor, the ceiling. She checks her clothing. Crimson streaks stain her dress. She stands on the sheet, removes her bloody gloves, and steps out of her dress and shoes. Handi Wipes remove the red traces from her arms and face. She takes a shift from her bag and slips it quickly over her head. Gold sandals follow. She rolls the soiled items in the sheet and places it into the plastic shopping bag. She raises her wrist. Her hand is steady.

"Six minutes." She slings the shopping bag over her shoulder and takes a last look at Jonas.

His eyes stare up like empty marbles from a white bowl. His body is laid open on the brilliant ruby sheets.

He stares at heaven.

CHAPTER FORTY-TWO

The lights come up slowly. Danielle looks at Hempstead. Both have tears streaming down their faces. As Danielle turns, Sevillas and Doaks rise to meet her, while Max and Georgia enter the room. She puts her arms around them all. They walk her to her seat.

Hempstead clears her throat and recovers sufficiently to nod at the court reporter. Her fingers prepare to take down the record. "Mr. Langley?" says the judge.

He looks as if someone has thrown a grenade into his foxhole. "Yes, Your Honor?"

"Does the State have a motion it would like to make?"

"What, Judge?"

She taps her pen impatiently. "On your feet. You have a motion to make."

He scrambles to comply. "I — uh — the State hereby moves to dismiss all charges against Max and Danielle Parkman."

Hempstead nods grimly. "Ms. Parkman,

please rise."

Danielle stands.

"Ms. Parkman, the Court hereby dismisses all pending charges against you and your son. You are both free to go." She stands and clasps her hands before her. "Before you do so, however, I must offer you the abject apologies of this Court and the State of Iowa. You have been subjected to a most terrible ordeal — one I most fervently wish could have been spared you. Unfortunately, when confronted with the evil and tragedy we have seen today, apparently nothing is as it seems." She sends a small smile to Sevillas. "The contempt charges against Mr. Sevillas are, of course, also dismissed."

"Thank you, Your Honor," he says.

"Although I could still make that one stick," she mutters. She gathers up her robes and sweeps from the bench. The bailiff puts his hands on his hips and bellows. "All rise!"

Doaks jerks his head toward the door. "Let's get the fuck outta here."

"Amen," says Sevillas. Tony wraps his arm around Danielle's shoulders to shield her from the onslaught of the press and well-wishers who swarm the aisle. She buries her face into his neck as exhaustion and emotion finally overcome her. She sobs as she realizes that Max will be all right. Although she never let herself believe it, a wave of relief so intense washes over her that she realizes how profoundly in the dark grip of that diagnosis she has been. Georgia hugs her hard — her eyes brimming with tears. Danielle releases her and holds Max so close, he grins up at her. "Hey, Mom, I'm not going anywhere."

She smiles through her tears. "And I'm not letting you out of my sight."

Tony holds her closer, his voice gruff. "Thank God it's over."

She looks up at him. "But Marianne got away with it."

"For now," he says. "They'll find her."

She shakes her head. "I don't think so."

Doaks tugs on her arm. "Hey, cookie, ain't you had enough? I need a goddamned drink."

She smiles. Shoulder to shoulder, the five of them march down the aisle. Danielle walks through the door. She doesn't look back.

EPILOGUE

Danielle leans back in her deck chair and shades her eyes from the blazing afternoon sun. She waves at Max, who has returned from a long hike through the wooded hills near their new home — just north of Sante Fe. The wind has whipped a healthy glow into his cheeks. The sun glints in his hair. He stops and waves back, a big grin on his face.

She left the firm a year ago and put out a shingle in this small town. Her practice is now low-key — wills and estates. Tony spends every free moment he can with them, shuttling back and forth from Iowa. Max has recovered from Maitland, although it took months to undo the harm Fastow's experimental chemicals wreaked on his system, much less the trauma he suffered as a result of the entire experience. After the hearing, Danielle learned from Reyes-Moreno that Fastow was finally found in an isolated fishing town in Mexico and that Maitland is pursuing criminal charges against him.

She watches Max — so strong and happy — and can't believe her good fortune. Once the poisons were cleansed from his system, Maitland confirmed that he was not psychotic, not violent, not crazy. Reyes-Moreno correctly diagnosed him as bipolar — which explained his wild mood swings and anger — and gave her back her boy.

Danielle gives him another long look and checks her watch. It is almost time to leave for the airport to pick up Tony. He just accepted a partnership with a firm in Sante Fe. She looks at the antique band on her left hand, the diamonds afire in the bright sunlight. Soon he will never have to leave her again.

She picks up her wineglass and makes the short journey to the mailbox. Inside is an envelope, forwarded from her old New York address. She opens it. A postcard falls out, the postmark smeared and illegible. Danielle holds it up. It is an African scene of bolting antelope and wildly colored birds flying across a veldt. She turns it over. A flowing, elaborate script fills every available writing space.

God moves in mysterious ways.
Adopted adorable twin girls.
All mine!
Love and kisses,
M.

ACKNOWLEDGMENTS

I would like to thank all of my family and friends who have steadfastly supported and encouraged me. They have read my manuscript ad nauseam — and still love me. For my brilliant agent, Al Zuckerman, for taking a chance on a new writer and for his insistence on excellence; for Donna Hayes and Linda McFall, for loving the book and making this happen. For Glenn Cambor, who first told me to write and then kept my head on straight while I did. For Beverly Swerling, my reader, without whom this novel would still be in a box under my desk.

My heartfelt thanks to Jim and Jeanine Barr, who provided their judicial and criminal-law expertise; Wayman Allen, for his police and private investigator savvy; for Cynthia England and Dawn Weightman — for their steadfast devotion and love; for Lane, Tom and Kelly — who made me laugh every day.

543

For Jim Sentner, my other father, who has supported me in every wild endeavor with love and patience. A special thanks to my three sons — Brendan, Sam and Jack — who have inspired me and given me the privilege of being their mother.

And for Bill — my editor, my love, my life.

QUESTIONS FOR DISCUSSION

We hope you enjoyed *Saving Max.*
To further enhance your reading
experience, please see the discussion
questions below.

1.) **What is the novel about?**
Does the book have a central theme? If
so, what? Does it have many themes? If
so, how do you think they interlink? Is one
theme more dominant than others? What
do you think the author is trying to get
across to the reader?

2.) **How important is the setting to the
story?**
Does the author provide enough background information for you to understand
the events in the story? What is unique
about the setting of the book and how

does it enhance or take away from the story?

3.) **Do the characters seem real and believable?**
Can you relate to Danielle's predicament? To what extent does she or the other characters remind you of yourself or someone you know?

4.) **How did the book affect you?**
Do you feel "changed" in any way? Did it expand your range of experience or challenge your assumptions? (For example, did it deepen your understanding of autism and what it means to raise an autistic child?) Did reading it help you to understand someone better — perhaps a friend or relative, or even yourself?

5.) **What do the characters do?**
Do they react the way you think you would in a similar situation? Are their actions consistent with their characters? If not, perhaps ask yourself if it is reasonable for anyone to be expected to act consistently in the situation confronting Danielle.

6.) What do you know about the author?
The novel is partly based upon the author's experience in raising an autistic child. Does she effectively convey the emotions you would expect her to have in the novel?

7.) Did certain parts of the book make you uncomfortable?
If so, why did you feel that way? Did this lead to a new understanding or awareness of some aspect of your life or the world you might not have thought about before?

8.) Discuss the mystery aspect of the plotline?
How effective is the author's use of plot twists and red herrings? Were you able to predict certain things before they happened, or did the author keep you guessing until the end of the story?

9.) How do characters change or evolve throughout the course of the story?
What events trigger such changes?

10.) How is the book structured?
Does the author use any narrative devices like flashbacks in telling the story? How did this affect your reading of the story

and your appreciation of the book? Do you think the author did a good job with it?